PAM FOX

To a Good Friend
PSFox
2023

This is a work of fiction. The names, characters, and incidents either are a product of the author's imagination or are used fictitiously. Any resemblance to actual persons, living or dead, business establishments, events, or locales are entirely coincidental. The different archaeology sites around the world are real, but the fictional story wrapped around them is a product of the author's imagination.

ISBN: 978-1-935356-69-1

Reach out to Pam Fox at psfox5@aol.com

Printed in the United States of America

To my father Gordon David Sample,
who taught me by example to always do the right thing
no matter the cost.

Other Books by Pam Fox

Agency Series

Lethal Hostage Book One
ASIN: BOON397551

The Sinister Holiday Book Two
ASIN: BOON3AOKS6

Operation Green Zone Book Three
ASIN: BOON3WHHT4

The Missing Manuscript Book Four
ASIN: BOON41U188

Captive Book Five
ASIN: BOON691ZGA

Stealth Series

Ester Book One
ASIN: BOON42HHNO

PART ONE

PRELUDE

A heavy energy filled the ornate room as the hired help moved about, making sure everything would be ready. The large crystal chandeliers had been dusted. The long tables had been prepared with rows of platters of colorful finger food. Each hors d'oeuvres was beautifully designed, resembling miniature pieces of art. The bar off to the far corner was aligned with crates of chilled champagne, the bottles popping their heads out of the sparkling ice. An array of expensive wines sat in rows, creating contrasting patterns with the crisply ironed tablecloths. Hundreds of shiny crystal glasses stood ready, their circular designs making patterns in the reflected light, decorating the surfaces of the white tables. Round tables filled the magnificent ballroom, the tops decorated with blue runners that raced down their centers. Huge long-stem white roses in crystal vases spread their petals over the place settings, making the space appear as sheer elegance.

The center of the room was left empty, making space for a dance floor. The early birds stood in the middle of the room, where the women swayed from side to side in their high heels, leaning against their husbands. They sipped their beverages and watched the door as they shared small talk with a group of strangers. All sipping...whispering...waiting.

The room hushed for a moment, wondering about the tall couple entering, thinking that they were important because their height gave them a presence. All eyes followed their movements, taking in the stunning women with auburn hair piled high on her head. Her long red gown hugged her svelte figure, making each man she passed turn his head in her wake, wondering who the beautiful woman was. The attractive man in front of her pulled her forward, weaving through the tables. He towered over the sleek women and all the other men in the room, his dark curly hair adding a few extra inches. *Was he an athlete?* They asked each other. He escorted the woman, moving her along, until they reached a table by the center of the stage. The "wannabes" watched as he put down a Reserved sign, took out a clipboard, and examined his notes. Seeing that the couple was of no importance, the observers looked away, returning to their socializing.

"You're sure he's going to make an appearance?" Eve asked.

"Yes…he'll be here. My new boss is a state senator, you know?" Scott teased, "He wouldn't go to all the trouble of organizing this table if he didn't know for sure."

"I know…I know…I'm just excited to see him in person…" Eve said, turning her head so he couldn't read her. She didn't want Scott to know what she was about to do. Eve understood that he would think it was a bad idea and try to stop her. For the past week, all she could think about was her mission. Tonight was the night. This might be her only opportunity to get close enough to the new President of the United States.

"Well I have it on good authority that he has left the last ball and is headed this way. He saved the best for last—just two hundred of his closest friends." Scott laughed, giving her a hug and kissing her check, glad that she came with him tonight. They had been through so much recently and the relationship had turned from friendship into something more.

"That's a lot of friends." Eve giggled, softly wiping the moisture left behind from his kiss.

"Yes, crazy...but many of the higher-ups in the Democratic Party are in this room. Look around." Scott caught sight of his boss making his way through the crowd that was getting larger by the minute. "Okay—work calls. Here comes my boss. I need to make sure his guests are taken care of...I'll be back." Scott said, and left her side.

Eve stood alone, leaning against the wall, watching the entrance, like the rest of the people in the room. The excitement level had risen with each commotion at the front of the hall. The time had finally come. Secret Service agents in dark suits with earpieces and sunglasses entered the room, first spreading out, looking into the crowd, searching for danger.

Moments later, President Conor and his wife swept into the ballroom, hand in hand. They raised their arms to the sound of cheers, blocking out the light jazz music that was left playing in the background. Everyone was standing, clapping, cheering; the energy in the small space was contagious, filling the crowd. The room started going crazy... seconds turned to minutes, until the President raised his hand in the air to silence them. The crowd calmed down, then broke again into load applause that finally turned to hushed whispers as they waited to hear what President Conor would say.

Scott's boss went on stage and grabbed the microphone, "A big welcome to the President of the United States!"

The noise in the room went ecstatic this time, bouncing off the walls.

The President and his wife made a slow procession through the crowd pressing around them as they made their way to the stage.

Eve knew this would be her only and best chance to get close enough to the new President to do what needed to be done. She let out her breath, finding that she had been holding it, and touched the gold medallion hanging around her neck. She felt its warmth as it heated up against her skin, reminding her what she had to do. The crowd calmed down, wanting to hear what President Conor was saying to people he passed.

Seeing Scott was busy, Eve moved through the tight spaces between people, making her way closer. The President was taller than she had thought and their eyes met briefly across the tops of heads as the crowd crushed in closer to him. His smile filled the room with his presence; he walked to the center of the space, waving, whispering in people's ears and shaking hands as he moved forward through the crowd. The Secret Service tried to do their job, spreading out, alert, scanning the surrounding people, attempting to put themselves between him and the crowd. It was a difficult task because so many wanted to get as close as possible to the charismatic man. But he didn't seem to notice or care, caught in the moment, already accustomed to their presence. Happiness filled the air; the adrenaline of energy carried by emotions flowed throughout the room.

As Eve grew closer, she could see the tiredness around his eyes, but he shook hands and listened to well-wishers with enduring compassion, working his way around the room toward the stage. Like a moth to a flame, Eve moved in, drawn to the man, not letting him out of her sight. Her slim frame slid between the partygoers until she stood in his path. Because of her height and elegance, he stopped and took her hand, looking into her eyes. For a moment Eve was frozen, forgetting her plan as she leaned in to say "thank you" when he admired her beauty. She touched the gold medallion hanging around her neck, feeling the heat coming from it. The stone in the middle had lightened, changing colors to match Eve's eyes. She clicked a dangling large red jewel hanging in the middle of her cleavage. It easily released from the heavy gold as she had cleverly designed it to do. As the President let go of her hand and turned to shake someone else's, Eve quickly touched his arm and slid the jeweled object into his tuxedo pocket.

Chapter I
Two Months Earlier

All morning, something had been in the back of Eve's mind, distracting her while she tried to work on her project in the lab. Her mind kept flashing to her parents and she thought it was just anticipation of their arrival that night. They should be home by the time she finished in a few hours. They were usually gone for a few weeks at a time. Both were retired professors and always found a reason to travel to out-of-the-way places, researching the latest discovery in astronomy, archaeology, and science. Eve often wondered what they were doing with all the information they collected, but she was happy it kept them busy. She didn't have time to get involved with their research, but had overheard their excitement many times when they returned with their latest discovery.

Looking at the clock, Eve realized it was about time to clean up her area. The others around her were still working on their own projects at the long black lab tables. This was an independent lab for graduate students and she could come and go as she pleased. Eve sat for a moment and wrote her findings and reactions for the day in her notes. She felt she was close to discovering the solution to months of work. Many had tried to create an anti-gravitational device that could carry the weight of a small plane; all had failed in their attempts. Eve had studied their notes and tests and tried to approach it from a different angle. Now she closed her notebook and locked it in her briefcase. *You can never be too careful,* she thought. She didn't want her ideas stolen. But today wasn't going to be the big day of success. Eve knew she didn't have much time to prepare for her parents' arrival.

Leaving the lab, Eve nodded silently to other students as she passed. Most barely noticed her as she went by, absorbed in their own work. Outside, the air was brisk and she picked up her pace. As she passed Grove Street Cemetery, she admired the old carved statues, worn by years of erosion. The dull granite stones now weathered with time showed their age. Eve passed today without looking at the dates on the slabs, rushing by and thinking that she would have to take a day to really explore the ancient graveyard. Usually she would make up stories about the different people as she read the inscriptions left on each tombstone. *A sweet girl, a loving mother, a missed father.* But today there was no time as she ran past, taking a shortcut through the cemetery.

Crossing the busy street, she went by the Yale Law School, then cut across High Street, walking past the Beinecke Rare Book and Manuscript Library. Eve thought if she picked up her pace, she could reach Blue State Coffee before they closed and then catch an Uber home.

New Haven was spread out and her parents had opted for buying a house close to the Yale campus when Eve had been accepted for undergrad. Being an only child, she was close to her parents and they had always done everything together. It wasn't a surprise when they announced that they would all be moving to New Haven together. As she aged, Eve realized her fortune, living in a mini mansion. Her father had inherited a large amount of money when he was in his late thirties and invested wisely, making the family not want for anything.

Eve had to think for a moment to remember where her parents said they were going. She sipped her warm coffee, smiling. They had said something about going to see Petrospheres in Costa Rica in Palmar Sur. They had told her the spears were still being found all over the area, perfect circles cut in stone, in all different sizes ranging from two to ten feet. At one point, theorists had said that they were made in molds because of the perfection of each stone. But after closer analysis, it was found that they had been carved. The mystery was how had it been done? They dated back further than the technology at the time. What had they been used for? Eve had heard her parents discussing that they might have been a representation of a different solar system. Each perfect stone, different sizes, mimicking a different planet in a different place. Eve laughed out loud and the Uber driver looked at her in his rearview mirror. She remembered their conversation. Her parents had said something about aliens or intelligent civilizations that had been on Earth, influencing human development. Knowing that this idea wasn't mainstream, she didn't know what she thought about it. As a scientist, she knew a theory was one thing but physical proof was a whole different story.

From a young age, Eve had grown accustomed to her parents talking about topics that weren't the norm. It had given her the drive to discover the impossible and embrace the unknown, letting her mind expand into ideas that the average person would think was crazy. She had always absorbed the books she read, filing the information away in her photographic memory. The books had taken her to unknown places, making her think about the world around her and all its possibilities.

Eve had always been tall and a little different than the other kids her age. Her large green eyes were unusual and they stood out in contrast to her auburn hair and white skin. She had been teased because she would pause when asked a question, thus making her retreat into herself or whatever book that she was reading at the time. She yearned for knowledge. By the time she was in tenth grade, her parents had her tested because her teachers had said that she was bored at school. They were told that her IQ was higher than they had ever seen at the school and wanted to give her additional tests, thinking she was ready for other possibilities. It had pushed her into college when she had just turned sixteen.

Now she was finishing her dissertation for her Masters degree in Quantum Physics and a second Masters degree in Mechanical Engineering, where she was working on an anti-gravitational device. It would be a tremendous discovery if she could figure out how to make it work. Sometimes she thought she almost had it and then had to start over. Many had tried to solve this problem, but Eve wasn't a quitter! She was already being courted by NASA, but she wanted to finish school and her project before she accepted a job.

Her ride pulled up in front of her house and Eve clicked the device that opened the gates and hurried up the drive, happy that she had made it home before her parents. She wanted to quickly straighten up the house; she knew her mother liked a clean ship and didn't want to hear anything about the week's worth of dishes she had left in the sink. For the past six years they had enjoyed the large white house, making it a home.

Approaching the porch, Eve jumped in the air, hitting a spot high on top of the pillar as she ran by. She had done this since they had moved into the house. Eve had told her parents that she could have played basketball; now it was a family joke that made them all laugh when she leaped on the porch. Eve grabbed the mail out of the box and noticed a loose piece of paper in the screen door. She put it on top of the pile, dumping everything on the table in the foyer.

Like a storm, she raced around the house putting things in order, washing dishes, filing papers away, tossing a pile of clothes left on the floor into her upstairs bedroom. She lit a fire, put on some tea, and was just sitting down to take a sip when she heard a knock at the door. She untangled her long legs and sprinted across the room, happy to see her parents.

chapter 2

Clicking the locks and opening the door, she was disappointed to see a mid-sized man sporting a short brown crewcut who was around forty. He fumbled over his words, not knowing what to say when he saw her looming over him. Her parents had warned her that she had to close the gate when she was home. Now she wished she had listened, not in the mood to be bothered by a stranger.

"Did you get the note I left in the door? I wasn't sure when you would be home. I'm…FBI," he said.

Eve saw something shiny in his hand and understood it was a badge that he was trying to show her. She noticed his nametag was a bunch of symbols that didn't make any sense, which was odd. He was dressed in a black suit with a white shirt and black tie. His eyes were covered with dark sunglasses and his whole look reminded her of the agents in the movie *Men in Black* with Will Smith.

"No, officer, I didn't see it…I was in a hurry. How can I help you?" Eve asked.

"I think it's best if I come in. Is that okay?" He asked.

Eve hesitated and tried to look closer as he flashed the badge again; she thought it looked official and noticed the seriousness of his voice so opened the door wider.

"Yes. This way please." She took him into the great room to the chairs by the fireplace and waited while he took a seat. She watched him look around the room as if he were taking pictures with his mind, not wanting to miss a thing. Eve was starting to feel that this was all really weird and wondered if she had done the right thing by letting him in the house.

"How can I help you?" Eve asked. She sensed something was really wrong and wanted this interaction to end quickly.

"Well, we have lost contact with your parents." He paused, watching her. Eve got the feeling that he was watching her reaction to see if she knew where they were.

"I don't understand. They should be home tonight." Eve hesitated for a moment, thinking about what he had said. "What do you mean that you have lost contact? Why would you be in contact with my parents?"

"They didn't tell you?" He asked.

"Tell me what?" Eve said.

"I just assumed that they would have mentioned it to you," he continued watching her closely.

"Look—you're making me nervous. I don't understand what's going on. Why are you here? You need to tell me what is happening! Where are my parents?" Eve jumped up and started to pace the room; an uneasy feeling had come over her. She started feeling something terrible had happened to her parents.

She should have listened to her "inner ear" or "voice," what her parents had called her intuition. From time to time in the past, Eve would feel things or ideas flashed in her mind. Often she would brush them off as coincidence. Her parents had told her that she needed to tune into them when it happened and embrace the images and information. Now she realized that was the reason her parents had been on her mind all day.

The agent hesitated, "All I can tell you is your parents have been...helping the government by looking into different...let's call it...mysteries pertaining to...scientific discoveries."

"What kind of discoveries?" Eve asked.

"Well...I've said more than I should have already.... Have you seen or heard anything about what they have been working on?" He asked.

Eve found this odd; if her parents were working for the FBI, then the agent should know the details of their work. She sat down and looked at him, sizing him up. He hadn't taken off his sunglasses in the house and she wanted to see his eyes to see if he was telling her the truth.

"No! I haven't," Eve responded.

"Well we have reason to believe that they might be gone..." He said.

"When you say gone...what does that mean? Gone as in disappear? Or gone as in dead?" Eve had resumed pacing the room, feeling anxiety and fear rise inside her. She was ready for this man to leave. For some reason she perceived they weren't dead. Eve knew if that were the case, she would have felt it.

"We aren't sure," he said, looking away.

"This conversation has been extremely unnerving to me. I would like you to leave." Eve moved toward the door and opened it. He looked surprised that this young girl would put him out, feeling he could maneuver her into getting the information he wanted.

"I need to try to contact my parents. You need to leave." She said, ready for this man to be gone. For some reason she was feeling DANGER flashing in her mind. He smiled at her, pushing the sunglasses to the top of his head. Eve noticed how the smile didn't reach his icy light blue eyes. They were cold and void of compassion.

"Okay," he handed her his card. "Could you call me if you hear from them or they show up? We are just concerned."

"Of course—I'll let you know. Can you do the same? If you find them from your end," Eve said, taking the card. She closed the door and locked it tight. She waited until he cleared the driveway and hit the button, closing the twelve-foot steel gates and flipping on the alarm as soon as he passed them. She watched the anger cross his face as he looked back in her direction before the gates locked in place.

After he was gone, Eve searched the living room, removing her cell phone from her book bag. She fumbled online, finding the number for American Airlines. Eve told the representative her situation and waited on hold while she checked. When the woman returned, she was kind and told Eve that the flight was to land around seven. Then Eve was asked to hold again. While she waited, Eve tried to recall anything that her parents might have said. Mad at herself for being so absorbed in her own work, Eve kicked herself for not paying more attention to what her parents had been doing. When the woman finally came back on the phone, she explained that they must have missed their first flight and hadn't been on the plane. Eve had held her breath and asked just to make sure.

"Can you tell me where their ticket originated?" Eve

could hear the sound of typing and was surprised at the answer.

"Yes, they were to board yesterday at 7 P.M. in Sanliurfa, Turkey, then on to Istanbul, from there to London and on to the United States. It looks like they weren't on those planes either," she said. "The way it works these days is if you're not on your first flight, then the rest of the trip is canceled."

"Okay—thank you for your help."The conversation disconnected and Eve sat silently thinking. Then she got an idea and focused on her mother, visualizing her face and reaching out with her mind. Many times over the years when she had thought of her mother, her mother then told her that she had felt Eve in her head. Then she would stop what she was doing and call her. It was weird but Eve had been told that sometimes when people were close, a person would keep popping in their minds. Then they would call and find out that the other person had been thinking about them. It was worth a try, so she concentrated on her mother and waited in silence for fifteen minutes. Eve sat thinking about her parents.

They had met in college when they about her age, at a college football game. Her mother hadn't wanted to go that night but a friend dragged her away from her studies, telling her that all she did was study and she was no fun. Her mother had denied that fact and to prove herself a fun person, had filled an empty peanut butter jar with vodka from her parents' stash and brought it to the game in her purse. After partaking in the stands, she had gone to the restroom and bumped into a young man, almost falling into Eve's father's arms. Later, when she couldn't find her friend, Michael had given her a ride home. By then she had sobered up while having a long conversation about life after college and what they wanted in the future.

Eve smiled to herself, remembering her mother telling the story. More time passed as she waited...Nothing! Eve knew she needed help and decided to call her friend Scott.

chapter 3

Scott was an incredibly smart student that Eve had met when taking some of her undergrad classes at Yale. He was a few years older than her, having starting college after he finished high school. Eve had admired his mind at first, before noticing that he was quite handsome. At 6'6", he towered over other men, with his dark curly hair making him look even taller. Scott was well built, having played basketball and football in high school. When Eve and Scott were together, other women tended to cast looks in his direction; he seemed quite popular. But his most endearing feature was that he didn't seem to notice. They had been good friends for the past five years. He was now in law school at Yale and their paths didn't cross as often as before, both caught up in their own studies, pushing forward into their uncertain futures.

Eve dialed his number and as she listened to the ringing, repeated *Pick up* over and over in her mind until she heard the phone connect and Scott's voice sounding like she had woken him.

"Hello?" He said, sleep in his voice.

"Scott…sorry to wake you," she paused, waiting for a response. "It's Eve." She heard the covers rustling.

“Hold on, Eve.” Eve heard him walking across the floor and the toilet flushing. When he returned, he sounded a little more awake.

“I’m here.…What’s wrong? I can tell from the tone of your voice that something is up.”

Eve hesitated, “Can you come over to my house? I need a mind to bounce a few things off and you’re the largest brain I know.”

He chuckled at the compliment, but turned serious when she was quiet. “Sure…I don’t have classes tomorrow.”

“I mean now! Can you come now?” She asked.

Scott sat straight up in the bed. She had never asked him to come over late at night. He had always liked her, but she had often pulled away, seeming disinterested in him. Once he had tried to kiss her and immediately felt, judging from her reaction, that it was best to leave things as they were. He had settled into being her friend until she might be ready for more.

“Okay—I’m up. I’ll be there in thirty,” he said.

“Thank you, Scott, I’ll see you soon.” Eve sat thinking… Scott…maybe she better call for a pizza…or two.

chapter 4

Outside down the street, the now grumpy agent entered a parked sedan with darkened windows. It was parked four houses down, across the street in a side alley. He moved into the passenger seat, quietly shutting the door before the overhead light cast a glimpse of luminosity over the shadows of the deserted street.

"Well, anything?" The driver asked.

"The neighbors said that they are pleasant people but don't know them very well; they seem to keep to themselves. Their house is the biggest on the street and surrounded by that tall brick wall; the neighbors don't talk to them. They said they are friendly when they do see them," the grumpy passenger stated.

The larger man in the driver's seat watched a lone dog pass in front of the car, searching for discarded food. "Dang! I don't understand where they could have gone! We had someone on them the whole time in Turkey and we were told that they didn't leave their hotel room that night. Their things were still in the room and there were no papers or notes left behind that could give us any clues to their whereabouts. You would think there would have been something, especially if they were doing all that research." He watched the dog, wondering if they had anything inside the car that he could toss to him. "What did you think about the daughter?" He asked.

"She was a little odd, but I didn't think she knew anything until she kicked me out. I thought that was a weird reaction." The passenger said, unbuttoning his shirt and loosening his tie.

"Well, everyone deals with things differently. How often do you hear your parents have disappeared?" The driver said. The skinny dog had found something and lay down on the sidewalk to chew on the bone.

"That's what I'm saying…I thought she would have asked for the FBI's help." He said. "What happened after I left?"

"Well it was kind of muffled—you must have put the bug far away," the driver said.

"Sorry—I had to dump it fast. I didn't know I was going to be kicked out." The passenger felt he was being told he didn't do a good job. He was defensive and hid it before his partner saw his anger.

"But she made two phone calls, one to the airline and the other to a Scott Alexander." The driver said, reading the name from his notes.

"Who is that? I didn't have him on the list." The agent said, frustrated.

"I'm not sure…maybe her boyfriend?" The driver said. "I'll drop you off and I'll take the first shift."

"Okay, thanks," the agent settled back in the leather seat for the ride back to their hotel.

chapter 5

By the time Scott arrived at the house, the pizza had come and Eve had put it in the warming drawer in the kitchen. She had spent the rest of the time looking for the key to her parents' hidden room. The room had been built a few years back, on the top floor of the house. Her parents had said it was to protect the valuables that they bought while traveling. At least that is what they had told her. After the weird encounter with the FBI agent, Eve had remembered what her parents had told her over and over, "If anything happens to us, find the key and enter the room."

Eve had never thought much about it before, because her parents weren't old or sick and she figured they had meant when they passed. She had only half listened, not interested in hearing that kind of talk. But now their words returned, pounding in her head. Eve felt this must be the kind of situation they were referring to. Now she would finally see why they spent so much time upstairs and had gone to so much trouble creating a hiding space.

Eve found the key taped on the bottom drawer of the large wooden desk in her father's office. She had remembered them saying to look in the office. Eve had pulled the desk apart with no luck until she came to the last drawer. Relief flooded over her when she found what she was looking for on the underside of the heavy wood.

Eve ran up the stairs two at a time until she stood at the end of the hall in front of a large printed picture. She ran her fingers along the sides of the thick frame...searching. The framed picture was a photograph of a statue. She had never thought much about it, other than thinking it was artistic. Now she digested the content. In the middle was a photograph of a figure carved in granite. At the time the photo was taken, the statue was already disfigured and worn from erosion. Eve's parents had said the statue was over five thousand years old and was a cosmic egg. Eve now took in the details, making out a weird looking person with an odd shaped head and large eyes, with long arms surrounding a smaller figure. Looking closer, she noticed a small shape inside the smaller person's embrace; it looked like a baby. Eve wondered about the meaning of the photo. At first she thought it had been manipulated in Photoshop, then disregarded that idea. She questioned, *Why did they think the photo was important?* Eve wondered. *What does it symbolize?*

Before she thought about those questions further, Eve's finger snagged a small button along the bottom of the frame. Pushing it in, she heard a click and the frame released on one side, opening like a door. Behind was a small passage. Eve stepped inside, following the curve into blackness within, taking baby steps as she felt her way along a two-foot walkway that stopped at a door. Standing in the dark in front of the entrance, she gathered the courage to move forward. She fumbled with the key, finding the hole, and pushed it in. The lock clicked when it turned and released.

But before Eve could move inside the wall, she heard the doorbell ring downstairs. She pulled the key out and quickly backtracked the way she had come. Eve pushed the picture back in place on the wall until she heard a light metallic sound and ran down the stairs. She pushed the button for the security system and when she heard Scott's voice over the intercom, ran to the front door.

Scott stood on the front porch, his briefcase flung over his shoulder, a bag of hot wings in one hand and a Nike gym bag in the other. His curly dark hair was sticking out in spots and sparkled with fresh snowflakes. Eve looked behind Scott out the doorway into the dark night; the weather had changed and now a heavy, steady stream of snow was coming down behind him, covering his footprints. The once sunny day had turned into a whiteout. Eve noticed Scott's mismatched basketball clothes; the oranges, reds, and blues along with his black hoodie ran together, creating a blur of color.

"Thanks for coming so fast! What's wrong? You seem out of breath." Eve said.

"Hey," he grinned, "Are you okay? I hurried."

Before Eve could answer, she saw the concern in his eyes and lost control of her emotions. The stress of the situation rose to the surface and she went into his arms and held him tight, feeling comfort in his strong arms as he dropped his bags and kept his wings far away from her hair. She didn't realize how alone she felt without her parents and this was the only other person in her life whom she felt close to. After a few moments she pulled away and wiped her cheek where a lone tear had trickled and dropped off her chin to the floor.

"Okay, Eve—what's wrong?" Scott stood there, lightly patting her back and smelling her hair until she pulled away.

"Come in; please shut the door," Eve said. She waited while he picked up his Nike duffel off the porch, shaking the snow off his jacket before closing the door behind him. Eve watched him look around and stop for a moment. She took a look at the room through his eyes, taking in the soft lights and the logs burning in the fireplace. Eve flipped on the overhead lights, not wanting him to get the wrong idea. "Sit by the fire in that chair and I'll grab some pizza."

"Where are your parents?" He asked, looking around. She had never had him here alone.

"Hold on and I'll tell you…put your things by the stairs." Eve had moved into the kitchen and Scott decided to do as she had instructed and sat in the chair in front of the fire and waited, trying to figure out what was going on.

Eve came back with plates of the steaming hot pizza, the cheese melting over the sides onto the plates. She grabbed two wine glasses and an opened bottle of red wine. Sitting opposite of him in the high-backed chair, she pulled up her feet and covered her lap with a blanket before looking up. Scott had opened the bag of wings and put a few on their plates. The room was silent for a few moments while they ate. Scott waited for her to speak, knowing how she was and suspecting she was thinking of how to say what was on her mind.

"Something has happened to my parents and I need your help to find them! I usually don't hear from them when they travel." Eve said thoughtfully.

"They don't call?" Scott asked.

"No, they just tell me when they will return and sometimes I get an email. But usually they aren't close to the

Internet in many of the places they go. So…you are the smartest man I know and very logical." Scott listened, waiting until she was ready to tell him the situation.

"Tonight I came home to an FBI agent on my porch saying some really weird things. Either I don't know my parents, or I haven't been paying enough attention. Sometimes I'm in my own zone when they are discussing what they're working on. This man said that they had been working for the government. I'm not sure what to believe. All I know is they have disappeared, and I need to find them." Eve said, taking a breath, trying not to become emotional.

"Okay—what can I do to help?" Scott asked, taking a large bite, watching her.

"Well, for a start…can you stay here at the house with me? I'm used to being alone, but right now being alone in this large house…makes me a little uneasy. I felt danger when that man was here. Not that I'm scared or anything. I just thought if you agree to help me it would be better if we were in one place. I'm not saying lock ourselves in…but almost like when we worked on that project a few years ago. Remember when all we did was research and eat?" Eve asked.

Scott thought about what she was saying and remembered how fun it was working together. That was when he really got to know her. After that, when he went on dates, he had found that no one compared to her quick wit and intellect. But because she had backed off from his advances, he fell into the friend role. He was happy being around her, hoping someday she would start to feel the same.

"Okay; I might need to stop at my house for more clothes. I only have classes on Tuesdays and Thursdays this semester and it isn't a heavy load. I'm coming to the end of my program and it's more or less prepping us to take the big law exam. Because it's a pass/fail, I'm not worried about that. Then I have to study for the Bar exam, so this is a perfect time for me to take on a project." He quickly corrected himself, "I'm not saying finding your parents is a project...I just mean it's a good time for me because I have plenty of time right now."

"Thanks, Scott!" Eve smiled at him.

Chapter 6

Scott felt his heart flip and tried not to move or show it in his eyes; he looked down at the pizza, jamming the rest of the piece in his mouth.

"You can have the room at the top of the stairs. It's a guest room. You will be the first guest to stay in it, so it should be ready for you."

"Okay...where are we looking for your parents?" He asked.

"Well, I thought they were going to Costa Rica and found out today they were in Turkey at some archaeology site called Gobekli Tepe."

"I'm not familiar with that...what is it?" Scott asked.

"While I was waiting for you to get here, I looked online and I guess it is a very old site. It is thought to be about 12 or 13 thousand years old. It's the oldest ritual structure found thus far and is called a 'Potbelly Hill.' It was discovered in the sixties, but nothing was thought about it until 1994 when they discovered many temples and rounded structures. Archaeologists are saying that each site was buried after they were finished using it and a new one erected close by. Now they are finding more every day, all on top of each other. The mystery is…what were they used for? One suggestion was that they aligned with certain solar systems or stars. There are carvings of animals on the stone pillars, but many of the animals hadn't lived in that region. So…it's weird." Eve stated, reading from her notes.

"Okay. I wonder what this all has to do with where they went?" Scott said. "Please continue."

"Where was I? Here's something…each structure had been built and then buried. Then close by, another was built and on and on. I wonder because it lined up with the stars, maybe it was a kind of observation place. And when the star system changed, the location changed. Makes you wonder how many thousands of years it was functional? It makes it sound like there was an advanced civilization that had lived there once and then disappeared." Eve said, taking a breath and waiting for his reaction. "I must have gotten that from my parents," she laughed.

"That is interesting, but why would your parents be looking into it? And what did that FBI guy say? That your parents were working for them?" He asked.

"I'm not sure myself! They were just happy running around doing their investigating. Are you finished? I have more pizza in the oven…I know how you can eat."

Eve stood, feeling a bit more relaxed after she had drunk a large glass of wine. Now she felt the warmth in her body and the heat from the fire. She refilled their glasses, finishing off the bottle. "Well, we can't let it go to waste!" She said, seeing he was watching her as she walked into the kitchen.

"I'll take whatever you have that's hot." Scott said, sipping the dark liquid and finding it smooth and dry.

Eve brought him one more plate with the last three pieces and watched as he inhaled them. She was silent, searching the Internet to see if she could find more information.

"Wow—here's something odd. Some people claim that the only possible answer to the mystery of who built the structures is that extraterrestrial beings had a hand in building them." Eve said, looking up and finding him quiet in thought.

"That doesn't sound logical to me—like aliens?" He laughed.

Eve had to smile. It was kind of funny. "Well, tomorrow is Friday—want to help me? Can you start then? Oh…I forgot to tell you. My parents told me that if something ever happened to them that I was to go into their secret room. I think it's where they hid valuables and hopefully cash. I haven't checked my account in forever and we might need to travel."

Scott looked up, "Okay, cool. Did you check the room?" He asked.

"I was getting ready to when you arrived. Want to come with me? I'm just a little uneasy. It might be better with two sets of eyes." Eve said.

"Sure, show me the way." Scott said, "And your parents' hidden room is between us. I don't want them to know that I was in there. They might not like it and I want them to like me."

"Well, they already like you!" Eve said. "But if it makes you feel better, we don't have to tell them when we find them."

"Maybe they just went somewhere else and they will show up," he said.

"If something bad happened I would feel it, but where are they?" Eve said, sounding sure of herself. Scott just nodded and hoped that she was right.

"Come on, follow me." Eve headed to the staircase and grabbed his bag as she walked by.

"Here, let me have that…I can carry my own bag!" Scott said.

Eve handed it over and raced up the stairs, seeing if he could make it to the top as fast as she could while carrying the bag. Turning at the landing, he was standing next to her, smiling and tapping his foot when she reached the top.

"You were lucky!" Eve laughed, "This is your room…put it in there and follow me."

They went down the long hall to the end, where the odd photo hung, and she opened the latch. Together, they stepped into the passage, pulling the art tight behind them. Eve stopped at the door and Scott bumped into her. She felt the length of his body against her before he stepped back.

"Sorry…" was all he said.

Eve pulled out the key, turning it in the lock. The door swung open into a large office. They could make out the walls that were lined with bookshelves, all filled with books and files. The moonlight now filtered in through the snow-covered skylight, casting shadows in the dark corners. In the middle of the room, a dim glow filtered down on a large table. In the center were stacks of organized papers. Using the light from her phone, Eve searched the wall for a switch. The lights turned on and brightened the cluttered room, showing the immense amount of files.

One of the walls had been painted black and was now covered with star systems. A closer inspection showed that the artist had painted the wall with detailed care, making sure that the solar systems looked recognizable. The other wall held a large painting of Earth; it was covered with many small yellow sticky notes and papers taped all over the surface. Lines of thin black tape crossed over each other, forming some kind of grid pattern connecting different places around the world.

"Well it looks like they were working on something!" Scott said, taking a closer look at the maps. "What do you think these maps mean?"

"I'm not sure! But who would have known that they were doing all this? I lived in the same house with them and never knew. This is crazy!" Eve said, walking over to the table.

Papers had been stacked in neat piles, anchored down with rocks. In the middle of the mess was an envelope written on with a dark sharpie. Eve recognized her mother's handwriting and saw her name had been written in bold black letters. The large "EVE" jumped out at her. Eve took a breath and traced her fingertip over the letters of her name. Her trance was broken when she felt Scott's hand on her shoulder.

"I'm all right," Eve half smiled and turned the envelope over. She saw that it was sealed, and nervously turned it over a few times, staring at the letters of her name as it contrasted with the white paper. "I hope this isn't their will! Well, it seems like we have a lot of research to do. How about we start early in the morning?" She asked, feeling the cold, thick weight of the envelope between her fingers. Eve felt she needed to be alone when she read the letter from her mother and was urgent to leave the room.

"Okay, sounds good to me. It's almost 2 A.M. and I'm always brighter after coffee in the morning and of course a large breakfast!" He laughed, trying to break her mood. "Come on…don't worry! We'll find them." Scott took her hand and pulled her behind him, closing the door and locking it tight before handing her the key. In the light of their cell phones they found the release for the art and stepped into the hall.

"Where is your room?" He asked.

"Right beside yours." Eve pointed to the open doorway a little farther down the hall.

"Okay, get some rest and we'll talk in the morning and make a plan." He saw the weariness in her eyes and the hesitation. "It will be all right! Don't worry—I'm here and we'll figure this out."

"Thank you, Scott," Eve said, "I really appreciate you coming."

"Of course…what are friends for?" He said, noticing how beautiful she looked in the dim light of the hall. "Sleep well." He pushed her toward her doorway and waited until he heard it close. Then he raced down the stairs and checked the door and the windows, confirming that the house was locked up. The fire was just embers and he shut the metal fireplace cover, making sure nothing fell out in the night. He turned down the lights, leaving one on in the entryway and was back up the stairs in less than five minutes. Leaving his door cracked, he went inside.

His room was large; the walls were cream with white trim. In the center was a king-sized bed that had been perfectly made and was covered with a matching cream comforter. A dark iron headboard contrasted against the light colors, making the room look modern and masculine. On the walls, black-framed pictures continued the theme. The large prints were of Eve's family smiling for the camera. As a teenager she was already a foot taller than her parents and towered over the dark-haired couple. Scott noticed Eve's red hair had been lighter when she was young and had deepened as she grew older. But what stood out were her large green eyes. *Everyone was awkward at that age*, he thought. He pulled back the covers and felt the flannel sheets softly touch his skin; it felt like heaven. *I need to buy some of these*, he thought. Scott looked over to make sure his door was still ajar, just in case Eve needed him in the night or awoke early. It didn't take long and he was soon asleep.

chapter 7

Inside Eve's room she was still awake…thinking. She had changed her clothes and climbed into bed but sat holding the envelope in her shaky hand. She was afraid to open it, but knew she had to take the plunge. Courage found her and she ripped the end off and shook out the contents. She recognized the familiar curve of her mother's handwriting.

December 5, 2020

Eve,

If you are reading this, don't be alarmed. Your father and I knew one day something would happen to us and we might not make it back from one of our research trips, which would lead you to finding this letter. We both knew that there were many things that we should have told you long ago, but the years just seemed to go by. We were afraid to tell you as you grew older . . . afraid that you would turn your back on us. Please forgive us—it was out of love. As you can tell by the pages, it is a long story. But the time was never right. One thing you need to know is that we have always loved you; you are our life and you are the reason that took us on this journey. The path that made us want to discover more.

About twenty-two years ago, your father and I had just married. It was a happy time and we were in love. We wanted children and set out to start a family, but nothing was happening. We went to the doctor and found out that the injections that your father received when he was in the military had made it impossible for him to have children. His sperm swam in circles and were cross-eyed. I know this sounds like a crazy way of describing them, but it was true. We had already accepted the fact that it would be just the two of us. Luckily we were very happy just being together.

We were on vacation in Arizona and went on a day trip to check out some cliff paintings. They were interesting because they had unusual depictions of animals and people that had been painted thousands of years ago. Walking around in the area, we met an Indian who told us the story of the Ant people. He was an older chief and told us that his tribe had been visited from outside our solar system for thousands of years. These space beings had saved his tribe by taking them underground during the last ice age. We studied the drawings of the beings painted on the rocks; they looked human but not quite. We noticed some of their heads had what looked like antlers coming out of them and some of their bodies were more elongated. They almost looked like they were robots. But the thing that caught my attention was their eyes. They were really large and wrapped to the side of their head. I put this off to the artists' depictions. The Indian said that the elders of his tribe had passed the story down for hundreds of years. He said to this day, there were many sightings of UFOs seen over the reservation. Some of the elders had even greeted the space beings as friends.

We thought it was really interesting but believed nothing more about it, figuring it was just folklore. By the time we left, the sun had gone down over the horizon and the night was overcast. It was a very dark night. We gave thanks to the man and made our way down the deserted dirt road toward the hotel where we were staying. As we traveled back to the hotel, we didn't see any other cars at all and wondered if we were going the right way. Then we noticed a weird light shining ahead of us and we kept traveling toward it, thinking we could get directions. As we drove closer, slowing the car, we watched the light start to flash around the sky in different directions. We thought it must be some kind of military craft that was being tested. But when we slowed the car, the lights slowed. When we went faster, the lights went faster. It was really bizarre and I was frightened. We stopped the car and the light stopped right above us, then the car began to shake and rock. I remember holding on tight to the side door. We were both worried, never seeing anything like it and finding it focused on us. We were terrified.

When we woke up in the car, it was daylight and we proceeded to find our way back to our hotel.

When we checked our messages on the hotel phone, we found out that we had lost a few days and had missed our plane to return home. We both found that we had a blank space of time in our minds and didn't understand what had happened. At home we went back to work and after a while we questioned if it had happened at all or if it was our imagination. But the loss of time had happened to both of us. We put it behind us, thinking that maybe there had been peyote in the drinks offered by the Indian that we had met. We thought this might explain the loss of time in our minds.

About eight weeks later I noticed that I hadn't had my period and took a test, finding out that I was pregnant. Both your father and I took it as a miracle; we were indescribably happy.

After you were born, we noticed a few things that made us question your parentage. Your eyes were incredibly large, you had red hair and we both knew that it wasn't in either of our families. Also you were so smart—by two you had taught yourself to read and had asked me where you could find more books. It kind of blew our minds. When I told my girlfriend about it, she sent me to a friend of hers that she said could help. I didn't understand at first, thinking I was being sent to a psychologist. I found this woman had special talents. She put me in a hypnotic state and soon the blank space that had been in my mind from that night in Arizona came to the surface and I remembered what had happened.

I remembered being in a room that looked like a lab; it had lots of machines, bright lights, and reflective surfaces. I looked around, just moving my eyes because my body wouldn't respond. I could see your father on a table next to me. We both looked in each other's eyes but we couldn't speak or move. I remember seeing an image over me and I shut my eyes. I was afraid, feeling a pain inside of me. I remember trying to focus on controlling the sharp shocks going through my body. When I got the courage to open my eyes again, I saw large, expressionless eyes staring into mine. The dark orbs didn't blink or have eyelashes and I felt they were boring into my soul through my mind. I remember closing my eyes again, now having to endure the pain that had moved to my head.

The next thing I remember is waking up in the car. Both of us felt sore in weird places and all we knew is we had to get out of there. It was scary and I felt that I had relived that horrific moment, understanding why my mind didn't want to remember what'd happened.

The woman asked me if I had heard of children called "Star Children." I told her I hadn't. She explained they were children that were birthed without having sex and suggested that we get your father checked out again, along with a DNA test on you. I was shocked and asked, "What do you mean . . . like Jesus?" I thought this had to be a joke and wondered how I got talked into seeing her.

At the time I was mad and to prove her wrong, we did the tests. The results came back a few weeks later. Then I was ready to hear what she had to say. The test revealed your father wouldn't have been able to sire a child. It was a hard time in our relationship because he thought that I had stepped out on him, wanting a child that badly. But it wasn't true! I persuaded him to see the woman. When he was under hypnosis, your father remembered what had happened to us. It brought us closer together and he asked for my forgiveness for not believing me.

But the part that I have been afraid to say is that the DNA test showed that you had my human DNA and something else.

The woman told me that in her circles for years there had been talk of these children who are extra talented. She explained that 5,000 years ago, humans took an evolutionary jump in intelligence. The idea had been presented that beings from outer space had visited our planet and gave us information . . . teaching us. At the same time, they created a better human by installing or mixing their DNA with ours. It is something not commonly talked about because we think more on the lines of evolution—where it takes a long period of time and selective breeding to create enough change to advance a species. She explained that time and breeding wouldn't have been able to account for that much of a jump in intelligence of the human race. She explained the theory is that at one time in Earth's history, the planet had been visited by space people who integrated or mixed their DNA with humans, causing the change. People don't talk about it and evidence has been hidden because of the fear of a society breakdown over where we came from breaking down their instilled beliefs.

So . . . For years your father and I have been doing our own investigation. This might sound crazy, but from what we have found we think that you are a hybrid of human and something else that isn't from this planet.

chapter 8

At this point, Eve cried out, dropping the letter. She gathered her knees to her chest, trying not to shake, and sat in a trancelike state, rocking her body, thinking about what she had just read. This was the craziest thing she had ever heard. She saw wet spots dropping on her blanket and realized that tears were streaming down her face. Her vision blurred and Eve couldn't see; she felt arms encircling her and the soft gentle hand of someone stoking her hair.

"Here now...it's okay. You're just having a bad dream," Scott's soft voice washed over her. Eve felt comfort, finding warmth in the physical contact of his strong body. She pulled away and opened her eyes. Scott's face was full of concern.

"I'm okay," Eve said. "I just don't know what to say."

"What's wrong?" He asked, gathering her fallen papers and stacking them neatly on the side table.

"It's hard to explain unless you read it. I now understand what my parents were working on and why." She paused, trying to work her mind around it. *Was this really possible? No...it couldn't be true.* "Here—I need a logical mind right now." Eve picked up the pages, found where she had left off, and handed him the ones she had already read.

"Are you sure you want me to know? It's your family," he asked, holding the pages in his hand.

"Yes…we're in this together, right?" She questioned. "But whatever we discover on this journey, I want to ask you to keep it just between the two of us. Can you do that?" Eve asked, waiting for him to decide.

"Okay…listen…Eve, look at me. We Are In This Together! Whatever we find out is between us…I give you my word." Eve reached over and gave him a big hug, crushing the papers a little before pulling back and sitting up straight.

"I trust you…but get ready to blow your mind." Eve pushed the crumpled papers into his hand, took hers, and said, "READ." The room was silent.

Eve read on:

I know it sounds like your father and I are disturbed, but if we are missing, they might have come for us . . . Or the government has? For some reason the government has been following us. Maybe they have taken us to protect the fact, which they have known for a long time, that we are not alone on this planet.

We found in our research that sometimes the same people or lines of generations are watched. The ones that seem to be taken or disappear are usually blond with blue eyes and have a certain blood type. So it leads us to think, why choose us? After researching others that have been reported being taken, we learned that many have the same story of being in a lab or medical atmosphere and not being able to move. Many have been aware of the beings and felt the pain of samples being taken. It seemed that the samples taken most of the time were sperm and a woman's eggs. These outer space beings were very interested in our reproduction system. Maybe over time they had lost their ability to reproduce?

The theory is that these beings have been using our planet like a petri dish, mixing our genetics. What we have been finding in our research is that the hybrids of human and space beings are very tall with red hair. We know you will have to research all of this on your own, because it is a lot to take in. Start with our file of the giants found in Wisconsin.

If we are missing, I want you to go see the woman we met with. Her name is Sarah Smiles; she is in upstate New York in a small town called Buskirk. She is easy to find. She will help you understand; she knows all about you.

We love you, my darling.

Mother

Eve handed Scott the last few pages and was silent, waiting while he finished. She didn't know what to think but was really glad he was here with her. She watched him read the final page and saw the wheels turning in his mind before he spoke.

"I'm not sure what to say. I have never thought about this kind of thing. I did hear some people at school talking about there being many advanced ancient civilizations that have been found around the world. Some of these sites were found on archaeology digs and others underwater. I remember them saying that the sites dated back further than they thought possible.

"The one I remember hearing about was Gunung Padang…they said it dated back at least to 15,000 BC. Now I recall your Gobekli Tepe that they say was dated around 13,000 BC. At the time I remember thinking that it was interesting because the question that researchers didn't understand was how man had moved the large stones into place on the pyramids in Cairo. The stones were so large, heavy, and precisely cut that they fit together where you couldn't fit a piece of paper in the cracks between them." Scott said, trying to pull information out of the corners of his brain.

"Okay, Scott, you're rambling. I have read some of that information online in my research for the anti-gravitational device I'm working on. I just don't know what to think. My parents have always been intellects and of sound mind. It sounds like they believe what they are talking about. But I guess I can't just believe something so far-fetched. I think I need to rest on it and tomorrow I can think of something." Scott took her cue to leave but her hand grasped his arm. "Please don't go! Not that I'm afraid...I just don't want to be alone," she said.

"It's okay...move over and I'll sleep on top of the covers," Scott said, tucking her in tight so she was warm. He fluffed a pillow, laying down next to her, pulling her afghan on top of him. Scott watched her and noticed tears in her eyes. He stroked her cheek, brushing the hair off her face. "Really, it's going to be all right...shut your eyes and get some rest." He hesitated, then leaned over and kissed her forehead.

Eve felt safe and did as she was told; soon she was asleep. Scott listened to her soft, even breathing. He lay there for a while wondering if any of this was possible. His logical mind said no, but he promised himself to try to be open-minded for her. He drifted off with visions of outer space and different creatures dancing in his head before falling asleep.

chapter 9

Eve woke up, stretched, then remembered the events of the previous night. Slowly opening her eyes, she reached her hand for Scott. His side of the bed was empty; the afghan was folded neatly at the foot of her bed. The letter from her mother had been put back in the envelope and sat on the side table. She tossed on her sweats and pulled on a large sweater after finding her socks. She hated to be cold. Eve found Scott downstairs starting a fire; the smell of coffee made her smile and in the kitchen she found he had made eggs, toast, and bacon. Hers sat ready in the warming drawer under the oven. She was surprised; Eve didn't realize he could cook. Her mother did most of the cooking in their home and had told her many times, "The way to a man's heart is to cook for him." Lucky for Eve she wasn't trying to snag a man. She had never felt the need to learn to cook or to try to draw a man in; she always felt her studies were more important and cooking didn't stimulate her mind. Eve found cooking a little boring when after all the work and effort of preparing it, the food was gone within a few moments.

"I hope you don't mind that I helped myself. Sometimes in the morning the tank is empty and if I don't eat, I won't feel right for the whole day," Scott said, smiling at her.

"Not at all. Thanks for this, by the way," she said, motioning to her plate. "You can cook anytime; I'm not much help in the kitchen." Eve took a bite, "And this is really good." She sat down in her comfortable chair by the fire and watched him add wood to the small blaze. The room started to warm, giving it a cozy atmosphere. Sitting back content, she sipped the coffee, enjoying the flavor; it had the perfect amount of half and half.

Scott had a pad of paper in his lap and she watched him writing something. Eve noticed his large hand encircling the pencil, almost making it disappear.

"What are you doing?" She asked.

"I decided to get a head start while you slept. I think we need to take this on, like we do when we research. I'm making a list of the different things that we need to look up and do."

"What do you have already?" Eve asked, munching on a piece of bacon.

"Well…we know why your parents started looking into this alien outer-space idea. And I think we need to start at the beginning and look into the giants in Wisconsin like your mother said. Also, I think we need to call the woman in upstate New York and maybe go see her. I have already looked up mysteries in Turkey and found something else that was interesting. Maybe your parents had investigated that as well. Did you know that there are underground tunnels that were found in Cappadocia?" He paused when he saw the question on her face. "That's Central Turkey. They are called the Derinkuyu caves. Listen to this…some family was renovating their house and dug farther into the rock face, then dug through into these tunnels. They now have found that it was a whole underground complex that went down 280 feet. It was full of living areas, religious centers, wine presses, stables for livestock, and it even had ventilation shafts that brought in fresh air from the surface. It is said that the place could hold 20,000 people. But the kicker is they don't know how old it is because as you know, you can't carbon date rock.

"So it is estimated to be built around 800 BC to 18,000 BC. But researchers think that they were used during the last ice age and that ended around 10,000 years ago. It is thought that the people went underground to protect themselves from the weather on Earth's surface. Sounds a little like these ant people that your mom refers to going underground to survive the last ice age. So I'm thinking we could check and see if this was one of the places your parents went?

"The other theory is that it dates back as early as 800 BC and the reason they think it was built in the first place was for protection from what was happening on Earth's surface. Maybe protection from enemies, because there was a 1,000-pound round boulder that was used to block the entrance from the inside. It was set up that only one person from inside could move the rock in place, totally blocking out the outside world." He read from his paper.

"But what does that have to do with us?" Eve asked.

He paused reading. "Well, it says here that the myth is that a being from the sky came down on a dragon and directed them how to build the underground structure." Scott was thoughtful. "We need to look into anything that has to do with anyone coming from the sky since there wasn't technology that allowed us to fly back then."

"I guess there are things that happened in Earth's past...what if there was an intelligent society that existed thousands of years ago, which had more technology than we have right now and people of today don't have any idea? What happened back then? What if all the technology of that time was lost and we are still catching up today? What happens if the information we find is different than what people believe, it would mess up the logic and idea that people have had in place for thousands of years. Hold on—I'll be right back. I'm going to find the file that my mother talked about, so we can start with that." Eve said, heading for the staircase.

Scott barely looked up, intent on reading what he had found. He watched Eve race up the stairs out of the corner of his eye.

Once inside the hidden room, Eve found stacks of folders lining the length of the table. They were well organized and in order, so she took off the first rock holding a ten-inch pile in place. She turned the stone over in her hands, noting the unusual markings. The rock didn't look like something that she recognized; taped to the bottom was a label saying it was a meteorite. *My parents are something*, she thought. Setting it aside, she looked at the files. The one on top was labeled Wisconsin Giants. Eve took the whole stack and left the room, locking the hiding place behind her. She tossed the key in a potted plant at the end of the hall as she ran past. Eve was back down the stairs, files in hand, in less than ten minutes.

chapter 10

"I found the Wisconsin file," Eve said, moving her chair closer to the fire. She pulled a floor lamp over, clicking on the light, and opened the first file after setting the others to the side. She was silent for a few moments while she read the article inside. "Listen to this—it's an old newspaper article.

"First reported in the May 4, 1912 issue of *The New York Times.* Two brothers find mounds with freakish skeletons.

"Burial mounds were found near Lake Delavan, Wisconsin. Two hundred effigy mounds that proved to be classic examples of 8th century Woodland culture. They did not fit very neatly into anyone's concept of a textbook standard. The skeletons found were enormous. These were not average human beings. Scientists are remaining stubbornly silent about a lost race of giants found in burial mounds near Lake Delavan, Wisconsin. In the dig site was found enormous skeletons with elongated skulls. Their heights ranged between 7.6 ft and 10 feet and their skulls 'presumably those of men, are much larger than the heads of any race that inhabits America today.' Most of the giants found in the Americas and across the world have a double row of teeth, 6 fingers, 6 toes, and like humans came in different races. Are these the giants that are mentioned in the Bible and many other civilizations where they have been painted on walls portraying their history?

"In the Christian Bible, Genesis 6:4 says, 'There were giants on the earth in those days, before and after when (the divine beings) the sons of God came and had sexual relations with human women and they bore children to them. These children were the mighty famous men of long ago.'

"Wow—crazy!" Eve said, "A side note on the margin says to look into the Book of Enoch. Wonder what that is? I have never heard of that book in the Bible. It says here, 'Giant skeleton finds have not made the local and national news since the 1950s. It seems in most opinions it is because of the fear that people would question evolution.' I feel like this is all news to me," Eve said. "Why haven't we ever heard of such a thing? We better put this Book of Enoch on our list!"

"I find this fascinating!" Scott said, "Who would have known?" He had been sitting back, listening with his eyes closed.

"Wow! There's one more side note," Eve said. "It looks like the Smithsonian Institution was accused of a cover-up. They showed up after the discovery and took all the bones and artifacts. It says, 'They have displayed some of the artifacts found at the site but the skeletons have never been exhibited.' It's almost like they just disappeared." Eve stated.

"I'm not sure what to say. Maybe we need to add the Smithsonian to our list to check it out. Wait!" Scott jumped up and loomed over her chair.

"What are you doing?" He had invaded her space and taken her hand. "Scott, what are you doing?" Eve giggled, "Quit!"

"Let me see your hand," he said, laughing.

"Oh no you don't! Stay on your side of the room!" Eve was laughing, trying to pull away.

"Can I see your hand, please?" Scott asked.

"What's your problem?" Eve asked, giving him her hand, waiting to see what he was about to do. He turned it over, examining the top and bottom and the sides.

"I'm checking for your sixth finger." Scott said and ran away when she chased him into the kitchen. "I was just teasing you." He stepped around her to open the refrigerator, grabbing a piece of cold lunch meat and jamming half of it in his mouth.

"Okay—I'm ready…next file." He was in his chair when she came back in the room acting serious but she saw the gleam in his eyes. "But I do remember the stray cats that were around my grandparents' orchards. They had six toes and my grandmother told me it was because of close breeding, like kissing cousins," Scott said, laughing at her expression.

"You are a funny man! And maybe that's what's wrong with you! Okay—the next file. It isn't much, just a chart." Eve quickly took a look and passed it over to him.

The next file contained a chart of documented giants found around the world throughout history. A side note on this one was of the story of Goliath (the giant) and David from the Bible. Many stories from the past had been considered myths that had been passed down over time. But an archaeology dig had found the place where Goliath was said to have lived. Among the artifacts was pottery. They found a piece that had the name Goliath signed on the bottom of it. It had been carbon dated and found to be the same time period that the story had been told in the Bible. It thus proved his existence and added truth to the myth.

"This is getting more and more crazy!" Scott said, "What do you think?"

"Well…I'm not sure. But the thing that keeps playing in my mind is the mention of DNA. My mother said that when mine was tested it showed human and something else…meaning what else? What the hell? How can that be?" Eve became serious. "I'm used to being a little different, but this is hard for me to wrap my mind around," she said.

"Don't worry about it," Scott said, feeling her pain. "We'll get to the bottom of this! You just seem a little special to me!" He winked at her. "Okay, next file," Scott said, changing the subject.

chapter 11

"Here we go..." Eve read the first few lines silently and then started reading it to Scott. "It's titled Paiutes Indians battle red-haired giants at Lovelock Cave." Eve flicked her hair and they both laughed before she continued.

"At one time the Lovelock Cave was known as Horseshoe Cave because of its U-shaped interior. The cavern was located about 20 miles south of modern-day Lovelock, Nevada. The cavern is approximately 40 feet deep and 60 feet wide. It's a very old cave that pre-dates humans on this continent. THE LEGEND was...

"The Paiutes, a Native-American tribe, was indigenous to parts of Nevada, Utah, and Arizona. They told the early white settlers about their ancestors' battles with a ferocious race of white, red-haired giants. According to the Paiutes, the giants were already living in the area.

"The red-haired giants stood 12 feet tall and were a vicious, unapproachable people that killed and ate captured Paiutes as food. The Paiutes told the early settlers that after many years of warfare, all the tribes in the area finally joined together to rid themselves of the giants. One day as they chased down the few remaining red-haired enemy, the fleeing giants took refuge in the cave. The tribal warriors demanded their enemy come out and fight, but the giants steadfastly refused to leave their sanctuary.

"Frustrated at not defeating their enemy with honor, the tribal chiefs had warriors fill the entrance to the cavern with brush and then set it on fire in a bid to force the giants out of the cave. The few that did emerge were instantly slain with volleys of arrows. The giants that remained inside the cavern were asphyxiated.

"Thousands of years later, the cave was rediscovered and found to be loaded with bat guano almost 6 feet deep. Decaying bat guano becomes saltpeter, the chief ingredient of gunpowder, and was very valuable. Therefore, in 1911 a company was created specifically to mine the guano. As the mining operation progressed, skeletons and fossils were found.

"The guano was mined for almost 13 years before archaeologists were notified about the findings. Unfortunately, by then many of the artifacts had been accidentally destroyed or simply discarded. Nevertheless, what the scientific researchers did recover was staggering: Over 10,000 artifacts were unearthed, including the mummified remains of two red-haired giants; one was a female 6.5 feet tall, the other male, over 8 feet tall."

"Among the thousands of artifacts recovered from this site of an unknown people is what some scientists are convinced is a calendar: A donut-shaped stone with exactly 365 notches carved along its outside rim and 52 corresponding notches along the inside." Scott read.

"Really incredible!" Eve said, "So there were giants here in America before 1492, when Columbus sailed the ocean blue."

"It does seem like it. I think anything is possible and if there is physical evidence, it seems like maybe there is truth in the story. What else do you have over there?" He said, eyeing the next folder. "Hold on..." Scott ran to the kitchen and returned carrying two sandwiches. He handed one to her.

"Hanging out with you I'm going to pack on the pounds!" Eve laughed.

"Ah, you can afford a few pounds...you're slender," Scott said.

"Well, thank you—that's the way I want to keep it!" She said. "Okay, let's see what this is." Opening the next folder, Eve looked puzzled. "Here we are again with the Smithsonian," she stated.

"What does it say?" Scott asked.

"Hold on—let me read it and I'll summarize; there's too much to read it all to you out loud."

"Okay, I'll finish off one more turkey sandwich if you don't mind." He messed up her hair as he walked by. When he returned, she shared the contents of her folder.

Chapter 12

"The Smithsonian also discovered an ancient Egyptian colony in the Grand Canyon that proved a race had inhabited the cavern. It was down by Yuma, Arizona, close to an Indian reservation. They think it had Eastern origins, possibly from Egypt, because the tablets they found were engraved in hieroglyphics. Wow—they found a cross-legged idol resembling Buddha and a large tomb filled with mummified humans of Egyptian and East Asian cultures." Eve said, "Who would have thought?"

"When did this happen?" Scott asked, surprised. "I never have heard anything like this in America."

"Well, listen to this...in 1908 a guy named Kincaid was traveling down the Colorado River, looking for minerals. A note says others speculate that he was looking for discovery sites for the Smithsonian. 'The Smithsonian's Department of Anthropology said there wasn't a paper trail at the Smithsonian detailing any artifacts gathered on this so-called expedition and that he wasn't working for them. It was stated that there weren't any Egyptian artifacts found in North or South America and they had never been involved in any such excavations.' Anyhow, the story continues...Kincaid saw some discoloration in the rock face about 2000 feet up and climbed to investigate. He found an opening to a cave that was hidden by an overhang of rock. Looking around inside by flashlight, he found a whole system of caverns and rooms perfectly cut in the rock. He took a few pictures of a mummy and gathered some relics, carrying them down the river to Yuma. He sent them to Washington with the story of his discovery. Soon after, President Theodore Roosevelt made the canyon into a National Forest, closing it for mining or prospecting activity. Currently FBI agents now guard Kincaid's cave and other archaeological sites in the Grand Canyon." Eve said, reading parts of the article out loud.

"See, I'm always amazed by the things that they didn't teach us in school. I haven't heard of any of this!" Scott said.

"That is crazy…now I wish I had taken that trip with my geology class. You know I could have gotten credit for rafting in the Grand Canyon and camping all the way down. Who knows what I could have seen!" Eve said.

"Yes, at least you would have had a nice vacation. What kind of class was that?" He laughed.

"Right…the reason I opted out. Seemed like a blow-off class. But you got four credits for doing the trip and writing a paper. The big downside was they only let a certain number of people down the river each year. I would have to wait two years to be on the list to go. Thought it would be fun if you were into that kind of thing." Eve watched him, waiting to get his response.

"Well…it sounds fun to me!" Scott said.

"What do you think thus far?" Eve asked.

"I think that the government/Smithsonian found the need to cover up the findings. That's one thing that I always find troubling, when they feel the need to hold information back. Like JFK's assassination—having to wait for 50 years to see the reports and they still haven't released all of the files. Knowledge should be something that is free to all to make their own opinions. We shouldn't have to question the facts. My opinion is that the Smithsonian and the government have been covering up discoveries and facts for a long time. Most likely they were gathering everything possible to hide the fact that there was a race here in America before we came and took the country from the Indians." Scott said.

"I know…I think it is their way of controlling us." Eve said, thoughtful.

"Well, it does mess with people's beliefs. It could crush the weak-minded," Scott commented.

"I would still rather know the truth. I feel the need to get out of the house. Are you up for a drive?" Eve asked.

"What do you have in mind?" He said, adventure shining in his eyes, ready for about anything as long as he could spend the time with her.

"I was thinking of trying to contact that lady that my mom said to go see."

"Cool—a road trip!"

Chapter 13

Eve unfolded her blanket and pulled out the envelope. She opened it once again, scanning the information and looking for the town and called information for the phone number. Taking out her phone, she dialed the digits and was about to hang up after several rings when she heard the click and a faint voice.

"Hello?"

"Hi," Eve paused, "Um...my name is Eve and my mother wanted me to contact you?"

"Yes...I know who you are. Your parents told me that one day I might hear from you. Are they okay?" She asked.

"Well...I'm not sure. My parents have disappeared." Eve heard the voice pause on the line and a sharp intake of breath.

"You need to come to see me. I think I can help. Are you still around Stanford?"

"Yale," Eve said.

"Yes—that's right...hold on," the woman said; Eve waited on the line.

"What did she say?" Scott whispered and Eve put up her finger when she heard the woman come back.

"Eve—are you still there? I had to go outside. I...felt something...anyhow, I'm off Rte. 67. I will meet you at the general store. It's not hard to find but if you blink you'll pass it. Once you cross the one-lane red covered bridge, the town will be close. Don't worry; the bridge will squeak and creak, but it will hold the car's weight as you cross. It's been there forever. Be careful; young people hang out under the bridge, so go slow just in case. It should take you about three hours to get here. Plan to stay the night. It's too dark once the sun goes down to find your way out." The woman explained.

"Hold on," Eve said, putting her hand over the phone. "Scott, we'll have to stay the night in a small town—are you up for that?"

"Sure, I have nothing going on right now—it sounds like fun!" He started to straighten their dishes, getting ready to take them to the kitchen.

"Okay, we'll call you when we get to town," Eve said, and the phone disconnected.

"How did she sound?" Scott asked.

"Well...she does know my parents and about me, so...let's hope we aren't wasting our time. I think she's an autodidact."

"That's okay—not everyone has a degree behind their knowledge. I always thought people like that must use part of their brains that we haven't yet developed. I always wondered why we have all that 'Junk DNA.' I think it must be used for something, or why would it be there in the first place?" Scott said.

"They do say that we have DNA that no other creatures on earth possess. Makes us interesting!" Eve said.

"Maybe if that's the case, it's because we're a hybrid of the space people!" He laughed, a sparkle in his eyes.

"Are you serious?" Eve laughed.

"Sure—why not? If we're expanding our minds, we have to be open to all ideas. That might explain our real existence. Who knows if what we've been told all our lives is the truth. Our government is always covering up information. What if this kind of thing has been happening for thousands of years? Especially with the Catholic Church. Talk about the Smithsonian covering things up; I bet the Vatican in Rome has a lot of secrets in their basement." Scott said.

"You're right!" Eve said. "I once heard that at one time priests were allowed to marry, but the reason the Catholic Church changed the rules is because of land."

"What do you mean?" He asked.

"When a priest died, the church wanted the land and if they were married, the wife and family would get it. So they made the rule of not getting married, so the land and wealth would pass to the church." Eve stood. "I'm going to shower and pack a small bag. Could you be ready to leave in an hour? We can take my parents' truck—it's very comfortable. But you're going to have to drive. I don't trust my skills in the traffic around here, so don't drive often." Eve said, heading for the stairs.

"No problem, I'll be ready." Scott went to the kitchen and cleaned up, just in case her parents came home when they were gone. He didn't want them to think that they trashed the house. He wasn't sure what they would think of him staying in the house alone with their daughter and he wanted them to like him. Going to his room, he found that she had left a bar of soap and a towel on the bed. He smiled, thinking about how she never left him bored.

chapter 14

The drive wasn't too bad, and soon they were outside the city. The scenery changed the farther north they went; the day was sunny and had melted the snow off the road, leaving it wet. Everything looked clearer, the trees were greener, the sky was more blue. The sun had come out, now peeping through the puffy clouds. After a while, the road had turned into one lane. Long dead grass was stiff along the edges of the road's shoulder, showing that winter hadn't left yet, keeping its hold on the deserted landscape.

Eve was enjoying the ride, watching out the window as they moved farther away from the hustle and bustle of the city. After a while they noticed that they were the only car on the road. Large fields with rolling plains were on both sides of the car. The brownish grass poked through the last snowy crystals left from the snow flurries from the night before. Old farmhouses once painted bright barn red now sat faded and discolored with the paint cracked and peeling from the lack of upkeep. They passed an old railroad track that looked like it was no longer in use. Most likely the trains took a different route to more populated areas. The iron tracks sat rusting in the sun, replaced in places with a large cement wall that looked out of place in the overgrown vegetation.

"I'm glad that we gassed up at that last station; who knows if this town of Buskirk has a gas station." Scott said, rolling down his window and feeling the cool breeze filter into the car. The smell of country came in, making them both feel relaxed and at peace.

"Look," Eve said, pointing. "I think we just went through the town—I saw a sign with 'Buskirk' at the last intersection. That store over there must be the general store Sarah was talking about." Eve directed Scott's gaze across the deserted street.

"Hold on; I'll turn around." Scott did a quick u-turn and pulled into a vacant space in front of the general store. The outside looked ancient; the glass in front was cloudy and warped; old advertisements hung around the edges, showing the once displayed items from years past. It was like a step back in time.

"Let me call her." Eve picked up her phone, saw that she just had one bar, and cursed under her breath. "I hope this works." She heard it ring once, then a click as it was picked up. The voice was harsh until the women realized that it was Eve.

"Hello…who is this? Eve, is that you?" The voice stated.

"Yes; we just arrived." Eve said.

"Okay, my dear. I'll be there in five minutes." The phone disconnected and Eve was left wondering about this stranger that had the trust of her parents.

"She's on her way…seems a little odd. Come on, let's get something to drink while we wait," Eve said.

"Okay now, give her a chance." Scott said, getting out of the car and stretching his legs. "Ready?"

"I'm giving her a chance—I'm here, aren't I?" Bumping Scott with her shoulder as she went past ahead of him into the store, she said, "Well, are ya coming?"

chapter 15

Inside, the place looked like they had traveled back in time. Antique toys and slightly rusted tools hung from the rafters. Old glass display cabinets, framed in worn wood, sat locked full of pocket knives and odds and ends with jars heaped with hard candy. They looked like they had been there for a long time and Eve wondered if the candy was fused together. The building had to be at least a hundred years old. The floorboards creaked under their feet, but were shined and scrubbed clean with beeswax. There were about four aisles packed with cans and general supplies. At the back of the store was a tiny post office that looked the size of a small bathroom; little boxes with numbers and keyholes lined one of the walls. By the door was a shelf that held a small lockbox labeled U.S. Mail. Beside it were small bottles in little rows; looking closer, Eve read them and laughed. The one potion said that it cured all kinds of things ranging from gout to headaches and snakebites.

They slowly walked through, looking for something to drink, and found an old soda machine. They pulled a few glass bottles from the bottom and moved to the front to pay. An older gentleman was behind the counter reading a newspaper, eyeing them over the top.

"Nice place you have here," Scott said, pulling the cash from his pocket. Eve spied a few Marathon bars on the counter and put them with the bottles.

"Thank you, son. Are you guys lost?" He asked, moving his glasses higher on his semi-bald head and eyeing them.

"No sir; we're meeting someone here." Scott said.

"Who are you looking for?" He asked, "I know everyone that lives within twenty miles of here."

But before Scott could answer, the bell rang at the front door of the store and a woman rushed in. She was wearing a long flowing dress of bright colors and her hair was light brown, curly, and sticking out in places from under a head wrap. She ran inside, patting her hair down and straightening her clothes. Seeing them, she slowed her pace to a walk.

"They're with me!" Sarah said, taking Eve's arm in a protective gesture and directing them to follow her. Scott paid the clerk and they left the store.

"He is very nosy and will tell anyone that comes in that you've been in his store. I've already been having someone creeping around my house lately. It's best to say nothing here…come, follow me," the woman said.

Curious, Eve looked her over and said, "Okay. We'll follow you." She hurried to the truck, jumped in, and watched the woman quickly take off in a black sport utility vehicle. Scott hurried to his seat, belted himself in after handing Eve the drinks, and followed the truck.

"What's the big hurry?" He asked, chasing the dust path down the road. Scott swerved over the gravel, trying to miss the potholes. They followed, turning off the main road on to a dusty dirt road. It led them through the woods; the tree branches here were very overgrown, reaching over the top of the large truck. The branches touched the truck as they passed, making screeching sounds and giving the dusky night an eerie feeling. They watched shadows dance in the headlights around the swirls of dust and bugs flowing in front of them. As they followed, Eve tried to remember what way they turned. Looking for road signs; she found none.

"We need to remember how to get out of here. You know, if we have to leave quickly...I feel like we should drop breadcrumbs to find our way back." Eve concentrated, trying to memorize the turns.

"Yes, you're right....Do me a favor and write it down, just in case." Scott said.

Eve found a pen in the bottom of her purse and detailed each turn, describing the landmarks. It wasn't long until they took a left turn into a long driveway that led farther in the overgrown woods. Because of the lack of light, they couldn't see the house from the road. As they approached, they didn't notice the structure until they were right on top of it. It was an older home and it made Eve wonder who would live this far off the grid 100 years ago. But from the outside it looked enchanting. The walls were made with large rounded stones cemented in place. A small porch in front had two rocking chairs that looked inviting. When they got out of the car, the wind blew lightly and Eve could smell the leftover wildflowers from last year that were growing on each side of the worn trodden path. The frozen colors of pinks and purples could still be seen as the wind moved them along the path. It was a forgotten place of long ago. Now the remnants of the past had been taken back by the forest and it was a beautiful setting.

As they approached the house, the woman came right up to Eve, her arms outstretched. Eve held her distance and looked her up and down, taking it all in, before giving her a hug.

"I'm Sarah. You look just like I thought you would! Amazing!"

"Hi, Sarah, this is my friend Scott." Eve said, stepping back a little, feeling uncomfortable with the woman's fondness…but she knew her mother would never send her somewhere that wasn't safe. Still she wondered. Sarah looked at Scott as if he didn't matter and motioned them to follow her inside.

The house was dimly lit, and Eve waited for her eyes to adjust before moving forward. She could feel the warmth of Scott's body behind her; she calmed, feeling comforted that he was there. She wasn't afraid.

"Here…sit by the fire." Sarah motioned, pulling up an extra chair off to the side for Scott, then disappeared into the back of the house. They looked at each other, silently questioning the situation.

Chapter 16

"I know you're wondering if your parents sent you to a nut. I'm not a crazy person, and I hope when I explain maybe then you'll understand." Sarah said, coming out of the darkness. "You see, I have been waiting to meet you for almost twenty years—from the time your mother came to me. She had told me one day she would bring you to see me, but the time just went by. I think there was never the right moment to tell you the truth. When too much time had passed, she was afraid that you would hold it against her for not telling you. But I knew that if something happened to them, she would send you to me. How long have they been gone?"

"I'm not sure. They went on a trip two weeks ago and when it came time for them to return, I was told they had disappeared," Eve said.

"Well, I'm not sure how much you know, but twenty years ago while traveling your parents had an encounter. You see, sometimes people who have encounters are revisited. Many times, people who have experienced some kind of encounter later have found a form of tracker had been put somewhere in their body." Sarah opened a side drawer, pulling out a small wooden box. She lifted the lid, and inside were a few small objects the size of a dime. She turned them in her fingertips, studying them before passing them to Eve.

"What are those?" Eve asked, looking them over before handing them to Scott.

"These were removed surgically from four different people who had claimed that they had lost time. These were from young women; two of them swore they hadn't had sex and found themselves pregnant. When I put them under and opened their minds, they were able to remember what happened and the stories are all about the same. All were taken to a ship and found themselves in a medical lab where they were prodded inside and out. Samples were taken and they were put back in place and found time had gone by, their minds wiped clean." Sarah said, watching their reaction.

"Well, how could that be?" Eve asked.

"Dear…think of it this way. These stories have been around for thousands of years, the biggest being the story of Jesus. You see, we are dealing with a more intelligent race of people from space, maybe thousands of years more advanced than we are. They have the technology, which at the time, we didn't have. But if you think of it today…if someone is having trouble getting pregnant—what happens? Ha ha—we harvest the eggs and the sperm, mix them in a dish, and put the fertile egg back in the woman," Sarah said.

"Yes, that does make sense…" Eve said, slowly thinking about it.

"Here is something else to think of," Sarah said. "Over time, as the space beings were messing with our reproduction, they were mixing not only with humans, but with other creatures on earth. Think of the petroglyphs found painted on stone walls around the world, all depicting different strange creatures. Some are of a human body and a dog head or human body and a snake head or a human on top and goatlike feet, or human on top and horse on the bottom. Well, you get the point.

"There are a lot of things that people in the past saw and recorded in their way. People chalked it up to the imagination of that time. But if you think about it, these cave paintings or drawings etched in stone were what the people saw. Maybe we should pay attention to the myths and investigate them further because maybe the core information could be founded on facts. It seems that technology was so much more advanced than what we have right now. The space people could have been using our planet as an experiment." Sarah smiled at Eve.

"Well…experimenting…hummm…yes, think about it.…Why were these space visitors so interested in our reproduction?" Eve asked.

"Well, some theories think that they had somehow lost the ability to reproduce themselves…but who knows? Hahaha," Sarah laughed at Scott's facial expressions.

"Interesting!" Scott said. "I've never thought of such things, but when it is explained this way, it does make you wonder…I guess anything could be possible!"

"What you're holding is what was taken out of the four women, your mother being one of them. I had it tested at the local university and found something interesting. They are all pieces of a meteorite and some of the elements found inside haven't been determined because they are not found on the planet Earth! Look closer at the small crystals; they hold energy. I have heard that you can record data on crystals, and it can last forever. They are doing that right now. Lately I heard that they have imprinted the whole Bible on a small crystal the size of a quarter." Sarah looked pleased when she saw the surprised look on their faces. "You see, the theory is that they were implanted to keep track of the people that they had taken."

"Incredible!" Eve said. "How were you able to open their memories?"

"Well, look at it this way. The brain is an incredible thing and cells make carbon copies of themselves. Copies of memories are almost like a shadow. Or think of it like when you remove data on a computer. We know the information isn't really gone; it is embedded in the hard drive. The information is really still there."

"Yes, we understand that," Scott said.

"Well I can unlock a part of a person's mind, as I did with your parents," Sarah said.

"But how will that help find my parents? Because I don't think that I have been taken." Eve said, looking doubtful that it would help.

"If you're part of these beings, we might be able to see or contact them through you. But I will need to put you in a trancelike state and see what is locked inside that mind of yours. I'm not sure, but I think there will be something that will be able to help us." Sarah said, closely watching Eve, waiting for her response.

Eve looked at Scott; he shrugged his shoulders, leaving the decision to her. "I can try…if you think it will help." Eve said.

chapter 17

"Okay, great!" Sarah went to the fireplace and looked through little jars that sat in disarray on the carved wooden mantel. She found a small bottle and returned, motioning for Scott to leave the house. Eve's hand shot out and gripped his arm when he started to move.

"He has to stay with me or I won't do it," Eve said. Sarah looked disturbed but covered it with a smile.

"Of course. He can stay, but he has to remain completely silent, no matter what happens or whatever you say, he can't move." Sarah didn't look at Scott, but he nodded, giving his word.

Eve turned to him. "Take my phone; I need you to record everything that happens. I need to see and hear everything that I do." She heard Sarah start to protest but Eve turned to her.

"I need to know it all.... Please, let's just proceed." Eve said in a soft voice. Sarah nodded and handed her the small vial.

"Go ahead, dear...swallow it all...it won't take long."

"What is it?" Eve asked, a little afraid. She glanced at Scott, who smiled with encouragement.

"I'll be right here." He said, "I won't leave you...I promise," he patted her hand.

"It's a mixture and all natural; the main ingredient is peyote." Sarah said.

"I've never done drugs," Eve stated. Before she lost her nerve, she tipped her head back and gulped the shot down her throat, tasting a slightly sweet liquid. A minute later she felt a little dizzy as the drug took effect. Then she felt herself slipping away.

Scott noticed a slight chill come through the room and the candles flickered. He looked at Sarah; she was in a trance. Her eyes had rolled back, showing just the whites. Eve's head whipped around as if looking for something and then she stared forward, a glossed over, blank look centered on her face. She looked right through Scott as if he weren't there. The room was silent before he heard a soft mumbling coming from Sarah's direction. The words were a language that he didn't understand and he hit the button on the phone and started recording.

chapter 18

Turning to Eve, Sarah spoke in English. "Are you with me, Eve?"

The room was silent for a moment and Eve's face seemed to change. The transformation was weird to Scott, but he remained still. Then a child's voice filled the silence. Scott felt his heart race with the unexpected and tried to remain calm, feeling he was the only one in the room in his right mind. He wondered if Eve had a split-personality, He looked down and his hand was shaking, he told himself to get a grip and make sure he captured it all on Eve's phone.

"Who is Eve? I'm Gola,"The young voice stated.

"Hello, Gola…I'm Sarah Smiles….Can you tell me what you see? Or what is happening today?"

"I'm afraid…Mother told me to run and hide in the caves…but I wanted to see what everyone was so excited about."The child's voice said.

"What happened?" Sarah asked.

"Men floated onto the beach today on a large stone with legs that moved them through the water. Their skin was light like a fish's belly, and they were dressed unusually, with things on their heads. My people hadn't seen anyone like this before. They had light hair and eyes but were tiny, like the small ears that live on the other side of the island. They were surprised when they saw us, pointing fire sticks at us. The fire sticks made a lot of noise. Then yelling, lots of yelling. We couldn't understand their words, but my mother told me to run and find my father, then go to the caves. I ran to the other side of the island and found my father cutting stone. I told him what had happened and ran after him, following him back to the beach, and hid in the brush.

"I watched from a distance as my father went into the water, walking to their floating stone. He went to them with open arms and their fire sticks went off. One hit him in the shoulder, making him cry out in pain. I saw his anger and he picked up the side of their stone, tossing them in the water, the fire sticks sinking under the waves. He picked the short ears out of the water and tossed them on the shore. At the same time, a large stone came around the bend and stopped a distance away. By now many of my people had come to the beach and surrounded the white small ears, forming a circle around them, looking at these different-looking creatures. They put up their hands and my people didn't know what to do but look at them. Then my father stepped forward, wiping the blood off his shoulder, looking down at them. He got on his knees and poked a finger at the closest one. The little ear put up his hand and shook my father's finger. That's when I ran to the caves. Many of our people were already hiding deep inside the earth to the core, where it was warm while they safely waited."

"You live on an island?" Sarah asked.

"We live far away...we are just waiting." The child said.

"Waiting for what?" Sarah asked.

"For our people to come for us." The child's voice stated.

"Where are you from?" Sarah asked.

"Far away…" Scott watched Eve point to the ceiling. "A place very far away. My parents said we were put here to gain an understanding. But we want to go home." The child's voice stated.

"What is holding you here? Why not just go home?" Sarah asked.

"They say we are being punished for caring about the little ears. Some found the little ear women attractive and lay with them, making children. They say we are mixed blood of the earth men. Seven brothers came to the island to wait out their time, but they are no longer with us. They were our people's fathers. It is said that they look out to sea because they are facing the home island they left. It was said they left their home not as punishment but because they had special powers and were being hunted. The little ears of their home had wanted to kill them and eat them to consume their power. They told us not to show the little ears that lived here our power or they would try to take it. They told us what to do while we wait and that we would return home in the future. They destroyed all of the trees so we couldn't leave the island. So…we wait, for our people to return for us."

"What do you do all day?" Sarah asked.

"The men work cutting the stone into heads of our people, making our protection stronger," she said. "The women fish."

Scott's mind clicked at the same time as Sarah's and he guessed where the Gola child was.

"Are you on Easter Island?" Sarah asked.

"I don't know that name. What is that?" The child's voice asked.

"Why are the stone heads so large?" Sarah asked, changing tactic.

Eve's face changed as the child's voice laughed, "Like you don't know...they need to see us from above, from our real home. So when the time is right, they won't forget to come for us. The heads are magnetic and form a protective circle, keeping us safe," the child said.

"That's why the stone heads are facing away from the water...they're looking up at the star system that they are from," Scott whispered.

"Quiet! Someone is coming!" Eve cried. Sarah looked at Scott, alarmed, and someone pounded on the door.

"Quickly! Carry her into the back room," Sarah said. The banging came again. Scott put Eve over his shoulder and ran down the hall to a side bedroom. He gently put Eve in a chair by the bed. The room was dark, and Scott put the phone, still recording, in Eve's hand. He went back to the door, cracking it, and peered out to listen. He could hear the sound of heavy boots and a man's angry voice. Sarah was yelling at him to get out. He could hear it was getting heated and thought it might be best if he went into the room to help Sarah. He slid out the door, silently shutting it behind him.

In the living room were two men in dark suits. There was something about them that didn't look right. Scott immediately remembered the story that Eve had told him. It must be the same man that visited her after her parents' disappearance. He could swear one fit the description she had given him. He backed into the hall and found Eve where he had left her, the phone still in her hand. Her eyes had opened.

"Hi, Scott...what's going on? Why am I back here in the dark?"

"I'm glad you're awake, I think we have to leave. I think your FBI man is here."

"What! Were we followed? Why?" Eve said, standing. They opened the door and she moved silently down the hall with Scott behind her. By the time they reached the living room, the door was slamming shut and the men were gone. No one moved; they just listened to the sound of car tires backing away from the house.

chapter 19

"What is happening?" Eve asked. "Why are those men following us?"

"Child, there is so much you have to learn. Most of it is locked deep down in that mind of yours. Those are the kind of men that are always sent out to defuse the situation. Governments have been trying to hide the fact that we have been visited from outer space for hundreds, or even thousands of years. You see it in the hieroglyphics of Egypt, the advanced writings of the Incas, the cliff paintings of American Indians, the Aborigines' rock carvings in Australia. There is even evidence in paintings from the Renaissance period. Many artists protested by hiding information in the backgrounds of their paintings. Some of the paintings portray spaceships flying with people painted in them. Many depict the same things...that at one point around 5000 years ago, space people visited and influenced mankind by not only having children with them, but giving them technology and intelligence." Sarah said, peeping through the drapes and making sure the car was gone.

"We did read the files about the giants in America and around the world." Eve said. "I thought it was interesting, at least proving that there had been people on this continent a lot longer than history wants to admit."

"That's because the children of space people and humans were very, very tall. You have to think about the fact that in space there is less gravity. With less gravity, the body elongates and with the darkness of space, the eyes grow larger to gather light. There have been skeletons found around the world that have been quickly hidden because they are hybrids or the real space people. The heads found are elongated and don't have the fusion of bone on the top like ours. When tested, the DNA has shown that they were part human, but the other part of the DNA hasn't been found here on earth in any other creatures. For some reason there has been a cover-up, not only by our government but from countries around the world. I think they don't believe people could handle the truth. Or it is hidden for a different reason. Nevertheless, they have been here on Earth for a long time and might be still living here right under our noses.

"Some have said that the legends and myths right here in America's Northwest were passed down from the Indians and current day hikers talk of encounters with Bigfoot. The creature has been described around the world under different names. Many entertain thoughts of them living undiscovered for hundreds of years in the cave systems around the world. Many have described the encounters with these beings and the descriptions have been the same. That when they ran across them in the Rockies and Appalachian mountain ranges or the plains of Montana, they were described as tall creatures that walked on two legs, with long reddish hair that covered their bodies. They are said to have a sulfur smell. One witness said some kind of large beast or animal was running though the brush and he could hear the branches breaking and smelled a foul odor before they saw the beast. As he drew closer, the animal screamed so loud that the sound echoed off the mountains, sounding like a cross between man, lion, and elephant. Large footprints in mud and snow have been found along with large nests made of brush imprinted with the depression of something large sleeping there." Sarah said, speaking fast, wanting to convince them with all the information that she had inside her head after all these years of research.

"Where do you think they came from?" Eve asked.

"There are a few theories.... One of them is that they are a product of gene manipulation between human and gorilla. Or they are from the time when the watchers came down from the heavens and had offspring with humans, thus creating giants. I think they were some kind of hybrid." Sarah said, taking a breath. Scott had been watching and saw the look on Eve's face. He tried to change the subject, knowing this hybrid thing was most likely a soft spot for her.

"This is all really interesting! Sarah...what did you say to get rid of the men and what did they want?" Scott said, looking out the window and not seeing any car lights.

"Oh...yes...the men. They said they were concerned for the girl and were just trying to keep track of her. But I don't believe them. I think they must have been watching your house or tapped your house phone because there is no way that they would just come to this town. I think they showed up last night. I had a feeling...I felt them outside my house. You guys need to be careful! They were following your parents and now are stuck on you. They can be dangerous... you need to shake them," Sarah said.

"Where can we go?" Eve asked. Sarah was thoughtful.

"Sometimes the best place to hide is in plain sight. Let me gather a few things...I'm coming with you." Sarah said, leaving the room.

"I'm not sure it's such a good idea to bring her with us," Scott whispered.

"I was thinking the same thing, but what if they're dangerous? We can't just leave her out here in the middle of nowhere by herself," Eve said.

"I guess you're right." Scott said, watching down the hall in the direction Sarah had gone.

"Anyhow, she could be useful. She knows a lot about this crazy thing we're dealing with...I'm not sure what to believe, but she does make a good case," Eve said.

chapter 20

Sarah entered the room carrying a briefcase and a small bag of what looked to be clothes. "Where are we going?" Eve asked.

"I'm taking you kids home," she said, laughing when she saw the looks on their faces. "Don't worry, we'll give them the slip. If there is a bugging device in your house, we can use it to our advantage." Sarah smiled and led the way to the truck. She opened the back door and got in. Eve and Scott looked at each other and followed the middle-aged woman, returning to their seats. The small group left the cottage, taking their time as they moved slowly through the forest toward the main road.

Scott backtracked down the bumpy, deserted dirt roads. It took twice as long on the return route. Sarah was right; it was hard to maneuver after dark. The forest had taken over, blocking most of the light. They might have been lost without Sarah there to direct them. At one point, they saw light illuminating through the branches down one of the side roads. Scott killed the truck's headlights, slowly maneuvering in the darkness until they had passed the area. He kept the lights off, making his way over the gravel potholes until they were back on I-67 and headed south. Eve had been holding her breath until they had made it out of the maze.

"Do you think that was them back there?" Eve asked.

"Yes, it was." Sarah said, touching her fingers to her forehead. "This will give us a head start and plenty of time on the drive to come up with a plan."

"Well, I vote we move all conversations upstairs when we reach my house. If some kind of listening device was installed, we can be sure it's safe upstairs in the secret room. Let's only talk about research when we are in that hidden space. There is no way that anyone has found it and we'll be safe to talk there," Eve said.

"Yes…they will know we're in the house, and when we're downstairs, we can feed them what we want them to know." Scott said.

"Not to change the subject…but Sarah, I was wondering…what do you know about the Book of Enoch? It was mentioned in one of my mother's files and I was just looking at it online. I was thinking I might order it. They have a few that have been translated into English on Amazon," Eve said, looking at Sarah in the back seat.

"You can order it if you want, but I can give you the overview if you would like," Sarah said. "I have been studying everything that I can get my hands on for a long, long time."

"How did you get interested in this space people idea?" Scott asked.

"Well from childhood…I was always different. It's almost like I had a sixth sense. My parents didn't understand me, because I just knew things. If the farmer down the road was beating his wife, or a girl had disappeared and was dead, or the neighbor was having an affair. I don't know how…but

I just knew these things. They would just come to me. My father didn't understand and would want to know who told me such things. He thought that I was making up stories for attention. But later, when he learned what I said was true, I think he was really just afraid of me. It had become a problem at home, so I started keeping it to myself. But my mother wanted to help me. She found a small boarding school that was for people like me and told me it was for the best. It eased things at home for her with me out of the house. It was there that I was able to understand and fine-tune my abilities.

"During this time, I met a girl who had also been placed there by her parents. She didn't have the same kind of talents I did. After we became friendly, she told me a story about being taken on a ship and what had happened to her. She said that no one believed her; they had sent her away because they didn't know what to do with her. I could feel she was telling the truth. She became my first subject, leading me down this path of investigation into the unknown."

"Incredible!" Eve said.

"So that's the reason for my excitement over you, my dear. I've never met a 'Star Child' and am curious about you," Sarah said, smiling.

"I see...I'm your new subject." Eve laughed.

"Something like that," Sarah said. "But I want to help you too, so you can find the answers you need by tapping into what is hidden in your own mind. I want you to understand why you're so special."

"I'm not sure about that...but if it helps to find my parents, I'll do it." Eve said, looking at Scott, who had been listening. "Scott, what do you think?"

He saw Eve watching him out of the corner of his eye. "I'm just keeping watch on the road behind us. I want to make it back without any interaction with our friends back there." The car was quiet for a few moments with everyone remembering their situation, watching the road behind them. It had only been an hour and Scott had them traveling at a fast pace down the dark, deserted road. Time had passed and they hadn't seen any lights behind them. Around 2 A.M. they reached the outskirts of the city and were able to easily get lost in the traffic on the lit streets.

Chapter 21

"Tell us about this Book of Enoch," Scott said.

"Yes! Could you?" Eve chimed in.

"All right, here's a story for you. Let me start at the beginning. It is said different people gave lists that were put together to create the books of the Old Testament. Eusebius, a historian from the 300s, and Athanasius, the Bishop of Alexandria, both gave a list of books for the New Testament canon. After Christ's death, the New Testament was put in order to be placed with the Old Testament. At the time, I believe the Catholic Church decided what chapters or books would be in the Bible and New Testament. Because of the times, certain books were found to be too racy or politically controversial for that time period and were taken out. One of them was Enoch. If I remember, I think that was around 4 AD. But that date could be wrong…anyhow…

"The discarded scrolls and books not included in the New Testament had been buried, hidden with their secrets safe, for thousands of years by the Jews of Qumarn who protected their literary treasures. These manuscripts and scrolls had been hidden in containers, wrapped in linen and sealed in large jars in the caves in Qumran, Palestine.

"In 1947, a shepherd was trying to find a lost sheep and saw a cave. He tossed a rock inside and heard something break. The next day, when he came back and investigated, he climbed up to the entrance. He found many jars, some were already empty or broken, but a few still had the seals intact. When he opened them, he found the ancient manuscripts. Thinking that they might be worth something, he took them to an antiquities dealer in Bethlehem.

"So 'The Dead Sea Scrolls' were found. One of the books included was named The Book of Giants and The Book of Enoch. Both are believed written by Enoch, who was the great-grandfather of Noah. By comparing other writings with ideas in the New Testament, scholars confirmed that another writer was Paul. Paul, among other disciples, had written his version of what Jesus had said. Most of the their writings showed that they were well versed in the Book of Enoch. It has been said that the Book of Enoch was written around the time of Genesis, in the 3rd century BC.

"After this discovery in 1947, around 800 ancient scrolls were pulled out of those caves…including the oldest copy of the Hebrew Bible ever found…a big find!" Sarah said, taking a breath.

"Yes! I heard about that discovery….My parents were talking about the scrolls at some point. Wow!" Eve said, excited. "What did this Book of Enoch say that got it kicked out of the Christian and Catholic Bible? I do remember that the Catholic Bible has seven extra books than the Christian King David Bible."

"Well, it was very interesting," Sarah said. "I read the Book of Enoch and was surprised. I understood why the church wouldn't want that information put out there. The book tells of the 'Watchers,' a certain renegade group of 200 angels that came from the heavens to Earth to watch over humans. They had to take an oath before descending to Earth to meet with the humans. The oath was that they would just watch over them and not interact. But when they came down the mountain, they found human women attractive and lay with them, producing children with them. The offspring were giants called the Nephilim."

"What do you think? Was it true?" Eve asked. "Here we go again with these giants!"

"I believe it, because in 1869, a British explorer named Sir Charles Warren found the deserted ancient ruins of the Temple of Qasr Antar. It was the highest place of worship in the biblical world, found on the top of Mt. Hermon in Lebanon. Other than finding the ruins, he found a 'Stele.' It was so large and heavy that he broke it in two pieces and brought it down the mountain. It sat in the British Museum for over a hundred years. The text was in Greek and said, 'According to the command of the greatest and Holy God, those who take the oath proceed from here.' Archaeologists were stumped, not understanding the meaning for a hundred years.

"But when the Book of Enoch was discovered, it gave details of the location where the Angels/Watchers had come down from heaven. The story of what had happened was then revealed. You see, back in those times, humans weren't that advanced. The Watchers not only taught them things reserved for heavenly beings, but also the fact that some of them had eternal life. But Enoch tells that the Watchers gave man through their women…instruction and information about: planting, tools, stars/space, spirits…really knowledge. That is why mankind went through a transformation and jump in knowledge and intelligence around 5000 years ago. You know that evolution couldn't have been the only factor in the human development. You realize it couldn't just be by picking their partners for different reasons...stronger, smarter, best hunter, and on and on...creating a better human over time. But here we have men in caves without tools and then—boom—everything changes.

"For example, in many cultures they describe angels coming down on a fire dragon or with lots of smoke and noise. Just as a spaceship would land today. In the past, the people of that time period thought the space people were gods or angels because they were more advanced and humans didn't understand the technology. In reality, they were space people from somewhere else that had taken an interest in Earth and advancing the human race for some reason. That reason is unknown still today." Sarah said, watching their reaction.

"So...they had physical proof that points to the fact that all this might have really happened?" Scott said.

"Yes, I would say so...but there's more," Sarah said.

Chapter 22

"The story continues in Enoch. It tells the story of Noah. When he was born, his eyes glowed like the sun, lighting the room. His skin was illuminating, glowing white and bright red. His hair was white as well and his face was 'glorious.' The big thing was that he levitated in the midwife's hands. At the time, Noah's father was afraid when he saw Noah. He went to his father; he had been away from his wife for a long time and the months didn't add up. He asked his father to ask Enoch, his grandfather, for the truth because it was noticeable that his son wasn't a normal human. He accused his wife of having slept with one of the gods. Enoch told him, 'This is your child! A gift!'

"One day Noah and his three sons would be spared from the wrath of God, which would be sent to Earth. His seed will live on and help populate Earth," Sarah said.

"What kind of glowing?" Eve asked, "I never heard that description of Noah in the Bible. And levitation?"

"I know...interesting, right? So...the story goes that the gods (people from outer space) weren't happy because the Watchers were sent to watch over mankind, not create offspring with them. Now their children (the giants) were causing trouble on Earth. The Book of Giants claimed that giants were not only killing humans, but having sex with their women. They were also having sex with animals and drinking their blood. Noah was told to build an Ark for him and his family, because he was found worthy of God. The flood was 'the gods" way of ridding Earth of the wickedness of the giants and Watchers and to start the human race over...like a reboot...killing them and their genetic mistakes.

"There was a story in the Book of Giants that told of a giant called Og. It was said that he was really tall and when the flood came, he clung on to the side of the Ark and Noah found him and fed him. After the flood, he disappeared. It is said that Goliath was one of his children. Thus the reason for the giant skeletons found throughout the world. After the flood there were still a few around.

"Some other interesting things have been said.... There's a different theory that the Ark wouldn't have been able to house two of every living thing on Earth including plants. Lately that was proven when someone in Kentucky decided the rebuild the Ark according to the measurements in the Bible. In 2016 it was finished and opened for tours. It was too small for all the animals and plants on Earth. It has been said that instead of housing all the animals and plants, it carried all their DNA and seeds. But it is only a theory. I would like to get a look at the real Ark! For years people have claimed it lays hidden in a snowcap on Mt. Ararat in Turkey." Sarah paused, taking a breath.

The truck was silent for a moment while Scott and Eve took in all the information and thought about it, wondering if it could be true or just a myth.

"Well, it makes sense," Scott said, slowly. "So, Noah was told when the flood would happen and how to go about saving and repopulating Earth. Meaning someone with information about the solar system and space would have known that something was going to happen. And like you said, people of that time wouldn't know that kind of information."

"I think I read somewhere that in Spitsbergen, Norway is a 'doomsday vault.' It is an underground facility that houses all the DNA of plants, animals, and humans, and can withstand a flood, earthquake, or nuclear blast," Eve said. "I think I heard England has one too! And if I'm right, the United States has theirs in Colorado?" Eve said.

"It would take something big to have the oceans flood Earth. But something must have happened because the great flood has been documented around the world in different cultures that at the time had no contact with one another. Think of it...Noah had time to build this ark, and claimed God told him to build it. Well, God or these beings from outer space knew that it was coming. Maybe a meteorite hits Earth, making a huge crater like the one they found in the Indian Ocean. The blast is so big—like a nuclear blast—it shifts the planet on its axis, causing the oceans to come out of their basins. It floods the land and then it takes about 40 days and nights to settle back out." Scott said. "Remember the earthquake that happened in Japan a few years ago? It was something like a 7 on the Richter scale and I heard it shifted Earth's axis a small amount...¼ centimeter? I can't remember the exact numbers. But if it was something that big, I think it could cause Earth to shift or wobble, allowing the water to be displaced enough to make something like that happen," Scott said.

"You know they discovered two cities off the coast of India in the gulf of Khambhat that are 25 miles offshore and 125 feet underwater. It is said that a comet must have struck Earth, causing a global 'deluge,' wiping out an advanced society that dates back further than we know of our existence on Earth. It has been dated to 9000 years ago. Right now, archeologists are mapping it and say they think they found seven temples. The myth is that a great flood covered it in one day," Sarah said.

"Yes, most likely a geological shift and some places were then underwater." Eve said, "Interesting!"

"Did you know that before Noah and the flood, people lived a lot longer? Some lived as long as 900 years. You see it in the Bible in the Old Testament. After the flood, human lives were much shorter—closer to today's life expectancy," Sarah said.

"I wonder why?" Scott asked. "Do you think after Earth was cleansed of the evil, there was a new strategy for our planet? Maybe that was when there was a real separation between the gods (people from outer space) and humans?"

"I'm not sure, but I'm ordering the Book of Enoch; I want to read it all myself," Eve said, pushing buttons on her phone. "It will be here in two days."

"I know there is a lot that isn't explained about the past, But some want to keep it that way," Scott said.

Talking had made the trip go by fast and soon they were back at Eve's house. Eve pushed the gate code and they pulled up the drive. She turned on the security system as the electric fence closed behind them. From now on, the gates would remain closed until her parents returned. The eight-foot-high stone fence had wire on top that carried a strong charge; it would knock someone out if they tried to enter coming over the wall.

"That should keep us safe while we're inside at least." Eve said.

They pulled into the garage and Eve waited while the large barn-type doors rolled back in place. The overhead lights came on, making it bright inside the clean space. Tools and outdoor equipment hung neatly on one side and a small sports car sat in the other space. Everyone grabbed their things and entered through the back of the house. It was 3:30 A.M. and they all were dragging from lack of sleep.

"Let's take to our beds and start new in the morning," Eve said, motioning for Sarah to follow her. Scott left ahead of them to check the house. Eve took Sarah to the third floor and opened a room that had sat unused for a long time. After checking to make sure the sheets were clean, she found an extra blanket and the remote for the TV.

"Will you be okay here?" Eve asked. "If you want to be on the same floor, I can change out the sheets in my parents' bedroom. That way you could be closer to us." Eve asked, making sure their new friend was comfortable.

"I will be fine, dear…I'll be asleep soon." Sarah took Eve's hand, "You're a good person, Eve." Letting go, Eve stepped to the door and watched Sarah unwrap the fabric around her head. Long, brown, curly hair flowed down her back, making the woman look much younger than Eve had thought. Sarah turned, "I'll find them—don't worry. Night, my dear. We'll talk in the morning."

"Well, I'm glad you're here…night," Eve said, closing the door behind her. She went back to the second floor and met Scott in the hall.

"Do you want me to stay with you?" He asked; Eve hesitated and took a deep breath.

"Go ahead next door…I'll be fine." As he turned to go, she touched his arm. He turned and she noticed he was really close to her.

"Thank you…Scott…for everything," she said.

"Hey…it's been an adventure and very enlightening." Their bodies were so close, Eve could feel the warmth coming from his and the smell of faint aftershave. She turned to leave and he lightly took her hand and pulled her into his arms. He held her, gently stroking her hair for a brief moment before pulling back. "Night, Eve."

"Night, Scott," she whispered, before closing her door. She felt her heart beating at a rapid pace and she thought, *What is wrong with me? Chill out,* she told herself. *He is a good friend.* But in the back of her mind she heard a faint… *He is an attractive man.*

chapter 23

Eve sat in bed and couldn't make herself fall asleep. A vision of an island entered her thoughts; she could feel the warmth of the breeze and hear the sound of the waves hitting the shore. She pictured it in her mind, trying to remember the place. Then it just came to her. It was the place she had visited in her mind and now understood why she was thinking about it. Curious, she found her phone, holding her finger over the button. *Should I wait until morning?* She asked herself, *Or just go ahead?* Eve hit the button and closed her eyes, listening to the recording. She heard a child's voice. *That doesn't sound like me*, she thought. Eve concentrated, listening.

Her mind raced, taking her back to a different place and time. She felt scared and could feel herself running up the beach, fighting the sand, her legs tired, but fear moved her quickly, rushing to the caves. She was moving fast and could feel her heart pumping harder the faster she went. When she came off the sand from the beach, she felt the wild vegetation between her toes and her pace increased, moving across the space at top speed. She was one of the last to enter the caves and rapidly moved through the entrance of the opening, making her way farther and farther underground. She followed the worn passages into Earth, where it was safe. She caught up with others moving along in a line, carrying food and water on their backs. Her mother came and she felt comfort; Mother would take care of everything.

"Mother, I saw Father..." she tried to say.

"It will be all right. He'll be along soon." Her mother said, "Come—we have to hurry! They might find us."

"Mother, who are those floating small ears? Their skin is our color and one had light red hair like mine," she asked. "I thought the Moai were positioned to keep us safe within the circle. But now will the gods from home have to come?" She asked.

"They were made to keep us safe on the island until the time was right. The gods will come when we are no longer safe. Now we will be able to go home. We won't be punished any longer for the Watchers not minding the gods. Hurry, daughter, we have much to do."

They traveled deeper into Earth, coming to a passage behind a large boulder. They entered an enormous cavern that was full of activity. A few dozen of her people were at work loading a disk-shaped ship. It took up the whole cavern's space. Wood burned around the edges, lighting the cave; golden objects and tools were being put on board as a gift to the gods. Her mother stopped in front of her.

"Your father needs his tool. Go—get it quickly and bring it to him. He is coming now....Go, child, hurry....He has much to do."

"Yes, Mother." She ran into their living space and grabbed the golden object. It was heavy but she couldn't let her people down. She put it on her shoulder, feeling the weight of the shaft pressing into her skin. The three sharp points were a few feet in front of her face. Balancing it on her body, she ran back toward the cave's entrance, making sure the points didn't touch anything.

At the mouth of the cave she saw her father and was proud of his stature. He was the largest of their people, standing almost 15 feet tall. He took his wand from her back and lifted it easily in the air. She heard a loud crackle of electric current and the energy filled the cavern; thunder filled the sky. With a sweep of her father's trident through the air, clouds moved over the island and the wind increased.

"Go on now! Back to your mother! I will be right behind you!" Her father said; he turned, leaving her standing there. She moved back and hovered in the entrance for a moment. At the last second she turned and followed him, wanting to see what he was going to do. She watched him raise the shaft over his head; currents of electricity shot sparks from the end of the wand. When he pointed it at each of the Moai heads, they toppled over. Their large faces were left lying on the ground, broken and uprooted. Her father raced around the island, making most of them fall and breaking the circle. The only ones he left on purpose were the seven brothers that looked out to sea. He touched them with the trident and a current flowed through each, connecting the electricity on the tops of their heads. Power flowed and smoke rose above the island, mingling with the storm clouds. Finished, he started back to the caves. Now the sky was black; rolling thunder boomed behind him as he ran. She watched as he leapt over the fallen stones that fell in his path, his long legs carrying him through the air. They both arrived at the cave's entrance at the same time.

"Why are you still here?" He yelled, when he saw her.

"Father...why destroy all of our work?" Will the gods still remember us if they are no longer there?"

"Don't worry—we're going home now....This is what was instructed long ago. When the floating machine came, it was the sign for us to leave and quickly before they return. Our punishment is over. Come, child, we must hurry! I can feel them coming." He cracked his device and the winds increased, making the magnetic storm more violent.

When they got to the large cavern, the area outside was deserted and they ran up the ramp, feeling the door closing behind them. Smoke filled the cave and fire burned the enclosed area. Her father yelled for them to go. The disk lifted off, bumping the side of the walls and the top of the cave. After two tries the roof opened and the ship pushed its way through the rock and roots holding it together. It rose, hovering above the island and in a flash of lightning, was gone.

Gola looked back at the island; it became a small dot as they rose through the clouds. They moved out of the hemisphere, making their way to space, the blue Earth getting smaller with each moment. They were going home!

chapter 24

Eve sat for a while under the warm covers. The sun was coming up. She reached over and shut the blinds and sat in the dark, thinking about all that had happened during the past two days. She tried to understand and logically think about what they had learned.

This might just be a case for reincarnation, she thought, *what else could it be?* How else was she able to connect with this child from hundreds of years ago? It was the only thing Eve could think of that might make sense. All she knew was…what she had felt at that moment was overwhelming happiness.

Who knows what happens to people after they die? There have been many who have described seeing a white light at the end of a tunnel when they had a near-death experience. Or surgeons and nurses reporting seeing something floating over a person when they were operating. Then upon waking, the patient would say that they had seen their body on the table being worked on by the doctors, looking down from the ceiling.

Eve wasn't sure what to think; this was all new to her. She lay awake for hours thinking. Sleep wouldn't come to her, so she decided to get up. While Eve was brushing her teeth, she heard the house alarm going off in her parents' bedroom. She tossed on a sweater and sprinted down the hall, meeting Scott at her parents' door. He looked sleepy and was only wearing his briefs and a white tank top. Eve filed that away and opened the door, going inside. She pulled a sheet off six computers, their screens now all aglow; something had triggered them. Clicking the mouse, Eve was able to close in on different places around the yard. The camera security system covered every location of the enclosure along with the outside wall. Both Eve and Scott stood searching the flat screens, finding the view that showed the house's entrances and the large walled-in yard. On the south corner by the deserted side of the street, they saw a man in dark clothing lying on the ground. By the looks of it, he had been blown off the wall by the electric current. They watched as he moved, trying to stand, removing the dark facemask that was covering his face.

"Well, it looks like he will be okay. Hey! That's the FBI agent!" Eve said. "Most likely he didn't know we were home. But why try to break in?"

"Or maybe he did know and was creeping up on us," Scott said. "He could have just rang the bell, but without a warrant for our arrest or a search warrant we don't have to answer," Scott said.

"It's nice to have a lawyer in the house. I told you we were safe inside," Eve said.

"You're funny…I'm not one yet. Well, we can't hide in here forever!" Scott said. "This isn't normal—it's a little extreme. We'll hold out until we can't take it any longer."

"Yes…let's get some food and go to the place." Eve said, pointing her finger upward, winking at him. Turning, she jumped, seeing movement in the doorway. "Sarah—you scared me!"

"I heard the alarm. Sorry. He won't bother us for a day or so.... He doesn't feel good." Sarah said, rubbing her forehead. Stretching her arms over her head, she suggested, "I'm in need of some coffee. Then to the place?"

They all stood for a moment watching the monitors. Scott had wrapped the discarded sheet around himself after seeing Sarah checking him out, making him remember he was half naked. Looking at the screen, they noticed no new movement.

"He's gone for now," Scott said. "Let's go do a few things..." He pointed to the heavens and they laughed when his cover started to slide. "Ya...and I need to get dressed."

"No you don't!" Sarah said, and pretended to slap his rear as he went past her. Eve giggled, amused by Sarah.

Everyone got their coffee and a few snacks and moved upstairs. Sarah was excited when she saw the room and the painted walls. She stood for a few moments, running her fingers over the painting, connecting grid lines with her finger and seeing how they encircled Earth.

Eve had moved the organized stacks of files to one end of the table. Taking the second stack, she started flipping through the files, reading the titles. She had made a clear working space and spread out the pages of the file on Easter Island. Finding an empty box, she put the already reviewed files inside and moved it off to the side of the table.

"Before we start, I think you guys need to listen to this." Eve pulled out her phone and handed it to Scott. The room was silent except for the voice of the child (Gola). Afterward no one said anything for a moment. "What do you think?" Eve asked, looking at Sarah. Her eyes were closed and both Eve and Scott waited to see what Sarah's reaction would be. She only blinked and had a weird look on her face, as if in thought.

"I know the voice was kinda crazy. But the odd part was that I felt what the child was feeling...like it was me from a different time," Eve said.

"If we believe in reincarnation, we would say that the spirit lives on after the death of the body and finds its way to a new person at birth. I have heard people say that this happens because the spirit is trying to work something out or be better than they were in a past life. For instance, sometimes a current person in your life might not be a good person, but you are still drawn to this person. You know it will never work, but you have such a strong connection and don't understand why. It has been said that the reason you can't shake them is that you had a connection from a different lifetime."

"So do you think that I'm reincarnated from this child from Easter Island that was a space being?" Eve asked.

"Well, I have come to the conclusion that anything is possible." Sarah said. "Most likely...I would say yes."

chapter 25

Scott had been looking through the Easter Island file as they spoke. "Take a look at this. It says here that the island was discovered in 1722 by a Dutch explorer named Jacob Roggevin. He tells the story of a very tall race of people that met his ship. He said they were 7 to 12 feet tall. Years later, when the next explorers returned to the island, those people were gone. But inside the caves they found large skeletons, tools, and artifacts from an advanced civilization. Most of the artifacts were taken by the Smithsonian Institute and never heard about again."

"Maybe what I saw is what happened. And then the island was just left with the small ears?" Eve said.

"I would bet you're right. Isn't it interesting that at the time the Smithsonian Institute was all over exploring and collecting artifacts that showed evidence of the giants' existence and burying it. Remember, we said we need to take a look at them. They seem to be everywhere back then." Scott said. "Are they or were they controlled by the government?"

"I'm not sure…but it is something that would make sense. I find it interesting that the girl's father had a device that seemed to knock over the Moai heads and they weigh tons. It seemed like this tool was able to control the weather also. Do you think maybe it was an anti-gravitational device or something with enough power to move mass? Do you think somehow that the energy was stored or saved in the device?" Eve asked excited. "And pushing this thought farther…I know it might sound nuts! But do you think other than reincarnation, it might be that I have this connection because I am to recreate this device? Think about it!" Eve said, watching both Sarah and Scott, hoping they weren't thinking she had a screw loose.

"I've read that some of the great advanced minds have claimed to have had thoughts of technology come to them in dreams. Or think the thoughts and diagrams just came to them and they were able to visualize them in their minds. Nikola Tesla and Da Vinci were among those few. What I read said that after each of their deaths, all their notes and work were taken by the government and might be the basis of what current technology we have today," Sarah said.

"Incredible! Who knows? It looks like governments around the world have all been covering things up for a long time," Eve said. "Could you imagine if they all shared the information that they have? What kinds of advancements could be made today! How else would they move the Moai heads?" Eve asked. "In the past year they have dug up some of the heads and found underneath the ground that many had bodies. I wonder why they were buried up to their necks. Do you think it had something to do with magnetic energy?"

"I'm not sure on that one. But this is interesting…many have wanted to solve that mystery. It says here an older woman who lived on Easter Island was asked how the heads were moved. She said that her great, great grandparents told her that it was with a mystical device that was called 'Mama.' It would make the stone weightless," Scott said.

"I think they've done different studies at universities trying to see if they could come up with a way to move the Moai heads, with ropes and manpower taking the heads from the rock quarry," Eve said.

"Here it says that the island didn't have any trees left, so maybe they used them all moving the heads?" Scott said. "A different idea is that the seven giant brothers had all the trees destroyed so that no one could leave the island. It was to keep them safe; they didn't want anyone to find them, because they were hiding there. Theorists say that they left their home island because the people there were killing giants," Scott said.

"I think the trees might have been used in the caves to create power. But to me it seems odd, that I would be working on this very thing for my dissertation. What do you guys think?" Eve paused, looking at Sarah, who had been still. She opened her eyes and they could see them glossed over before clarity came to them and she focused on Eve.

"Yes, it was a device that the leader used…I saw it…" Sarah said. "The trees were used to create energy that stored power for the ship. I think they had come up with a way to create hydrogen, so they were ready to leave quickly when the time came."

"When I was doing my research, I found a case that might have defied gravity. Have you heard of the 'Stone Garden'? It is a structure that was made out of cut stones in Homestead, Florida. It is the only modern monolithic structure. It was built in 1923 by this slight man who weighed around a hundred pounds. It is said that he would work on moving the large rocks after dark, because he didn't want anyone watching him working. He said that he only used a wooden tripod and chains. But the tripod looked like there was no way that it would hold anything that heavy. After he died, his notes claimed that he had found the secrets of the building of the Pyramids. In his notes he stated that he had found a reverse force that was electromagnetic. The certain frequency would transform the stones into weightless objects. That's what I have been studying," Eve said.

"Does it work?" Sarah asked.

"Not yet, but I'm close...I'm just trying to find the right frequency that when connected with an electric charge can switch or reverse the force to an anti-gravitational force." Eve said, looking proud of her work. She twisted a loose piece of hair around her finger and stopped when she noticed Scott watching her.

Chapter 26

"Wow—I didn't know you were that close! Here's something that might help. I found this about frequency...hold on." Scott was quiet for a few minutes, reading from his file. "Scientists at Bristol University in England have been doing research on the effects of sound and frequency to levitate small objects and have crafted a small handheld device they call a 'portable tractor beam.' They say they are able to move very small, light objects the size of a corn kernel. I remember you talking about the hover trains and how they didn't touch the tracks and were using some kind of magnets." Scott said.

"Yes, it's hard to get the right amount of force from both directions to create an equal balance." Eve said, thinking out loud. "Can you let me see that file? I'm going to have to look into what they really did. It might be a combination of sound and reverse magnetic force. Incredible!"

"Eve, was there any kind of sound when the father used this device?" Scott asked.

Sarah and Eve looked at each other and said "Yes" at the same time.

"Okay, listen to this. I think I might have found something else. Here's a different study. This one is recent—2017!

It says here that a scientist thought to test the ancient sites around the world, checking the acoustic frequency. He found that when tested they had all been built to have the same 110 Hertz frequency," Scott said.

"What is Hertz?" Sarah asked.

"It is the number of vibrations per second. This is unbelievable! I never thought of using sound! I have a lot of work to do!" Eve said.

"Hold on. There was an experiment done March 25, 2017. The scientist wanted to know the effect that different frequencies had on the brain. They used an EKG machine to record the activity in the brain, testing it between 90-120 Hertz. What they found was crazy. When they dialed in 110 Hertz, the brain lit up in a different area showing a large amount of activity. The subject was asked if any of the frequencies felt different when applied. The male subject said, 'One of them made me feel different, as if I was floating away from my body.' He could feel it in his blood, almost percolating his skin. The scientist running the test found it was the same 110 Hertz. Further testing found that same frequency makes the water in the body and the tissue respond.... Wow—Science!" Scott said, smiling at Eve, enjoying her excitement and finding her irresistible. "It also says here that the technology came from an ancient civilization not found on earth." Scott said, quiet for a moment, reading the file in front of him.

"What else do you have?" Eve asked, sitting on the edge of her seat.

"Well...have you guys heard of the Dropa Stones?" Scott asked.

"I haven't," Eve said.

"Me neither," said Sarah.

"Okay here goes…in 1938 a Chinese explorer came across a cave where he found many skeletons. They were all under four feet tall and had larger elongated heads. The DNA testing found they weren't children. Half buried at the back of the cave, the explorer found 716 round disks about a foot in size, all with a hole in the middle. There was hieroglyphic-like writing around the edges that you could see with a magnifying glass.

"After about five years one was deciphered; it told the story of a race of people coming from the heavens and crashing on Earth. On the walls of the cave, they found drawings of small people in spacesuits; also there was a drawing of a solar system with planets circling. Not far from the caves was a small town that had been cut off from civilization. In the town was a race of people that were all under four feet and were thought to be the descendants of the people from outer space. Maybe these are the grays? You know the ones they talk about?" Scott said.

"What are the grays? And how does that help us? Besides making the case that we've been visited by people from space," Eve asked.

"It does sounds like the grays. Some claim our planet was visited from space people from different solar systems. So they didn't all look the same. The grays were described by people who said they were abducted. These beings were small with large heads and had very large eyes. I would like to see them myself," Sarah said.

"Hold on—listen to this. After their discovery, the disks weren't heard of again until the 1960s when two were put on display in China. But soon after, they just disappeared out of the museum. The next time they were heard of was in 1968 when a Russian scientist published an article talking about the research he had done on the disks.

"He said that when testing the disks with an oscillograph, he recorded a rhythm. The scientist said he thought they had once been electrically charged or had functioned as electrical conductors. Does that help?" Scott asked.

"What? Really! Let me read that…" Eve had gotten up and was looking over Scott's shoulder, reading.

"Maybe that's it…yes! That must be it!" She kissed his cheek. "I think you've solved a problem I have been having."

"How did I do that?" Scott asked, smiling up at her, watching her lips move, thinking they were so perfect.

"I need to try it with an oscillograph or spinning the object. See, it says here they were made of granite with high levels of cobalt." Eve said, as if talking to herself.

She looked up, smiling. "Granite contains a lot of small crystals, and crystals are energy conductors…I need to get to the lab," Eve said, getting up.

"Look, it's Sunday, Eve. We can go tomorrow when the building opens at 9 A.M." Scott said.

"Okay, sorry…I forgot!" Eve said. "I need some paper." Scott handed a few scraps that were in the trash and she started drawing and working formulas, forgetting the others in the room. Both Sarah and Scott watched her. Eve was in her own world now, tuning them out as she focused.

"What is an oscillograph?" Sarah whispered to Scott.

Without looking up, Eve said, "It's a machine that observes electronic current and voltage. The machine draws a graph of the signal as a function of time."

Scott and Sarah smiled at each other, watching Eve work.

"Hey…here's something that might help. The scientist who wrote the article said that he put the disk on a turntable and spun it." Scott said, laughing as Eve stopped, thoughtful for a moment, then continued scribbling. "It looks like the Russians stole the disks when they were on display and when the article came out, they had to return the disks to China." Scott laughed, "All this intrigue!"

Hearing that, Eve looked up, "Did it say anything about the speed? Or sound? Because that might have caused a different frequency. Maybe that is the answer to getting the anti-gravitational to work! Who would have thought what I have been looking for would be in my parents' files?" Eve mused, not looking up from the paper she was working on.

"Okay…you do your work and we'll continue going through these files to see if we have a clue to finding your parents." Scott said. Eve didn't even look up; he saw a long drawn out formula that had already covered two pages.

chapter 27

Scott, absorbed in reading, didn't hear Sarah move over to Earth painting on the wall. She had kept staring at the lines that covered Earth's surface connecting different ancient places around the globe. Scott looked up, watching her trace her fingers over the lines, reading the places that she stopped on.

"I think this might help you," Scott moved over to the wall. He carried an open file and was comparing the notes he had found. "I think it's an energy grid," he said, "Look at this."

Sarah looked at the pages Scott was holding, trying to make it out. Graphs and drawings were inside, showing pyramids among other early civilizations all connected in straight lines around the planet. The other was a chart of obelisks showing how they also connected.

"Maybe you're right," Sarah said, thinking.

"Did you see this one connecting the pyramids? Look—the lines connect to Easter Island as well." Scott said, tracing his fingers along the line. "Your 'Space People' or 'Watchers' had to have shown ancient man where to build these in order for them to be connected. They could only map it from the sky."

"Look—these are on the same longitude and latitude lines around the globe. You're right.... It would take someone looking at the planet from outer space to make them so accurate," Sarah said.

Scott studied the lines, seeing how they connected and was thoughtful. "Look at all these. Her parents put every archaeological discovery and the estimated time frame of the civilization. The older ones are the largest and all set up mimicking a certain star system...is that Orion's belt? Or Sirius B solar system?" Scott asked, looking at the file, turning it sideways and comparing it.

"I'm not sure—we will have to look it up. That's not my expertise," Sarah said.

"Yes...I think it is Sirius B, which is weird because it wasn't discovered until this century!" Eve said from across the room, as she continued drawing something.

"Hey, it says here that the UFO sightings have been more common in these areas around the planet. It's thought that they are running along these energy lines. Maybe they use the energy to power their ships?" Scott said, "Because the reports I have read on UFOs say that the disks in the sky don't fly in normal patterns; they are extra fast and move in unusual directions. Pilots interviewed said that kind of movement is some type of technology that we haven't yet developed," Scott said.

"Most likely they are returning to safe places to gather energy and they have been traveling there for thousands of years." Sarah said, "I've heard that they also are seen frequently flying over power plants, nuclear bases, and rift zones in the earth's crust. Maybe somehow they can gather energy that way?"

"Look at this newspaper article from last year. It says that the pyramids weren't a burial chamber after all, like they had first thought. They were some kind of energy plant. They discovered this at the Giza Pyramids in Egypt. There are small shafts that come from the King's chamber. On closer investigation, they found they weren't air shafts. They were used to send chemicals down where they met in the main chamber, mixing together to cause a reaction. The chamber was lined in lead.

"The shafts were only about a square foot and a team of scientists wanted to see where they led, so sent a robot with a camera down them. At the end was a small door with electric symbols. They took test samples from the sides of the walls and found that one had a zinc hydrate residue and the other had residue of hydrochloric acid. When the two were run down the shafts at the same time, they mixed together in the chamber and combustion happened, creating hydrogen gas that came out the peak of the Pyramid. I think you're right about it being some kind of energy grid giving power that connected around Earth," Scott said.

From across the room, Eve spoke, her head still focused on her notes, "I read once that they had found giant lightbulbs painted in Egyptian hieroglyphics and wondered if the Egyptians could have had electricity. It didn't make sense that they were painting on the walls with just reflected light from mirrors." Eve said, turning over one of the pages she was working on, looking at what she had written.

"At this point I think that anything is possible," Scott said. "Look at these sticky notes on the side of the map. They show where Eve's parents went to see each ancient site. They are dated...and going in a circle. This one is in

Turkey at the place you said your parents were going, and the last one marked is in Malta," Scott said. "It is some ancient underground caves or tunnels."

"That must be it!" Eve said, jumping up. "They most likely knew they were being followed and gave the FBI the slip. This is where we need to go!" She had moved across the room and stood by them, running her fingertips over the map and stopping on Malta. Eve looked from Scott to Sarah. "What do you guys think?" Eve asked, "I bet that's where they went. Do we want to check it out?"

"I'm in!" Scott said, "I'm always up for an adventure…just need to finish a few things for my class and email it to my professor. How soon do you want to leave?"

"Is tomorrow morning too soon?" Eve asked, jamming her scraps of paper into her worn briefcase and locking it tight with the extra files. "I just need to go to the bank to check on the funds."

"Tell you what…I'll drive you to the bank and we can stop by my apartment so I can toss some clothes in a backpack and we can be back within the hour," Scott said.

"Sarah, are you coming with us? I'm sure I have plenty of money to pay for everything we're going to need," Eve asked. Sarah was standing in the middle of the room with her eyes closed and her hand on her temples.

"Yes…I can see…I need to go with you. This I can't miss!" Sarah said.

"What did you see?" Eve asked.

"I'm not sure, but it is a dark place. We will need to bring lots of solar backup and remember that conch shell on the table in the living room? We need to bring that with us," Sarah said.

Thinking that was odd, Eve just nodded, feeling that they might need this woman's help. She seemed to know a lot about the beings that might have influenced mankind, but Eve's main objective was to find her parents.

"Anything you need while we're out?" Scott asked.

"No, I'm ready to go. The coast is clear right now...the men won't be back until nightfall. Now I must rest. Care if I stay here while you're gone? Just in case?" Sarah stretched her arms over her head and moved to the couch. The sun was in a different position overhead and was shining on the pillows through the skylight. They noticed her brown curls flowing around her face with different tones of browns and natural highlights. Her eyes closed, the sun warming her face. Scott and Eve closed the door behind them, locking her in, and went downstairs.

Eve started to put the key in the planted pot and Scott put his hand on hers, "Just in case, maybe we should bring it with us."

"Good idea," Eve said, smiling at him.

"Sorry you can't go to the lab. I know you're feeling the need to figure out your research with all the new information." Scott said, touching a piece of hair that had fallen on her face.

"It will be there when I return. I don't know what I would do without my parents...they're all I have," Eve said.

"They aren't...all you have," he said, looking into her eyes. Eve gave him a quick hug to break the moment and stepped back.

"You're really sweet, Scott. Hold on—let me change and I'll meet you at the truck in five." Eve turned and was gone.

chapter 28

Driving out the front gates of the house, Scott waited until he saw the eight-foot ornate steel move back into place behind them before pulling out onto the street. He took a few extra turns, checking his mirrors, making sure that they weren't being followed. Like Sarah had said, the coast seemed to be clear. It was already 11:00 A.M. when he pulled in front of the Chase bank. The sun was out, making it seem like a nice day until Eve opened the door and the brisk air flowed inside the cab.

"Man! It's chilly today! Can't wait until the weather finally changes; it's just teasing us. Did you want me to go inside with you?" Scott asked, watching her zip up her hoodie.

"Yes, you aren't kidding. You know how I feel about the cold! I'll be all right; this won't take long," Eve said.

Scott watched Eve cross the street and enter the bank. He found a station on the radio, tuning it to the news. A new headline had just broken; a Playboy model was telling her story of an affair with the current President. Scott wondered how men of power could get away with everything and people would just look the other way, putting aside their moral convictions. He had never seen such a divide in American society as it was now in the United States. He wondered about the future of the country. He was glad when Eve returned, turning off the station. It was better to think of something positive. He had wondered about this "Make America Great Again." He felt after being able to travel to other countries while growing up, that America was already great and didn't understand the concept. Maybe it was his age.... Anyhow, they were going on an adventure. He just hoped that they could find Eve's parents. He wasn't so sure of the outcome, but he would follow it through, no matter what...for Eve.

"Everything go okay?" He asked, when Eve fought the wind opening the door.

"Yes...we are all set," she said, tapping her purse with her fingers and smiling. "We have plenty of money! I didn't realize that my parents have been putting money in my account and I hardly have spent anything."

"Did you forget your briefcase?" Scott asked.

"No, I put it in the family safety deposit box, just in case. What if those men break into the house when we are out of the country? I can't have my work fall into the wrong hands or get lost in the mix. Do you understand how big this discovery could be?" Eve asked.

"I understand! I'm really proud of you. I know it's been a lot of hard work," Scott said. "I give it to you for not giving up."

"Yes, about two years' worth of experiments and research. So I hope I can get it to work." Eve said, not wanting to fail. "I keep telling myself that I can do it...Nothing has ever stopped me before. And I do love the feeling you get when you make your goal become reality." Eve said, smiling at him.

"I understand that feeling as well. I know you'll do it! You're the smartest women I know!" Scott said, meaning it.

"Well, thank you...you're not so bad yourself," she laughed.

chapter 29

The plane left early in the morning for Barcelona, Spain. The usual night flights had all been full and the seats had been limited at short notice. They had put Sarah up in First Class where she had immediately made friends with a businessman around her age. By the end of the seven-hour flight, the man was sure to know everything there was to know about their new friend Sarah. They thought she had been in that small town too long and was very chatty with everyone she met, interested in their lives.

Scott and Eve had opted for seats across the aisle from each other in coach, where they both tried to sleep; they wanted to be ready when they arrived in Spain. But it was too early to doze, so they opted to play gin-rummy, keeping track of points, both being competitive and not wanting the other to get the best of them. By the time the plane landed, Scott was up by 50 points and they hadn't slept a wink.

"Come on, one more quick game!" Eve begged. "I know that last one you had to have cheated…I had you!"

"Oh no you don't! I just outsmarted you on that one! I am the champion!" Scott started to sing, "I am the Champion…I am the Champion of the world."

"One more game!" Eve said, ignoring his little song, perplexed that he had triumphed.

At that moment the overhead speaker told them to prepare for landing, making them put away the cards and upright their chairs. Eve stuck out her lip and Scott laughed at her.

"I'm sure you'll get a chance later to try to beat The CHAMPION!" Scott harped, laughing at her expression. "I know you're not used to being...a loser!"

Eve slugged him in the arm and he fell back, acting like she had carried a strong punch, knocking him into the chair. They both laughed, enjoying each other's company.

Disembarking the plane, they gathered their bags, went outside, and found a cab. Luckily for them Sarah was pretty fluent in Spanish. She sat up front directing the young driver, finding out he was newly married and had a young baby at home. He easily found their hotel in the middle of the city. It was an old brownstone redone with an art deco flair, mixed with the old carved wood of the past. They had opted for two rooms that joined together, knowing that in Europe the hotel rooms were a lot smaller than in the United States. They had taken the driver's phone number and arranged for him to pick them up in the morning to take them to the docks to catch their ship. Eve had rented a private boat to take them down the Mediterranean to Malta.

In the morning they met their driver in the front of the hotel and piled in. When he learned where he was taking them, the driver told Sarah that they had an extra hour to kill and he would give them a quick tour on the way. She translated the information to Scott and Eve, and they all agreed that it would be nice to see the city while they were there.

He took them to one of the main attractions built for the Sagrada Familia. The large church had been under construction since 1882. It was a giant basilica designed by Gaudi, who was known for his artistic architecture.

"That's incredible!" Eve said, looking out her open window at the tall peaks forming what she thought looked like small mountains. The car was silent while they all stared in awe from their seats at the different stones, colors, and figures hanging off the building. It was a lot to take in and every detail was truly a piece of art. Their driver smiled with pride at their reaction and circled the building slowly, showing them the outside of the structure that was still being worked on all these years later. They saw the lines of people waiting to go inside. "Maybe on our return we can take the tour," Eve said.

They left the area and a few minutes later the driver pulled up to the front of Gaudi's park. They were learning that Gaudi had many places that he had designed and built, filling the city with works of art. They noticed the large animals crouched on the steps made out of carved stone. Their bodies were covered in small mosaic tiles, creating patterns and color. Stone trees swirled, curving along the walkways, each detail done with care.

"This guy's mind was something else," Scott said, taking a few pictures with his phone.

"Our driver told a sad story about Gaudi. He was hit by a trolley car and left to die in the street at the age of 74. Onlookers hadn't recognized him and thought he was just a bum," Sarah said, being the interpreter.

The driver looked at his watch and said it was time to catch their boat and everyone got back in the car. Sarah had gone to the top of the steps where different vendors had spread sheets and were selling jewelry with small cut stones, the designs resembling the Gaudi style of art. Some were quite nice, so Sarah carried a full bag when she returned to the car. She picked out a necklace for both Eve and Scott and put them around each of their necks. Eve's was beautiful silver inlayed with red stones swirling around a silver circle. Scott's was a square with a matching design with brown stones, which made it look more masculine. They looked well made and very expensive and Eve dug in her purse, wanting to pay for them.

"No dear, these are a gift from me. Some say crystals have protecting powers." Sarah said.

Eve tried once more to hand Sarah a hundred-dollar bill over the car seat. "They are too expensive!" Eve said.

"No. It is my treat and they were just five euros. So put your money away! Anyhow, you paid for everything else!" Sarah dug in the bag, finding one with green stones that she liked. She put it on, looking in the rearview mirror and admiring their beauty.

"Well, I see why you got a bunch of different ones at that price…I should have bought some myself," Eve said. The driver looked back at her in the rearview mirror, and hesitated at the curb.

"You go…" he said in English, smiling at her. "We have time." Eve looked at Scott and they both jumped out of the car and sprinted up the stairs to the top. They were back in five minutes, satisfied with their purchases.

"These will be great gifts when we return home," Eve said.

Chapter 30

"Thank you, Sarah!" Scott said, "My mother and her friends will enjoy these. Look at the back, Eve. It has the name Gaudi imprinted in the metal."

"Cool," she said, flipping hers over and touching the name. "I hate to admit that I don't know too much about Barcelona or even Malta," Eve admired her crystals sparking in the light from the window.

The driver surprised them all by speaking English with a strong accent. "Malta is a small island that has been a neutral place for hundreds of years. It has stayed out of the wars that have surrounded it; it's located off the coast of Italy in the Mediterranean Sea. It's a safe haven. It has one of the oldest stone structures on Earth, on the Maltese island of Gozo dating back to 5,200 BC. It is thought that the people that inhabited the island came from Sicily. But if you ask many of the citizens, they'll explain that they are descendants of the Roman Empire. The ancient civilization found on Gozo is said to be 1000 years earlier than the Pyramids of Giza. What is interesting about the structure is that it was built before metal tools and the wheel had been invented. People have wondered how it was built because the monolithic stones at the site weigh over 20 tons each," the driver said, speaking like he was used to giving tours, and was full of information. He laughed at tricking them, smiling with a toothy grin, proud of his English.

"Thank you," Sarah said sweetly. "You could have told us that you speak English. We could have had even more fun!" She winked at him and watched him blush. "How far is Malta off the coast?" Sarah asked, in English.

"I would say around 80 miles. The Mediterranean Sea is rather large, almost like an ocean. It has been said that at one point it was part of the North Atlantic Ocean." The driver had pulled up to the curb and jumped out, pulling the few bags out of the trunk.

"Thank you. We really enjoyed the tour!" Eve pulled a hundred-dollar bill from her fanny pack and saw the grin that would keep the dogs away as she put it in his hand.

"Call me when you return, and I will come for you." He pointed to the small thirty-foot ship down the wooden walkway.

"Thank you! We will call you when we return." Sarah said, kissing him on the cheek. Laughing at his expression, she took her bag, leading the way.

chapter 31

The group moved down the boat ramp, hearing the thump…thump…thump…of the wheels of their suitcases as they rolled over each weathered wooden plank. They stopped at the ship, looking it over. It didn't look all shiny and clean like the ad that had been on the Internet. Eve wondered if it really was the right boat. A short, chubby little man rounded the corner, followed by a small boy with brown, longish hair. The child looked to be around seven years old. He held a sign with Eve's name on it and she nodded that it was her.

"I guess this is us," Eve said, disappointed that her money hadn't bought something better.

Reading her mind, Scott stepped in front of Eve and addressed the man. He really didn't understand one word that Scott said. Seeing the problem, Sarah smiled and talked to the man, leaving Eve and Scott to wonder what they were saying. The man started laughing and motioned them on to the boat.

"Are you sure that this ship is safe to go as far as we are going?" Eve asked, not sure she wanted to get on board.

"The owner said he takes people to Malta all the time," Sarah said. Taking her fingers from her forehead, she continued, "It will be safe…I saw it…but bumpy."

"Bumpy?" Eve said. Sarah had already stretched her leg over between the boat and the dock. Quickly standing on the deck of the swaying boat, Eve watched her rocking with the boat's movement. She motioned for Eve to come on. "Okay...OKAY! Here I come," Eve said, and felt Scott's hand steady her as she crossed over to the rocking boat. He handed the man their bags before crossing over himself.

On the boat they were motioned to go below deck and followed the boy down the steps into the small dining area. There was a little kitchen with built-in seating around a table. Here everything seemed to be nailed down. Eve noticed that they had an older coffee machine with the pot pinned down to the wooden counter. Eve was relieved knowing that she would get her caffeine fix in the morning. Off to the side was a dark hall; Eve hesitated when the small boy took her hand and pulled her forward. He pointed where to put her bag, and when she didn't understand, he took it from her and put it off to the side of the bunk beds. He pointed to the top bunk and she understood this was where she would be spending the night. It was a tight space about two feet from the ceiling, but looked to be the size of a double bed. The boy eyed Sarah and pointed to the bottom bunk; the bed was the size of a twin. He eyed Scott up and down, taking in his size and looked at both women. Making a decision, he pointed for Scott to sleep on the upper bunk.

"Well, I guess we're sharing..." Scott laughed. "Hope you don't snore!" Eve slugged him in the stomach, and he pretended that it hurt, falling to the side. The small boy's eyes got wide before he realized that they were playing.

"You know I don't snore!" Eve said.

"How do you know? When you're asleep?" He asked.

"You better watch out or I'll switch places with Sarah!" Eve threatened and giggled at his expression.

"Yes...I would have my way with him, if we were in the same bed," Sarah said, pretending to slap his firm butt, making her hand look like it was bouncing off. Eve heard a noise and saw the little boy laughing. Scott remained quiet, a twinkle in his eyes, and winked at Eve.

They felt the boat get underway. It rocked with the current, moving forward into the deeper, cooler water. The boy made a noise over the sound of the loud engines, drawing their attention and signaling them to follow him back into the kitchen area of the ship. On the table were plastic cups with a bottle of red wine, a bottle of limoncello, and a bowl of fresh fruit.

Eve reached for the ice and Scott stopped her. "Better to drink it warm than be sick," Scott said, pouring all three of them the limoncello. "Come on guys, let's go above deck and watch the sunset," Scott said.

The sun was indeed setting on the horizon; the orange, yellows, and reds contrasting with the dark blue water was beautiful. The three sat on the wooden platform until the shore was no longer visible. The boy had returned with the open bottle and filled their glasses. Sarah had moved to the front of the ship, standing tall on the bow, spreading her arms. Her hair had come loose of her wrap and flowed in the breeze as she did a *Titanic* moment. Soon all they could see was darkness and the waves as they crashed over the hull of the ship. The wind had picked up, making it impossible to remain up top any longer. The boy took Eve's hand, pulling her and signaling her to come below.

"You guys ready to go in?" Eve looked back over her

shoulder. "I think he wants us to come inside…I'm getting chilly anyway. The breeze is blowing through my sweater." Eve said, her words fading in the wind. "Scott, are we going to play a game of cards before bed?"

"I'm right behind you. Let me collect Sarah." Scott yelled over the sound of the waves now smashing into the boat. The wind was getting stronger and louder with each minute.

"I'm coming," Sarah said, hearing him. She arose, straightening her hair and pulling it into a knot at the back of her neck. Scott watched as she skipped across the deck like she was a young woman, almost floating when the wind picked her up. He wondered how old she really was. He had assumed that she was Eve's parents' age. Sarah smiled as she approached, "I'm 42, not that old!" she said, as she passed, shocking him to silence.

chapter 32

Inside, Scott addressed Eve, "I didn't realize you wanted to take another beating tonight!" He said, going below.

"I might not mind a beating from you!" Sarah stated, skipping past him and taking her seat.

"You are a funny woman," Scott said, "Maybe we can find you a man on this trip...it seems like you need one."

"Are you offering?" Sarah said, making him slide in on the other side of Eve, putting her between them. Inside, the table had been set; the room was warm and toasty. They all watched the young boy as he stirred the food cooking on the stove.

"Wonder what we're having?" Scott whispered.

"I think we're having fish," Sarah said, leaning in closer and crowding Eve, "And some kind of rice with vegetables."

"Well, I'm hungry," Eve said, and scooted over closer to Scott, feeling crowded with Sarah leaning on her arm. The boy brought plates steaming with food and set it down in front of each of them. He made a motion for them to eat and smiled at their expressions when they tasted his food.

"This is really good," Eve said, "A great flavor."

"You're right," Scott said. "It is good!"

Sarah was quiet for a few moments, "Don't eat too much, a storm is on its way and you don't want to feel ill." She spoke to the boy and he nodded and brought them some ginger, slicing it and putting it on their plates.

"What is this for?" Eve asked, eyeing the small pink slices. "I didn't know that it was a root. I've only had it already prepared with sushi."

"It's to keep us from getting seasick." Sarah said, "This is really going to be a storm. We will need to take to our beds early because once it hits us, we will get no rest."

They ate quickly and Eve took out her cards. She was standing by the bed in her jammies (that really were a pair of running shorts and a t-shirt). Scott came in the small enclosure, ducking his head so that he didn't hit it on the ceiling. He had given the girls a few moments to collect themselves before coming in and had changed in the kitchen.

When he had taken off his shirt, the boy had stared at his strong abs and athletic body. He pointed to a magazine from Athens. Opening the pages, he motioned at photos of Olympic athletes that would be going to the next games in two years. Scott understood his meaning and shook his head "No." He smiled at the small boy that he thought was asking him if he was an Olympian.

When he entered the room, Scott found Sarah was tucked in her bed, her eyes closed. She had put on her sound-canceling headphones. Eve was waiting and stood to the side of the bed with her cards in her hand. She had waited for Scott to figure out how to approach getting on the top bunk without stepping on Sarah.

"Here, let me give you a boost." Scott put his hands around her small waist. "Ready…On three…One…Two…

Three." Eve hopped in the air and launched herself on to the top bunk, hitting her head, her long legs dangled in the air. For a moment Scott almost bust a gut thinking her legs looked like a baby giraffe trying to walk. He stopped himself when he saw her rubbing her forehead. He suppressed a giggle and looked away, not wanting to laugh at her.

"Are you ready for me to come up?" Scott asked.

"Hold on. Okay, I'm all the way on the back wall…come on," Eve said.

Scott tried to ease his way in and didn't give it as much force as was needed. Eve had to grab his leg and arm at the same time and laughed because he too ended up hitting his head. He tried to hold on to the edge of the bed, not wanting to fall and crush Sarah below and get her talking nonsense. Eve pulled him inside the small space, now laughing so hard that she couldn't talk. Every time she tried to say something, she choked on her laughter. It was contagious and by the time they both were laying side by side, they were holding their stomachs because they hurt.

"Stop! You're making me laugh harder and my jaw hurts." Eve said, breaking out in uncontrolled giggles again. "Well I guess this is a funny situation…I feel like I'm in a coffin over here; good thing I'm not claustrophobic!"

"Yes…you've put me in a tight spot. I don't remember laughing this hard in a very long time!" Scott said, enjoying her smile.

They tried to play cards but after two hands, the ship's rocking was making it hard to concentrate. Their cards keep getting displaced. The swaying from side to side continued, increasing until they were holding on tight to the ceiling and wood sides of the enclosure.

After a while, Eve closed her eyes and fell asleep. She woke in the middle of the night to a loud crash. Sarah below them had fallen to the floor of the cabin. At the same time the boat's momentum had rolled Eve into Scott. If he hadn't been there she would have fallen on top of Sarah on the floor. Eve saw a flash of motion. The young boy ran through the cabin with a ropelike mesh and helped Sarah back into bed, locking her in with the fishing net, hooking it onto the side of her bed. Then he climbed up onto their bunk like a little baby monkey and hooked the mesh in place so that it would hold them in bed as well. They felt the boat rock harder.

"Where is your father?" Eve yelled. He stopped and looked like he didn't understand, then disappeared. But she didn't have time to think about it. A big wave carried the boat onto its ridge and let them fall, almost going to one side. The weightlessness for those seconds made butterflies fly around in her stomach before the ship uprighted itself. Eve was grateful that she wasn't sick but felt a little frightened. Reading her reaction, Scott pulled her into his arms. Eve hesitated for a moment, not wanting him to get the wrong idea. But she found it harder to keep her body away from his with all the rocking and then just went with it out of fear. Or the fact that his body was warm and was heating her cool skin. Clinging to Scott, Eve felt safe in his strong arms and just prayed that the ship held together. She closed her eyes, feeling out of control.

chapter 33

The night had worn on and on and finally they had all drifted off to sleep. When Eve awoke the next morning along with the sun, there was a great amount of humidity. She felt the skin on her leg sticking to Scott's and she tried to detangle herself from his embrace. She moved away, not wanting to speak until she had some distance between them. Eve knew she would have to wake him to get out of the bed.

Pressed against the wall, she tapped his arm, then poked it—nothing happened. He didn't even stir. She could only hear the lapping of the water against the ship and his light snore. After about 15 minutes, she decided to crawl over him to make her exit. She leaned in, unhooking the mesh. Judging the distance between his body and the ceiling, she had about a foot of clear space. Glancing over the edge to the bed below she saw Sarah's bed was empty and neatly made. *Okay. That's good,* she thought, *In case I fall.*

Eve squeezed on top of Scott, trying not to put all her weight on him, moving a few inches at a time. She felt him stretch and his hands encircling her waist, pulling her tight against his body. She looked to see if he was awake, doing that on purpose, and found that he was truly still sound asleep. She pried his hands off, releasing herself, and continued making her way across his body, until she found that she was stuck.

Great, what now? She thought; in these close quarters, she could only use her hand to touch his face and she lightly tapped it with a few fingers. "Scott…Scott—wake up." She felt his body move a little and something came alive by her leg as she tried to wiggle her way loose. Before she knew what was happening, his lips had found hers and he was kissing her. It wasn't like a peck that you would get from Grandma, but an open mouth, strong, passionate kiss, the first Eve had ever experienced. It was soft at first, then grew stronger and she felt his fingers kneading her ass, moving his hips in sync with hers. He was firm and she felt the hardness pressing between her legs, through her shorts. Her legs felt weak; her body came alive, taking over with each motion. But her mind was stronger, and Eve knew, even with it feeling good, that she had to get away from him.

"Scott! Stop…" She yelled, squirming like a wild cat. His eyes fluttered open; he tried to pull away but was trapped under her. He had thought he had been dreaming, and here she was with her face six inches from his. Scott didn't know what to do or say and just lay still, not responding, watching her frustration. Out of breath, Eve whispered, "I need to get up."

"Eve, please don't be mad…I really didn't realize what I was doing." He touched her face and saw her pink cheeks and reddish swollen lips. His finger brushed her bottom lip as he looked into her eyes. He was surprised at what he saw…lust.

"I'm not mad—could you help me get down?" She asked, looking away.

"Are you sure you want to go?" He whispered, pushing a loose strand of her wavy auburn hair from her forehead.

"Yes…I'm…hot!" Was all she could say; her mind was feeling foggy and her legs were shaking. She hoped she would be able to stand and not be humiliated. Scott helped her down and watched her take some clothes out of her bag.

"I need to freshen up." Eve said, not looking back. She went into the small bathroom that was the size of an airplane restroom. She stood inside, looking at herself in the warped mirror, seeing her flushed checks and darkened pupils through the distorted image. Eve waited a few moments, taking a deep breath until her pulse started to slow. *What was that all about?* She asked herself. *Okay, I'll go up top and just act normal…like nothing happened. Like it's no big deal….You're fooling yourself…you know you like him!* A voice said in her head. *But if I admit that, then I will lose all my power and I'm not going to allow him to make me weak. But the kiss was kinda nice, he tasted good.* Eve thought about him and what had happened; she just stood there talking to herself in the mirror. Looking at her reflection, she noticed that she was smiling and told herself to stop that.

Eve moved into the unkempt, worn shower, wearing her flip-flops after seeing the soiled floor. The water was chilly; Eve stood there, letting it flow over her body until she thought she would be waterlogged. Feeling better, she glanced at herself in the mirror; a grin smiled back at her. She corrected her expression, immediately practicing her game face; checking it again, she was satisfied. *That's better,* she told herself, but the sparkle was still in her eyes.

chapter 34

Scott waited until the door closed before getting out of bed, then he quickly cleaned up, putting on some fresh plaid shorts and a white t-shirt. He found his sandals under Sarah's bed. He left the cabin and went to see what was happening topside. The sun was rising on the horizon and he pitched in, helping the young boy put the seating area back in order. The chairs had blown across the deck and were in a tangle by the bow. He separated them and found none were broken; one was bent a little and he straightened it out. The water was calm now and glistened with small ripples pooling away from the boat.

Scott noticed he was able to see the shore on the horizon. The outline of a city sparkled with golds and reds when the sun hit the light cream brick. The boat drew closer and he could make out large pots filled with green vegetation that surrounded the old breaker wall; their rims overflowed with bright pink and purple flowers, outlining the bay. Scott noticed Sarah sitting at the other end of the boat enjoying the view, her face uplifted to the sun, the breeze blowing her hair in the light wind. He waved at her and she waved back, then returned to enjoying the rays.

Eve came onto the deck and noticed Scott at the other end of the boat looking over the side. She took a breath and squared her shoulders, feeling her long wet hair hanging down the middle of her back, and moved in his direction. She had changed into a Maxie dress and sandals. Holding the hem of her dress, Eve moved forward, swaying with the rocking of the boat, gripping the rail as she went.

"Wow—look how beautiful it is!" Eve said, peering at the bright colors of the sailboats docked in the harbor. A little way down the dock was a full line of houseboats bobbing against the ropes that tied them securely to the dock. A path had opened up and their boat coasted slowly past. They watched the Maltese going about their everyday lives. A busty woman waved as she was hanging clothes to dry in the sun; a boy playing with a small dog watched them pass; and an older man in bikini briefs slept in a hammock.

"It looks like a nice place to live. It has the slow pace of an island." Scott said, looking at her and then where she was pointing, seeing the beautiful landscape off in the distance.

Their ship moved into the quaint harbor surrounded by high whitewashed walls that went up about three stories from the bank. In the harbor, there were many smaller boats that lined the wall docked in numbered slots. Other boats waited in a line for their turn to unload. They soon were able to pull into a vacant spot, tying to the dock until the boat was secure. The boy motioned for everyone to move from the boat to the weathered wooden planks that led to the sidewalk. They waited until the boat was tied to the dock, and soon the boy and his father joined them.

"You will wait and take us back?" Eve looked at her watch, then at the boat's captain.

The boy said something quickly to his father and the man nodded. "We will meet you here at 5:00?" Eve said, walking over to the boy and pointing at the five on her watch. Scott came over beside her, took off his watch, handed it to the boy, and pointed to the five. The boy smiled and put the large watch around his wrist; he pushed it up his arm where it fit around his bicep.

"You sure you want to leave your watch with him?" Eve asked.

"It will be all right." Scott said, winking at the boy.

They walked to the road and found a line of taxis; the drivers were down the block, hanging out playing cards. Eve could hear a few arguing about the last play. Their heads all turned when they saw the tourists approach the line of cars. One stood, telling the others that it was his turn. He moved forward, speaking English. Eve's small group gravitated to the older man with the large brimmed hat. He pulled it down as he spoke, blocking out the sun.

"Taxi? Tour?" He asked, leading them toward a green four-door that was parked on the side of the street. It looked like an older car; the heavy metal and polished steel made Eve know they would be safe. She wasn't sure what kind of car it was because the front was a different make and model from the rear. The paint didn't quite match, as if certain spots had been spray-painted over the top where the sun had faded the finish. But inside it was clean and neat. Scott and Eve took the back seat and Sarah jumped in front, smiling at the driver.

"Where would you like to go, my lady?" He asked Sarah, "I'm Roberto." He smiled at her, smoothing down one side of a full mustache, making it match the other pointy side.

"We would like to go to Hal-Saflienti, Malta's Hypogeum. We see that they reopened it to the public last month," Sarah said, flipping her long hair over her shoulder.

"Yes, that is true…a good choice. Do you have tickets?" He had stopped mid-sentence to watch her. "Sometimes you have to buy tickets a few weeks in advance. You see, they limit the amount of people that they allow to enter each day. This is because the bodies alter the CO_2 levels, airflow, temperature, and humidity inside the cavern. But we will check. It is still early and I might be able to get you in. I have a friend who works there and for a price we could move you to the front of the line." He paused, waiting for her answer.

"Yes. Please see what you can do to get us in today. Whatever you can do, we would really appreciate it. We would like to see the Oracle Chamber," Eve said. "We have heard a lot about it."

"If it doesn't work, pretty girl, if not today then tomorrow." He said, adjusting his rearview mirror so he could see her better.

"Don't worry…let's just see what happens." Scott said, patting Eve's hand, watching her blush when the driver had said she was pretty.

"Yes, a few weeks ago, after we had just reopened, the visitor center had to be closed to tourists and only offer a virtual tour. A couple had gone down with a group and when the tour returned to the surface, this couple was missing. They had to sweep the whole area down there and we have yet to find them. The guide was sure of her count before going down and remembered the two people," the driver stated.

Sarah put her fingers on her forehead and after a moment she looked in the back seat and nodded at Scott and Eve. All remained quiet, not wanting to speak in front of the driver.

In the silence Roberto started talking again, telling them about the site and becoming their tour guide. "The Hypogeum is a complex excavated cave chamber that includes a temple, cemetery, and funeral hall. It is one of the world's best-preserved prehistoric sites, dating back 6,000 years. It's an underground network of alcoves and corridors carved into the soft limestone," he said.

"What do you know of the Oracle Room?" Eve asked, "Does it really have acoustic effects?"

"Yes, it does my lady—it is quite unusual. The walls were cut out a certain way to create amplified sound and it really echoes. If you speak in this room, the sound will travel through the whole complex...almost like a loud speaker.

"Also, the third tier goes 10 meters farther underground and has small rooms that served as mass graves. The weird thing about it is that around the 1920s, 7,000 elongated skulls disappeared from the five burial rooms and no one knows where they went or who took them. A friend of mine told me that there was an article in *National Geographic* in May of 1920 that told the story of the disappearance." The driver said, knowing that the more information he gave would build a relationship with them, thus getting a bigger tip at the end of the trip.

"What did the story say about the skulls?" Sarah asked.

"Well, they thought at the time it was a different race of people who had built the underground structure. But history doesn't know what happened to the people because they just disappeared, leaving it all behind. It is said we are descendants from that lost civilization, but also that we are mixed with the different nationalities that have taken us over at different points in history." He explained, looking at his watch.

"What do your people think about the underground structure?" Scott asked, "Or the one that they found above ground that dates back to the same time period?"

"Well, it was just rediscovered in 1902 when a builder was expanding a few homes and dug into one of the caves. They had sat untouched for thousands of years and it was a big discovery. People wanted to understand the history. When they dated the underground structure, it went back 1000 years farther than the pyramids. It wasn't understood how it could have been built in that time period because of the engineering capability. So it created a real mystery. Workers won't go too deep into the lower levels because a few have disappeared, like the couple that didn't come back out. They say that it is haunted," he said, looking at Scott in the rearview mirror.

"What are they doing about the missing people?" Scott asked. "What did they think? That they just got lost?"

"Well, I heard it was searched and they found nothing. It was as if they just vanished. Ah, here we are." He pulled the car around by the entrance and parked under a tree in the shade. "Hold on…I will be right back. I see my friend over there."

It was noon and there were only about ten people waiting outside the visitor center. They watched from the car as the driver approached an older man in a uniform. Hands waved in the air as they spoke loudly and the driver pointed in their direction. Money looked to be exchanged and he returned holding three tickets. "We are in luck. They only allow 75 people a day and it is early. When they hit that number, they close for the day and he gets off work early." He pointed at the new building. "The tour leads you down to the first two levels, where they have built walkways. Just stay on the path with the group and you will be safe. I will wait for you over there and take you back when you're finished. Hurry on now; they looked as if they were ready to depart," he said.

Eve glanced to where he was pointing and saw a few other cars parked under the large trees, which shaded the cars from the hot sun.

"Okay, we'll see you soon," Eve said.

They walked across the dusty field. Small tuffs of grass had tried to grow, but many had died under the footfall of many visitors. At the new visitor center, a small group had formed and the trio joined them, standing a little apart. They waited with the rest of the visitors with anticipation of the tour.

Chapter 35

"All right, what do you guys think about the missing couple? The timing would be right. I think that we're going to need to check the lower level," Eve said. "Scott, did you bring your flashlight?"

"Yes, I have it," Scott dug it out of his bag, checking to make sure it was ready. "I agree, it does sound like it could be possible."

"Your parents were here," Sarah said. "I saw it…we are on the right track." She patted her large bag, making sure she had everything.

"Are you sure?" Eve asked, feeling her heart pound in her chest.

"They are in no danger," Sarah paused, "but we don't want to take their path. It has something to do with the Oracle Room."

"I'm sure that's part of the tour," Eve said, as Scott and Sarah nodded in agreement with her.

A small, dark-haired woman rounded up the group; she had a little pink umbrella blocking the sun from her face. The group was told they were to follow the umbrella even if they couldn't see her. They found their place at the back of the line, following the other tourists as they moved slowly forward. They were told the rules while the guide counted the group and led them down into the caves.

Small golden lights lit their path, reflecting off the walls and giving it an eerie presence. Wooden steps and walkways had been inserted into the rock leading the way down into the earth. Everyone stayed close together as they moved down the steps, making sure not to trip or fall. They were told not to touch the walls or speak when in the Oracle Room because of the CO_2 levels. The guide told them the Oracle Room had been built like a speaker system that could take the sound to every underground room in the complex.

When they entered the main room, everyone was quite in awe, fascinated with the high cathedral ceilings. They observed the beautifully designed cuts that curved their way up the smooth stone walls. When Eve stepped into the center of the space, something happened; she heard a buzzing in her ears and put her hands over them, trying to block out the noise. She fell to her knees…everything and everyone was tuned out. Flashes of light rapidly passed through her mind, as if downloading information.

The guide and tour group started to move closer to her; Eve raised her hands and everyone stopped, frozen in time, except Scott and Sarah. They both came and knelt beside her. Each took hold of one of her hands. The vibration went through her to them and they all felt the static as energy filled the room.

Before Eve knew what was happening, her voice rose into a weird childlike sound, almost screeching like a dolphin. It made the space start to turn and an area to the right side of the room opened up as the floor fell away. Eve concentrated, her mind spinning to a different place, making her feel as if she were flying; a force pulled her. The energy was moving her in the direction of the open hole. Eve stood and began to walk toward the dark open space, pulling Scott and Sarah along with her, until all three stood on the edge looking down into the darkness below. Still holding hands, Scott turned on his flashlight, trying to judge the distance below. He could only see a continuous void of light and space as they peered into the dark hole. The flashlight didn't help at all and he turned it off, pushing it back into his bag.

"We have to just step out," Eve said, moving forward. Scott looked in Sarah's direction to see what she thought. Sarah didn't look sure that she wanted to go any farther and he wasn't sure either. "It will be okay…trust me," Eve said, pulling them forward with incredible strength into the darkness. They levitated above the hole, buoyed by static; their bodies started turning, spinning out of control, as they descended into the ground. Scott grabbed Sarah's other hand, forming a linked circle and they spun more controlled. The hole above them closed, blocking out any light from above. But as they quickly turned, the energy created some kind of electricity. When they stopped rotating and their feet touched the ground, they found themselves in a different chamber. They could see now, because the crystals in the granite walls glowed a dim light leading the way.

chapter 36

"Come! Quickly!" Eve said. She moved them down the curved hallway at a brisk pace. They could hear the sound of moving water in the distance. After five minutes, the cave path opened into a large chamber where the walkway ended on a ledge that looked upon a small river below. For a moment all three just watched the flowing water, looking through the haze around them, trying to understand where they were and what they were seeing. It looked like a different world. Stalactites hung from the roof, forming light calcium deposits that looked like icicles. They created rounded structures that dripped down the cliff and walls to the river below.

"Look over there!" Sarah said. Scott and Eve jumped at the sound of her voice because it sounded so urgent. They turned and saw her pointing, rubbing her temples, then her eyes when that didn't help, trying to believe what she was seeing.

Scott and Eve looked in the direction Sarah was now pointing. They saw what had made her speechless. A cluster of tall creatures stood on the other side of the large trench. They resembled humans, but were taller with longer limbs, larger heads, and dark eyes. They were completely white. Their skin glowed, illuminating the darkness around them; their faces were covered with long white hair and beards. They stood so still that they had blended in with their surroundings.

Scott jumped when they moved to the edge of the cliff across from them. He had thought they were statues. Everyone stood silent, peering across the space at each other, all waiting to see what would happen. The larger one that stood in the front looked at Eve and she felt something happening in her head. It was a little painful, but she understood. He was asking her why she brought these humans.

"I didn't mean too," she whispered out loud. "It just happened." Scott and Sarah looked at Eve, not understanding.

"You know that once they have seen us, they can never leave. We are the protectors…the Watchers," the leader said in her head.

"I will not leave them," Eve said with her mind.

"Then you must stay also. Come to me," he said in her head.

"I must have your word of our safety," Eve said.

Sarah had seen inside Eve's mind and put her hand on Eve's arm. "He is a Watcher…but not the one to make that decision. I can see we are safe," Sarah said.

"Who is this woman? She is not one of us!" He yelled in Eve's head, making her fall to her knees with the strength of his voice.

"What is going on?" Scott asked, observing some kind of interaction that had turned angry.

"He wants us to come to him," Eve said, out loud. She looked across the divide and shut her eyes, using her mind. "Are my parents here?"

The creature didn't answer at first; Eve looked across at his dark blue reflective eyes…surprised.

"Only one has your blood. Why do you look at the man as your father?" He asked.

"I guess they are here," Eve transmitted with her mind.

She spoke to Scott and Sarah, "My parents are here; they have been holding them. I have to go across to get them back. You guys can wait here."

"Are you sure they're here?" Scott asked, and watched Sarah and Eve nod their heads. "Then I'm coming with you."

"And I am too!" Sarah said.

"How do I come to you?" Eve asked with her mind.

"Don't you see the pathway?" He asked in a sarcastic tone, "Maybe you are not the one I was told of."

Looking over the side, Eve didn't see anything but the cliff dropping off and the water far below. She closed her eyes and focused for a moment. Then, leaning down, she picked up a handful of dirt and tossed it over the edge.

"Scott, hand me your flashlight," Eve said, kneeling down. She took the light and aimed the beam in the direction she had sprinkled the dirt over the edge. The invisible path was now visible; the sprinkled dirt hung mid-air and she saw it would lead the way. Eve turned and looked at Scott and Sarah.

"Okay...if you both are set on coming with me, you'll have to trust me." Eve watched as they both nodded. "Follow me single file; we are going to cross here and find my parents. Are you guys ready?" Eve asked, squaring her shoulders, not feeling afraid, but determined.

"Yes, I'm ready," Sarah said, "but I'll go first; I'm smaller. Everyone pick up a handful of dirt and when we don't see the way, we'll sprinkle as we go." Sarah pushed her way in front of Eve and stepped out onto the invisible walkway first.

Eve thought Sarah would be happy to stay and study these beings, but she wasn't going to be leaving anyone behind. She followed Sarah with Scott behind her. They moved out onto the path, taking their time, making sure their footing was sound before each step, creeping forward slowly.

"Try not to look all the way down; just keep your eyes on the floating dirt," Eve said, balancing, concentrating on her footing. She had always been clumsy, having such long limbs; it had taken a long time for coordination to arrive while growing up. That was the reason she hadn't tried to be an athlete in high school.

When they were almost to the other side they ran out of dirt and Sarah took the last few steps by faith, slowly sliding her small foot forward. When they reached the other side and stepped on the flat rock by the edge they were surrounded by the white creatures. Some had come out of the background and Eve thought there might be about twenty making a large circle around them. They all just stood there for a while, sizing each other up.

"Move out of my way!" Eve said, walking between a few to the tallest one that was standing in the center of the group. The others looked at him for his reaction. Eve took in his eyes, finding they were very dark blue instead of black. The large creature didn't know what to do, so he stepped out of her way, not wanting her to get too close to him. Eve felt a higher power directing them. They stepped aside and Eve reached over and took ahold of Sarah and Scott's hands. They walked past the beings, finding a side path around the rocks. The group of Watchers followed closely behind them. Eve felt something in her head showing her the way. The group entered a large hall cut in the stone; the ceilings were about fifteen feet high and here the crystals in the rock walls glowed brighter, sparkling like diamonds lighting the room. Eve moved into the center of the space and stopped, waiting to see what would happen.

chapter 37

"The crystals are energy conductors," Eve said out loud, talking to herself. The room looked similar to the Oracle Room. When Eve stepped in the middle of the space, she had felt the vibration of hertz frequency like she had before, calling her to move forward. She wasn't afraid. Eve felt happiness fill her; it was almost like returning home after a very long time. Inside this chamber was stone seating around the sides of the space and Eve pulled Scott and Sarah to a large rock that held a being sitting in the center. He had to be about 15 feet tall; his skin was almost iridescent like the others, but was glowing, almost illuminating. When he opened his eyes the space physically brightened.

"My Child..." he said, kindness coming from his voice and shining from his eyes. Eve felt a sense of peace. She stepped closer, dropping Scott and Sarah's hands. Drawn to the voice...searching to see if it was him.

"Is it you?" A child's voice carried her question. It was high pitched, echoing off the walls of the chamber. She saw him grin and Eve ran to him, climbing up onto his lap, encircling his face with her arms. "Father! I have missed you!"

"Why are you here, Gola?" He asked

"I think you have my human parents," she said.

"But they aren't really your parents...you are one of us. They just tended to you for us. We have a great amount of work to do on Earth or these people will end up killing each other and the planet," he said.

"I know, Father. You think they are the weaker race... but they have a purpose on this planet. It is their planet... we destroyed ours. I have come to love them." Eve said, not knowing where the information was coming from.

"That is why we are here. We are to watch over them to make sure that they don't do the same thing we did to our planet," the being said.

"In that case, why would you give them the technology to destroy themselves?" Eve asked.

"We wanted them to be free to choose...a free will. It is our biggest experiment...seeing what happens to them. We want to see if they choose good or evil. If they kill themselves, it is like a reset. It isn't the first time," he explained.

"I know we have been using the humans and animals for a long time, breeding with them to create a race of giants and combining creatures developed on our ships in test tubes. I understand that we were searching for the strongest and smartest to mine for minerals for us to take home. I know the resources are needed to restore the energy to our dead planet. But you remember how it got out of hand and we were punished for their wickedness." Eve knew what she was saying when spoken by the child's voice and understood as if it were the first time hearing it.

"Hush, child...these things are not to be spoken in front of them," he said, gesturing to her companions.

"Don't worry, Father. Humans on earth are starting to figure it out on their own, without anyone telling them. Letting the humans think that you are gods or angels to be worshiped. Shame! All you're doing is stealing their resources and stripping their planet."

"Quiet!" He yelled and the walls vibrated; smoke and fire filled the space, making it hard to see two feet in front of them. Eve had moved away from the being and took Scott and Sarah's hands, standing tall, a fire in her eyes.

"No more! It is time for us to go!" Eve yelled back and felt a rush. Smoke filled the chamber, sucking out the air in the room. It became calm once more and there was silence. Eve stood with Scott and Sarah, so close she could feel their hearts thumping along with hers.

"It will be okay, my child. Come back to me—no one will harm them," he said. Eve looked into his eyes and dropped their hands. She moved forward, jumping into his embrace again, feeling safe and happy.

"Father, it is you!" The child's voice stated.

"Yes, it is I," he said, "I have missed you as well."

"How can this be happening?" She asked.

"We all have our mission…you do as well," he said.

"Is that why I have been far away from you, Father?"

"Yes…it is not all about the minerals on this planet. We know we made some mistakes that we have had to pay for over time. But we have been trying to help the human race, because they are our future as well. We want them to expand their knowledge so that when they are ready, they will come to us and help repopulate our planet. We don't have the ability to reproduce offspring anymore among ourselves and we will die out if they don't come. Your assignment is important."

"What do you mean? Are you talking about my anti-gravitational device?" She asked, starting to understand.

"Yes, Child, but that is just the first part. It will lead them to levitation and further on the path to finding us. You must finish it and give it to the world."

"I understand, Father. I've been having trouble getting it to work."

"You will get it. You need to reverse engineer one of our units and then you will have some of your answers. Also, look at the sound frequency. I need to go back—I am being called. Here, take this…it will help you. This will lead you to one of our ships that the humans have in hiding." He handed her an object the size of a silver dollar. It had a point at one side and a dark stone in the middle; curved symbols were engraved with Egyptian hieroglyphs written around the edges. The medallion hung from a thick gold chain. "Here, let me help you put this on; it will help lead you. You will be able to talk with me though the object and I will help you." He hung it around her neck and Eve felt something hot under her hair. Eve put it under her shirt, hiding it. She could feel the cold metal against her skin between her breasts. He kissed her forehead, holding her tight for a moment and looking deep into her eyes before letting her go.

"Where are you going, Father? Will I see you again?" She cried out.

"Someday, Child, we will be together again," he said, moving away.

Chapter 38

"Wait! Father! What of my friends? And my human parents?"

He paused, "In this time, we are not allowed to interact with them and if they know of us, then we don't let them go."

"Father, I need their help to finish my mission," Eve said.

He looked across the room at the Watcher leader. "Let her leave with the humans…I will answer for it myself." The Watcher nodded. The room filled with smoke and a bright light flashed and he was gone.

Eve wiped a tear that had fallen down her face. She was thinking *How did that just happen?* The Watcher answered in her head, "It was a wormhole, a portal that makes it possible to travel between dimensions by twisting time." Eve wasn't sure she believed that wormholes were possible, or how time was really bent. But now she knew that it had to be true, even if she didn't totally understand how it worked. It was hard to wrap her mind around the thoughts of time travel. But before Eve could think any longer, she was standing back with Scott and Sarah. Out of the left side of the room through the leftover smoke, her human parents emerged. They were somewhat dazed, as if they had been in hibernation.

"Mother...Daddy!" Eve said, hugging them hard.

"Eve! What are you doing here! Hurry—you have to go back—it's dangerous!" Eve's mother stated, fear in her voice.

"It will be okay! Come with me right now!" Eve's parents looked at each other and said nothing, but did what they were told. The group raced after Eve at a fast pace back to the cliff. The white beings let them pass as instructed, following at a distance. Eve tossed the dirt on the semi-invisible path and took a step forward, leading them across. She knew she had to hurry. She could feel it coming from her being father, knowing he would be punished for letting the humans go. She didn't want the Watcher changing his mind before they reached safety. She could feel the conflict going on in her head, almost as if she could hear the conversation that was happening right now. No one stopped them and when they reached the other side, Eve looked back, seeing that the beings were moving quickly to the other side of the cliff.

The larger one called Eve with his mind, telling her that they had changed their minds and the humans had to stay. Sarah read his mind and removed the conch shell from her bag, putting it to her lips. At first nothing happened as she tried to blow through the opening. Then she inhaled and blew really hard, clearing the inside. The noise bounced off the walls, echoing through the chamber, carrying the sound. They heard a loud cracking sound and then vibration shook the ground. They all ran. Eve looked back behind them; the glass walkway had crumbled away, crashing to the water below. One of the beings fell and clung to the other side of the wall, quickly pulled to safety by the others.

"Stop!" They yelled loudly in Eve's mind. She put her hands to her head, gripping each side, falling to her knees.

Scott picked her up, tossing her over his shoulder. He ran, carrying her.

"Hurry!" She tried to speak but the pain was so intense she barely got the words out. "We don't have much time! They've changed their minds." Scott was strong, running with her in his arms leading the way. The group followed with Sarah taking up the rear. They jogged down the stone hall and found the spot where they had fallen through the floor. Eve closed her eyes, feeling the frequency hum through her body. The sound was silent; all five were sucked up through the floor into the Oracle Room above. Inside, the tour group stood frozen where they had left them. The small group went and stood in the middle of the room. Eve felt the hum of electric energy snap and the people were released. They had weird looks on their faces as if bewildered.

Eve looked at the guide, "Isn't time we go?" She asked, righting herself on her feet, testing if she could walk, leaning on Scott.

The guide looked at her watch and the extra two people hugging Eve.

"Yes, it is time to go. Come along, everyone; that concludes our tour for today."

chapter 39

The group moved out of the caves into the bright sunlight. It had turned into a nice, sunny, hot day. They walked toward the car, wanting to put some distance between them and the guide before anyone noticed that they had extra people emerging from underground. They could see her pink umbrella up ahead; she continued giving the group more information. The tour ended in the area where souvenirs could be purchased.

The small group found their driver waiting under the trees with a homemade fan he had constructed out of some wood and a piece of paper, He fanned himself rapidly, trying to stay cool. When he saw the group, he started the car and turned on the air. He noticed the older man and woman and was curious. But before he could ask any questions, Eve was giving orders for everyone to squeeze in.

Eve noticed the driver's confusion and made a quick introduction, "I found my parents were on the same tour! This is my mom Janet and my father Michael. They will be riding back with us."

In the backseat, Eve sat on Scott's lap with her arm around his shoulders, making room for her parents. She could feel his strong arms engulfing her and calmed herself, feeling a little flustered as she remembered the kiss. The events of the past few days had left her wondering about herself; the images of both past and present kept spinning in her head. Eve wondered if it was having the same effect on him. She tried to block the slow-moving pictures that kept distracting her. She was drawn out of her daydream when she noticed a familiar man that she hadn't seen earlier. He was walking with a bigger man; both were wearing sunglasses, polo shirts, and long cargo shorts. Eve hadn't placed the man before; out of their surroundings, she didn't recognize them.

"We need to go! We're in danger!" Sarah said. "They will kill us to keep the information from getting out. They think that being in a foreign country it would be easy for us to just disappear. I saw it."

"Go! Go!" Eve yelled. The driver didn't question her and pushed the gas, giving the large 8-cylinder engine a power surge. It tore across the dusty, bumpy field before finding traction on the paved road and speeding down the hill.

"Hurry! They're coming!" Scott yelled at the driver. The men were now alerted to their movement and ran to their car. Jumping in, they followed rapidly after the taxi. Eve's parents were looking behind, trying to figure out what was happening, wanting to know why their daughter and everyone was in such a panic.

"What is happening?" Janet asked, holding on tight as the car took a turn and she was forced to crush her husband up against the side of the door. She reached over and locked the door so Michael didn't fall out and turned toward Eve.

chapter 40

"I saw the men! Hurry, we have to get to our boat!" Eve said above the noise of the large engine.

"What men?" Her mother asked.

"The FBI agents are here…I just saw them!" Eve yelled. Scott and her parents turned toward the back window. Through the dust, a car was barreling down on them at a fast pace.

Sarah put her fingers to her head concentrating. "Yes, it is them. They must have tracked us. Why were they following you guys in the first place?" Sarah asked, addressing Eve's parents.

"We weren't sure who they were, but always felt their presence. One day someone had gone through our things at the hotel and then we noticed that we were being followed. We were cautious and when the time was right we were able to give them the slip. Why would the FBI be after us?" Janet asked.

"We weren't doing anything illegal." Michael said, "Just research. The FBI, you say? What would they want with us? Nothing we are researching is secretive, anyone could find it. We are just trying to connect the dots and put together what really has happened in Earth's past! You would think people would want to know the truth!"

"That's where the man said he was from. He came to the house. He was looking for you both and led me to believe you were dead," Eve said.

"What an ass!" Janet yelled above the roar of the engine, now mad.

"He had some kind of badge that he flashed. But at the time I didn't study it, I just let him in. It's not every day someone comes to the house and says they are from the FBI. Why would the man lie about that?" Eve said.

"Well, we'll get to the bottom of this!" Michael said, also angry.

The driver took a turn extra fast and a cloud of dust filled the car through the open windows when the wheels hit the shoulder of the road. The driver had turned off the air to give the car more power. The back of the car skidded around the curve of the road, losing traction, then righted itself. The dark car behind them had caught up and the men were signaling for them to pull over. The passenger had a gun in his hand and was taking aim toward them.

"What do you want me to do?" The driver yelled, not slowing down, giving the car more gas.

"Drive! Get away from them! Don't worry about your car! I will give you money to buy a new one!" Eve yelled over the noise of the engine.

The driver pressed harder on the accelerator and the large engine shot like a rocket across the road. They left the men behind, racing around the sharp turns, taking them back toward the port. He was able to put some distance between them and the other car when they hit the straight patch of road and just slowed down when they entered the small city. Just to make sure he lost the pursuers, he took many turns, blending in with the traffic, making sure they weren't followed, before taking them to the dock.

At the harbor, Eve felt relief when she saw that their boat was still parked at the waterfront where they had left it. Scott jumped out, taking charge, running to the ship. He alerted the boy and his father that they needed to leave right away. The boy translated the information to his father and he ran to start the engines. Scott helped the boy pull the anchor and untie the ropes, hurrying the process.

Sarah, Janet, and Michael rushed on board and Eve jumped the distance into Scott's arms as the boat started pulling away. She had given the driver about $2,000 and told him to hide for a few days so that the men didn't find him. He understood and kissed her cheeks saying, "Thank You, Thank You! My lady!" He was really happy seeing the amount of cash, not believing his luck, and hurried off to find a local bar.

The group watched the shoreline as the boat pulled into the shipping lane, leaving Malta. They searched the banks waiting to see if they had truly lost the men. Once in open water, they relaxed somewhat, hoping to put some distance between them and the island. They didn't see any boat following and proceeded to sit on the deck to keep watch, breathing a little easier. Everyone had just composed themselves when the young boy showed up with some cool drinks in a small worn cooler. Eve now was able to focus on her parents.

"What happened when you were in the caves?" Eve asked, "We were lucky to have found you!" She hugged her mother as her father watched them, smiling.

"Well it was quite an adventure!" Michael chuckled.

"You should have told me years ago; I could have helped in your research," Eve stated.

"We didn't understand ourselves, until we started looking into the idea. Your mother had to really convince me, with the help of our friend Sarah here." Michael said, "But it has been a great life and we had plenty of time in retirement. It really has kept things exciting for us. We have no regrets… right, dear?"

"Yes, we have enjoyed it all," Janet laughed. "We figured if something happened to us, you would be just fine. It was all so interesting, and it has helped us stay young." Janet rubbed her husband's hand and smiled at him.

"But what happened when you went into the caves?" Eve asked again.

"That's a story…I'll let your mother tell you; she always was a better storyteller." Michael chuckled, looking at his wife with love in his eyes. Everyone turned toward Janet.

Janet took a deep breath and began, "Malta was one of the places on our list to check out. We had found that there were many underground cave systems around the world that had been carved into the stone by a highly intelligent race. These sites had been recently discovered and excavated over the past 50 or so years. We set out to check them all. We wanted to see if there was any lost evidence of these space beings or 'Aliens' as people call them, coming to Earth.

"The one that we haven't checked is in Antarctica, but I wasn't sure about trying to find it in that cold, desolate place. I think it was the 1940s…?" She looked at her husband, checking to see if the years were what she had remembered. He shrugged his shoulders, not knowing the exact year.

"Anyhow, we found information that stated there was some activity there. You see around that time, the U.S. military had gone to check it out, thinking to put a base there. They found a large entrance to an underground cavern that went deep into the earth. You could fly a plane inside where it was said there was a whole ancient city. At the time it was hushed up and a plane had flown in and saw a whole complex before being chased out by unknown aircrafts."

"Mom…focus…what happened in the caves here?" Eve's patience was fading.

"Oh yes…the caves…I have so much information in my head I'm getting sidetracked. We came to Malta to take the tour and see what was underground. We split from the group because we wanted to check the lower levels. We had read an article about a lady who had gone down there and she stated she had seen some tall white creatures. She thought at the time that they were still living down there. You see, we think beings from outer space instructed humans on how to build these places. Our research showed that all these underground places were built around the same time frame. Theorists have said they were built about 10,000 years ago as a means for the humans and these beings to be able to survive the last Ice Age.

"We went to the lower level with our flashlights and were surprised that we were able to see. There was a kind of energy that dimly lit the walls as we walked forward; after we passed, the lights went dark behind us. It was almost like we were being led. We came to the trench with the water below and were admiring the beauty of the place. It looked like a different, beautiful world. Across the water I thought I saw a flash of movement. I questioned myself if I had really seen anything at all. But when your father jumped in the air and scared the pee out of me, I saw what had frightened him. On the other side of the trench were these weird looking creatures." Janet took a breath.

"Well it wasn't that funny! I was caught off-guard; I didn't expect to see anything alive down there. Dear, please continue…the kids are waiting!" Michael stated.

"Yes, yes…where was I? Oh yes…we see them across the trench and we are frozen, caught off-guard. We just stared at them, not moving as they stared at us. Then this big one signaled for us to come to them by waving us forward. Both of us shook our heads "No," but we felt a pull in our heads telling us "Come to us now!" Physically I felt them using our minds to make our bodies move to the edge. I thought they were going to toss us over. But when we took a step over the edge, we found the invisible path that they had in place. They moved our feet with their minds like a tractor beam! Almost like we were zombies. Looking back, it was kind of cool," she said.

"Well, it was scary at the time!" Michael stated.

"What happened next?" Sarah asked, sitting off the edge of her seat, leaning forward. Janet turned in her direction.

"It was quite incredible. We got across to the other side and were surrounded and taken to this rock room. It had to be some kind of portal…looking back. When we entered there was no conversation, the beings just stood around us waiting for something to happen. But they didn't touch us."

chapter 41

"Then there was a bunch of smoke and a flash of light and we woke up in a modern, stainless steel room. Everything was streamlined; there was no softness to it, just hard, smooth surfaces. We thought it must be a spaceship, but now I think it might have been an indoor civilization on a different planet. One day we left our room and we were walking down a long hall. At the end there was a commotion and a bright light might have burned one of the beings. I think the door to the outside opened and the sun might have touched the being; in an instant, he was burned. We smelled the burning flesh and were hustled out of the hall and put back in our room," Janet stated.

"What did you do most of the time?" Scott asked, curious and finding he couldn't remain silent any longer.

"Well, it was like we had a computer in our brains. You just had to think of a subject and all these articles would come up in your mind. You would choose one you wanted to read and pick it and it would come up in English. It was crazy because they had so much information—newspapers, magazine articles, anything that would be on a computer. It was like our minds were the computer processing the information. They had access to all of Earth's information like they were tapping into The Cloud. So really we could do everything we do today on our phone or computer, just in our heads," Michael said.

"Amazing!" Eve said.

"When you came for us, we were taken to a room and it filled with smoke like before and we were teleported back to the room that we had been taken from. How did you come for us so fast?" Janet asked.

"We had to figure out where you might have gone next. But it wasn't that fast—it took us about four days," Eve said. "I'm not sure how long you were gone because I just found out you were missing around the time you were to return home."

"What? We were gone maybe two weeks?" Janet exclaimed, looking at her husband. "It felt like we had been gone two days. I don't remember even sleeping. Time must be different there."

"Well, I'm glad to be back," Michael said.

"We're glad to have you back, because they don't let humans go after they've seen the beings. It's not like back before the flood, where they lived among the humans and were worshipped as gods and angels," Eve said, puzzled where that information had come from. It just popped into her mind.

"How did you get them to let us go?" Janet asked.

"I think that I am reincarnated from a child that was on Easter Island and they've given me the task of finishing my anti-gravitational/levitation device and want me to give it to mankind," Eve said. "I told them that I need you all to finish my task."

"Why would they do that?" Michael asked, "I mean, why give humans the technology?"

"I think they have been giving us technology for a long time, to advance our civilization. I think it is to save both of our races." Eve said, "They need us to evolve at a faster pace to be reunited with them. I think from what I was told, they can't reproduce. But they do live longer than we do because time is different on their planet. This is the reason for the abductions. Remember how people that were taken said their sperm and eggs were harvested from them?"

"Been there…done that!" Janet laughed, "So where are we going now? What's next?"

"We have to go home. I need to finish my project," Eve said.

chapter 42

They arrived back at the house on Sunday night. Everyone was really tired from the flight from Barcelona. They had taken a taxi from the small White Plains airport in Westchester, NY. The group was dragging. Unloading their suitcases into the house, Eve's father checked the security system, finding that it was in place and no one had entered the house while they were away.

"Well, it looks like our FBI friends didn't come in and search the place. I was worried that they might," Eve said, yawning.

"We'll look at the camera feed tomorrow, just to make sure. Tonight, I think your mother and I need to find our beds. We aren't as young as we used to be," Michael said, moving toward the staircase.

"Good night then. We'll talk in the morning." Eve kissed her parents' cheeks as they passed and watched their slow climb up the stairs.

Turning from the top step, Janet remembered her hospitality, "Sarah, you're all set in a room?" She asked.

"Yes—the best room in the house…all the way up. Eve took good care of me. Good night, All." Sarah said, following them up the stairs.

Eve and Scott stood for an awkward moment watching them disappear. There was a moment of silence. *What's next?* Eve thought, not wanting to go to bed yet.

"Do you want to share a pizza? I'm tired but food is calling me." Scott said, rubbing his stomach.

"You're always hungry!" Eve laughed.

"Well, a growing boy." Scott said, flexing his muscles and kissing his bicep.

"You are too funny! I think you're done growing!" She gave him a fist to the midsection and only felt the hard abs. "I would love to! Could you call it in? I'll be right back. I want to change—I'll be quick." Eve said, using the last of her energy to sprint up the stairs.

In her bathroom she rinsed off in the shower and put on some fresh, comfortable clothes. By the time she returned, Scott was waiting by the fire with a bottle of red wine and two glasses. She noticed that his hair was damp and that he had changed into his red snowflake flannel pajamas. He looked like a Christmas gift to be unwrapped. The thought made her laugh out loud, especially when Eve noticed his bottoms were very short, almost up to the middle of his calf.

"What are you laughing about?" He smiled at her.

"Nothing," Eve suppressed a giggle, sobering up when the bell from the gate rang. Eve clicked the doorbell to silent and checked the monitor, not wanting to disturb her parents. "Pizza is here!"

"Eve, could you keep an eye on the gate and the pizza guy just in case? We don't want to be tricked by those men if they made it back," Scott said.

"Yes, you're right. After we got away, I wouldn't be surprised if they showed up here. I get the feeling that they were really trying to kill us." Eve watched the monitor and the man getting out of the car. It was indeed a pizza boy around 17 years old, hurrying up the steps, rushing while balancing the pizza in one hand. Scott met him at the door and the transaction was done in a few seconds, Scott not needing any change. They both waited until the gates were locked and the alarm was back in place before moving to their seats by the fire. Both devoured the large pizza and sat back in their chairs, satisfied, drinking their wine. Scott refilled her glass, seeing it was almost empty.

"Well—what's the next move?" Scott asked.

"I was thinking the same thing. I think we have to find out where the government is keeping the spacecrafts that have crashed in America. We have a few choices. There is the place called Area 51...or was it 52? Hold on, let me look it up."

Scott waited while she read, sipping his wine, watching how the firelight highlighted the color in her dark red hair. "There was this scientist who claimed to have worked there and when he left, he reported the research that he had worked on. He came out to the news and said he had worked close to Area 51. It was a place that they had taken the spacecrafts that had come down in the 1940s at Roswell. They also found four small, child-size bodies.

"There was documentation around the time of the crash. It stated that a nurse had been close by and was asked by local law enforcement to give aid to the bodies in the crash. When she approached, at first glance she thought that they were children. After a closer examination, she found that they were adults with large heads and weird eyes. Soon after the military showed up and took over...everything from the crash site was removed and the area totally cleaned up. The nurse stated that all the beings were dead from the crash, but she knew by the way the bodies looked they weren't human, and their eyes were something that she would never forget," Eve said.

"The scientist had worked at the location that the military had brought the crafts and the bodies. His new assignment had been to work on reverse engineering the ships. But it was a hard job because the technology was so much further advanced, and it was taking a long time to figure it out. When the man left working for the government, he told the newspapers of the beings from a different world that had crashed on Earth. He stated he had been working at the secret military location to figure out their technology. The government came out and said that this man was crazy and didn't even work there. But they never explained why he had pay stubs showing that he had," Eve said.

"Cover up—not the first time, I'm sure. As Americans we can only believe half of what the government says. They think we're a bunch of dummies." Scott said, taking a gulp of his wine.

"Well, Area 51 is the United States Air Force facility and is highly classified. No wonder why it's in the middle of nowhere. It says here that it is a detachment of Edwards Air Force Base in Nevada." Eve said.

"That's a good place to hide something that they don't want the public to know about. What is the other option? I'm not so sure about breaking into a base…that would be big trouble it we get caught." Scott said, logically. "The other option is the Smithsonian archives. Or what do you think about the Smithsonian Air & Space Museum?"

"I'm not sure," Eve said. They were both quiet, thinking for a few moments. Then Eve jumped up, almost spilling her wine. "I know what to do!" She said, pulling the medallion from under her shirt. "I wonder how this works."

chapter 43

Both of them watched as the medallion sparkled in the firelight, gleaming. Eve hadn't looked at it closely and now turned it over in her hands, inspecting the round edges and the sharp little point that had a hole in the middle where the heavy gold chain went through. In the center of the medallion was a stone. It was dark, cubic in shape, and came alive in the warmth of Eve's hand, the firelight changing the color somewhat. Scott looked on, curious to see if anything would happen.

"I know what the stone is," Eve said. "I think it is a Galena!" Scott looked puzzled. "It's a natural semiconductor in mineral form of lead (II) sulfide. You know what that means? Wasn't that what they found in liquid form in the air shaft going from the king's chamber in the pyramid in Cairo, Egypt?" Eve asked, not remembering.

"You better tell me what you're thinking on this one… I'm lost!" Scott said.

"You see how the crystal is kind of cubic in shape? You can extract silver from this mineral. But most of the time this stone has been called a 'lead glance.' Anyhow, because it is a semiconductor I think if I hit it with a charge of electricity it will transmit some energy and we'll be able to see what happens," Eve said, flipping it over in her hands and looking at the hieroglyphics. "I wish I could read what this says…but I'm sure I could look it up in the rare manuscripts part of the school library. For now, we'll just see what happens. It's like an experiment. Could you hand me that lamp by your side table?" Eve instructed.

Scott handed her the older Tiffany lamp and watched as Eve removed the shade and turned off the light. "Can you unplug it for me?" Scott did as he was told and watched to see what was next; this was her expertise. Eve took the lamp apart, exposing the wires. "Okay, plug me back in please."

"Are you sure? You aren't going to burn the house down, are you?" He teased. Eve gave him a look that said *Are you serious?* and waited for him to flip on the switch.

"Let's see what happens." Eve touched the two wires together and it sparked, showing it was a live current. She put one of the pillows on the side table and tried to pull the necklace over her large head, finding that it wouldn't fit. Eve tugged on the metal and ran her fingers around the chain, looking for a clasp, and found there was none. "It looks like this is meant to stay on for life!" She crouched on the floor and stretched the medallion across to the pillow. "Scott, could you hand me the lamp?"

"Hey—wait! Are you sure this is safe?" He asked, putting it in her hand.

"Yes, it will be fine. Here goes!" Eve touched the stone with the wires and at the same time a bolt of electricity sparked the stone's point. There was a burning smell and Eve thought she might have burned some of her hair. She was getting ready to try it one more time when she heard a voice in her head.

"What is it?" Scott asked, seeing her face change.

"Yes, my daughter?" Eve jumped and Scott sat back in his chair, trying not to move or cause a distraction.

"You said I could call on you for help." Eve said, out loud.

"What do you need?" A masculine voice sounded in Eve's head; it was full of authority and by the sound of it, didn't want to be bothered.

"I need to know where the spacecraft is being held so I can finish my mission," a young girl's voice said.

"BB206," the deep voice said.

"Where is that? Father, please, I need your help!" The child whined.

"My daughter, go to the basement of the Smithsonian Institute…Door BB206. Turn on the electric fence. A man is trying to come over the wall." Then he was gone.

Scott raced to the door and flipped the lights outside, reestablishing the fence's power. They heard a scream and pop as someone got a shock. "I thought you turned on the system?"

"I thought I did…maybe this interfered with it?" Eve questioned, her voice back to the woman he knew. "Don't talk anymore down here," Eve whispered in Scott's ear. "Come on, we need to take our beds, we have a lot of work to do tomorrow." He felt her breath on his ear and the word "bed" had set him in motion. He pulled her in his arms, pressing his lips to hers, softly at first and then they gripped each other tightly, hands roaming, kissing roughly, full of passion.

"Dang, girl, you're making me crazy," he said. Eve was speechless, feeling the same way. Confused, she ran up the stairs to find her bed…alone.

chapter 44

In the morning, Scott and Eve were up early trying to plan what to do next. They had been researching the floor plans of the Smithsonian to locate this BB206 room. They had found that the oldest archives contained files of American history in Science, American Life, Art, and Culture and were all housed at the Smithsonian Institution Castel building.

In the 1800s the Smithsonian had funded a group of men they called the Megatherium Club. They were a group of explorers that worked for the institution. These were wild outdoorsmen known for their parties and drinking. They lived together when in town at the Smithsonian, using it as a home base. But they spent most of their time on expeditions gathering artifacts and information that started the collection for the Smithsonian. It was a top-secret group; the men took their jobs seriously, recording all the information for the history of mankind.

"I think I found something that shows that there is a second basement. See this shadow on the blueprint? It looks like it leads to a lower level. I think there is a deeper basement in the Smithsonian Castel building. Look—it's near the Egyptian exhibit housed on the floor above. Right now, the building is being used as the Smithsonian Institution's administrative offices and information center." Scott said as he looked up from his computer at the group in the upstairs war room.

"Great—it looks like they still have tours in that building." Eve said, looking away shyly when Scott caught her eye.

Janet, Michael, and Sarah had joined Eve and Scott upstairs when they woke, bringing their coffee and breakfast. Her parents, being retired scientists, enjoyed the research. They loved the challenge of understanding what chemical elements and minerals were found at archaeology sites around the world and seeking knowledge to understand what had happened in the past. Now they focused on looking for a common pattern.

"You know, I'm finding the most common denominator is each society's interest in gold." Janet said, as everyone stopped to listen.

"Yes, I see that too." Michael said, flipping the page on something he was reading from a file. "Maybe the gold is the reason that Earth was visited in the first place. There are many references that suggest that these gods came here to gather it, and then modified mankind so humans could work as laborers for the gods."

"Maybe they were using gold as a conductor for energy?" Eve said. "We have to think about why they would want gold, And thinking about it, to this day humans have a fascination with gold. Even our money is backed with gold. I wonder if that has been installed in our collective memories over time."

"Okay, think about it. Gold is an inert material; it doesn't react to anything." Janet said, "And it is a good conductor for electricity. But do you remember the third property of gold?" Janet asked Eve.

"I remember! Yes, that makes sense! It is a reflector of infrared energy!" Eve said, excited.

"Help me out here…what does that have to do with your project?" Scott asked.

"In space, gold can be used to make thin blankets that could cover a spaceship. The blankets would protect it from not only the infra-red energy but could be used to protect the spacecraft from a heat source, like the sun," Janet explained.

"Yes…makes sense," Michael looked thoughtful. "Remember those pictures of the spacecraft crash in the desert? I think a few pictures showed a kind of foldable material that was found at the site. It was lightweight and would fold around things and then go back to its original form. I think I saw a video of it in black and white. I wonder if the material was a foldable gold blanket like you suggest?"

"I think that I saw that too!" Janet said.

"Also, because of the way gold reacts, it is used a lot in technology…like microchips. I have to try using it as my conductor in my device…something that I haven't thought about," Eve said.

Sarah was helping by researching old files that had any mention of the "gods" using a device that had power…a gravitational wand? Anything that mentioned movement of the heavy cut stones that were used in the construction of structures around the world. Engineers of today still haven't figured out how these stones that weighed tons had been cut and moved in place, even at Stonehenge. They said that the type of stone found was brought downriver a few hundred miles away and placed at the site, forming the round enclosure. The legend or myths from that area said that "giants had moved the stones."

"I found something interesting as well," Sarah said, "But nothing to do with the moving of stones. In addition to myths saying that giants had moved them in place at Stonehenge, this mentions that there was a glowing light that cut the stone. It sounds almost like a laser to me."

"Most likely that's how they did it." Janet said, looking back down and continuing on with what she was reading. "But I did read lately of a new discovery of giant bones. They were found buried under a church on the island of Sardinia, Italy in 1979. They were dug up and put inside the church and disappeared in the night."

"That's crazy! All this covering up of the facts!" Michael said, looking over his wife shoulder. "Yes, it is referenced by the type of structures called cyclopean. The side note tells of 'Cyclops,' depicted by Homer in the Odyssey. I think this is the place for us to check out next, dear."

"Yes, Honey…I think you're right!" Janet smiled at her husband. "I wonder if the Cyclops really had an eye in the middle of their foreheads or if it was reference to a third eye like in enlightenment or the 'all seeing eye'? No matter—I find it interesting."

Scott and Eve were still working on how they were going to find the crashed spaceship inside this BB206 room.

"I think we should take the train down to Washington, D.C. early tomorrow," Scott said.

"What? Do you think we should take a tour of the The Castel?" Eve asked.

"We could do that…but then what?" Scott asked.

"Well, we go on a tour and slip away from the group and go to the lower level and find this room," Eve said. "Just like before."

"Okay. But we have to remember that they will have cameras." Scott said, typing on his laptop, trying to locate a better layout of the map. Every one that he found didn't show a lower level. "It won't hurt to take a look. I think that small shadow on the map is an elevator." He said, looking at different blueprints and comparing the area.

"I think it looks like a hidden doorway by a 15-foot-tall Egyptian statue." Eve said, studying the layout.

"Around the back is a hidden door; when you open it you will find a slope, which will take you down to the lowest level." Sarah said, rubbing her temples. "You will find it."

"You aren't coming with us?" Eve asked.

"No…my place is here. Your parents and I must stay here to create a diversion so that you won't be followed," Sarah said. "You know the evil is waiting."

"Are you sure?" Janet asked.

"Yes, I see it. We must think of a way for them to leave in secret," Sarah said.

"What about the brick wall in the back that goes into the woods?" Michael asked, looking at Sarah. "We could order some food tonight and when the delivery arrives, the kids can sneak over the wall at the back of the house."

"Do you think it will work?" Eve asked, looking toward her father. "What if they get in?"

"You don't worry about that! We'll take care of them if they try," he said.

"Scott, are you in? You sure you can miss a few more days of class?" Eve asked.

"That works for me; I already texted my professor letting him know that I will be back next week…a family emergency," Scott said. "I'm not missing anything. All my work has been done for a while. Really, I'm just studying for the Bar exam and waiting to see where I will get my internship."

Eve looked around the small room at the people she cared for most sitting around the table, not wanting any harm to come to any of them. She could feel the heat of the metal on her chest, reminding her of her mission. "Okay… as long as you're all sure that you will be safe, then it's a go."

chapter 45

That night around 9 P.M., everyone took their stations. Michael was upstairs in front of the monitors in the master bedroom. Scott and Eve were by the back door of the house, dressed in black Nike running gear; each had dark backpacks and shoes. Janet and Sarah were in the living room waiting by the fire for the alarm on the gate to alert them that the delivery boy had arrived with pizzas.

Earlier that day, Eve's parents had gone shopping for what the kids needed. They hadn't seen a tail on their way to the Nike outlet. They returned with bags of sporting gear for everyone…all in black. It had been a fun time as Janet made everyone put on their clothes, modeling their new matching outfits.

The doorbell rang on the gate and everyone ran to their positions. Michael turned on light jazz music that played throughout the house, blocking any extra sound. They knew there had to be a bug in the house and hadn't yet found it. Janet pushed the button and the gate opened. It closed behind the small Honda, its lights illuminating the drive as it came around the curve. The car parked in front of the long porch and a man dressed in a pizza uniform came up the steps past the pillars.

Sarah opened the door, reaching for the pizza. The man pulled a gun and she was ready; her quick reaction might have saved them. She flipped the pizza box at the man, blocking him and throwing him off balance. Slamming the door, she locked it tight. Both women ran up the stairs, stopping at the top to catch their breath. They heard gunshots outside and sank to their knees on the top step, hugging each other on the landing.

At the back of the house, Eve and Scott heard the bell ring at the gate. The sound echoed through the house. The noise was like the start of a race, sending the couple running into the dense woods. Eve led the way; her senses seemed better tonight. She could feel the heat of the metal against her chest, moving up and down under her shirt as she pushed forward into the darkness. As she ran, she wondered if it was intensifying her senses. They ducked in and out of the bushes, jumping and diving over logs, feet falling on uneven ground. Eve slowed her pace, letting Scott catch up. They made their way to the back of the five-acre property where they stopped at the eight-foot brick wall. Eve hesitated, then launched herself up the flat surface, catching the top with her hands, dangling for a moment before pulling herself up to the top. Behind her, Scott had grabbed her foot, giving it a shove. The momentum kept her moving until she went over to the other side. Scott took a few steps back before running at the wall, jumping in the air. Not stopping, he flipped his body over to the other side, joining her crouched on the ground. They caught their breath, staying down in the bushes.

"Hold on—let me take a look." Scott crawled on his belly to the end of the wall and looked around the corner. In the street in front of the house was a man waiting in a dark sedan. Scott crawled back to her.

"Come on, we need to go this way." He said, leading her in the opposite direction.

"What did you see?" Eve whispered.

"One of them is waiting in a car near the gate. Come on—don't worry, they're fine. We don't have much time," Scott said.

Eve hesitated but then fell in beside him. They jogged down the side streets, making their way toward central campus. Lost in the sea of people, they slowed their pace and mingled in with the other students walking in different directions to their dorms, the bar, or off to study at the library. They briskly walked through campus where they located a few Ubers hanging out by one of the main dorms and jumped into the back seat.

"We need to go to Stanford Train Station," Scott said. On the way, they both were quiet, riding in silence.

When they arrived, they fell in line at the ticket counter and purchased round-trip tickets to Washington, D.C. on the Amtrak. They ran up the stairs to Platform Number Four and didn't have long to wait before the train arrived. They sat in the first railcar that they entered and found two seats together in a silent section of the train. It was quiet; many businessmen and women were traveling for work into the Capitol in their business attire. Scott and Eve put their phones on mute, following the posted signs.

"We have about two hours until we get there. Do you want to text your parents?" Scott whispered, pointing at the sign.

"I will but it might take them a while to get back to us because they don't always carry their phones around like we do," Eve said. "I've tried to explain to them that they need to keep their phones on instead of turning them off after making a call."

"Why don't you try the mental thing and see if you can connect with Sarah with your mind?" Scott said.

"I'm not sure if I can do it…but I'll try," Eve said.

"I'm sure you can do it." Scott said, and watched the woman across the aisle hush them, putting a finger over her lips, telling them to quiet down. Eve closed her eyes and focused on Sarah, reaching out with her mind, sending the message that they were okay and on the train.

chapter 46

From the top of the stairs, Janet and Sarah heard the doorknob rattling below. Sarah moved back to the door, looking for something to put in front of it. She pushed the chain in place moments before the door started to open. She pressed her small body against the door, slamming an arm in the crack, watching the fingers searching. Janet joined Sarah and the two small women pressed their weight against the door. Sarah stretched her arm, reaching, and grabbed a letter opener off the table by the door. In one fluid motion, she brought it down, stabbing the arm. They heard a surprised scream and the man pulled his arm back. The women were able to close the door, locking it back in place. Michael, hearing the ladies' screams, ran down the stairs to help.

"I should have stayed down here! They're still inside the gate. I've called the police!" He leaned against the door.

"Oh, no!" Janet screamed at the sound of a crash in the kitchen. The women held each other in fright and Michael stood in front of them, facing the sound of breaking glass. The distant sound of a siren could be heard drawing closer. At the same time, the crunch of glass under feet in the kitchen was getting closer, along with the sound of a man cursing. The steps were coming in their direction. Sarah ran to the front door, unlocked it, and pushed the button making sure the front gate was open. All three of them ran into the yard and around the side of the house, hiding in the tall bushes.

They could see flashing lights coming around the corner over the other side of the wall and then police cars with loud sirens blasted into the driveway. The three of them moved from the bushes and waved until the officers got out of the car. Michael approached the police. They saw the dark clothes and drew their guns, taking them for the intruders. Eve's father put his hands in the air and called out.

"Please—we've had a break-in and the man is still in the house," he yelled. One more back-up car pulled into the drive, blocking any escape. The flashing lights surrounded them, bouncing off the tall walls and the white pillars of the house. The other officers had concluded the same as the first officer and now there were four cops with guns drawn moving forward slowly, surrounding them.

"My license is in my pocket with our address." One officer saw the two women and lowered his gun, patting Micheal down and checking for weapons before finding his wallet in his back pocket.

"What's going on here?" The sergeant stepped forward, taking charge. He noticed their dark running attire and their age.

"We've had a break-in and the man is still in the house. He has a gun and I think shot through my kitchen window," Janet said, standing behind her husband. The officer looked at the address on the license and saw that they were telling the truth.

"Why are you dressed this way?" The officer asked.

"We're taking up running and just got new outfits. We were getting ready to leave after we took in some carbs from the pizza that we ordered," Michael said.

"Okay—stay here." He joined the other officers that were now slowly moving toward the front door into the house. They returned a few minutes later.

"We found evidence that someone has broken in your back kitchen window and left the same way they came in. We tracked him through the woods and think he must have jumped the wall in the back. I have called for the dogs to be brought in to make sure he isn't hiding on your property. It might be a few hours before we finish. If you can take a seat in the last squad car, my partner will take your statement."

"Yes, officer," Sarah said, gathering the older couple and following the young officer to the car. After the lights were turned off, introductions were made. The officer asked them questions, writing down what had happened and taking their statements.

They told the officer about the break-in, explaining that when they opened the door to get their pizza, a man with a gun had tried to rob them. Or that was what they thought, seeing someone holding a gun. The young officer wrote quickly and soon he was finished and left the car.

From their seats in the back of the police car, the trio watched a van with dogs and their handlers arrive. The dogs started barking, pulling on their leashes, ready to do their job. The other pups sat silently next to their masters, eyes alert, ears up, waiting to be turned loose. But they were ready.

The officers released four German shepherds. Two circled the area and finally took off in the same direction as the yapping ones, disappearing into the woods. A few minutes later the barking had changed to a frenzy of noise, then the handlers were yelling orders and there was silence. The officers came out of the woods leading a man in handcuffs. His shirt was torn and hanging from one of his fit shoulders. He was yelling and struggling, trying to break away, telling them that he was one of them. They didn't listen, ignoring his cries. He was pushed into the back seat of the car parked in front of theirs. Sarah recognized the man from the chase in Malta. He eyed the trio through the glass, turning around in his seat. He had an evil, cocky grin and the group stared back at him, not flinching or backing down.

The officer saw that the man was trying to intimidate them and turned back to the older people sitting in the back of the police car. "Don't worry, he'll be off the street for a while. We're going to take him downtown to process him. You're safe, but I would turn on your alarm system after we go. You can never be too safe.... Ladies, Sir."

The police car left with the intruder. The three of them waited outside, watching the Honda being put on a lift and towed out of their driveway. After the driveway emptied out, the neighborhood was quiet, flashing lights gone, the lingering neighbors had returned to their yards, and the gate was closed. The electric fence was activated and the show was over.

Inside the house no one said anything; they worked together cleaning up the glass. Michael found a piece of wood from the shed and nailed it in place over the broken window. They cracked open a bottle of wine and sat by the fire, watching the flames grow before speaking, analyzing the night. The realization set in of what had just happened and they absorbed the danger they had been in.

"This isn't a game—these men are serious! I can't believe they would kill to keep the secret safe. Do you think the kids made it to the train?" Janet whispered.

"They made it and will be in Washington soon." Sarah said, keeping her voice low. They all knew that it was possible that someone was listening.

chapter 47

The Washington, D.C. train station was full of people even at the late hour. The hustle of people coming and going was a steady stream in and out of the large building. Many didn't even notice the old crystal chandeliers that hung from the high ceiling, sparkling at all hours. At the curb, Scott and Eve found a taxi and instructed the driver to take them into the city to the center of the tourist area. They wanted to be close, within walking distance of the Mall where the Smithsonian Castle was located close by.

They had booked an older hotel. After checking in they took the elevator to the tenth floor. Their room was really small; the bed took up most of the space, leaving a little path around the edges. But it was clean, smelled good, and the shower was hot. The kitchen had been closed for a long time and they resorted to a few bags of nuts and a can of Coke from the small refrigerator.

Eve curled up close to Scott's side for warmth and closed her eyes; she felt safe, exhausted, but hungry. She had to stop her mind so she could rest. She knew at some point they were going to have to have a conversation. She liked their relationship the way it was and didn't want to ruin it.

She had grown used to having him around and would feel lost if he no longer was there. She let it all go as she fell into a deep slumber.

In the morning, refreshed after finding a large buffet, Eve and Scott walked to the Smithsonian Castle and stood in line with the other tourists, waiting for entrance into the large museum. The building was vast, bigger than they expected. Its rounded rooms and tall peaks showed the 19th-century architecture. The Smithsonian had many different outbuildings and tours took place daily.

"Here we go," Eve said as she took Scott's arm and they moved forward with the line. They looked like a typical couple seeing Washington's sights. They had dressed in baseball caps, khaki shorts, t-shirts, and tennis shoes. The woman at the desk didn't look twice as she took their money, stamping their hands with invisible ink. Once admitted, moving forward with the line, they waited as a woman counted people and closed the velvet rope behind Eve and Scott. The rest of the line would wait their turn.

They followed the tour inside, listening to the guide as she explained about the museum and how it started. A British man named James Smithson had donated a large amount of money to fund the Smithsonian. But it had taken years after his death before the groundbreaking of the building took place. It took a while for the government and committees to decide what kind of museum would be built.

"I didn't know that his tomb was here," Eve said.

"Look at this." They pushed a button and were electronically told the history of the man. "Kind of cool," Scott said.

The group started moving downstairs to the floor below. Eve and Scott followed, looking at the large room, trying to find anything familiar that they might recognize from the video they had watched online. The room had been rearranged and they didn't see the Egyptian statue that they remembered as a landmark. They searched for anything large that could block the view of the secret door. The room was crowded and full of many cases packed with interesting collected artifacts.

"We need to come back here when all this is over…lots of cool stuff. Hey! Look over there! Those pillars coming out of the wall—they were in the room that we saw online and they can't be moved. I think the statue had been in that space to the right!" Eve said.

The group had spread out, each looking at different things. They had gravitated to the other side of the large room, staying close to the guide. Scott and Eve moved to the pillars unobserved, searching the wall to the right side. Scott ran his fingers over the surface, finding an outline of a door frame about in the middle.

"Look here…I think the door has been covered by this piece of painted canvas." Scott said, checking the seam of the wall. He moved a table to the side using his leg. The canvas was painted with an old circus advertisement of a snake man, its length taking up the whole wall.

Eve saw what he had found and moved to the corner. She peeked behind the thick cloth and could see a small lump in the middle. She checked across the room; everyone was still occupied, not looking in their direction.

"Scott, come on…" Eve pulled the bottom of the canvas carefully from the wall, making sure not to damage it. If the corner was pulled a certain way it allowed just enough space for them to squeeze behind. Side by side, they flattened their bodies against the wall, slowly side-stepping to the doorway. Soon they crowded in the door frame, giving them six inches of extra space. Eve breathed a sigh of relief and calmed her heart, feeling it beating hard against her chest. Scott was pressed up against her and she could feel the warmth of his breath on her neck as she trembled.

"What's wrong?" Scott whispered, rubbing her arm, thinking that she was cold.

"Nothing…I'm good," Eve said. "Kinda…exciting," she said, then thought again that she didn't mean it to sound that way. "I mean…it's like treasure hunting!"

"I know. Look at the trim around the door. It's really old; see the way it was carved, you don't see that kind of craftsmanship these days. Back in the day, things were made to last." He focused his phone light on the surface. He touched the thick carved wood, tracing the grain lines and carved details with his fingertips.

This part of the castle hadn't been refinished yet and looked like the original structure built in the 1800s. Eve remembered reading that there had been a fire that destroyed a large area. But the fire hadn't reached this spot; it mostly destroyed the picture gallery on the second floor. It had started from an incorrectly installed stove 150 years ago, she recalled.

Eve tried the door, feeling the old latch with her fingers. It was dark and she felt her way around the old heavy metal. She almost giggled and suppressed it, finding their situation funny if anyone were to catch them. At first, she thought the access was locked and jiggled it, disappointed. When the lock clicked and started to open inward, they were both surprised. Eve pushed the door forward, almost falling into the inside room, finding the open passage into the darkness within.

The smell of moist air and mold greeted their noses and Eve held her breath for a moment before adjusting to the rank odor. It smelled of old books along with years of dust arising in the undisturbed room, making her eyes water. Scott turned his phone light brighter and in the glow they could see the swirl of dust circling in the blue beam. He moved Eve behind him and took her hand, leading her down a slight slope as they descended farther into the abyss.

The old wood squeaked under their feet as they passed through the room. It was filled with discarded objects used to decorate the museum for the holidays. Antique bulbs wrapped in yellow newspaper lined the floor stacked in wooden crates. A large tree lay on its side, taking up most of the room, half covering a six-foot Santa. They moved forward, following the path through the stacked storage boxes. The room became cooler and they could feel the area change, finding dirt under their feet.

Eve and Scott shuffled forward in the dark. She felt the old wallpaper, touching the dusty patterns of velvet. In the light she could see the faded reds discolored with time. A dust coating covered it and Eve pulled her fingers away, feeling the grime now on her fingertips, wiping them on her shorts. She decided to count on Scott to pull her along in the darkness. They stopped when they came to another door. Eve figured out how to use the flashlight on her phone and illuminated a circle around them, lighting the space. With both phones they could see the room better and found that it was like taking a step back in time. Dusty books filled the bookcases from floor to ceiling, along with glass-encased displays. They saw a group of Native headdresses surrounded by arrowheads, leather objects, and painted bowls.

"What is that?" Eve asked, focusing the light on the case that held a few dark objects.

"I think those are scalps," Scott said. "Look at the different colors of hair!"

"Yuck! I think you're right!" Eve said.

"Come on…this way. Try not to touch anything." Scott gripped her hand and led her past the cabinets, moving between stored antique furniture and more stacks of random items off to one side of the room. They walked past a large, heavy, wood desk in the center; it was loaded with cast-offs waiting to be put away. Making their way, they saw a light across the room. It was coming from under a thick dark door at the other end. Moving toward it, they found the doorknob. They turned it, finding that it opened on creaky hinges into a modern lit area.

chapter 48

The space they entered was new, full of stainless steel and advanced scientific equipment.

"Well, this area has been redone. I wonder what floor we're on? It wasn't on the diagram. There must be a different entrance," Eve said. "We have to be careful—there's no place to hide."

"Yes—come on. Let's see if we can find this special room," Scott said, moving forward. Eve followed him down the modern hall; it was lined with industrial lighting above each numbered doorway. They checked the doorways as they passed, listening for any movement on this side of the building. They came to a row of glass windows; inside were workers dressed in outfits resembling spacesuits. They were busy working with some high-tech equipment in the middle of the room. Scott and Eve passed quickly unnoticed. Walking in the other direction, they found a staircase that went to a lower level.

On this floor they didn't hear any noise; the lights seemed much dimmer and the smell of earth increased. Eve put her hand to her nose. They quickly checked the door numbers. Finally, they found Room BB206. Eve could feel a throb in her temples, pulling her toward what was inside. The medallion around her neck became hot and she pulled it from under her shirt, seeing the stone in the middle glowing in her fingers.

"Scott!" Eve said. "Look!"

"What's wrong?" He asked, seeing her face change. Her eyes looked larger and brighter green. He took the disk out of her hand and looked at her singed skin, feeling the warmth. "Put it on the outside of your shirt," Scott said. He tugged her cap down, covering most of her face from the overhead cameras that he had spotted. They moved in front of the computer keyboard that was off to the side of the door.

"I'm not sure what to do now," Eve said.

Scott hesitated, thinking. "What if…do you think what's inside recognizes your device? You might want to try putting it by the panel. See if anything happens."

"That's a good idea…I'll give it a try." Eve leaned in closer; the medallion hung in the air between her and the keyboard. She moved it against the panel, and they noticed that it began to glow in the center, but the door remained closed. Disappointed, she stepped back.

"We were so close!" Eve said, feeling disappointed.

"Try the panel again?" Scott said.

Eve stepped up, laying the gold against the keypad this time. Again she saw the device glow and nothing happened. Then she felt a surge go through her body making her heart rate increase; she shut her eyes, concentrating, feeling the rush intensify. A gust of air blew past them, funneling down the long hall and cutting the overhead lights. Eve could feel the energy moving through her; Scott took her hand and she felt the energy go through his body as well. Time stood still and they heard the door click. The lights flickered, then everything returned to normal as if nothing had happened.

"The door is open!" Eve said, opening her eyes, surprised.

They entered the room and the door snapped closed behind them. Inside held a circular, disk-shaped spaceship that now was alive, greeting her. Eve could feel the vibration flowing from it with energy. It was about 12 feet long; the outside shone with a kind of metal that looked different than anything that they had seen. Eve dropped Scott's hand and moved forward, feeling drawn to the ship. When her fingertips touched the craft, images went through her mind, showing her the beings that had been inside. Blueprints of information flowed from the craft into her mind, filling it with knowledge. It was as if her mind was downloading stored information from a computer to a port in her brain, creating a file in her head. Eve saw the turning of glass spears, spinning like a top on its axis. It contained a metallic magnetic composition that wasn't familiar to her. The faster it spun, the more it lifted off, There was something different about the spears that her human mind couldn't comprehend.

"It's giving me a lot of information. I think I better take a sample of the outside of the ship." Scott handed her his pocketknife. Eve pulled out a piece of paper from her backpack and had Scott hold it under the directed area. Eve used the knife to scrape the outside of the ship, taking a sample of the metal. Folding the paper containing the metal scrapings, Eve stuffed it in her back pocket.

A young voice filled the room and Scott stepped back, alarmed. Eve's eyes opened widely, "We need to go—they saw us on the cameras." Eve grabbed Scott's hand and pulled him to the door. Energy filled the room and the door blew open. The lights in the hall were blinking, going on and off in a line.

"Which way?" Scott shouted above the roar of the ship.

"This way! I can see the way!" The child's voice said, with anger. Hands still locked together, Scott was pulled down a different way than they had come, amazed at Eve's strength. They followed the blinking lights, turning left and right, the lights showing them the way. They came to a spiral staircase and quickly ran up the stairs. Their footfalls clanged on the metal, echoing through the space. It seemed loud and they rushed forward, running as fast as they could.

They heard voices below and behind them and didn't stop. The staircase ended and they found a door open at the top. Going through, they found themselves in the sunlight. It had taken them outside; the heavy door slammed shut behind them. Eve and Scott found themselves in a garden maze and ran down the paths, searching for a way out. Eve felt the heated metal around her neck moving up and down as she ran, giving her a shock when she made a wrong turn.

Understanding that it was leading them, she allowed the device to move them through the high hedges. They found their way out of the maze into a crowd of people waiting in line to go on the tour. Slowing down, they tried to blend in, walking through the groups of people, making their way to a side street and moving away from the Mall.

Eve now knew the secret that she had been looking for.

chapter 49

They went straight to the train station and found the extra items that they had removed from their backpacks stored in a locker where they had stashed them. Quickly filling their packs, they rushed for the train. Running, they looked for their gate number. Steam and humidity blew past them from the train's engines as they searched for the right track. They found Track 14 and rushed through the door, barely making it before the doors closed. Relieved when they found their seats, they fell into them as the train pulled away from underground into the sunlight. They relaxed, happy they had accomplished what they came to do.

The Amtrak moved north back to Stanford. It was a nice day; pieces of blue peeped through the clouds, casting brightness over the shadows in the landscape as they drifted overhead. It didn't take long for Eve to fall into a deep slumber, leaning up against Scott. He watched her hair moving in the breeze from the cracked window and pushed it from her face with the back of his hand. He studied her face as she slept; it had gone back to normal. He had to admit that it freaked him out a little when it changed and that weird childlike voice had come out of her.

He wondered about all they had learned in the past week and went through the information, trying to wrap his mind around it. It was hard to believe when she had first told him, but as they progressed on their information journey, he had come to believe much of what they had uncovered. Who would have known that the general population had been kept in the dark by governments around the world for so long.

Before the 1950s, UFOs were common, written about in articles in the local papers. But when Truman was president, something happened that had changed that approach. It was said that President Truman had a secret meeting with aliens at an underground location.

After that, the government and military had been hiding the evidence that showed something had been happening for thousands of years. Scott remembered their findings about space travelers being depicted in cave paintings, figurines, pictographs, and the earliest forms of writing. These beings were easily recognized in spacesuits all around the world in Hawaii, Tassili, Algeria, and Goblin Valley, Utah. All were said to date before the great flood, talked about in almost every culture around the world.

Scott now thought of the Renaissance paintings in the 15th century. He remembered how the Catholic Church was against anything scientific and people were put to death for heresy. So many of the artists had hidden spaceships, disks, and alien faces (like Da Vinci's reverse mirror images) in the backgrounds of their paintings, leaving it to personal interpretation. All this made sense to Scott as he went over it in his mind. It was all really logical.

But the big news that recently came out was the fact that President 45 had signed papers in August of 2018 to have a new branch of the military created called "Space Force." It was to regulate space and protect our space stations and satellites. In the news, the American people were told it was because Russia had destroyed one of their own satellite stations by blowing it up in space. It made Scott wonder if that was really the reason or if something was happening in space that the general public had no idea about. Scott also found it interesting that this year President 45 had also dropped a lot of money into NASA and space developments. It made him wonder if something or someone were really out there, and it had been determined to be a threat.

He had wondered how people that were hunter/gatherers could have had the technology to build the pyramids found around the world, not only in Egypt but in Mexico, Bosnia, and China. But the biggest thing that had been hard for him to believe was the fact that the space people's DNA might have been added to humans, advancing the human race and creating a human hybrid like Eve. He had read in their research that the blood type that might have a connection to these beings was RH negative and was rare. He looked down at Eve, studying her sleeping face, wondering if it was really possible. But it had to be; after all he had seen, it had to be true!

The thoughts that the aliens might have never left, but took residence in our oceans or Antarctica, blew his mind. He remembered reading that a scientist looking at topographical maps had located a pyramid in the glaciers in Antarctica.

He looked over at Eve softly breathing at his side and wondered about her and what it would mean to have children with her. He couldn't stop the thoughts of making her his. She was the only woman that interested him. He knew that she must have felt it too, when they had kissed. But he didn't know what to do; women had always chased him and he didn't have to make much of an effort. But with Eve he felt her pull away, trying to keep her distance. All he knew, looking at her, was that he wanted to protect her forever. This acknowledgment made him feel a little insecure, and he thought if he could win her over, he would never have a dull moment. Scott closed his eyes and tried to clear his mind. *Rest,* he told himself. *This isn't over.*

Chapter 50

Eve had fallen asleep soon after they were safely on the train. Her mind was exhausted; a terrible pain was in the middle of her forehead and she couldn't stay awake. It was as if her mind had to reboot, like restarting a computer after a download. She quickly fell into a trancelike state.

She was aware of Scott next to her, feeling the warmth of his skin and his heartbeat pulsing through her body. She closed herself off to it, becoming afraid of what that might mean: That maybe she wasn't as normal as she had once thought. As her trance deepened, it tuned out everything around her.

Eve heard the thud…thud in her temples, beating to a rhythmic beat. *Was that the sound of drums?* She thought. Their steady rhythm thundered in her head. The sound of chanting drew closer, surrounding her, pressing in so tight around her she could feel bodies as they passed by. An excitement was in the air; the crowd pressed closer, moving her with them. They stopped at the bottom of the Pyramid of the Feathered Serpent.

"They are here!" The crowd shouted. Eve turned to see what was happening. "The gods are here!" They chanted.

Eve looked up to the top of the pyramid; a large disk had landed. Fire, sparks, and smoke shot out from the sides, raining down on the waiting people. But they didn't seem to mind, their eyes transfixed on the ship above them. Eve looked up, amazed, smelling the burning exhaust. She covered her mouth with her hand, trying to block out the toxic odor, not wanting to breathe the foul air.

In her dream, she looked around, seeing the metropolitan city of Teotihuacan, Mexico. She was standing in the center of an ancient city. Tall mounds of stone pyramids arose around her. Eve was amazed at the vast structures. Looking around, she saw a beautiful dark-haired child around 10 years old, signaling for Eve to follow her. When Eve didn't respond, the girl approached, taking her hand, pulling her along with the crowd, moving her closer to the center of the steps, where she could see better. Eve now understood what she was observing. No wonder these space beings were worshiped. *These beings were thought of as gods or angels. This pyramid must be some kind of electrical compositor device used for transmitting and storing energy.* She wondered, *Did these beings land on top of this pyramid somehow to gather an electrical charge? Does it release a static charge, creating a electric discharge?* Not understanding this technology, the people had come to the conclusion that the beings were gods coming from the heavens. Her thoughts were interrupted as the chanting stopped. She looked around to see what had happened.

The noise had ceased and silence fell on the crowd. Eve watched through the smoke; coming down the pyramid steps was a group of large beings. They were about 8 to 12 feet tall with long spindly arms, legs, and fingers. Their hair stood out, reflecting in the sunlight, bright reds and blonds cascaded down their shoulders. They were an incredible sight, carrying their helmets. Their spacesuits made them look huge; they towered over the dark-haired crowd that stood close, surrounding them.

Information flowed through her mind; every thought was backed up with formatted information downloading into her brain. Eve recalled the Sumerians having one of the first written languages known to man. It portrayed the gods mixing with humans and being a tall race of people, 8 to 12 feet tall. The pictures of large beings with wings sitting among the humans had been carved in stone thousands of years ago. The text had implied that these space beings had come to earth to harvest gold and got tired of doing all the work, so created a race of humans to do the work for them.

Eve's mind switched when the beings drew closer; she could make out the shape of their heads and saw that they were noticeably larger than humans. An article came to her mind. It was as if she were reading it in her head at the same time. The information was just flowing to her mind. In 2012 a new look was taken of the DNA from an elongated Paracas skull #44. Not only did they find that the head was 25 percent larger than a human head, but it weighed 60 percent more. The DNA showed that parts of the segments were not known to be human, meaning part of it wasn't from any species found on Earth. The eye sockets were larger, the jawbone stronger, and it didn't have a satchel suture like humans do. The weird part was the two holes toward the back of the head; blood and nerves had flowed through them. A picture popped in her head of a creator that looked like an ant. Eve wondered why this was on her mind. It was as if something wanted her to understand that these were advanced beings she was looking at.

In the crowd of people, Eve watched the beings come nearer and felt the pulsing of energy the closer they got to her. The hushed crowd started a weird hum; the pitch vibrated the area. She could feel it through her body, controlling her movement, making her heartbeat fall in sync with the rhythm. Eve thought, *I need to get away from this space so I can think.* She felt her mind fight for control as the beings tried to enter her mind. The medallion around her neck started to glow, a warmth coming from it. Eve could feel the tension in the air around her. The beings continued to pull on her brain and the fight hurt; she put her hands to the sides of her head.

"Stop it!" Eve screamed, in a tongue that she herself didn't recognize. "I am one of you!" She stood up, proud, making her stature known, her long red hair blowing in the current of energy. She watched as the leader's head snapped in her direction; it reminded her of the way a lizard moves.

"You are not pure!" He bellowed. The crowd fell silent and everyone stopped and turned, looking in her direction, studying this person that they didn't recognize. "Was she a god too?" They questioned each other; Eve could see their thoughts in her head.

"She is not one of us!" The being pointed at her. "Remove her! She cannot come with us!"

chapter 51

Men that had been standing up front moved through the crowd in Eve's direction. She could feel the child at her side take her hand, trying to pull Eve to safety, but her feet wouldn't move. Planted in place, she faced them. When they were about to touch her, an electric current struck out from the medallion, knocking them to their knees. The crowd looked at her in fear.

"You will remain still!" Eve yelled. The thousands of people surrounding her froze, not moving, and waited to see what would happen next. "I have been sent here for a reason," she addressed the being. "I'm not here to challenge you!"

"Where did you get that?" The leader asked. "I see," he said, reading her mind. "I do know your father...well, this is a surprise. I wasn't informed that you would be coming. You have come at the last moment. I have been sent to take this group home. They are now needed."

"I understand that. I am here for almost the same reason. I am from the future to gather the knowledge to help the human race. I'm here to advance the technology so that they can come home to us," Eve said.

He was thoughtful, seeing she spoke the truth. "Come with me and you will see what is needed," the large being said.

Eve moved forward and stood in front of him. The child still held her arm and she looked down in question. But the child just smiled, encouraging her to move forward. Eve stood at the bottom of the steps, surrounded by six beings that looked somewhat human. She noticed their fingers were oddly long and that they had six. Their bodies were slender and she remembered that being in space for a long amount of time, with its lack of gravity, would lengthen a body. She noticed their eyes were dark blue and larger than normal. A book popped in her head and she paused, scanning the information coming to her. It was "The Day After Roswell," a 1998 deathbed confession of Phillip Corso. Eve paused, taking it all in, flipping the pages in her mind.

"I understand that there are different races of beings that have come to Earth," Eve said, out loud. The man that wrote the book witnessed an alien body when working as a classified officer for the government. He thought at first it was child because the body was small; it had spindly arms and legs and a large head. But there was no mouth or nose, just large eyes. Later he saw the report of the autopsy, showing that there was no digestion system or reproductive system.

"You're right. We are all not the same. Just like human beings are somewhat different. But like them, there are good and bad and many have different motivations," he said.

"What are you going to show me? I am running out of time," Eve stated.

"Come!" The leader said. The crowd spread, making a path, not wanting her to touch them. Eve joined the beings entering a side opening in the pyramid bottom, and followed into a tunnel going underground. She found herself in a man-made cavern. It was dark and the beings moved forward without stopping; her eyes adjusted to the lack of light and she was able to see. She followed closely behind them.

They descended about 60 feet underground, coming to a large room encased in sheets of mica. Eve noticed the shiny pieces perfectly placed on the walls and wondered about the purpose. *Was it used as a protective shield for radiation, making it able to take the heat?* Eve thought, going over elements and different igneous, metamorphic, and sedimentary rocks in her mind, trying to remember what category mica fell into. Then she remembered it was a metamorphic rock and used in electronics as an insulator. The walls sparkled with a brilliant shininess and she noticed that the mica had been painted with gold dust. At first, she thought they were gold, knowing it was a conductor, but soon realized it was pyrite (fool's gold). She noticed golden metallic spheres of two to six inches in size lying around all over the floor. Off to the side was a large pool of mercury. Eve was thinking about the minerals found here and wondered *What would they be using these for?*

The beings positioned themselves around the room in a circle and held hands. Eve was on the outside of the circle and just stood there, watching, feeling energy fill the room. Her necklace heated and she moved it to the outside of her sweatshirt where it gleamed in the dim light. The pool of mercury in the middle of the circle began to take shape, forming a large, metallic ball. It reflected off the walls and rose from the ground a few inches, then started to spin. The room lit with the energy reflecting light off the golden walls. The orbs on the ground lifted and began to spin around the beings as the mercury ball lifted higher until it was almost to the ceiling, spinning faster and faster until Eve thought it would make a hole through the rock above. The static energy increased; the beings in the middle weren't affected, protected by their spacesuits, but Eve thought she smelled burning hair and realized it was her hair blowing back, away from the power. There was a large flash of light with a booming sound and Eve was left standing in the darkness alone. She waited for a few moments, hearing just the sound of the thump, thump of her heartbeat pumping blood in her head. She felt a tug on her arm and saw the child pulling her toward the doorway and allowed the girl to lead her back outside into the sunlight. The village was deserted; everyone had disappeared and Eve was left standing alone in silence. She looked above to where the spaceship had landed and saw that it too was gone.

"You have to go," the young girl said.

"What about you?" Eve asked.

"I will go later. There is another way." The girl said, pointing to a place that looked like a rock doorway.

"What is it?" Eve asked.

"It is a portal…a wormhole…in time. It will take me home soon."

"Why didn't you go with them?" Eve asked.

"Because I am here with you. I'm here to help you with your mission and I have to hide all the relics left behind. The people's history is here to be found, when the time is right." Eve watched with blurred vision as the child moved quickly. All Eve saw was motion and felt the air move as the girl sped by. She watched the girl gather all the objects made from jade, shells, and pottery. She threw them down the tunnel before closing it up by stacking rocks over the entrance, until the passage was closed with the tons of stone. Eve thought there must have been 50,000 abandoned objects. The child was soon finished and back at her side.

"You must go!" She said, trying to hurry.

"Okay, how do I go back? What year is it anyway?" Eve asked.

The child looked puzzled...hesitating as if getting information. "It is 700 AD and you have to just wake up and you will be back in your time."

Not knowing what else to do, Eve hugged the young girl and watched her look up at her with kindness. "You humans...no wonder we fell in love with your race...you have an inner goodness."

"Thank you!" Eve said and watched the child move to the rock doorway. Standing in the middle, she put her small hands on the frame and Eve watched as she became transparent, before disappearing all together.

Eve stood for a moment and looked around the large plaza that had housed around 20,000 people at one time. She realized the reason that they had never found the bodies of the rulers of this civilization and never would. She touched her medallion, closed her eyes, and felt someone shaking her. Eve awoke to Scott lightly touching her arm.

"Eve, you were sleeping hard. Come on, we're pulling into the Stanford station. Time to get you home," Scott said.

Eve looked at him and noticed how handsome he was and was happy that she was here with him. Now she understood a few different things she could try to make her antigravitational device work. She understood the importance of her task. It would make a difference in humanity. She was ready to get back to her lab.

chapter 52

Eve and Scott returned to the house and the group went to the upstairs room, closing the door. They exchanged stories of what had happened.

"We're so glad that you made it home safe!" Janet said, "Your father and I were worried!"

"Well, it was quite an experience. This medallion really did help us. Without it I'm not sure if we could have been able to get into the room with the ship."

"What did it look like?" Sarah asked. "And it recognized you?"

"It might have just been responding to my necklace," Eve said, "I'm not sure."

"It was communicating with her." Scott said, "As soon as she touched it. It put her back to that child voice and energy filled the room. It was controlling the environment."

"Yes, maybe you're right…it did get us out of there." Eve said, thoughtful.

"I think this intelligence is a lot stronger than is realized. The part that I find disturbing is that we don't understand the end game. What are their intentions? Sure…I see that they want us to advance as a race, but really, what is the real reason?" Scott said.

"Yes, and how much time do we have?" Janet said.

"I'm not sure of the answer to those questions, but inside I feel like what we are doing is to help mankind. I think by advancing and moving forward it is the right thing. It gives us a choice, doesn't it?" Eve said, hoping that she was right. "Tomorrow I'll go to the lab and try to work on my project. If all goes well, I'll be able to come up with the answer of how to make it work. I have a few ideas that I'm going to try."

"Well, we're all behind you. We've come this far...you just have to remember that technology in the wrong hands could make things worse instead of better. Just keep that in mind." Janet said as they all nodded.

"We're going to take Sarah home, spend the night at her house, and then come back. Scott, you won't mind staying with Eve while we're gone?" Michael asked. "We don't want any trouble while we are out of town, but I have the feeling it will be all right."

"I would be happy to. I'll cook dinner while Eve works. I don't have to report to my advisor until day after tomorrow," Scott said. "She told me that there was good news for me. I hope it is about my internship!"

"That's exciting! Let's keep our fingers crossed!" Eve said, smiling at him. "How about I meet you back here tonight around 7 P.M.? That will give me all day in the lab. I have a few tests in mind."

"That sounds like a plan to me," Scott said, rising from his chair. "I need to check on a few things at my place." He gave everyone hugs and lingered at Eve, hugging her tight and kissing her check. They heard the front door close and the gate roll back in place after he left the driveway.

"Well, he is a real nice boy!" Michael said, breaking the silence. "I like him."

"I do too," Janet said, looking at Eve, trying to read her. When Eve said nothing, her mother added, "And he is really smart and good looking."

Sarah closed her eyes, putting her fingers to her temples. When she opened them, they were clear when she looked into Eve's. "Yes, tonight the house will be safe."

Eve watched Sarah, waiting to hear what she had seen, but she said nothing. All Eve noticed was the glee in her eyes. "Well, let me gather my things and we can get on the road." She hugged Eve tight. "I am so glad to have finally met you. Now don't be a stranger—there is a lot of good we can do together. Bring Scott for a visit before he starts his internship in Washington."

"What did you see?" Eve asked, not able to stop her curiosity.

"Search your heart, child…I don't have to tell you. It is there inside of you." Sarah said. Eve looked at her, puzzled, and left her thoughts unsaid.

"Well…we need to get ready to go also. We'll drop you at your lab on the way," Eve's mother said.

chapter 53

Eve had been working for hours, trying to figure out and process all the information she had learned. She knew the answer had to be there inside her head. But she found her mind was full of jumbled information.

SOUND...at 110 Hertz sound frequency, the body and tissues responded. The same frequency is found around the world in the underground cave systems that had been built to have that same acoustic frequency.

SPINNING...if mercury is encased in a glass ball and spun at a certain speed, weightlessness is created and it lifts.

MINERIALS...certain minerals, such as crystals in granite and gold, are electrical conductors.

What is the answer...she pondered it for hours, putting all the information down on paper to make it clear in her mind. She noticed people coming and going around her and she kept at it until the clear ideas were written down. Then she decided to move on to the sample from the ship. Eve opened the paper and looked at the iridescent shaved material. She noticed the way the light reflected off the white paper.

She prepared a small amount on a slide and put it under a superSTEM microscope. This was new to the university and she found it incredible; with this newest electron microscope she could see down to the individual atoms.

Looking at the slide, she saw something was different.

It was a crystal formation that she hadn't seen before. Eve found a reference book that her professor kept on a shelf outside his office and thumbed through, searching for what she was seeing. She found nothing. Puzzled, she looked closer at the crystals, finding a combination that she wasn't familiar with. It violated the mathematical constraints on how crystals are structured.

Interesting...she thought and went online to see if there was anything current that she had missed. Science was always pushing forward and it was impossible to keep up with every area of study. After a while she found something interesting. It was an article about a meteorite that had crashed in Siberia, Russia in 1979. In 2016 samples were studied at University of Florence, Caltech, and Princeton; researchers found a rare formation never before discovered in nature. It was called a Quasicrystal; this crystal had 60 points of rotational symmetry. It was made of aluminum, copper, and iron. Eve looked at the pictures of the formation and back at her slide and smiled. She knew now what she was looking at and why it was important.

The spaceship had been made out of these ancient alloys and now Eve set out to test them in a different way. She encased some of the material inside a container to keep the environment of the lab safe and tried a few different things. Nothing happened at first. Then she had a thought and hit the sample with an electrical current. She watched as the matter became weightless, lifting inside the container. She had figured it out. Now she had to perfect it before it was ready for mankind. Eve was excited now, understanding how to make her anti-gravitational device work. Now how to give it to the world...like her family had said, it couldn't get into the wrong hands.

chapter 54

That night when Scott came to the house, he had decided he had to make his intentions clear to Eve. When she opened the door, he was suddenly nervous, making the greeting awkward.

"Hey…" He paused.

"Well—hey to you! Are you going to come in or just stand out there? What's up? You seem weird," Eve said.

"I have something to tell you." Scott said, feeling his palms sweat.

"Come on in. I have pizza in the oven, and I opened some wine. I thought it was too late for you to be cooking. It will be nice to just hang out. I have something to tell you, too!"

Scott dumped his bag at the bottom of the stairs, remembering the night days ago when he had done the same thing. He came in and took his seat by the fireplace. A lot had happened and it felt different now, sitting in the same chair that faced hers; everything had changed.

Eve brought them both a plate of pizza and took her chair across from his, pulling her feet up and getting comfortable. She took a bite of the steaming pie and felt a string of cheese break a foot from her face and laughed. He watched her, thinking that she was so beautiful and he didn't have the nerve to tell her.

"You go first," Eve said. Scott about choked, forgetting what he had rehearsed to say and filled his mouth, chewing slowly.

"You go ahead," he said, between chews.

"Okay…I figured out how to make it work!" Eve said, excited.

"You did? That's great! That was fast!" Scott said.

"It was the sample from the ship. It was made with these crystals that have only been made in a lab. The formation isn't found here on Earth."

"Seriously?" Scott asked incredulously.

"Yes, after I figured out what the samples were made of, I searched the Net for anything related and found a few articles from scientists. It told how they had made the crystal formation in a lab. But they really didn't know what they had." Eve said, excited.

"I knew you would do it! That's great, Eve. Now what's next?" Scott asked.

"I have to first process and make the device, which shouldn't be hard now that I understand what I have to do. The big question is how do I give it to the world? What do you think about making a video detailing the information?" Eve asked, "Maybe you could help me with that part of it?"

"I could help you set up the video camera so you could film whatever you want. But I don't think I will be able to physically help you. I also have some news," Scott said.

"What is it?" Eve asked, getting up from her chair.

"I'm going to be moving to Washington, D.C. soon. My internship came through and I am going to be working with a Democratic senator. Remember when I interviewed on campus? There were lots of people interviewing…but I got the big one! It was my first choice! It will really look good on my resume!" Scott said.

"That is so exciting!" Eve ran over and gave him a hug, holding him close. "Look—both of us are getting what we want!"

"Well, there's something else…something else that I want," Scott said.

Eve pulled back a little in his arms and looked him in the eyes. "What is it?" Eve asked, breathless. But before he could answer, Eve leaned in and lightly touched her lips to his, sending chills down both their bodies. The medallion around her neck was crushed between them and they could both feel the warmth.

Scott couldn't hold out any longer and kissed her hard, picking her up. Still kissing her, he carried her up the stairs and took her to her bedroom.

chapter 55

Early the next morning, lying happily in his arms, Eve asked, "What was it you wanted to tell me?" She giggled.

"I was wondering if you might want to come to Washington with me?" Scott asked, now serious, holding his breath.

"I was thinking that I would take that job at NASA headquarters. You know they've been trying to have me sign on with them for the last year," Eve laughed.

"Wow—that would be great! Both of us…together in Washington!"

"Yes—now stop being so serious and kiss me again." Eve said, pulling him closer and putting her lips to his.

chapter 56

The weeks had passed quickly. Scott had found an apartment in Washington and started his job. Eve had visited him a few times and enjoyed the fast pace of the city. She loved the style and watching the young people that hustled around going for cocktails after work, trying to network and make connections. She had accepted the job with NASA, not telling them about her project, but knowing that working for them she could do a lot of good. She was starting in two months, after the next semester finished, giving her time to tie things up and have access to the college lab on campus. At night when she was home, Eve worked on editing her video.

Her family hadn't been bothered by the so-called men from the government after the police had gotten involved. When Michael had contacted the officer that had taken their report, he had been told that the man hadn't been in the system. That he hadn't worked for the FBI and that someone had posted bail a few days later and he had disappeared. The group had come to the conclusion that someone didn't want any of their research getting out to the mainstream public. They figured the house was most likely being watched and they had to be careful and not let their guard down.

Eve had called a meeting with her parents, Sarah, and Scott, making it for the end of the week. She looked forward to having everyone together again. She told them she had something that she wanted to show everyone.

On Friday night they arrived at the house. Janet had ordered Chinese food and they all sat around the dining room table with chopsticks. Everyone was careful with their conversation, waiting until they moved upstairs to the war room. Once dinner was over, they went into the private room with a few bottles of wine. When the door was closed everyone looked at Eve.

"Did you figure it out?" Her parents said, in unison.

"I've been working on a few things…but I did figure it out from the ship's sample we took. Other than a new crystal formation, I found something interesting. I thought if I spun mercury, I could get a weightlessness. But I found when the elements Tellurium, Germanium, and Palladium are combined and spun at a certain frequency, you can get lift." Eve looked at their blank faces. "Let me show you. Please everyone, let's join hands in a circle," Eve directed.

Eve reached and took Scott's hand, feeling an electric current rush through her body from the physical contact. She concentrated, trying to remove the thoughts of their encounters from her mind. She tried to calm her mind so she could focus on the task at hand. They all felt the power as the circle was completed.

"Now close your eyes and clear your minds…thinking of the ocean usually works for me. See the waves and the crest of the water as hits the shore. Now hear the waves and let your mind relax and kind of float," Eve said.

Everyone did as they were told and felt the energy increase in the room. It pulled at their minds, revealing what she had done. They saw the beings' interactions with mankind in the past and the building of the pyramids. They saw the device that she had made in the lab and felt the power that came from it. They saw how she had moved a desk in the air with a flick of her wrist aiming the wand. At first it had been hard; then she got better at it and was able to put the desk down gently. They saw Eve leave the lab and go outside and use her device on a car. She made it move up and down until she had control, then made it raise high in the air. She lifted it to the treetops and then as high as the campus buildings and gently brought it down. They saw her making a video of her progress. When Eve was finished, she released their minds and waited for their response. The room was quiet for a moment and then a cheer went up. Everyone hugged, excited, understanding that this was a tremendous breakthrough.

"I'm so proud of you!" Michael said, "You really did it!"

"Yes! But we all knew that you would make it work." Janet chimed in. "What are we going to do next?"

"I'm not sure yet. I was thinking it might not be a good idea to patent it and show it to the panel for my dissertation. I can come up with something simple for that. If I did show them, I think it would get out to the press and everyone would know about it," Eve said.

"But isn't that what you wanted? Or the reason for all of this? To give it to the world?" Scott asked, still holding her hand, not wanting to let her go.

"I know...but I'll think of a different way...a better way of doing it," Eve said.

"Yes," Sarah said, taking her fingers from her forehead. "It could be misinterpreted or stolen and buried, putting you in danger. It is better to think of a different way. I saw it!"

"That's what I thought," Eve said. "I'll think of something." The room was quiet while everyone was trying to think of a solution.

"While we're trying to figure that out, I have some news," Scott interrupted the silence. "You know the presidential election is coming up." Everyone nodded. "Well, the Democratic Party will be preparing for the Inaugural Balls in Washington if they win." Scott paused, now feeling a little uneasy, thinking he should have asked her alone. *What if Eve says no?* "The senator I've been working for is going to have a table at one of the parties. I will have to work the event…but if the Democrats win the presidency, the new president will be attending." Scott turned to Eve, still holding her hand. "I was thinking…I was wondering…if you would…"

Before Scott could get the words out, Eve was in his arms, giving him a hug. "Of course, that's it…I would love to go with you!"

"Yes, that would be a wonderful night, Eve. There is still plenty of time to come up with a beautiful dress." Her mother said.

"Well, it's getting late…I need to catch the last train back to Washington. How about I call you tomorrow and we can talk about the details?" Scott said, moving toward the door.

"Sure! That sounds great!" Eve said, "I'll be right back, I'm going to walk Scott out." She announced to the room.

Going through the house, both Scott and Eve were quiet

as they moved downstairs. At the door, Scott turned and pulled Eve into his arms, looking in her eyes.

"I've missed you, Eve. I know I shouldn't say anything to scare you off, but these weeks away from you…I couldn't think of anything else. I want you to think about having a future with me. I'm thinking not only living together, but a future. I want it all…you don't have to say anything right now. Just think about it." He gently touched his lips to hers and they both felt a surge of power go through their bodies, pulling them closer together. The medallion around her neck heated and started to glow, the warmth heating her chest. Eve heard a voice in her head.

"What is it?" Scott questioned.

Eve gripped her temples, closing her eyes. Scott shook her.

"Eve! Come out of it!" Scott's voice snapped her head back. For a moment Scott had been a little scared, not knowing what was happening.

"I'm all right," Eve's eyes cleared, and she smiled up at Scott and whispered, "Yes, he is handsome!"

"What are you talking about?" He said, smiling.

"I have to get used to my father listening in," she said.

"Well, what did he say?" He asked, feeling that this was weird.

"In not so many words, he is pleased with my choice." She pulled herself further into the embrace and touched her lips gently to his. Passion grew and the kiss became deeper. Scott had to stop himself before he couldn't hold back and took her right there in her parents' foyer. He stepped back, breathing hard, kissed her forehead, and went out the door.

Eve stood for a few minutes, regrouping before going back upstairs. Her parents and Sarah were waiting, smiling at she entered the room.

"Perfect opportunity—we'll help you. You're right—he doesn't have to know until it is over!" Sarah said.

chapter 57

It had been a long day. The new President and his wife had been in and out of the protected limo, surrounded by Secret Service security, all night. After many parties and first dances with the new First Lady, the President was tired. Tonight would be their first night in the White House; workers had already moved their personal effects into the living space prepared for them. The President went into his new walk-in closet, looking around at the racks of organized suits, ties, shirts, and shoes all categorized in lines by color.

The new President sat in the comfortable chair and took off his shoes, neatly placing them with the others. He removed his tuxedo jacket and put it over his arm, looking for a hanger. He didn't want to just toss it on the fabric bench in the middle of the room, leaving it for someone else to put away for him. He straightened the fabric on his arm and felt something heavy in one of the pockets. As he flipped it over, something fell out, landing on the light carpeted floor. He looked down, seeing a large red jewel sparkling back at him from the white carpet.

He picked it up, turning it over in his fingers, inspecting it. It was a tear-shaped, red gem that sparkled in his large hand; the object had a small black end. He found his glasses in his shirt pocket and looked closer, seeing that it was a decorated memory stick. Disregarding his jacket forgotten on the plush chair, he quickly changed into his comfortable nightclothes and went into the bedroom.

His wife was in bed and he smiled, seeing that she had already fallen asleep. The President pulled the sheet higher on her shoulder, pausing for a moment and thinking how thankful he was to have her in his life. He had known she was the one for him when he first met her and discovered her inner goodness. He noticed in her haste she hadn't even pulled the bobbie pins from her hair. He slowly removed them, releasing the curls and setting the pins on the side table. A few of the long blond strands flowed over her pillow and he hesitated, seeing how beautiful she was. She had been a real trouper that night; it hadn't been easy and she had done well. Smiling down at her, he counted his fortune.

He went to the large desk and clicked on the computer, booting it up. Curiosity had pushed him to see what was on the fancy memory stick. Pushing it into the slot, he watched a file pop up on his screen. Tapping on it, he saw many files. He knew it should be given to his new detail to check out first. He paused for a moment, then decided to take a quick look. There was one video file and he clicked on the video, opening it up.

The woman he had noticed from the last party appeared on the screen and he almost clicked it off, thinking that the woman just wanted to get his attention and he wasn't that kind of man. But he waited to see what she said.

"My name is Eve. I have a story to tell you and something I wanted to give to you, to help humanity."

After ten minutes, the video finished and the President sat for a while, thinking about what he had just seen and what had been said. He picked up the phone. "I need a outside line. Connect me with Robert Bigelow.... Yes, from Aerospace! Get him up." He paused, waiting until he heard the click on the line and was told by the operator that she was putting him through.

"Robert Bigelow? This is the President of the United States. I want to meet with you...I need you to look at something for me."

"Who is this? How did you get this number?" A sleepy voice asked.

"This is your new President of the United States! I have some information that I need your expertise on and I couldn't wait to try to reach out to you. How familiar are you when it comes to people from space visiting our planet?"

"Well, sir, if I can speak freely..."

"Yes, please continue!" The President said.

"I think the universe is so vast, that we would have to be small minded if we think that we are the only game in town. That's why I have always had such an interest in furthering our space program," Bigelow said.

"Something has been brought to my attention and if it gets out, we might have a real big problem. I don't think the human race is ready. Can you meet me here in my private quarters for dinner tomorrow?"

"Yes, sir!"

Before Bigelow had a chance to say anything else, the line went dead and he was left holding the phone, wondering if the call had happened at all. He tried to call back the last call he had received on his phone and found that it went to the White House switchboard.

PART TWO

On August 9, 2018, Vice President Pence under the Trump Administration announced a new sixth branch of the Armed Forces. This established a command as United States Space Operations Force as a new joint organization called the Space Development Agency…SPACE FORCE.

chapter 58

Eve thought she felt someone aggressively shaking her; she tried to move her hand to fend them off, but the strong vibration continued. A loud rumbling sound rang in her ears, making them hurt. She tried again to lift her hand, but found it very heavy and stuck to her side. Her body wasn't responding to anything her mind told it to do. Opening her eyes, Eve saw that she wasn't dreaming; something was wrong. She focused, concentrating on making her brain rid itself of the cloud that surrounded her mind. Pulling hard on her memory, she tried to remember where she was. All that came to her were the feelings of being trapped. The last thing she remembered were flashes of her thoughts saying DANGER! GET OUT OF THERE! Then fear had filled her. Eve now told herself to get a grip, there had to be a logical explanation of the situation she found herself in.

Looking straight ahead, she tried to make out what was in front of her. Light reflected off a rounded curvature of glass covering her face. Eve could see through to the other side. It was like looking through a small airplane window. *Why would I be looking through a window?* Her head wouldn't move so she tried to turn her eyes to see what was on each side of her. When she understood what she was seeing, Eve felt her heart start to flutter, beating hard against her chest.

She tried to slow the rapid beating as the blood pumped in her brain, sounding like distant drumbeats. Her mind started to calm, feeling comfort from the heavy necklace that hung between her breasts. It proved to her that she wasn't dreaming—this was real. She knew that whomever had put her in this confinement hadn't been able to remove the necklace. The necklace was an unbreakable chain made of solid gold and something else. In the middle hung a medallion with a large odd stone that was about two inches in circumference. She remembered her father from the past putting it around her neck. Because of the length it wouldn't go over her head. She knew it had been made to never come off. At the time she didn't understand the power that the object possessed, thinking it was just a means of contacting this ancient being. But when she had been working on her anti-gravitational device many times she had felt the power. One time she had been doing an experiment and a surge of bright, blinding light in the form of a lighting bolt had came from the center, knocking her to the ground.

Shocked, she turned her eyes again and made out a line of four bodies wrapped head to toe in white puffy cloth. All were encased in their own capsules, with only their closed eyes visible; she noticed they all seemed to be asleep. Eve saw wires running from each pod to a small machine in the center of the room. Eve understood why she couldn't move. She had to be wrapped up tight like the others beside her.

Before she could figure out an exit plan, the door to the room burst open with a loud bang as it hit the wall behind it. Two lifelike robots, petite in stature, rolled into the room on large wheels instead of legs. They rushed in and moved in front of her, looking through the thick glass. Eve watched them in wonder. She tried to turn her head to get a better view. One of the robots was obviously a female. She had been built with a figure and a small breastplate covering her chest. Underneath were exposed metal wires and steel pieces of a machine that shone in the dim light. *Robotics have come a long way,* Eve thought. She remembered seeing some of their development when she had passed that department. That was the reason she loved her job at the Kennedy Space Center in Florida at Cape Canaveral. She had found the new technology developed there incredible and felt pride in the fact that she could help mankind move forward into the stars.

The female robot had a pretty face; her metal hair-plate was styled close to her head in a tight bun surrounding her delicate facial features. The other was a male with the same kind of construction except masculine features and high cheekbones. They had given him a metallic-plate comb-over style hair and a physique with an abs-like plate across his chest.

The two robots set to their tasks and Eve could only watch. She remembered reading that they had been developed to resemble humans because that made humans more relaxed and able to trust them. The male pushed a button, removing the glass from in front of Eve's face. For a moment they all just looked at each other, then the male made a screeching noise that Eve didn't understand, reminding her of the old-fashioned computer modem. The female robot, understanding his command, started working around her. *Were they talking in their own language?* Eve wondered. It made her think about something she had read about computer systems that had been set up to monitor Facebook. It had been discontinued for a time, after the computer systems had started communicating with each other, talking in their own language, and evolving on their own. The programmers hadn't thought to write in the program that they were to only communicate in English. The robots had evolved and created their own system of communication.

Eve heard a beeping noise and the robot pressed her metal fingertips to Eve's neck, reading her pulse through the fabric. The robot made a sound to the male and removed an IV bag hanging on the side wall. Eve watched as she filled a syringe and shot it into the bag. Eve's eyes followed the liquid as it went down the clear tube. It flowed quickly from the bag. Eve was calm until she saw that it was attached to her arm.

"No!" Eve yelled. She watched the robots snap their heads in her direction in a reptile-like movement in unison, blinking their large metal eyes. Before the glass was put back in place over her face, Eve had noticed their pupils had focused in and out like the lens of a camera.

Eve could feel the drugs starting to take effect; she fought them mentally, trying to stay conscious. They were too strong. Before she was pulled under, Eve reached out with her mind to her friend Sarah, concentrating, trying to send her a message. Before she passed out, all she could get out was...*Help...tell Scott I've been taken.*

Chapter 59
Months Before

It had been a long day at work and Eve was tired and struggled with her key in the door of her house. Before she could click back the lock, the door opened and Eve was greeted by her new husband Scott. They had been married for six months and tonight was the night they set aside to celebrate their union. One night each month, they both stepped back to make time for each other. Eve always looked forward to the 10th of every month, not knowing what surprise Scott would have for her.

Scott took her bags and set them aside, pulling her into his arms. He kissed her and smelled her hair, finding the lingering smell of engine oil; he tried to keep the smile on his face at the funky odor.

Eve saw his nose turn a little. "I know…I need to go shower. Don't go anywhere, I'll be right back." Eve kissed his lips and lingered two seconds before she ran up the stairs.

"I made your favorite!" Scott yelled after her.

Eve stripped, showered, and put on her comfy sweats. She was back in the kitchen to help with the salad within ten minutes. They always liked to stay in on their night and have a good home-cooked meal with some wine.

"How was your day?" Scott asked.

"It was good. It's coming along; there is a lot of testing to make sure that they will work in any atmosphere," Eve said. Crunching a piece of carrot between her white teeth, she continued, "I know it feels like it has been taking forever. But my team is good, everyone is really talented."

"That's a compliment to them coming from the smartest person I know. Building a new space remote vehicle I'm sure isn't easy. How are they dealing with you being so young?" Scott asked, setting the plates on the table and lighting a candle in the middle, then dimming the lights. "I think it's all ready," he said, smiling at her.

"They have been really nice," Eve laughed. "But they are old-school and I know it's been hard for them to accept me at first. I've learned that seventy-year-olds don't like change. But Gordon Turner is something else! He is the one I was telling you about. At first, I thought he didn't like me; he reminds me of one of my professors at Yale. You know the type…over-the-top smart, trouble communicating, carries a spare tire around the middle, balding on top, and lets his hair grow on the sides like a madman. He was the hardest to get to know but I like him the most…I think he is a genius! We have been partnered with this project for NASA's Mars mission for 2026. The U. S. will send robots to build a habitat before we send humans to be aliens on that planet. Gordon and I are working on the land transport that astronauts will use to get around the planet. The rest of the team is working in the Nevada desert assembling the module pods and figuring out how the robots will set them up remotely." Eve said, before sitting down in front of her dinner, feeling the warmth of the silver cover.

Eve started to look under the lid. "What did you make?"

"It's a surprise! No peeking." Scott laughed, holding her lid down and teasing her. "Okay!" He lifted both their lids at the same time.

"It looks so nice, Scott! Next time I'll cook." Eve said, pouring the wine in their glasses.

"Well, let's make our toast. To happiness...love and what else you have been talking about? Oh yes...children." They both laughed. "Well, I'm glad things are working out at NASA. No regrets on the other thing?" Scott asked.

"No regrets. I know—it had been a really good offer to work for that private company, but I felt I could be of more use with NASA. Anyhow, it worked out for us to be in Florida. With you opening your law practice, it's nice we are both working close by," Eve said.

"Yes; I'm glad it worked out the way it did also." Scott said, smiling at her from across the table.

"Anyhow, it makes us able to see each other more, especially with the other thing we are working on. I know it will happen!" Eve said, clinking her glass to his before taking a long sip. "Yes, this is nice," she said, holding up the deep liquid and seeing the colors swirl in the bottom.

"Go ahead before it gets cold," Scott directed. Eve screeched with joy as she tasted the sauce covering the salmon.

"Ah—you know me so well! I love salmon!" Eve said, digging in.

Chapter 60

"Hey—did you end up going to the doctor today? I remember you saying you had an appointment," Scott said.

"Yes, I took a long lunch. It was interesting, as we knew it might be. The test came back and I'm not pregnant yet. But I learned that if I do get pregnant—or when I get pregnant—I have to go to the doctor as soon as I know for more tests. I found out that I have to get a shot."

"What for?" Scott said, looking concerned.

"I have RH-negative blood; funny I didn't know before. Anyhow, because it is rare, my body might fight to kill the fetus because the two of us don't have the same blood type," Eve answered.

"No—I think I have AB or something like that. Is it dangerous for you? I don't want a child if it's a risk." Scott said, looking at his plate. Eve reached over and took his hand.

"It's normal—don't worry! Okay. I already have been doing some research because I knew you would think this way. I love you, too!" Eve got up and sat on his lap, kissing his cheek. His arms went around her long waist and moved a piece of her thick auburn hair from her face as he looked into her large green eyes.

"You have to understand my concern," he said.

"I know, Honey, but nothing to worry about! People with RH-negative have been having children for a long time," Eve laughed.

"What did you find out? I've heard of this RH-negative blood but never thought much about it."

"Well it's really interesting. Only 15% of the population have it and they don't know where it came from, because it just appeared about 3,500 years ago."

"Okay," he said, waiting for her to go on.

"Most of the people who have it have red or blond hair, blue/hazel or green eyes." Eve blinked her eyes at him. "Also usually left-handed, have low blood pressure and are psychic or in-tune emotionally and are sensitive to heat and get this…a higher IQ." Eve laughed, stroking his dark curly hair and adjusting herself in his lap. She was glad he was so tall because she wasn't a little delicate flower. At 6'2" she had a lanky build and had always felt awkward. But Scott at over 6'6" had been drawn to her and wouldn't give up until he had won her over with his intellect when she seemed to not notice his dark good looks.

"Well, that sounds like you! You know what it makes me think?" Scott said.

"Yes, that crossed my mind too! 3,500 years ago, there were travelers from a different planet visiting Earth. They changed the DNA of some of the humans they abducted," Eve said. "Their descendants might have been left with a new and improved blood. Maybe mixed with theirs. Thus, the reason for Haemolytic disease that makes the woman's blood build up antibodies to destroy the (fetus) alien substance in her body, thus destroying the child. So maybe the idea was an experiment? You know this doesn't happen anywhere else in nature, where the mother's body destroys its own child." Eve said, taking a breath. She paused, silently thinking. "The doctor gave the example of a horse crossed with a donkey; they are similar but not the same. Most of the time the donkey aborts the fetus."

"After all of the evidence we found last year, and the ancient civilizations we looked at, it makes me wonder about the Sumerians of Mesopotamia. You remember the interpretation of their ancient texts? If the experts are right there might be a thirteenth planet in our solar system that rotates where we can see it every 3,600 years. When those clay records were deciphered, they told the story of the seven tablets of creation and how they made man in their image. Remember the other name was Anunnaki, that means the sky people, the givers of civilization of mankind. The old text said that they were gods but referred to them as 'Giant people that came from the stars.' I wonder about their blood," Scott said.

"Yes, I remember! This will blow your mind because it is similar...funny of all things for you to bring up! What I read said that the Sumerians had a high percentage of their population with RH-negative blood," Eve said.

"Really! You don't have to convince me—I believe it! You know they were said to be giants." Scott winked at her.

"Yes! I wonder if they had six fingers also, like the information that we found about the children of the Watchers or the research we found about giants around the world. Anyhow...what I found interesting was that the other 85% of the population that doesn't have RH-negative blood can be traced back to the Rhesus monkey or primate."

"I see—you have special blood and mine comes from a monkey!" Scott teased.

"Very funny! Well, you know how special I am!" Eve laughed. "You're going to really think you're lucky to have found me, when I tell you that the 15% of the population that has RH-negative blood come from a royal blood line, pure blue blood, they call it."

"Yes, Honey…I know you're special!" Scott tickled her.

Eve giggled,"Wait—I have more!" She paused, backing away from him before she said the last part. "All of the British royal family has it and what is really weird is that almost every U.S. President has been RH-negative. Trump, Obama, Bushes, Clintons—all the way back. But the people that do have RH-negative blood aren't linked genetically to any primates." Eve said, picking up their dishes and putting them in the sink.

"Okay, that is really weird!" Scott said. "What do you think?"

"I found one theory that the people who have it.… Thoughts are that at one point in their family tree in the past 3,500 years, someone had been abducted and their DNA or their child's DNA was changed by people similar to us but not completely alike. Thus the reason the body attacks the fetus." Eve smiled and loosened her tie on her sweats provocatively.

Scott got up and encircled her with his long arms, kissing her ear. "Anything else?"

"Well, it's hard to think when you're doing that," Eve said, closing her eyes. "Yes…3% of blacks have it, 1% of Asians, and 45% are of European decent."

"Interesting," Scott whispered.

Eve had taken his hand and was leading him to the sofa. "Oh, I almost forgot...I read about a Basque tribe that once lived secluded in the Pyrenees mountain range between Spain and France. They are the oldest population in Europe. Thoughts are they go back 40,000 years to the Cro-Magnon man. They have the highest levels of RH-negative blood in their population and it might be where it originated."

"It doesn't surprise me; they were most likely in an isolated area like Easter Island. Earth visitors must have modified the DNA and then left them to see how their modified manipulation changed and advanced the humans. Remember the advanced intelligence of humans jumped in the past 5,000 years and it couldn't have been just from natural selection. I think it was like a science project," Scott said.

"What I found interesting was that studies were done on the Basque skulls and they were somewhat different than other humans. Also, their bodies were characteristically larger, thick-chested, broad-shouldered, with straight noses and long ears. Stories said that they used to be very tall and over time their bodies compressed with the gravity of Earth, but that they have denser, heavier bones." Eve took a breath, feeling the chills go through her body when Scott tugged at her ear and then nibbled it.

"I like your ears, Honey." Scott's warm breath was making her shake and she rocked in his arms.

Eve giggled and kissed his forehead. "Let me finish."

"Okay...okay...get it all out!" Scott stopped and waited, but the sparkle was still in his eyes.

"Almost done—you want to know it all, don't you?"

"Yes, Dear...please go on." He said, trying to be serious, but the corners of his mouth had formed a smile.

"Okay...where was I? Some who have studied the Basque say that they are from the lost thirteen tribes of Israel; others say maybe survivors of Atlantis. But remember the story of the Indians and blood?" Eve hesitated, "Remember growing up you could be 'blood brothers'?"

"Yes, I remember—I think I did that with a few friends when I was about ten," Scott said.

"What did you do? To be blood brothers?" Eve questioned.

"Well, we both cut our fingers and then rubbed the cuts together," he said.

"Yes—think about it...could this tradition have been started for a reason? Could they have really been checking to see if they were blood brothers, with the same kind of blood?" Eve asked.

"What are you saying?" Scott asked.

"I found out that when you mix Rh-positive and Rh-negative blood, you can see clumping (agglutination). Could it have been a way to see who were really their brothers and sisters? Because they had been told that their blood was different, almost special, than the rest of mankind?" Eve said, smiling.

"Wow...I didn't know that. You aren't going to make me go there, are you? Ah—who cares. I'll go wherever you want." Scott said, pulling her on top of him. "Okay...is that all?"

"Yes—for now," she shivered.

"Then let's make a baby!"

chapter 61

The phone was ringing again. It wasn't the first time in the past six months; Robert Bigelow had been receiving a lot of late-night calls. He knew he had to answer when the President of the United States called. But here he was being awakened again tonight.

"Did I catch you asleep?" The masculine voice asked.

"No, sir, I was laying here thinking…you must never sleep!" Bigelow stated.

"Well, I catch 15 minutes here and there. I was just wondering if you have had any luck getting her to come work for your company. She is too much in the open working for NASA. At some point they will discover her talents."

"I know, sir, I have gone to her more than once myself, making her a big offer to come work at my company. But she refuses; the money won't move her. Her family has money. Really, I don't think she even knows the possibilities of her talents—or how to use them," Robert said.

"Well, offer her a project, if money won't move her. You saw the video she sent me and the device that she created, an anti-gravity device. Who would have known that a college student could come up with that; NASA and all you aerospace companies have been working on it for years. The reason I came to you is because of the relationship NASA has with your company!" The President said.

"Sir...I promise that I am working on it. I know she's special. But as I recall, she did give you and NASA the formula of how she did it. Now we have the best people working on perfecting the device. Remember, we already have the tractor tow working in space similar to hers. Also, sir, if you recall, she gave it for free. Why not let her live her life... she seems happy," Robert said.

"Well, I don't care how happy she is...she is too valuable and I want her on the team. I know the race to space is on...I just don't want us to be left behind. Now these billionaires are building their own rockets. That Richard Branson funding his own fleet of Virgin rockets...he is going to take civilians on a flight around the moon and back!"

"Yes, sir, I heard. But shouldn't we be happy for the technology we can all gain from his success?" Robert asked.

"What I have learned from history is that we have to be the best and be there first! Jeff Bezos might be the richest man on earth with his fleet of rockets in Texas. But building his own space port! We need her! She would be an advantage for us."

"I understand! I'll get her!" Bigelow said.

"Okay, let me know when she's on our team!" The President hung up and Robert lay in bed, now wide-awake, thinking. *How did I end up in this situation?* He had two months to get Eve to come on board. How was he going to be able to do this? He started going over figures in his head. It would take 240 days to reach Mars, if we slingshot from the moon. But it had to be the right time frame, when Mars and Earth were at their closest point. They would have to be able to have a live feed from the International Space Station, which was 250,000 miles away. And then would have to get close enough, but not too close, to pass the space station with a wide berth because of the solar panels that branched out on each side. He remembered recalling each were the length of a football field.

His goal was just to be able to make it easy to travel in space. He had always been excited to see what was really out there. In building his company off the money from his hotel chain, he had been working for years on his idea of expandable spacecraft modules called the B330. The B330 was a set of module space habitats made for expanding the square footage on the space station, but were also capsules that could independently travel through space.

He remembered April 2016 with pride...Launch Day. His Bigelow inflatable module was attached to the International Space Station, where it now had been tested for two years. He was excited and nervous at the same time because the technology was almost ready to take man beyond. He fantasized of the day of a manned spacecraft setting down on Mars. He knew that the gravity was close to Earth's and with the planet being smaller, the temperature fluctuation was extreme. He had heard at one point the law of nature was: We leave the planet, adapt, or perish.

Robert couldn't go back to sleep and he got out of bed after checking the clock...4:30 A.M. He wondered about this new President who should have other things more important to think about.

He sometimes wished he wouldn't have partnered with NASA because of the pressure he now felt being put on him.

He wanted to launch his manned ship into space when he was ready and felt it was safe. But politics had pushed him, and time was running out. Now he would have to think of a workaround to give the President what he wanted. How could his goals be back in the balance, with the President's obsession with Eve? She didn't have any idea of what was going to have to happen. He would try to have a serious meeting with her and maybe her husband. Yes, that was it… bring in her husband…. He was a lawyer; maybe he could talk some sense into her. Maybe he could convince her to come on their team. But he found himself wondering, because he couldn't say what the team would be doing. If he couldn't get her to come, he understood what he would have to do, but he didn't like it.

Chapter 62

Eve left the house early that morning, wanting to get an early start. Scott was still in bed and she kissed his cheek and pulled the covers higher over his muscular arm. She paused for a moment, wondering how she had gotten so lucky to have a man she loved in her life. She hoped soon they would have exciting news to share with her parents.

Eve and Scott were flying up to Connecticut Friday night for a quick visit. Eve's parents had asked Sarah to come for the weekend as well. It had been a while since they had made it home and Eve looked forward to seeing what her parents had been working on. After their disappearance the previous year, she had tried to make it a point to call more and listen to what they were doing. Eve had made her parents promise to tell her when and where they were traveling before they went. After last time they had easily agreed. She was excited to tell them about her new job, the work she had been doing, and the new friends she had made.

Friday morning at 6 A.M., Eve pulled into her parking spot at NASA's Kennedy Space Center. She had been assigned to the vehicle assembly building, where she was working with a small group. Happily, she gathered her briefcase and made her way through the parking lot. Sometimes it surprised her how many cars would already be parked there, thinking it should be deserted at this hour. She noticed that her advisor and mentor was already there, and she picked up her pace. The sun was just starting to come up and she could feel the humidity already in the air. She found Gordon Turner bent over the wheelwell of the transportation vehicle, trying to adjust something.

"Good morning, Gordon! Did you spend the night?" Eve chimed, making Gordon jump. He squinted at her from behind his dirty, thick glasses. Before he could say anything, Eve noticed him squinting through the grime and handed him a tissue from her pocket. He made a face with displeasure at being interrupted. "Okay, there you go," Eve said, "Now can you see better! And I know you're happy that I'm here to help you!" Eve joked.

"I told you to quit doing that!" Gordon said.

"And I told you that I'm here to help you. Now quit acting like a grumpy old man," Eve said, putting on her work bibs.

A small smile broke on the corners of his mouth and his eyes sparkled before his face returned to the serious man that had been at NASA for at least 30 years.

"We have a lot to do. They want this done in six weeks," he stated.

"Don't worry—it will be ready! We're almost there! Now tell me the rest of the story of the way you met your wife while we work." Eve said, teasing him.

"Well, it's not that exciting..." Gordon laughed.

"Remember, you said that you wouldn't be here if it weren't for her. So I need to hear how she found the smartest man I know," Eve teased.

"Eve, you are something else!" He continued to tinker, putting his hand out, silently laughing as she filled it with the right tool, wondering if other than being smart she could also read minds. "My wife and I were in college. I had come from a family that didn't have a load of money, so I had to work my way through to get my degree. She was from one of those families with lots of cash and real estate and I didn't think she would ever even look in my direction. She was too pretty and refined. But in Chem class, she was having a little trouble in the lab and I had been assigned to be her partner. I would look forward to class every week just to be near her and have her talk to me.

"One day we were working on a project. I'm not sure what she did, but a fire started; the beaker had broken and we had a small fire at our station. Without thinking, I extinguished it and saw that her hand was burned. Before I knew what I was doing, I rinsed the chemicals off, and seeing the redness, I kissed it, like my mother used to do. When I looked up, horrified at what I just had done, I saw her smiling. She told me 'It's all right,' and we laughed.

"After that, Jane was a lot more talkative, telling me of her childhood and her dreams for the future. She wanted to be a teacher. The next thing I knew she was asking me to go to a park with her. When I arrived, she had prepared a picnic lunch and I don't know what happened…I guess we fell in love. After that we were always together. One day she told me we were going to get married. She then proceeded to push me to expand my horizons. She made me apply at NASA! I told her there was no chance they would want me. She said, 'NASA would be a fool to not take a guy like you.' So here I am! Can you hand me that oil can? I'm going to bleed the brakes. How did you end up here?" Gordon asked.

"That's a nice story! And you and Jane have been married 34 years?" Eve asked.

"Yes, 34 or 36—time goes so fast!" He said.

"And you have a son and daughter?" Eve asked.

"Yes; they are about your age. My son is in grad school and my daughter is planning her wedding."

"That's exciting!" How big is the wedding going to be?" Eve asked.

"I'm not sure. I try to tune out all the excitement. My daughter and my wife are always working on the details, plan after plan, change after change...I try to steer clear and let them enjoy it. I go into the other room and find peace with the news," he laughed.

"That looks good on you, Gordon!" Eve stated.

"What do you mean?" He asked, serious.

"Your smile!" Eve said.

chapter 63

Gordon laughed; *She is something else*, he thought.

"I'll tell you a secret," Eve said.

He put his glasses on his head and now looked at her, paying attention. "Okay..."

"We are trying to get pregnant. But you can't say anything—I'm not sure what the bosses would think, seeing I haven't been here that long."

"Congratulations! I won't say anything. I don't think they could hold it against you; times have changed," Gordon said.

"Well, I hope not...I like it here. But I found out something interesting. Have you heard of RH negative blood?"

"Yes, I have...that's funny, I did my dissertation for my Masters degree in genetics all those years ago. I found some of the research interesting. People with RH negative blood have to get a shot, right?"

"Yep. I didn't know much about it myself, but I've been looking into it," Eve said.

"If I remember right, there are many interesting things that have shown up in people's genetics over time. Some they aren't sure where they originated from. One of the things I came across was that people with RH negative blood usually have an extra vertebrae," Gordon said, pausing.

"You're kidding! You're so funny!" Eve laughed.

"No, I'm serious! It is called atavism. It's when a lost trait of a distant relative re-emerges in a modern organism."

"Yes—I think I've heard of that. All right, I'm feeling nervous."

"Nothing to worry about; it doesn't happen often," he said.

"What other things re-emerge genetically?" Eve asked, wanting to know what else was in store for her, just in case.

"Let me think...well, hundreds of tails on humans have been documented since the 1800s. This is from our distant relatives, the reptiles." Gordon smiled, seeing that Eve was pondering the thought.

"What kind of tail?"

"Well, there are pictures on the Internet. Hahaha," Gordon chucked. "There are also webbed fingers that look more like claws. The fingers look almost fused together. I think if I remember correctly, they are called syndactyly ectrodactyly and they say it is a link to our ancient ancestors that were commingling with reptilian aliens."

"What! Are you serious?" Eve asked, turning her body so he couldn't see her face as she adjusted a few of the bolts, oiling them until she could turn them freely.

"Well, I'm not so sure I believe all that, but I remember reading about a man in Houston, Texas, who was having chest pains and came into the emergency room. They found that he had a three-chambered heart like reptiles." Gordon said, enjoying the shocked look on Eve's face.

"Do you really believe that we are mixed with reptiles?" Eve asked, now really wondering, remembering the research they had done the previous year. Usually nothing really surprised her, but she was thrown off by this older man's easy attitude about it.

"Who knows for sure? But there are a lot of stories all around the world, in Japan, Greece, and South America—all talking of creatures in mythology and ancient texts. I think that mythology might be things that the people really did see at that time and wrote them down so the generations wouldn't forget. But so much time had passed that the new generations don't believe the stories that were passed down, instead thinking they are just myths."

"Yes, I'm with you—that seems to make more sense. Okay, I finished this side. I'll get the other side adjusted as well. Here's something for you…what do you know about Genetic Memory?" Eve asked.

"Not much…it's weird to think of. But I think the idea coincides with reincarnation. Kinda like we know things that we have never experienced or learned." Gordon said, looking under the wheelwell with his small light, making sure it was clean. "Think of it like this information is embedded in our psyche and is passed down for generations. We react to things that we have never been exposed to, because it has been in our genes so long. For instance, backing away from fire and not eating foods that are poisonous. It is part of a collective consciousness, like fear of certain predators or sense of taste. Do you think intelligence is passed down through genetics? Certain regions of the brain are under genetic control. Think about it as of today, the less time we spent on survival, the more our intelligence grew." Gordon said, climbing in the cab, "Come on—get in. Let's take her for a test drive."

Chapter 64

"It does make sense," Eve said, wondering about the child she would have and if the baby would be different. She took a breath and put her worries deep down inside her. Eve climbed in the cab and belted herself in the wraparound seat, putting on the computerized helmet. With the device she could see great distances and the information was recorded. When the vehicle was on Mars, the images would be sent back to Earth to be analyzed.

"Think about it," Gordon said, carefully backing the large vehicle out the hanger. He turned wide, driving slowly, heading toward the hilly testing area. "The DNA markers from the past show genetic evidence in our DNA. They found that 90 percent is junk DNA. The markers aren't understood yet. As time passes, I think we will understand more and it will show us what has been embedded or programmed into us. Because if you think about it, why is it there? If it's not used for anything? What do you think gives us the desire to go to space? And what is our fascination with Mars and gold?"

"That's a good question. Why do you think we are always looking up to space?" Eve asked.

"I know—I've wondered, too! What is inside of us that we sit here waiting for something to return?" He asked. "Working here makes you always think about space and the possibilities."

"Even the Bible talks about it. Revelation describes the second coming of Christ, talking of his return, coming back to Earth," Eve said pausing, "I sometimes think…could it be possible that these beings might have come from space? And maybe the people of the time didn't understand it. So they worshipped these space beings as gods or angels. I wonder if the Bible were read with that in mind, would people have a different point of view? As a society we are always looking for answers. You know like…Where did we come from? Where is that final link in our evolution? Was our planet visited in the past and in the process, the evolution of mankind projected forward by space beings tinkering with our DNA. And if so, why?"

"It's a lot to think about, child. We don't have to solve everything today! But slowly we are making progress. Look at us. This equipment will be going to Mars soon and the robots will remotely prepare a colony for humans to survive in. Wouldn't I love to be one of those people to first set foot on Mars. Think of the adventure!" Gordon said, moving slowly over some large boulders, watching his panel, making sure everything was working correctly.

"Yes, it does sound exciting! But scary! I heard they are taking applications to be on the team for the Mars One mission. It's a one-way trip," Eve said.

"Yes, I heard the same thing. I'm not sure what the name of the mission is; they keep changing it. In the past it has changed from going to really explore the moon, to going to Mars. It depends on the administration in the White House. It goes back and forth so we just adjust. But I think this time it won't change, because we are so close. You know it will take 240 days to get there. The ship has to be in the right position, when Earth and Mars are the closest. So, there is no quick there and back. But I think I heard that they will go to the moon first and then slingshot off to Mars. I would go, but they aren't looking for someone like me. Most likely young people that can still have children… a colony…wow! You know they are going to train them in Hawaii in a remote place. I guess the new ash is like the Martian surface," Gordon said.

"I read something about that…but I'm not so sure I share your excitement! I'm happy here on Earth," Eve stated. "And to never return! You know I read that space time is different than on Earth. The article I read said that 10 years here are equal to 108 years in space."

"Yes; I think they figured out a formula for that…something like velocity = v, speed of jet = w, speed of light= c," Gordon said, thoughtful as he drove down the embankment. He tested the hydraulic lift, moving it easily across the large rock face.

"Well, that could account for the space beings' ages." Eve said, adjusting her chair. "Here, let me try to drive her. Don't worry, I'll be careful with your baby."

Chapter 65

Gordon moved over to let Eve drive, then continued their conversation, "Okay, but be gentle—she's sensitive. How do you know the space beings' ages?" He asked, laughing at her. He paid attention to the monitors, watching her maneuvering up the side of a rocky cliff face, ready to take over if he saw her falter. The terrain testing site was near an abandoned mine.

"Well, from what I understand in the Old Testament of the Bible, people lived longer. Some were recorded to live 900 years. Then in the New Testament, the second half of the Bible (after Christ), people only lived maybe 100 years. I wonder if that has something to do with space travel and time in space. You know, because of the speed of light? For instance, if I went to Mars and returned a year later, about 40 years would have gone by on Earth."

Gordon was thoughtful, "Very interesting! What is your fascination with the Bible? Most scientists can't logically put creationism alongside their scientific theories."

"The way I see it, the Bible is more like historical documentation of that time period. I really believe that long ago, because of technology, the people might have misinterpreted events. It might have been space beings giving mankind information and reshaping their thinking," Eve said.

Gordon was quiet. "Okay, I see your point of view.... This I'll have to think on," he laughed.

"I've read a few things that I've been trying to understand. Why do civilizations around the world all have the same kind of ideas, when there wasn't communication between them? You know, things like the idea of gods returning, or the idea of reincarnation preparing the body after death for the afterlife. They have found mummies all over the world. Where would that come from? And you know the elongated skulls found in different places—at first they thought it was people wrapping the babies' heads. But after investigation, they think they were trying to imitate the gods," Eve said.

"I think there are a lot of discoveries that just add to mysteries instead of solving them. Maybe the idea of mummies was misinterpreted. The people could have seen the space beings preparing for space travel, going to sleep in the pods on a ship. Then they leave Earth and when they returned, the person is now awake. It all leaves us wondering about the past and searching for answers. Hey—did you know about the site that was discovered in 2011 in West Java, Indonesia?" Gordon asked.

"No, I don't," Eve said. "There is so much out there that we will never find the answers for."

"Don't worry, little bird! You're too young to have it hang over your head. We do what we can to discover the truth. I think you're young enough that you will see things develop in space that I won't be here to see," Gordon stated.

"Thanks, Gordon. I just worry about bringing a child

into this world." Eve said. Gordon patted her arm in a comforting gesture.

"You will be just fine! Now, listen about the discovery that was found in Indonesia. It's a step pyramid known as Gunung Padang, or 'Mountain of Light.' Anyhow, they found that a lava tube goes right up the middle and inside they found evidence that humans had been using it. They carbon dated it to 25,000 BC. It is the earliest civilization found and is blowing scientific minds. Head back toward the hanger. You're doing fine...she drives really smoothly, doesn't she?"

"Yes, I think we've done a good job with her. I like the way she can go sideways if she gets stuck going forward," Eve said.

"Well, the astronauts' lives are in our hands. We're going to have to check the air and the seals next to make sure they don't leak. I was told the astronauts need to be able to survive inside for weeks, because they will be exploring far away from the colony." Gordon said, "We have six vehicles to get ready."

"We'll get it done. I think we just haven't found much evidence of past civilizations because the flood got rid of a lot of evidence. But today, because of our latest technology, we have been able to see what is underground. Satellites have been finding all kinds of pyramids and ancient sites around the world," Eve said.

"I know; we're living in an exciting time. Ready? We're back—time for lunch." Gordon took over the controls, pulled inside, and shut off the engine.

"Yes, I'm hungry," Eve looked at her watch; time had passed quickly.

Chapter 66

After work, Eve and Scott had taken a plane to the Westchester County Airport in White Plains, New York, and caught an Uber to New Haven. Eve's heart quickened as the large, iron gate opened and she anticipated seeing her parents. It had been about six months and she really missed them both. Before they could get out of the car, the front door opened, illuminating the driveway with a warm glow. Eve jumped out before the driver had completely stopped, running into her parents' waiting arms. Scott laughed, shaking his head, and took care of the driver and the bags.

"Mom, you look so nice! You have a new haircut and color!" Eve said, touching her mother's highlighted shoulder-length hair. Turning, she hugged her father, admiring his perfectly pressed pants and dress shirt; it had always been his conservative attire. Eve smiled as she watched her parents hug Scott, pulling them both inside to the large great room. Extra chairs had been moved around the fireplace, making room for them. Sarah sat smiling at them; her long brown hair streaked with gray flowed down her back. Eve could see the dark red highlights reflecting from the dim glow of the embers.

"You kids look so vibrant and tan! I see Florida is doing you both well!" Janet said, patting a seat next to her, motioning for Eve to join her. Scott had put the bags at the bottom of the stairs and sat with a plate of food that had been set out on the table.

"What has been happening? What have you guys been working on?" Eve asked, looking around the circle at the people she loved the most.

"We've been trying to plan a trip to Egypt to the Pyramids and Sphinx. We want to see them for ourselves. A new chamber has been found; I think a large void was found inside above the King's Chamber. They say it is so large that the Statue of Liberty could fit laying down," Eve's mom said.

"That's wonderful!" Eve said, "That's an exciting trip!"

"I might want to go with you," said Sarah.

"Yes—come with us! Why don't we all go?" Janet said, looking around the circle.

"We would love to go!" Eve said, glancing at Scott, who winked at her between bites of a large sandwich. "I think I remember hearing about a psychic from the 1960s? I can't remember exactly, but he dreamed that there was a secret room under the right paw of the Sphinx. He said it held the records of man's real origin."

"In the past, they say information has came to people in dreams…it's almost like part of a person's brain is unlocked when their subconscious mind is at rest." Sarah said.

"I once read that the Sphinx is thousands of years older than the Pyramids. You know when they first found the Sphinx it was buried up to its neck? When it was uncovered, they found that the body was much larger in proportion to the head. After many years of considering the dilemma, researchers said that they believe that the head had been a dog." Scott said, smiling.

"How did you know that?" Eve said.

"I read! After being around all you big brains, I have been reading some archaeology magazines," Scott said. Everyone clapped, teasing him. He hadn't even thought about these kinds of things before Eve's parents had disappeared and he had helped with research. Scott almost fell off his chair laughing. "Also, the pyramids were built out of granite and granite has crystals. The top was a large quartz crystal. It does fall in with our theory, that the pyramids were some kind of power plant gathering energy and focusing it to space. Or maybe it was a signal that could be seen from Earth." Scott sat looking pleased with himself, happy that he had been able to contribute to the conversation, but it looked like the information provided was already a fact among this group. He sat back in his chair.

"You're so cute, Honey!" Eve said, kissing his cheek. "Here, let me get you some more food."

"What is happening with the…you know?" Michael asked. The room fell quiet, waiting for Eve's response. Scott was even watching her, wondering if this was the big reveal and he wouldn't be the first to know.

"Well…we've been working on it. I did find something out—I have RH negative blood." Eve proceeded to fill them in on what she had learned. After a few moments, they all looked in Sarah's direction. Her eyes were closed, and her fingers were on her forehead. Everyone waited and watched her open her eyes.

"It will be fine…I saw a child. But there was a haze over something that was blocking me…I couldn't see it clearly." Sarah looked at Eve and came by her side. She touched Eve's stomach and after a few moments she opened her eyes.

"Not yet...but soon," she said.

"Thank you, Sarah. That's great news." Eve said, looking down, realizing she was holding her breath and Scott's hand. She breathed slowly, looking into his eyes where all she could see was his love.

"Sarah...did you see the sex of the child?" Scott asked.

"No, I couldn't, but I saw blond hair and light eyes."

"Well, I'm sure it will be as beautiful as the mother," Scott said.

"Okay...okay! Now what have you guys been researching? I know you're up to something," Eve asked.

"Have you heard of the idea of Panspermia?" Janet asked, patting her husband's hand.

"You go ahead dear, you do tell a better story." Michael chuckled, knowing she loved being the one to deliver the updates.

"Okay, okay...Panspermia is the idea that our planet has been seeded from outer space. We are looking into the idea that bacteria and other living organisms have been transported by comets or meteorites to Earth, thus changing our DNA. Thoughts are that some viruses are brought to Earth this way and exposed to humans, changing us. It's kinda the idea that life exists throughout the universe," Janet stated.

"That's incredible! Are you saying that it was space beings doing it on purpose or this is the way life starts throughout the universe?" Eve asked, trying to understand.

"We haven't gotten that far. But we did find something that might prove the case. On August 19, 2014, on the outside of the International Space Station, they found living sea plankton. Now we know that sea plankton can survive in space, exposed to radiation and extremely low temperatures," Janet explained.

"So, what are you looking for?" Eve asked.

"The same thing. We wonder if this is the way life starts throughout the universe or if Earth selectively had help," Janet stated.

"It sounds fascinating!" Eve said, and yawned. "I think I need to get some rest; it's been a long day. Do you mind if we retire?"

"Not at all, dear...you know where your room is. We will see you both in the morning. Then we'll go shopping for your new place!"

"Mom, we don't have to do that—we both have jobs." Eve said, getting to her feet and signaling Scott to get a move on.

"We can just look. Anyhow, with a baby coming soon, we are going to need to at least look at furniture."

"Okay! We'll see you all in the morning!" Scott took Eve's hand and led her up the stairs to her large bedroom.

After they were gone, Eve's parents sat looking into the flames. "Okay, Sarah, what did you see? We've known you for a long time and can tell when you're hedging."

"Really...I wasn't sure. It was like looking through a fog. You know, where I could see shapes...but the child did look healthy. I'll have to meditate on it," Sarah said.

"Okay. We're just worried because we don't know what to expect with her being a Star Child," Janet said.

"I understand." Sarah excused herself and headed to her room.

"Come on, my beautiful wife, let's take to our beds; we want to make this a fun weekend for the kids," Michael said. The subject was dropped but the question lingered in all their minds.

chapter 67

Eve felt groggy and she smelled something foul. Struggling to wake, she pushed her mind to come to the surface of her subconscious. She had been dreaming and tried to open her eyes; loud noises rattled in her head and throughout her body. When she focused her eyes, she was able to see what was in front of her and her memory returned. She found herself shocked when she realized that it hadn't been a dream. Reality was now returning to haunt her. She had been taken! "Sarah!" Eve reached out with her mind, "Sarah—help!"

Eve felt a crash as she was jolted forward and thrust side-to-side, bumping her head. Then an eerie silence surrounded her. She opened her eyes and searched the darkness, trying to see anything moving in the void of light. Shutting her eyes tightly, wishing that she was wrong, she tried not to panic. Moments later a door burst open, illuminating the space. The pair of robots rolled in the room, quickly adjusting monitors and pushing buttons on a computer screen. The glass covering her face popped open and Eve could feel moist air dampening her skin, making her hair cling to one side of her face. An IV was removed and the top of the capsule holding her opened. For a moment she just lay there trying to get her bearings, looking around the room. Four other capsules were open as well and she noticed some slow movement. All were wrapped like mummies with white jumpsuits covering almost all of their skin. Each body had been completely covered except for their eyes. They all looked around the room and at each other, slowly starting to remove the wraps covering their faces. Eve followed suit, finding her hands were stiff and her mouth was dry. It took her a moment to uncover her hair and sit up.

There were two young women; one was blond and the other had brown, wavy hair. They were petite and about the same size. A dark-haired man sat between them; he wasn't much larger and had a handsome face with a goatee. The last was a large man who looked to be struggling getting the wrap off his head. He was rubbing his knees that had been cramped inside his enclosure. As the gauze came off, Eve noticed the dark curly hair—it was Scott!

"Scott! Scott!" She screeched; her voice was hoarse, but she found him looking at her in recognition. He seemed disorientated, not understanding where he was.

"Eve…what is this? Where are we?" Scott asked. Tears fell down Eve's cheeks and she struggled to get out of her wrapping. She stripped the extra material off and ran to him, circling her arms around him and holding on tight.

The others were looking at the couple, wondering who they were. They had practiced with a certain team for the past three years. The blond girl stood, testing her legs, and then helped the other two astronauts untangle themselves. She went to a panel on the wall and started a check, making sure the oxygen levels of the craft were running correctly. Then she turned to look at the strangers.

"Who are you?" She asked. "Why are you here?"

"We could ask you the same question." Eve said, "I'm Eve and this is my husband, Scott. We don't know why we are here and when you say here...where is here?" Eve asked, not liking the girl's attitude.

Scott patted Eve's back, trying to calm her, but inside he was freaking out a little, seeing he was in a spaceship and Eve's necklace had started to glow with her anger. He was afraid any moment her space father might pop in and cause more of a problem.

"What! You really don't know?" The blond woman asked, looking at the others. "Okay, since it looks like we are in this together, let's first introduce ourselves. I'm Britney, the Commander of this ship. This is Courtney, she's a doctor and scientist and that Italian stallion over there is Markus, he's electronics and technical. To answer your question as of where we are..." She laughed, "We just landed on the rim of the dark side of the Moon."

"What! It can't be!" Eve yelled.

"Well, for some reason you both were switched out with the two other men that were members of our team. So, I'm sitting here wondering if you're an asset or a hindrance on this mission. Because if you haven't been training, I'm not sure what we are going to do with you. I wonder why we weren't told." Britney said, eyeing them like it was their fault.

"Well, we aren't sure of our value here or why we were kidnapped and put on board," Eve said.

"Who would do this?" Scott asked. "It would have to be someone with a lot of power."

"We'll get to the bottom of it." Eve said, now mad as she started to pace. She could feel the stone in her necklace start to warm and she told herself to calm down. Eve wasn't ready to show outsiders or strangers her father's power; she didn't really understand it yet herself. She moved her hand to the heavy gold and covered the stone with her fingers until it cooled.

"Come on with us. We have a procedure that we need to go through and might need your help, seeing we are missing two of our team," Britney said.

chapter 68

Eve and Scott followed the small group, leaving the room with the sleeping pods, and found their way to the control center. The robots were already fast at work, racing around the room on their speedy wheels. They both stopped when the group entered and stood awaiting their orders.

"Proceed," Britney said, and Eve and Scott watched as both robots went back, moving quickly, doing their jobs. Eve and Scott looked around the compact room full of equipment and watched everyone work.

"Let me give you a rundown about the moon," Courtney said, talking as she checked some of the levels on a large panel. "The surface is scarred with evidence of collisions from meteors that have crashed to the surface for around 4.5 billion years. It has no oxygen or atmosphere. When the first astronauts landed on the moon, they went back inside the ship after gathering their samples. They found that their suits were covered in moon dust that was moist and clinging to their clothes. It was deep gray and very fine-grained and clingy; when they took off their helmets there was a smell in the air of the cabin. It was described by Buzz Aldrin as the smell of a 'firecracker after it has gone off.' The fear was that the moon dust might be explosive once oxygen hit it. So the team did their own experiment and found that it wasn't chemically reactive. By the time they reached Earth, the smell was gone. But the night they spent in the ship, on the moon, the astronauts slept in their suits with gloves and helmets on just in case the air was toxic," Courtney said.

"Wow—I didn't know that!" Eve said, thinking it was incredible the things that she didn't know and enjoyed learning.

"Yes, we have came a long way in the past 50 years," Courtney explained.

"Yes, we have!" Britney said, "At the time, thoughts were that the dust on the moon might be so deep that the lunar module and astronauts could sink and not be able to be retrieved. As you might remember from Earth Science class, the moon is a quarter the size of Earth and because of its slow rotation, there is 41 percent of the moon that can never be seen from Earth. Also, the moon can cover the sun, forming an eclipse. But the sun is exactly 400 times larger than the moon, and can appear in the sky the same size. It also has a perfect circular orbit."

"I didn't know that," Eve said, thoughtful. "Okay, I would like to know the mission we're on and the reason Scott and I are here. Are we harvesting rocks? Or checking the dark side for aliens? I heard the moon rocks brought back to Earth were fine grained basalt."

"As astronauts, our minds have to be open to the possibilities. Don't worry—we'll get to the bottom of it. For now, we need to move to our transport area. Come on—follow me, time is limited. We have a small window of time to make contact because of where we have landed." Britney said.

They moved to the bottom of the ship and entered a room that held six vehicles and were motioned to enter the one closest to the rear door.

"Scott, these are the transports that Gordon and I have been working on." Eve said, puzzled. "That's weird. Why are they here? I thought they were on the way to Mars."

Markus overheard her, "They are on their way to Mars.… We all are."

"What! That can't be!" Scott said, shocked. "What is happening?"

"I'm not sure why we have been kidnapped! Why would someone think we could help on this mission? But I might have an idea," Eve said.

Deep inside, the realization had started to hit her. She knew that it might be because of the information she had given to the President. She remembered the man that had showed up many times after she planted the video and tried to get her to join his company. He had said his company had government contracts with NASA, and he was working with them on the Space Station. But Eve hadn't really listened, happy with her position already with NASA. She leaned over and whispered in Scott's ear, telling him what she was thinking. Scott patted her hand, trying to calm her anxiety. He knew she was feeling guilty, thinking this situation was her fault.

"Don't worry! We are in this together. You did the right thing and it will be okay," Scott said.

"There must be a reason," Courtney said, overhearing them. "Don't worry! There has to be a explanation. We'll find out soon enough."

"But the human mission to Mars was to go next, after

we send robots to build the colony on the surface first," Eve raised her voice, frustrated.

"Well, someone high up changed the plan." Britney said, "Look on the walls! We were told two weeks ago that the mission was going early, and we had to train quickly on basic robotics."

Eve and Scott looked to where she was pointing and saw 20 seven-foot robots hanging on hooks stored for the journey.

"Well, we can't go! They can't take us against our will!" Eve said. "We want to go back to Earth!"

"Sorry—you're going to have to put that out of your head, because this is a one-way mission. In about twenty hours we will be in the right position to slingshot from the moon to Mars. It is the closest point," Courtney said.

"This is not happening!" Eve said. "What are we going to do?" She asked Scott.

"I don't know! One-way mission! They have to have lost their minds!" Scott yelled and felt his pulse beating rapidly in his chest. He caught Eve's eyes and knew something was about to happen and pushed back his fear. He didn't want her necklace to blow them up and kill them all. He softened his voice and moved to trying to calm her.

"I'm not sure but we'll figure it out. Honey, relax for now, let's just help them do what they need to accomplish right now. They are short-handed and might really need our help." Scott locked her eyes with his. "We'll find a way out of this," he whispered in her ear.

"Okay," Eve saw the love in his eyes and thought as long as they were together, she would be okay. She followed suit and strapped herself in her seat inside the modular vehicle. She noticed that they could have fit three more people.

chapter 69

Britney was up front trying to turn over the engine and Eve noticed she was struggling, not familiar with the procedure. Gordon would have been upset with her heavy-handed approach to his baby girl. Eve smiled, thinking of what he would say.

"Switch places," Eve ordered. Courtney and Markus watched, knowing how Britney would respond to giving up the controls.

"I don't think you're qualified to drive; we can't have anything happen. We will need everything on this ship for us to be able to survive on Mars," Britney stated.

"Chill, girlfriend! Glide to the side! I helped design this ride," Eve said. The astronauts looked at each other in silent communication. "Scott, check the seals around the doors to make sure they are sealed correctly; we have to make sure there aren't any leaks," Eve ordered.

"They look good, Honey. Don't forget your seatbelt," Scott said, as he tightened his.

Scott trusted his intelligent wife to be in control of this situation. He hoped she didn't have to knock Britney out, because if the astronaut didn't listen, he wasn't sure what Eve would do. The reluctant commander hesitated. Markus nodded at her and gave up his seat in the front; he moved to the second row beside Scott. After everyone was strapped in, Eve gently started the engine and listened as it purred perfectly.

Beside her, Britney ordered, "On board Command, open the hatch." The sound of pumps fizzed and the ship's hatch slowly started to rise. The team looked out from their seated positions into an abyss that was void of light. Finding the truck's headlights, Eve pulled out and watched the door close behind them. She listened to the airlocks as they went back in place and the room filled with oxygen before she pulled out.

"Okay, where to?" Eve asked Britney. She watched the astronaut study a monitor in silence and pointed in the direction of total darkness. Nothing could be seen outside the dim glow from the headlights; they would have to trust the computer.

Courtney from the backseat was looking at a handheld GPS device. "It isn't far; we landed right on target. It is about 100 yards to the west," she said, pointing in the direction.

Eve moved across the uneven ground and found herself along the ridge of an enormous crater. Slowly she moved forward, keeping the truck pointed in the direction she was told.

"Okay, here we go…by the way—where are we going?" Eve asked.

"We are going to a space station, an outpost on the dark side of the moon. What, you didn't get the classified memo?" Britney said, sarcastic.

This girl was getting on Eve's nerves and she tried not to let the little blond know that her bossy, negative attitude was getting under her skin. "When did we put a space station on the moon?" Eve asked, suppressing her emotions, now surprised.

"I think it had to be the late seventies; that was when we were last on the moon as far as we know. They said the reason was the lack of broadcasted missions to the moon. But we think there were weird things happening on the moon. We were told when the astronauts first landed in 1969, they saw spaceships on the edge of the crater, like they were being watched. Also, there were structures—like obelisks or spires that were too tall to be natural. One was about 15 stories high," Britney said.

"One of the missions in the seventies found a base that wasn't ours. It went inside to underground tunnels and looked like it had been recently abandoned. The astronauts discovered that energy was running throughout but they didn't see anyone. They noticed high peaks on the landscape and thought they resembled the ancient pyramids and structures in Egypt. On closer inspection, they found tunnels close to the largest formation, where it led down under the surface of the moon for about three miles," Markus said from the back seat.

"What they found inside was a shock! It was full of semimodern equipment and some technology we had never seen before and didn't know how to use. Some of the advanced technology was brought back to Earth and reverse engineered. At first, we thought the Russians had been to the moon before us. But samples were taken of the fuel from one of the crafts that was left behind. From what we heard, a new element was found, one that we didn't have yet on the periodic table. So, it couldn't have been the Russians," Courtney continued.

"I wonder how much the governments around the world really know and hide from the main population," Scott said.

"I know...we were briefed last week, most likely because we aren't coming back. The new element is called McMoscovium 115. It is unstable and only stays together for a few seconds. But it is the same element that Bob Lazar said he worked on in Area 51. It affects gravity by producing its own gravitational energy that surrounds the ship, creating distortion and allowing the craft to move forward and side-to-side. It's a kind of anti-gravitation proportion," Courtney said.

Eve looked back at Scott, catching his eye, starting to understand more why she might be there. She slowly meandered over the landscape; the moon dust wasn't much of a problem, but on the rim of the crater, she could feel them slide a little. Eve knew she needed to be careful so that they didn't get stuck. Up ahead the lights picked up something large in the darkness. It grew in size the closer they got to it and Eve noticed the weathered stones now devastated from asteroids. But it was still magnificent! They all sat for a moment in silence, admiring the powerful structures, realizing they were among the few to see them.

"I wonder if these structures have been used to produce energy like the ones in Egypt. Interesting!" Eve slowed down. "Okay, Courtney—where now?" Eve asked.

"Around the right side of that big one. There should be an opening in the side—that's what we were told," she said.

"Okay, here we go." They rounded the corner and Eve thought she saw something out of the corner of her eye—a flash of light? She put it down to nerves and soon found the large cavelike entrance in the backside of the weathered pyramid.

chapter 70

"We are to pull inside and then move forward on foot when we can't drive any farther," Courtney said.

Eve could feel the tension inside the cab while everyone wondered what would happen next. She pulled inside and could feel the surface change as they moved down the large smooth cavern. Everyone was silent while they looked through the blackness, only seeing where the vehicle's lights would allow them to see. Eve stopped when she couldn't move any farther; the tunnel had narrowed, and they found themselves in a large cavern. In the center were huge stone pillars that formed a circle. Around the sides of the cavern the space was full of discarded machinery parts—spaceships? Everything was covered in a layer of thick moon dust. The party sat looking at the remains of a civilization, trying to figure out what it all meant. The headlights reflected off the shapes that formed the circle, their tops reaching high above the group's line of sight, covered in darkness. The equipment didn't look familiar; it was unlike anything they had seen on Earth. The metal was a weird color with a seamless surface, making them all wonder.

Britney broke the silence, "Okay…ah…let's prepare to leave the truck. We have a job to do."

Eve and Scott looked at each other. They had never been in a spacesuit before. They knew they had to make the best of this situation, because even with being unfamiliar with how the suits worked, Scott and Eve weren't about to be left behind. They struggled with their suits, finding them tight. They clearly had been made to fit each astronaut. The ones that they were replacing must have been a lot shorter. Markus made his rounds, checking to make sure that everything was in the right place.

"Now when I put the helmet on your head, don't panic! You won't be able to breathe at first, but it just takes a moment and a mixture of oxygen and nitrogen will fill your suit. You also will be able to communicate with each other; the devices are like a bluetooth that I'm now putting in your ears. Scott, we'll put yours on first," Markus stated.

Scott saw Eve hesitate, "It's the same kind of mixture that goes into a dive tank and I'm sure the O ring is in place," Scott said, and watched Markus nod. "See, all will be fine—you can do this," Scott reassured Eve.

Eve had been nervous for Scott and then remembered he was an athlete and a certified diver and thought she had better worry about herself. She could feel her heart beat harder as the helmet was placed on her head. But soon she was able to breathe normally. The young astronauts rechecked each other and then Scott and Eve. Once Markus was satisfied, they all moved toward the door.

"Ready?" Britney asked. Everyone nodded and Eve pushed the air release button on the door. It opened, allowing them all to get out. Once on the ground, everyone was instructed to take a few steps and get used to the change in gravity. They soon found they were going to be able to walk with ease. Some needed more weight and Courtney strapped a small weight belt around their ankles. Then she proceeded to put up her hand and motioned for everyone to line up. They were to place one hand on the person's shoulder in front of them. Everyone moved through the darkness with just the lights from their helmet units showing the way. They passed the stone circle and came to a large doorway that was about 15 feet tall and entered, following the chamber, going farther underground.

Eve noticed the walls here were covered in Egyptian hieroglyphics as they passed; the colors were still vibrant, and she saw that many were painted in scenes of everyday life. Eve wondered what was so important that they had put the images in stone. *What messages were these beings trying to tell them?* Some of the ancients were depicted taller than the others. Eve took a breath, remembering the research that they had done last year. Some of the ideas were still hard for her to believe. Eve wondered what these inscriptions said and fumbled with her outside pocket where she had put her cellphone. She knew there wasn't an Internet connection but found the camera still worked and she snapped a few pictures, then flipped it to video, filming as they walked. No one said anything, so she continued taking pictures and gathering as much information as possible. Eve hoped one day she would be able to show her parents. She felt a pang of sadness with the thought of never seeing them again and put it to the back of her mind.

chapter 71

The group came to the end of the long hall. Eve wasn't sure how far they had gone underground because it was slow moving in the suits. She was sure they must be carrying around 100 pounds including the air tanks, which were the size and shape of a small briefcase. They all stopped at once and Eve watched Courtney produce a code that she typed into a keypad on the outside of a large door. Everyone stepped back, waiting to see what would happen. They heard a rumbling noise and a hiss of airflow when the huge piece of stone started to roll from the entrance and stopped in place on the right side, allowing them to enter.

Once they were inside the room, the space started to lighten, illuminating around them. They turned off the headlights on their suits, wanting to save energy.

"It has an internal energy source," Eve said. "I wonder what kind it is? It reminds me of Malta." Eve looked at Scott to see what he thought. The room was now full of glowing light coming from the crystals in the walls.

"That's what I was just thinking," Scott said.

"I wonder where everyone is?" Courtney asked, "I thought we were told that this base was active, and someone would be here to greet us."

"Look over here," Britney said, as they all gathered around a clear, dust-free panel of controls. "Should we flip it on?"

"Yes. We have to contact NASA," Courtney said.

"Why didn't we hear from them after we landed?" Eve asked.

"They said it would be hard depending on where we landed. The dark side of the moon doesn't face the satellite," Markus said. "That's why our orders were to come inside and make contact." He turned toward Scott and Eve. "I'm not sure if you know, but from Earth we only see about 58 percent of the moon."

"Yes—that we understand," Scott said

"Also, the weather on the moon varies. The side facing the sun can be around 253° F and on the dark side as cold as –243° F," Markus said.

"Then it's weird that the temperature inside this room seems comfortable," Scott stated.

"I know—that's what I was thinking. I wonder what's controlling it. Maybe that's why we're underground. I'm sure you know the moon controls the tides and Earth's tilt make life possible—without it we might not be here," Courtney said.

"There have been many questions about the moon. Mostly where did it come from and how was it formed… I'm sure you remember the theory that at some point Earth was hit by a large meteorite that broke off part of Earth. It formed the moon and then it got caught in Earth's gravitational orbit. But new wild theories have been around that say because of the moon's perfect distance from Earth and its orbit being as it is, that it was placed exactly where it is… making life flourish on Earth," Markus said.

"What do you mean 'placed'?" Scott asked.

"Tests were taken to figure out how old the moon is, and it has been determined that it is as old as the universe, messing up the meteorite theory. Now thoughts are that it was towed through the universe and put where it is now. That it is a giant space station or has been hollowed out," Markus said.

"Why hollow?" Scott asked, enjoying the exchange with this knowledgeable man.

"On one of the Apollo missions when they were leaving the moon, they decided to drop their lunar vehicle back to the surface to see what would happen. When they dropped it, the sound of a bell was heard ringing for over an hour. Then on a different Apollo mission, they had decided to drop a heavier one when leaving. It sounded like a gong and echoed for three hours. Crazy, right?" Markus laughed. "I just don't know the answers that mankind is looking for, but maybe we can help solve some of the questions that we all want to know."

"That's really interesting, Markus. Thanks for telling me—I didn't realize that," Scott said.

chapter 72

Their attention was drawn back to the others after their deep conversation. Britney flipped the switches. The panels started to light up. She stood in front of a camera; she had connected to the main computer and waited. Soon a rasping noise could be heard sounding like they were in a wind tunnel. A clear voice echoed over the background noise.

"Greetings! Is all well?" The voice asked.

"Yes! We are all fine," Britney stated; in the background, they could hear a cheer go up. "Just one question…what happened to the rest of my team?" Britney said, looking over her shoulder at Eve and Scott.

"What do you mean?" The voice on the other end asked.

"For some reason two of my team members were replaced. We are standing here now with two people who haven't been through any training and aren't prepared to make the journey to Mars," Britney stated.

"What do you mean? I wasn't advised…hold on." The connection broke and then the voice was back a few moments later. "Let me see them." Britney moved to the side and Scott and Eve took her place.

"Could you tell me your names, please?" The voice asked.

"Eve and Scott Alexander. Why were we taken from our home in the middle of the night and put aboard your ship? And now I'm told we are going on a one-way trip to Mars! This is unacceptable! I would like to know who has the authority to kidnap us and send us away without our consent!" Eve yelled. Scott reached over, took her hand, and cut in.

"Look, legally it is against the law to do what has been done to us and you're going to have to come up with a solution because we have a life on Earth, and we want to come back." Scott said, pushing Eve behind him.

"Well, son, there's nothing that can be done now. In 18 hours, the ship is leaving with or without you both on board. You get on the ship or you stay for a long time on the moon. I don't think there are supplies to keep you both alive for 50 years!"

"How come no one knows we have a base on the moon? No one has been here for about 50 years...right? What is this place and what country runs it?" Eve asked.

"This outpost is a secret because...put it this way, we didn't build it." The voice vibrated.

"Who built it? The Russians?" Eve asked.

"Well...no one from Earth built it." There was silence in the room while everyone realized what the voice was saying. "Some have said that the moon is a large spaceship, put in place to rotate around Earth 4.5 billion years ago, making it possible for life to exist as we know it. Without the moon Earth would be wobbly on its axis and it would cause devastating weather that would make it almost impossible for advanced lifeforms to exist. Others have said that it is an ancient satellite from an advanced civilization that was once on Earth. But whatever it is, we never stay long. It has been determined that they allow us to come to the moon, but are never far away. So, I suggest that you now go back to the ship and get a good night's rest, because you leave tomorrow."

"One last question," Eve asked. "Who has the power to put us on this ship?"

"I'm sorry, the orders came from high up, from the President's office. Okay—get going. We will be in communication in 12 hours, when we will be able to help your ship get on its way."

"I think I now understand why…I knew it," Eve whispered to Scott. "The information that I gave to the President. I believe he thinks that I would be an asset to this mission because of…you know. No wonder the owner of that space tech company with the expendable pods was trying to get me to come work for him. I think he was planning to send people to Mars on his own and then joined forces with NASA. The President is not taking no for an answer. We have to think of a workaround, because I'm not spending the rest of my life on a dead planet. I'm sure the reason you were brought along was to make me do their bidding. My parents are going to be worried when they can't reach us." Eve was starting to stress and could feel the necklace start to pulsate with burning heat. She didn't want any incidents happening, so she tried to control her emotions.

"It will be all right." Scott took her hand and followed the others back in the direction that they had come.

chapter 73

Something didn't feel right. Eve kept thinking she heard something. She felt she was being pulled mentally to the other end of the room with the large stone pillars, moving her in a different direction, toward a dark hall. "I need to check something out; it won't take long," Eve said, and the team stopped to look at her. "Look, we have time. He said 12 hours."

"But I think we really should get back," Courtney said. "What if the ones that built this place are really still around?"

"This won't take long. How many times are we going to get a chance to check out a colony on the moon that is from space beings?" Eve said, leading the way.

The group hesitated and then followed Eve to an opening that looked down into a large cavern. It was filled with log-sized quartz crystals. Eve could feel a hum in the air from the transferred energy. When she touched one of the crystals, they all started to illuminate, lighting the room. It was so bright Eve was almost blinded and flipped the golden visor on her helmet over her face.

"Your visors!" She yelled and everyone followed suit. She knew the covers must be lined with gold to reflect the radiation. The sound was familiar. "This reminds me of Malta," Eve stated. As the words left her lips, Scott too could feel the hum of hertz frequency; the static was making his hair stand up inside his helmet.

"Oh lord, here we go! Take my hand...quickly!" Eve shouted, and Scott tightly grabbed ahold of her arm. The others started to rush forward, seeing their distress. Eve put up her hand to stop them and they stood frozen in place. "Hold on tight!" Eve yelled above the sound of rushing air that was moving them off their feet. A thick gray fog surrounded Eve and Scott. They were propelled into the air and started rapidly spinning, faster and faster. When they stopped, they were in a lit stone room. Around the edges they could make out tall, light, transparent glowing creatures that just stood there watching them. Their heads were larger, their big eyes were ice blue, their skin and long hair was white. Eve noticed that they were waiting for orders and stood with blank looks on their faces as if listening to something.

She could feel the heat on her chest and put her hand to untuck the necklace, then remembered that it wasn't possible because it was inside her spacesuit. A large, 15-foot being moved forward to stand in front of her.

"Daughter! What are you doing here?" He asked. The room was quiet, waiting for her to answer. But she didn't have to say anything; she could feel him in her mind. "I see."

"Father, is it really you?" A childlike voice screeched like a dolphin, echoing off the walls. Scott gripped her arm tight. He knew for some reason to maintain physical contact with her for fear that otherwise he would lose her.

"Yes! It is I," the being replied. Eve reached her free hand toward the large being, pulling Scott along with her across the room. Her other hand found the being's and when she touched him, Scott felt a surge of energy flow through his body as well. He held on. "Child, it has been so long; one day we will be together again."

"I know, Father…I have my mission to help the humans move forward. Why are we helping them with knowledge? Is it an experiment? Or are we preparing them for the future with us?"

"You will know in time…you have to understand. We have been watching them for a very long time. Grooming them, preparing them, teaching them. Some disagree with what we are trying to do. They fear with the humans free will, they will destroy themselves and the planet along with them. Then the past will repeat itself," he stated.

"Father…I just want to go home to Earth until my work is finished," Eve said.

"I know you love them as we have grown to. Some have an inner goodness. But there are others that are filled with evil, causing the dilemma that we argue with the others about," he explained.

"Yes, Father, I do love them." Eve said, thinking of Scott and her family, but also thinking of this being in front of her.

"Daughter…you have to understand that there was a time thousands of years ago when we lived openly on Earth among the humans. But some disagreed with the treatment of them. You see…we are a highly intelligent people, and some were using the humans for slaves to mine resources. Others were using them for research, genetically tinkering with their DNA and also mixing them with different species found on Earth, trying to make them more efficient for our work. But some were falling in love with mankind and having children with them, causing all kinds of problems.

"At one point my people started to disagree with the treatment and it prompted a war among our people and the others that had come from different places. Many were interested in this young planet you call Earth. The war was so great, because of the power that we held, that it went out into the solar system. The war found its way to Mars, where a nuclear bomb was dropped. It caused an electric current so great that it scarred the planet, making it uninhabitable for life to survive there. But worst of all, at one time there was a planet between Mars and Jupiter. It was totally destroyed around the same time, creating a meteor belt," he said.

Eve was thoughtful. "Yes, like in the Icelandic legends of Ragnarok," Eve said, wondering how she knew that. "I remember the stories, talking of rocks of fire raining from the sky on Earth's surface. It said something like 'Earth was turned upside down.'"

"Something like that…yes, Daughter, you do remember! This is why you must go with these humans to Mars; without you they won't discover what they must. Besides the moon, this is their first stop, moving them into the solar system." He touched her helmet, looking at her face, for a moment looking into her eyes. "You always were special." He looked in Scott's direction and back at Eve. "You have chosen well…. Now go!"

"Yes, Father…until we meet again." Eve and Scott stepped away and disappeared back into the haze. They found themselves in the same crystal room that they had left. The energy had moved from the room, making just a dim glow off the walls that led them back to the others. The three astronauts were still as the pair had left them, frozen in time. Eve touched each of them, watching their eyes open with questions.

"You guys ready to go to the ship?" Eve said. They all blinked with confusion and followed Scott and Eve to the vehicle.

chapter 74

At Eve's parents' house in New Haven it was the middle of the night. The house was awoken to the sound of banging on the front door. Feeling alarmed, the couple jumped up, dressing quickly, running downstairs to the door. They wondered how anyone had gotten in the gates. Michael was sure he had turned on the alarm. The knocking continued and he fumbled with the locks, opening the door as Sarah Smiles rushed inside.

"Sarah! What's happening? Why are you here?" Janet asked. "What is it?"

Sarah was out of breath. "I came as soon as I knew," she babbled. "It's Eve! She and Scott have been taken."

chapter 75
space

That night everyone went to bed early, not knowing what the next day might bring. Every detail had been planned for them and all the team had to do was follow the procedures. Eve and Scott just followed what the others directed.

Eve had hung a sheet around Scott's sleeping pod for privacy and got in with him. It was cramped but she felt comfort in his embrace and cuddled up close.

"I'm so glad you're here! I couldn't do this alone. I'm just really worried about my parents. Time in space is different than time on Earth. I'm not sure I totally understand how it works. Scientists say that time can slow down when traveling the speed of light, making time go faster. Like a time warp? What are we going to do? I have to get back to them and from my calculations, once we get to Mars, we will have to wait almost two years until we are aligned with Earth where the distance is the shortest. It will take us about eight months to reach Mars from the moon," Eve whispered.

"Damm…eight months! Boy, we have a problem! I wonder if your friend at NASA could help?" Scott said, trying to help solve their dilemma.

"Yes—you're right! Gordon would help me! You know… I wonder if he installed communication systems in the vehicles. Gordon had said that he was working on it for emergencies, but I'm not sure if he got it approved through channels in time. He told me we needed to make the vehicles totally self-sufficient, able to keep the astronauts alive for long amounts of time. Because if something happened while they were out, it would give the others a chance to rescue them. His thoughts were in case of trouble while out exploring. The only problem is, if he did install something, he would have to turn it on from his end before it could work. I think it was an experiment that he hadn't told NASA about. I just remember him working on something. But I'm not sure because we were so rushed to have all six trucks prepared and tested in time. So I don't know if he did it," Eve said.

"Okay…that's an idea. So how about after we're in space, we check each of them. Maybe he did do it," Scott said. He rubbed her back, trying to comfort her, feeling it was a long shot.

"But how do we contact him? To get him to turn it on?" Eve pondered, her mind looking for a workaround.

"I have an idea!" Scott sat up, almost bumping his head. "How about you mentally focus on Sarah and send a message?"

"Yes! You're right! I could tell her to go to him." Eve said, excited, and kissed him. "I'll work on that! I'm not so good at that telepathy thing, but I will really try!"

"I know you can do it…I've seen you in action. By the way, what did you think about the idea of the moon being a spacecraft or satellite?" Scott asked, "I wasn't sure."

"Well, you have to wonder why the moon's craters are so uniform. The depth looked about the same. What do you think? It could be a metallic barrier? I thought it was interesting about the gong and sound waves that came from it."

"I know—it shows how much we don't know," Scott said.

"And the complex underground was something. Did you see the large granite stone blocks and how they fit together? They were perfectly smooth and aligned like the pyramids. Well…from what I read in books about the pyramids." Eve said, feeling sad as she thought of the upcoming trip to Egypt they had planned. She tried not to cry when she thought of her family.

"I also read about a couple of Russian scientists that wrote a book called 'Is the moon the creation of intelligence?' The thesis of the book was that the moon is an artificial Earth satellite, put into orbit around Earth by some intelligent beings," Eve said, smiling.

"Honey, you're so smart!" He teased. "Hey—I remember something. I'm not sure where I got this…I could be wrong. But it was suggested by one of my professors that the moons that circle Mars aren't moons at all…I think. What was it? Oh yes…the larger of the two is called Phobos. It is about ten miles long and goes around Mars twice a day. And Deimos is the other moon and half the size…I think it is about five miles long and goes around Mars once a day. Anyhow, they circle Mars right at the equator. It has been suggested that they are both ancient satellites," Scott said.

"I didn't know that. So maybe it is possible that the moon might be the same. If my (space) father was speaking the truth about human origin alongside theirs and what happened, maybe they did have advanced technology in the past and it was lost when they went underground for the last Ice Age. The ancient Sanskrit texts from India even have diagrams of the solar system. When I was studying and doing my research for my dissertation on antigravitation, I found diagrams in the ancient texts that looked like a system of flowing magnetism that encircled the craft, allowing them to overcome gravity," Eve said.

chapter 76

They were both silent for a few minutes, then Scott suggested, "I wonder if your being father was telling the truth about mankind destroying themselves in the past. Almost like a bottleneck, where mankind was made to start over or reboot. Maybe that is around the time when the Neanderthals who were larger and stronger disappeared. Science hasn't been able to explain their disappearance when they were on Earth at the same time. But maybe that is around the time when advanced science and technology was lost." Scott said, watching to see if Eve understood what he was saying.

"I know—that makes me think about the reason space beings wanted us to evolve. I think there were different groups of aliens experimenting and mixing their DNA with ours. Instead we need to look at things from a different perspective and then we might be able to understand the different possibilities. It is hard for us to imagine, because it seems like such a large task. But yes…we need to try to understand what their goal is for humankind. They could have set up satellites that helped control the planets, making them habitable. I remember a different theory about the moon, saying it had been towed into rotation around Earth. Maybe that is really what happened." Eve was thoughtful, wondering what they would discover on Mars.

"I know it's hard to understand because our minds question if it could be possible to do something so great. It makes us doubt. But look at me…I wouldn't have ever believed it possible, or understood even what a star child or hybrid was, if I hadn't done the research with you and saw these beings myself." Scott said, pulling her close. "But I'm so glad I did." Scott laughed and held her tight, not wanting to let go. "I knew being with you would never be dull!"

"I love you, Scott! Without you I would never have had the courage to accept who I really am." She snuggled closer and put her face in his neck.

"Try to rest—we don't know what will happen tomorrow," Scott said.

"Yes, you're right." Eve closed her eyes and tried to put her worry aside.

Scott lay there for hours feeling her warmth; he knew when she fell asleep. He couldn't rest. His mind wouldn't turn off. He looked out the window blankly into the darkness. He now questioned everything he knew and wondered about their future. What if it wasn't possible to go home? He knew that if they didn't leave Mars quickly, by the time they reached Earth their families would most likely be dead. Then what was the point of going back?

He reached deep in his mind, trying to remember something he had learned in one of his history classes. He recalled his professor saying that there was a time around 5 BC when the Romans had written a text referring to a time before the moon. His teacher had said that the Hebrew

Bible also described a time before the moon was in place in the sky. Some legends stated that the moon was put there to keep an eye on humans. He remembered the story of Moses and that he had described the curve of Earth as if he had looked down upon it from the heavens. This was a time before they discovered that Earth was round. Scott laughed to himself. He knew that the answers to those questions would most likely be thought of as myths. But now he understood that with myths there was most likely a seed of truth in all of them.

He suddenly sat up, pushing Eve off of him and focused out the window, his heart racing. He thought he had seen something. There it went again, he was sure this time. He saw lights and reflections on the moon's surface. He watched the flashes and streaks before they disappeared. Yes, he remembered there was activity on the dark side of the moon. He calmed down. Of course there was activity—he had just met some of them. Scott stayed where he was, watching as the lights faded and the window was left to darkness, making him question if he had really seen something. But deep down, he now knew that they were not alone, that the human race wasn't as special as humans had thought. He was sure there were other goldilocks areas out there where life was possible. Humans would be fools to think that they were the only intelligent lifeform. Scott closed his eyes and focused on images of Earth in his head, hoping someday to return.

chapter 77

The ship lifted off right on time; they had no complications. The team trusted that the calculations had been done correctly—NASA had been working on them on and off for years. Looking out the round window, Eve and Scott watched with the others as the beautiful blue Earth became smaller and smaller. It amazed them all how it lit up the dark space around it, glowing and sparkling as it got farther away. They all watched until Earth disappeared from their vision. Ahead all that could be seen was the void of light; the darkness seemed to go on forever. It was a scary feeling, thinking that they might never see their home again. No one said anything, but they all knew; they were all thinking the same thing as Earth disappeared from their vision.

"Come on, let's see what we can do to help the others; we want to carry our weight." Scott said, and took Eve by the hand and they floated back through the tight passages, making their way to the control room.

"I'm not sure if I'll ever get used to this!" Scott said. "Markus told me that orientation only comes from your eyes in space, because your inner ear can't tell you what way is up or down." Scott said, motioning her to go in front of him.

"I know!" Eve stated, "I wonder what this space travel will do to our bodies with the lack of gravity. I think we are going to have to work out every day to keep our muscle mass intact. I heard the others talking. Courtney said that by the time we get to Mars, 10% of our bodies' muscle will be lost. I remember seeing some film footage a while back. It showed when some of the astronauts returned from the Space Station to Earth's gravity, they had to be carried because they couldn't walk. But one exciting thing is with the lack of gravity, our bodies are going to elongate. I have heard that astronauts who stayed on the Space Station for an extended time gained about two to three inches in height." Eve said, trying to stand up straight.

"I guess we're going to be really tall!" Scott laughed. "I'm already 6'6"! We are probably the tallest astronauts ever! Well, at least the ones from Earth. What else will happen to us? My smart wife!"

"Well, there were two astronauts that were twins. One stayed on Earth and the other went to the Space Station. When the one in space came back to Earth, they ran lots of tests and found out that his DNA had changed 7% from his identical brother," Eve said.

"Seriously? Incredible! Well, here we are…there's no one I would rather go to Mars with! Hey—we could have really tall kids…they could be giants!" Scott ducked as Eve tried to punch him and floated past, frowning. "Ah, Honey, don't get mad," Scott tickled her and floated by too fast and crashed into the back wall. By then he had her laughing.

chapter 78

It was late on the United States East Coast. The white Lincoln made a good pace down the highway moving south. The small group had been traveling for the past six hours with Sarah behind the wheel. Eve's parents had fallen asleep in the back seat. It was a damp night and the weather had started to change as hurricane season had begun. There weren't many cars on the road at this hour and Sarah pushed on, wanting to reach Gordon Turner's home by 7 A.M.

Sarah had been getting images in her mind since Eve and Scott disappeared and she hoped that she understood them correctly. The sun had started to come up on the horizon and she looked at her GPS and saw that it wouldn't be long now. She turned into a McDonald's parking lot a few blocks away from their destination and stopped the car.

"Okay, wake up…" No one stirred. "Wake up!" Sarah said again.

"What is it?" Janet sat up, looking around the truck, spotting small Sarah still behind the wheel.

"We are five minutes away. Did you need to use the bathroom? I stopped at McDonald's. I'll get us some coffee." Sarah said, opening her door and dropping down from the tall truck onto the damp pavement. Looking around, she saw other travelers who were also identifying the golden arches as the place to stop. "They have the cleanest bathrooms," Sarah said, closing her door.

"Put cream in mine," Janet said. She started shaking her husband awake. Both stretched and slowly made their way to the restrooms. They found Sarah sitting at a table, staring out the window, watching the sunrise.

"Have you decided what you're going to tell him?" Eve's mother asked.

"I'm not sure...I didn't think about that yet, with all the rush. I hope he'll be able to help us," Sarah pondered. "I hope the kids just haven't gone on vacation. But the message had been clear, coming in every day, and sometimes I can see what Eve is seeing. But I haven't managed to use my mind to talk back to her...there's some kind of blockage and I'm wondering why. I've never before had a problem reaching out to her," Sarah frowned, sipping her coffee.

"We can just hope that Eve's friend Gordon will understand and be able to help," Michael said. "Come on, ladies, there is no time like the present. I need to know."

They left the parking lot, driving into a subdivision a mile down the road, and pulled up to a large, red brick house sitting back from the street. They expected to see a house that was dark and asleep at this hour and were surprised to find the driveway full of cars. They watched as people were already coming and going from the house. Many looked at them strangely when they passed, wondering who these strangers were. Sarah lightly tapped on the door and waited. Soon the heavy door opened, and they moved aside to allow few younger women to pass. They noticed most of the young ladies had hair in rollers and their arms were loaded down with bags. They chatted excitedly as they passed them, smiling at the newcomers. Eve's parents looked at each other, exchanging a puzzled glance. Sarah pushed the half-open door wider, showing a room full of activity inside. People were moving about, some were dressed in their Sunday best and others organizing, doing their assigned tasks.

"Come on…follow me." Sarah said, stepping into the room and looking around. No one looked up or noticed that they didn't belong. The small group stood for a moment up against the wall observing, searching the crowd of people for a middle-aged man…Gordon. "I think that might be him over there. Wait here and I'll go check." Sarah said, and was gone, maneuvering between tables, smiling and nodding as she went. No one gave a second glance, thinking if she was there, she belonged there.

"Okay…I pray he can help!" Janet said, taking ahold of Michael's arm, backing both of them out of the way when a girl moved through the open space between people. She was loaded down with flowers arranged in crystal vases overflowing from a large box.

"I think someone is getting married today," Janet whispered in her husband's ear and he nodded.

They both watched Sarah from across the room. She stood in front of a large man with a balding head. They observed the sides of his hair had been slicked back, giving him a neat appearance for the big day. They waited to see what would happen. Sarah tugged on his sleeve to gain his attention and they watched as he leaned down to listen. Eve's parents saw a shocked look pass across his face, and he turned his head in their direction, finding the strangers in a crowded corner of the room. His eyes stopped on them and he made a beeline toward them with Sarah following in his wake.

"Come with me to my office, where we can talk. As you see, my daughter is getting married today." Gordon said, looking around the room. Locating his wife, he saw her back was turned. He kept moving before she saw him and wondered what he was doing.

"Yes, a big day! We are so sorry to impose!" Janet stated. "We could return tomorrow."

"No! I would love the distraction! Between my wife, my daughter, and about ten bridesmaids, I'm happy for some peace of mind." Gordon closed the large oak door of his office and the noise outside was instantly muffled. "Now... what has happened to Eve? I was told that she had taken an extended vacation...or honeymoon to Europe?"

"Well, extended, yes. Vacation, no. What do you know of the Mars mission that left a few weeks ago?" Eve's mother asked.

Gordon looked puzzled, "I know a lot...I work at NASA." He chuckled and saw that they were serious and grew concerned. "I don't understand—what has happened?" He asked.

"Well, this might be hard to believe...but Sarah here is a telepath, among other things," Janet stated. Gordon looked at the smaller woman, sizing her up.

"Okay," Gordon said, still wondering what this was all about.

"Start at the beginning." Janet directed Sarah.

Chapter 79

"For the past two weeks I have been getting signals, messages from Eve." Sarah saw doubt cross Gordon's face. "Eve and her husband disappeared two weeks ago, and I have been contacted from her in my mind. I see what you're thinking…I am not a nut! I won't get into it, but you understand that the brain is 80-90% junk DNA. My brain uses more than 10-20%, allowing the neurons to reach places in my brain that the normal person wouldn't understand. Just listen for a moment! Eve has been telling me that they were kidnapped and put on the ship that is heading to Mars."

This got his attention. "What! No, that couldn't happen! That couldn't be possible!" Gordon looked at Eve's parents, seeing the confident look on their faces, seeing that they believed what Sarah was telling him.

"Listen to me!" Sarah said, slamming her hand on the desk, making a loud sound that demanded all of their attention. She watched Gordon jump a little. Everyone stopped and looked at her. "There isn't a question of did it happen. The reason we are here is that Eve said to come to you for help. She wants to know if you got around to installing the separate communication device inside one of the trucks.

You know—the ones that you were working on with her to get ready for Mars? And if you did install the device, Eve needs you to turn it on, so that she can communicate with you," Sarah said.

"How did you learn of that? No one knew about the device. Who are you people?" Gordon stated, angrily. "That was a secret! I think I only told Eve and my wife!"

Janet stepped forward and put her hand on his arm, drawing his attention. "She's my daughter…wouldn't you do anything to make sure your daughter is safe? My daughter needs your help and you are the only one that she trusts. She said to come to you. Please help us!"

Gordon looked into the tear-filled eyes of the older woman and thought of his only daughter. "Okay, maybe I did install something in one of the trucks just in case. But this is top secret…I don't think I can get you into NASA. I could get in a lot of trouble," Gordon said.

"We don't even have to go inside. We just want you to check and see if what Sarah is saying is true. Please find out what you can. If they are on this spaceship headed to Mars, are they safe?" Janet said.

"The earliest I can get away today is around midnight; we have the hall until 11:00 P.M. Meet me at the McDonald's parking lot down the road at 1:00 A.M. and you can follow me. There are many hotels down that way; you might want to get a place for the next few days. I'll get to the bottom of this," Gordon said.

"Thank you! Thank You!" Michael said, shaking Gordon's hand. "Here, take my cell number in case something changes." Gordon found a scrap of paper on his desk, jotted the number down, and jammed it into his overflowing wallet.

"Okay—see you tonight. Now back to work…I have my list!" Gordon chuckled and was a little thrown off when Sarah and Janet hugged him from both sides. "Okay, ladies—have to go." He smiled and was gone, feeling a little uncomfortable at the close contact.

"At least he didn't kick us out!" Janet said.

"Well, I think he was surprised," Michael said. "Come on, let's find a nice place to stay."

chapter 80

Onboard the spaceship they all fell into a daily routine. Eve had been focusing on her visualization techniques, trying to send messages to Sarah. Telepathy might not work for her; it was said to be mind to mind. She wasn't sure if it was even working, because she wouldn't get any mental response from Sarah. But she kept trying every day, reaching out to Sarah to tell her parents.

Eve and Scott had fallen into the role of farmers. One room of the ship was full of plants in different stages of growth. Britney had assigned them the task of tending to the plants that would feed them. It was a large responsibility for the couple who had never had a garden and they both took their job seriously.

They had been told because of the lack of time and that the mission had changed to accommodate humans, the garden had been added at the last minute. The Space Station that was 220 miles above Earth had been doing experiments on growing food in space for some time. They had come up with an advanced hydrophonic system, growing plants in sand, gravel, or liquid by using human waste, thus providing a continuous supply of nutrients. They were experimenting, trying to find a way to make a self-sustaining ecosystem in space. The scientists on the ISS had focused on growing micro algae. By growing algae, they were able to balance the carbon dioxide breathed out by the astronauts, allowing for the algae to grow at a rapid rate. Thus, the plants could take in the waste products of the humans and release oxygen in the process. Eve and Scott wondered if this was the magma system of the past, when Moses was in the desert for 40 years with the Israelites.

They had found a book on growing plants, canning, and how to dehydrate the food. The book was a real help explaining and instructing them on the basics of growing plants.

"Eve, listen: Plants collect sunlight and have been using it for billions of years. Plants eat sunlight, thus turning it to starch that helps the plants grow. The leaves are like the batteries absorbing and collecting the energy. Animals eat a plant and capture the energy that the plant collected. Plants look green because the sun is green (blue-green wavelength)," Scott read.

"Okay, that makes sense. What I'm trying to figure out is—is this a canner or dehydrator?" Eve said, looking at the directions and wishing she had been interested when her mother had tried to teach her a few things in the kitchen.

"They both preserve the food, because as we harvest, we need to put food away for when a crop isn't coming in," Scott said. "But how do we know what to harvest and when?"

"Here's a plant book showing the different kinds of crops we're growing, and it has pictures. Let's start with what we recognize and look it up and figure out how to preserve it. I know that this is a tomato plant. All these are ready to pick because they are red. So, let's start with these. We'll pick the ones that are ready and then can them and save a few for dinner. And then let's plant tomato seeds and put them here with the rest under the grow lights. We'll rotate harvesting and then seeding some and move to the next plant." Eve said, putting her face under the warmth. "I wonder if I could get a tan under this light. I think maybe not a tan, but the sunlight does give us vitamin D and make us feel better."

"Okay, Honey. Come from there—it might age your skin," Scott said. "Let's can…here's a recipe. We are going to need a pepper and an onion, salt and pepper."

"Green pepper or red?" Eve asked, looking around.

"I'm not sure…let's go red, it will match," Scott said.

"Look this is a red pepper and it looks big enough. Do you see any onions?"

"I think they are those over there…it looks like the picture. Gently pull that up and check," Scott instructed.

"It is an onion! Who would have known it grew underneath? Here, we just need two." Eve said, feeling proud that she was figuring it out.

"Yes, pat the small rocks back down. Could you please make a label and stick it in the middle of those plants? We'll label them, so we don't have to remember. Look at those… smell them. I think that's celery," Scott said.

"Yes, it smells like it! Hey, this isn't so bad—it's like figuring out a formula in the lab," Eve said. "Funny, the celery doesn't look like it does in the store; it's more like a bush."

"Well, cut some of it off and put it with the rest of our ingredients," Scott instructed.

"Leaves and all?" Eve asked.

"Yes, it will give them a good flavor. Here we are all organic!" Scott said, laughing.

"Okay—it's kind of fun!" Eve said. "We can do canned tomatoes and what about tomato sauce for spaghetti?"

"Well, it looks like we have plenty of time. Nothing is too hard for two Yale grads. Ha Ha." Scott laughed and she kissed him.

"We will have a green thumb and be chefs by the time we reach home. When we're finished for the day, let's sneak down to where the trucks are parked. I want to check them to see if Gordon had done anything special that I can detect. I'm trying to keep hopeful," Eve said.

"Do you have any idea of what to look for?" Scott said.

"I don't…I need to see if there's something different when comparing them. And then if we find something, figure out how it works. Don't worry—I think that will be easier than the gardening." Eve said, smiling at him. She noticed the sand on his cheek and wiped it off with the back of her glove.

Both Eve and Scott were excited when they saw some of the leaves coming up from the seeds they had planted. Eve's friend Gordon had once shown her pictures of flowers that his wife was growing for the wedding. Eve remembered asking if they grew them from seeds, he had told her that he had helped. His idea had been to put small bits of cotton in each hole. Then he put the seed on the cotton and covered it with the soil mixture that was comparable to the volcanic ash from Hawaii. He had told Eve that the cotton helped to keep the seeds moist to allow them to germinate. Eve had searched the spacecraft and finally found cotton in a cabinet that had medical supplies. Thus far, Gordon's technique had been a success.

Chapter 81

Daily, Scott and Eve watered and worked on carefully preserving the food and seeding new plants. After they were finished for the day, they would go to the storage area. Eve hadn't found a communication device yet. But she had not lost hope, going over each vehicle carefully. She believed that she knew her friend well and it had to be there. She had started to focus not only on the message to Sarah about finding Gordon, but also asking him where the device was hidden.

Every day Eve would etch a small scratch on the glass of the bed pod, keeping track of time. She wanted time to go by as fast as possible so she could figure out a way to get home. She had noticed that their circadian rhythm had changed from a daily rhythmic activity cycle that was based on 24-hour intervals on Earth to 24.9-hour intervals, the same as a day on Mars. At first Eve wondered if it was just her, but after monitoring the team, she noticed that they had all fallen into the same time frame as well, soon after they were on their journey in space.

Interesting...it made her wonder if Mars might be humans' original origin. She wondered if life had started on Earth or if it had come from somewhere else.

The astronauts were on their way to Mars. Their assignment was to set up a colony with the help of the robots. They knew for now the modules would only be temporary. Eve recalled hearing about the "Mars One" mission. Around 200,000 people had applied, and they only had chosen 24 individuals to train and send to colonize Mars. She had heard that that mission had been abandoned when funds ran out. But she wasn't sure because of the lack of information coming from governments around the world. She was positive that sending this group to Mars was a secret from other countries.

The plan seemed to be the same as the other missions. NASA would send the spacecraft to the moon where it would refuel and wait for Mars to be the closest to Earth. Then it would slingshot to where they could fall into Mars' orbit. But the plan at first was to send robots to Mars and then remotely set up a colony before humans would arrive. Then every two years more colonists in teams of four to six people would add to the population.

They weren't sure if it was going to be an equal male-female ratio because they were finding that women might be better suited for space. They were smaller and needed less food than men and thus there would be less waste product. Usually women weighed less, meaning less fuel to carry. Also because of their demeanor, women were easier to get along with in close captivity. But the main advantage when thinking of populating a different planet, women could carry a sperm bank of different nationalities and were able to produce children.

The colony's habitat would consist of an atmosphere designed to supply oxygen and water and minimize the effect of radiation to humans. But the living pods weren't meant to be permanent quarters.

Eve remembered Gordon telling her that they had found organic life on Mars. They had done many tests of the soil using SAM, or Sample Analysis at Mars. The test was done remotely by taking soil samples to determine the composition. But most of all, they were looking for life on Mars. The samples would be sent back to Earth to be further tested for microbial life. Gordon had said that astronauts were also looking for oil and carbon. These rocks, billions of years old, would be tested for organic materials embedded inside.

Eve also remembered reading that NASA's Opportunity rover had worked and sent back information for 15 years. It was designed to only last 90 days, but continued to send back information and run using its solar panels. It found sulfur, which acts as a protection for organic matter. Eve remembered a controversial test. Soil was placed in water and left for a few days. The idea was if there were microscopic living organisms in the dirt, there would be bubbles released of carbon dioxide. They did find that the soil had bubbles, proving organic life. The research showed that the Mars atmosphere was thin and made up of carbon dioxide CO_2, Argon Ar, Nitrogen N_2, and small amounts of Oxygen and water vapor.

So maybe what her space being father had said, about there being a war that had destroyed Mars, was true. Stories or ideas had surfaced in the past few years. One was after the Sumerian written texts had been deciphered. The Sumerians were an ancient civilization that had resided in Mesopotamia around the fourth millennium BC. It talked of a cosmic battle where planets were fighting planets. Thoughts were that there were different aliens trying to control Earth. It was said that people from the sky destroyed their world and had to come to ours to survive.

From what Eve now understood, the team's main objective was to start the terraforming process. It was the first step in making the environment suitable for humans' habitation on the planet. It was a long process—Eve had been told that it might take a couple hundred years—to make Mars a safe environment. The idea was to make the atmosphere not only breathable but to create a barrier atmosphere to protect the planet from radiation. The other objective was to spread microbes on the surface of Mars; these would help in the process by releasing carbon, nitrogen, and phosphorus used in preparing for new plants and animals. *A big job*, Eve thought.

chapter 82

Every day Eve and Scott started their morning with a workout; they helped each other put weights on their ankles and then ran on the treadmill. Then they cleaned up with water and soap that would float in large balls and bubbles that sometimes would get away from them. They would laugh, amazed, catching them with a washcloth. Once a week would be cleaning day. All surfaces and the air had to be cleaned and filtered of dead cells that shed off all their bodies. It was a huge task sucking them up as they floated in the air covering everything. The first time Eve had taken off her socks, a puff had floated like a cloud in the air. She remembered thinking that it reminded her of flour tossed in the air. It was crazy to see, because without gravity it stayed suspended in the air.

Time on the ship had passed with no incidents. Then NASA informed them that the ship had started to slow a little. They were told that they needed to go outside and check the solar panels that were partially fueling the ship with energy from the sun. They were still moving with enough velocity not to worry, but Eve could hear the concern in the man's voice from NASA. She understood that if they didn't fix the problem right away they might miss Mars and continue on farther into the solar system. Eve could tell the astronauts were tense and this was their concern as well. When Eve and Scott entered the control room, Markus, Courtney, and Britney were arguing about who would go outside the spacecraft to fix the problem.

"All right—I'm done arguing with you two! I'm the one who needs to do it. It's my ship!" Britney said.

"Well, we were trained to go in pairs when going outside the craft," Courtney stated.

"I understand that! But my partner isn't on the ship and I need the two of you to stay onboard. If something happens to me, the mission must go on! Do you hear me?" Britney yelled, leaving the room and heading for the airlock.

Eve could see the fear in Britney's eyes when she passed her, so she followed her to the bay with the large window porthole. Eve found Britney preparing to go outside the ship; she was struggling to get into her spacesuit.

"I can help! We can do this together. I can be your partner," Eve said, "Just tell me what to do."

"No!" Britney looked at Eve. "I said I'm doing it! But could you run get Markus to check me first?"

"Yes—I'll be right back." Eve floated quickly back to the main cabin, using the walls to propel her faster, zipping in and out of the close halls. She found Markus and Scott and told them to follow her.

"Britney is going outside…right now! She would like you to check her," Eve said over her shoulder. The men looked at her, confused. "She has to switch the battery backup and clear the left solar panel," Eve stated and left the room. Markus and Courtney exchanged a glance, and everyone followed Eve to the hatch, where Britney was already suited up. Markus, cursing, went through his safety check and found the spacesuit was fine.

Britney looked at Eve, sizing her up. "Will you suit up and feed the tether for me? You're taller—more leverage," Britney stated.

"I'll do it!" Scott said, moving in front of Eve.

"No! I'm more comfortable with her," Britney said, looking away.

"It's okay, Scott—I can do this," Eve pulled Scott close, "Let me do this," Eve whispered. "Give me a moment." Eve directed at Britney. She waited for Scott's response.

"Okay…but no risks!" Scott said, "Let me help." Eve waited while Markus and Scott both checked her suit. She held on to a silver bar, close to the round door that would soon be opening.

"Clear the room; you know the routine," Markus said. He moved to the outer chamber and motioned Courtney and Scott to come with him out of the room.

Scott looked concerned at this development.

"It will be all right…go ahead," Eve said. "I'll be just fine."

"Please be careful! I love you!" Scott said.

"Come on!" Markus said.

"Go!" Eve said, "I love you too!"

Scott stepped into the side room and watched the door close between them. The three gathered around a small connecting window that was the size of a porthole on a ship. They waited and watched as Britney opened the hatch to the outside. She looked at Eve.

"Now…you stay right here and anchor yourself inside the opening. Whatever you do…don't let me go!"

chapter 83

"Okay! Don't worry! I got you!" Eve said. With that said, Britney floated through the open hole. Eve could hear the astronaut breathing hard in her earpiece. "Calm yourself down; you're breathing too hard. Think of something else…I think of the ocean and the sound of the waves hitting the shore."

"Okay—quiet, please…I found the solar panel that is indicated. I see something hit it and left a large black smudge. That's what it looks like. It's easily wiping off and thank goodness it's not broken," Britney said, narrating her actions.

"That's good! Now what?" Eve asked, ready for her to come back inside.

"Now I have to go to the sector below it and replace the batteries with the powered ones. Just putting it in now… closing the panel. Good. Oh no! Something is wrong! I can't see out of one of my eyes! I dropped the old battery! Hold on—I have to grab it!" Eve felt the tug on the tether. "I got it! But now I can't see! Both of my eyes are stinging! It's like I'm being poked in the eyes with needles! I'm blind! I can't get back! You hear me! I can't see! Eve, don't let me die out here! I'm afraid! What if I float away and I run out of air? Who will find me?"

"Listen! Pull yourself together! I'm coming! You got this! You need to calm down…it's going to be all right…. Come on…you are the commander of this ship and I'm not letting you go anywhere!" Eve screamed. Eve looked around the small space and saw the pipe that she had been holding and pulled on it, testing its strength.

"It will have to do," Eve whispered to herself.

"What did you say?" Britney's panicked voice asked.

"Look—I'm coming! Just hold on!" Eve said. She hooked the steel clamp with the tether around the pipe and pulled on it, making sure it would hold.

Eve was now untethered and tried not to look toward the window where she knew Scott was watching her. But she did see a reflection of a tear floating in front of his face. Eve held on to the tether and went hand over hand, not releasing it until the other hand had a hold. The gloves were thick and clumsy and it was slow going. Eve tried to stay focused and tune out Britney's crying. She moved forward, hand over hand, until she reached Britney at the other end. She was about fifty feet from the open hatch.

"I'm here…it's all right…give me your hand and don't get crazy or you're going to kill us both!" Eve said and watched Britney slowly stick out her arm. Eve wrapped the tether around one hand, securing it tight, and grabbed Britney's arm, pulling her close to her side. "Now…I'm going to place your hand on the back of my suit, and I need you to hold on, like you're my baby monkey. Got it?" Eve said.

"Yes, like a baby monkey," Britney repeated.

Eve tried not to laugh at that. "Okay, hold tight." She felt Britney holding on and started to slowly pull them along the line toward the spacecraft. Eve stopped a few times, her fingers hurting, and continued forward. She looked up at one point and saw they were halfway there.

"How are you doing, little monkey?" Eve asked.

"I'm okay. If I'm blind who's going to fly the ship?" Britney asked.

"Pull yourself together…stop thinking! Let us get back to safety first! If you don't quiet down so I can concentrate, I'm going to make you my little bitch!" Eve heard a half giggle and smiled to herself.

"Okay, here we are. Duck your head." Eve entered first. Turning, she pulled Britney inside with the tether and pulled the latch for the door, waiting until it was closed tight. She pushed the airlock and the room filled with oxygen and temporary gravity. Both women fell to thc floor, breathing hard. When the light was green, the door burst open and Scott, Markus, and Courtney rushed in and helped them both take off their helmets.

"You can't see? What's wrong with your eyes?" Markus asked, putting drops into them, then checking and wiping them clean. "That happened to me once in training; it really stings doesn't it? What happens is the condensation from your breathing extra hard went to your eyes and with the lack of gravity, the moisture just sits there and builds up."

"Yes, you're right! I can see now!" Britney said, feeling ashamed for being so scared.

Eve and Britney looked at each other. "Little bitch, huh?" Britney said. "Thank you, Red," she whispered.

"Well, now we know…never cry in our spacesuits when there is no gravity or you're temporarily blind," Courtney said.

"Very funny!" Britney said, handing the used battery to Courtney as she rushed by. "I need to check to see if our effort worked." The group followed her to the control room.

"Well I'm going to be crying if you do that again!" Scott said to Eve. "But you did a good job—I'm proud of you! But don't do that again!"

"I love you too, Honey! Come with me…that gave me an idea." Eve said, moving by him.

Chapter 84

At 12:45 A.M., Sarah, Janet, and Michael sat waiting in the McDonald's parking lot. It had 24-hour service, and they watched travelers come and go from the highway until Gordon pulled up in a red convertible wearing a jogging suit.

"No laughs—this is the best I could do at such short notice. My car was blocked in and Uncle Ned was already passed out in my bedroom from too many drinks. Tonight the couch was assigned as my bed and I had to pretend I was asleep to sneak out. I ended up tripping over the dog while taking out the trash and woke my wife, who was sharing a room with her sister.... Anyhow, I was able to get away. I thought at first, I had forgotten my pass to get in to work." Gordon looked up and saw they were all watching him with smiles on their faces.

"We will take you however we can!" Michael said. "What now? Do you want us to follow you?"

"Yes, that's a good idea. Follow me. There is a truck stop not far from the NASA entrance. I'll go inside and turn on my device. I set it up to communicate to the spacecraft by bouncing off the Space Station. I only had time to put the emergency system into one of the trucks. Let's hope it works! I really didn't have much time to do many tests on it. It was a last-minute idea on my part. I didn't even have a chance to get it approved," Gordon said. "Okay—follow me. It's about twenty minutes.

"We'll be at the truck stop when you're finished," Michael stated.

Gordon led the way to his job and watched them pull into the truck stop when he motioned them with his arm to the parking lot. He went a few more miles and pulled up to the manned gatehouse. He had never come to work at this time of night and there was a different guard on duty than the usual one.

"Gordon Turner," he said, showing his badge.

"Well, you're either real late or real early for work, Mr. Turner," the guard joked.

"Just trying to finish some important work," Gordon said, smiling at the guard as the gate went up. "You have a nice night."

Gordon pulled up to the dark building and walked across the dimly lit parking lot, finding the side door that he used most mornings. He pressed in his code and waited after hearing the latch click as he was allowed through the door. The building was very large; he had about a seven-minute walk to get to his wing. As he passed, motion-censored lights turned on and off. Finding his closed lab, he again had to punch in a code and wait for the door to open.

He thought, *They now have a record of me being here.* Gordon moved to the back of the hangar; locating his office, he went right to work. He unlocked his personal locker that was the size of a closet and moved inside, finding the device he had been working on. He moved to his large wooden desk and fumbled in his haste but found it didn't take long to connect the device to his laptop. Gordon knew that it wouldn't be hard for NASA to detect if they knew what he was doing and hoped he would come in under their radar. He didn't want any trouble, but there wasn't time to cover his tracks and at this point he didn't even care. He was close to retirement age, but knew he would be lost without the work he enjoyed, giving him purpose. He crossed his fingers, turning the device on and watching the screen. A box came up and he entered his classified password and waited.

He wiped the sweat from his forehead and reached out to the beyond. "Eve…where are you?" He asked out loud.

Then he remembered the feed wouldn't be instant because of the distance and typed out a message that would hopefully be received on the other end when the transport unit was turned on.

chapter 85

Eve,

I've had a visit from your parents and Sarah. I am told that you are on the spacecraft now headed to Mars. This message will be time delayed, but if you get it please let me know if you are safe and that you received this contact. If there is something I can do to help you, please let me know. ps If this is the case and you are on that spacecraft, think of the positive side and bring me something interesting upon your return. I remember you saying that you didn't want to go to Mars. Think of the opportunity to understand the unknown and answer the question of our human existence. Gordon

Gordon closed his laptop and locked it in his top drawer. He ran the cable still connecting his device along the edge of the desk, locking the connection box still running into the top side drawer of his desk, leaving it on.

That was the best he could do at this hour. Tomorrow he would snoop around and see what he could find out. He wanted to know if they had secretly sent astronauts to Mars before the planned mission, even with the risks involved. He locked his office and returned to his car, driving to the parking lot of the truckstop where he found Eve's parents waiting, as directed. He pulled alongside the white Lincoln. Before he had a chance to speak, he saw the anxious looks on all their faces and wished that he had some kind of news to tell them. He waited while they rolled down their windows.

"I just sent a message to Eve that she will get if she finds and turns on the transmitter," Gordon said.

"Could you tell if the message went through?" Janet asked, wringing her hands with worry.

"No, I couldn't tell. Before the trucks were picked up, I put a small white flower sticker on the control panel of the one where I had installed the device." Gordon said, looking at the backseat window at Sarah. "If your telepathy really works, try to tell her to find that truck and peel off the flower and she will see what she needs to do."

"I'll try," Sarah said, trying not to cry. "I just haven't been able to contact her."

"You'll do it! I know you can...you did it before," Janet said hopefully.

"I'm off today, seeing it's Sunday and the day after my daughter's wedding. But I'm going to do some snooping around, and I'll find out if they put astronauts on that spacecraft. I have friends inside that circle. In the meantime, I suggest you all go home. I'll call you with what I find out," Gordon said. "Sorry I forgot about the time delay. Sometimes transmissions are a few months depending on the position of the satellite in relation to Earth and Mars."

"But what if she sends a message back?" Janet asked, not wanting to go home.

"It won't be instant…the message I sent might take a month to get there and if she responds, about the same amount of time to come back. But once functioning it takes 30-45 minutes. It takes time because of the distance." Gordon said. "Tell you what…I'll call you next Sunday when my wife is in church and give you an update. Unless I find out anything before," Gordon said.

"Okay. We'll go home and wait on you," Janet said, wiping a lone tear away and setting her jaw in a strong posture. "Thank you for your help, Gordon!"

"Hey, Eve is more than my co-worker—she's my young friend. Goodnight…talk Sunday." Gordon pulled the car out of the lot and saw the white truck pull out soon after, heading north. He prayed his device would work.

chapter 86

Scott and Eve had just finished their workout: 30 minutes on the treadmill and 70 minutes of resistance training with giant rubberbands. They had been told that they had to do this every day to keep their muscles and lungs in shape. After they finished, they made a quick stop at their sleeping pod to change before they headed to the other end of the ship. Scott saw the serious look on Eve's face when she came out of the restroom and wondered what was up.

"Okay, where to?" He asked, not being able to read her mood, thinking she had a new idea. Their day had become a routine of half the day in the plant lab and the other part of the day in the lower storage level. Scott had become tired of looking for a communication device, but he hadn't wanted to suggest that it might not be there. Eve had checked so many times, he had started to come to the conclusion that they were out of luck.

"Plant room," Eve said, moving past him in that direction.

"Plant room it is," Scott replied, following her. Inside, Eve flew into his arms and he just held her as they floated, carefully making sure not to knock over any of their plants.

"What is it? Want me to turn on the gravity?" Scott asked, pulling her face close to his and watching her reaction.

"I have something I need to tell you—it's good and terrible at the same time," Eve said.

Scott could see the vein pumping in her throat. In space, your pulse slows down. He knew she must be having a panic attack.

"What is it? Just tell me," Scott said.

"There's no other way to say this than to just blurt it out—I'm pregnant! And we have 24 more weeks to reach home so I can get the shot. Remember my RH negative blood?" Eve said.

"We don't have the shot on the ship?" Scott asked, starting to panic himself. "What happens again if you don't get the shot?"

"It could endanger the baby and my life."

"What if we abort it—would you be safe?" He asked.

"No! I would still have to get a shot," Eve said.

"Eve, please slow down and start at the beginning and tell me everything!" Scott said. He knew he couldn't do this or anything else without her in his life. A child was on its way!

"As you remember, I have to get a shot if I get pregnant. It is to protect both me and the baby. Our blood types are different—we have what they call RH incompatibility. In the 28th week of pregnancy, I need to get a shot and one more shot 72 hours after giving birth. We have about six months to figure it out. It's a vaccine called RhoGAM. It will stop my immune system from killing or fighting the baby. After giving birth, some of the blood could interchange in my body and cause me harm," Eve said, watching him closely.

"And why can't we just abort it?" Scott asked; he wanted nothing that would risk her life.

"After an abortion I would need the same shot, because the process would mix our blood," Eve said.

"I see…" Scott was silent for few moments, thinking. "So…we're a month pregnant? And you know for sure? You took a test?"

"Yes! I did—positive—I got the plus+. They had some in the cabinet with the meds," Eve said.

"Then we're going to need to go home or find out what's in that shot…maybe we can make it?" Scott said.

"That's a good idea! I just wonder if it's possible. We're having a baby!" Eve said.

"Yes…we're having a baby!" Scott said, hugging her, "We'll work it out!"

"We'll work it out!" Eve repeated.

That night, with Eve asleep in his arms, Scott prayed for the first time for God to take care of her and their child. He wasn't sure who would even hear him, the gods or the angels, but it did make him feel better.

The next morning Eve woke up rested and in a good mood. In the kitchen area she found some dehydrated milk and cereal that she put together and sucked out of the prepared package.

chapter 87

Gordon Turner could hardly sleep the night before and now sat in his home office at 4 A.M. He wondered if it really could be possible that Eve was on that spacecraft. He had been with NASA for thirty years and had never heard of them changing a well-thought-out plan. Except when a new president was voted in and they would switch the plan of going to the moon again or going to Mars. Lately it had been the slingshot from the moon to Mars that the team had been working on the calculations for, so he didn't think that had changed.

This morning as Gordon laid in bed, he had tried to think of how he could find out. Usually they had meetings to keep his team updated in case there was a problem with the trucks or crawlers. But those updates now wouldn't start until they were safely on Mars. Gordon remembered he had a friend who had worked with his department and had been moved to the launch team. Gordon quickly looked up his number in his work Rolodex. He had kept numbers at home for such occasions when he needed information. He sat at his desk, thinking, waiting until 6 A.M. to dial the number.

"Alex, it's Gordon Turner."

"Yes, how are you doing, old boy? I heard you had a wedding," Alex said.

"Yes, a real affair...my daughter. Sending her off today on her honeymoon," Gordon said. He hesitated, trying to think of how to ask Alex. He knew the young man was a stickler with policy.

"Well, what's up? You usually don't call me at home or really ever this early. So, it must be important," Alex stated.

"It kinda is...um...I'll just say it. You worked on the launch team for the Mars mission. I need to know something," Gordon said.

"Yes, I'm still on that team. We're monitoring it closely. But you know it's classified," Alex said.

Gordon had a quick thought. *What if NASA monitors private phones?* He had never had cause to wonder or care before. "Yes, I understand that...I was just wanting to know how my babies are doing and if they all made it fine on lift-off," Gordon said.

"Far as I know. They all did well, no problems that we can see as of yet. Hey...I was wondering since I have you on the phone—are you still golfing? My wife went to visit her sister in Seattle, so I'm free today. I've been wanting to get in a round while she's away. That way I don't have to hear about all the time I spend golfing—ha ha. Do you want to golf with me this afternoon? We could just do 9 holes, say around 1:00?" Alex asked.

"My clubs are a little dusty but I'm sure I could give you a run for your money! It would be nice to get out of the house with all the extra people staying with us. You'd think that the relatives from Kentucky are going to whip out a banjo soon. It's a perfect day for it!" Gordon said. "Where do you want to go? My favorite is the small club down the road. I think it's still open to the public."

"I know the place. Yes, that's a good one! I'll call and get us a tee-time," Alex said.

"Okay—I'll see you there at 1:00…I look forward to beating you! Ha ha ha!" Gordon hung up the phone. He had six hours to find his clubs and something to wear. His wife wasn't going to like it, but maybe she wouldn't notice him gone. *Yeah, right!* He didn't look forward to breaking it to his wife that he would be gone for a few hours. Gordon wasn't sure which was going to be harder, because he knew she wasn't going to be pleased. But he would be back just in time for the small party she was planning, only 50 of their closest friends and relatives. He had been told it was the tossing of the rice to send his daughter and her new husband off to Barcelona, Spain, for the honeymoon.

chapter 88

At noon Gordon was dressed and putting his clubs in the trunk of his car when his wife caught him. Jane looked him up and down, observing his clothes.

"Gordon—where do you think you're going?" She asked, shutting the side garage door behind her. She stood there with her hands on her hips waiting for his answer.

"Honey, there's something that I need to do today," Gordon stated, *When did my life change that I had to ask permission to go anywhere?*

"I think you need to march back inside and have lunch with your daughter and her new husband! Were you just going to sneak out of here and not tell anyone?" She asked.

"Ah…no one is going to miss me. I was just getting ready to tell you! I have a meeting with someone from work on the golf course. I won't be gone long, we'll just play nine holes. So that's just two hours," Gordon said, stepping toward her. "You can handle it without me. I won't be long, hunner bunner!" Gordon pulled her in his arms. As she resisted the embrace, playing like she was pulling away, he kissed her neck, tickling her. "I won't be long," Gordon repeated.

"You'll be back before we send her off? You know she's daddy's girl, it would hurt her feelings if you missed seeing her off," she said.

"Jane...I understand, and I promise to be back in time," Gordon said. He kissed her lips and got in the car, smiling at her. "You did really good yesterday. It was a nice day." He started the car and slowly let go of her hand and backed out the drive.

At the golf course, Gordon had time to check in and load up his cart before Alex arrived. He pulled the cart around to the back of Alex's car so he could strap his clubs next to Gordon's.

"Hey there—it's a great day for golf! What a perfect sunny day and it's not too humid." Gordon said, feeling happy to be outdoors to enjoy the nice weather and the friendly competition.

"Ready to weep?" Alex said, smiling, then giving the parking lot a once over. He tightened his golf bag on the back of the cart beside Gordon's.

Alex jumped in the passenger side of the cart and they took their place in line waiting for their turn to tee-off the first hole. Gordon didn't say much; he would approach the subject after they were in the fairway away from anyone who could overhear them. He noticed that his old friend was jumpy and kept studying the others around them. A group of four men had just finished and moved along down the dirt path to the fairway. Gordon and Alex got out and found the colored markers showing them where they were to drive from. They waited until the group in front had made it to the green and took their turns sending the ball far into the fairway.

"That was a good drive. But I think mine might have beat yours! Ha!" Gordon said, observing that there were two women around 60 that were going to be following them.

"We'll see!" Alex said, jumping into the driver's seat, Gordon barely got in and they both sped off in search of their balls.

"Okay—what's going on? This was a good idea to go golfing," Gordon said, feeling free for the first time in weeks.

"Where's your phone?" Alex asked.

"I left mine in the car…I don't like distractions when I'm playing golf." Gordon watched as Alex started to relax.

"Okay. A few weeks ago, we were preparing for the launch when we got notice that we had to readjust the weight calculations because there was going to be extra weight in the amount of 8650 pounds. Many of us wondered what could be that heavy that they were adding so we tried to figure it out."

"Here's your ball," Gordon said. Alex jumped out and took his shot, landing in a sandpit close to the green.

"There's yours," Alex said. Gordon got out and hit his with his 5-iron and was pleased when it landed on the edge of the green.

Back in the cart they picked up their conversation. "So, did you guys figure out what was being added?" Gordon asked, grabbing his putter and waiting for Alex to hit his ball out of the sand with his sand wedge. It went high in the air and landed close to the hole.

"We saw different kinds of plants and grow lights. We were all thinking the same thing, but were afraid to ask. But when we saw evaporated food that we transport to the Space Station being stocked and different oxygen generators and sleeping pods being added, we understood what was happening." Alex said, looking behind them and watching the women catching up.

"Come on, let's pick up the pace." They finished putting the ball in the first hole and went in search for tee-off number two, finding it close by.

"How many astronauts went on board?" Gordon asked.

"Here's the odd thing...three walked on board and later two were carried on as if they had fainted. I'm not sure but I've never seen anything like it," Alex said.

"Did you get a look at the ones carried on?" Gordon asked, his heart pumping. "Here, pick up your ball. Let's take these to the green; those women are pressing close behind," Gordon said.

Chapter 89

On the green they both putted while Alex continued. "I couldn't see their faces; they were totally wrapped head to toe. But I did recognize one of the attendants that carried them on. After the spacecraft was safely on course, I saw him in the hall and pulled him aside to ask him what had happened. We went inside the bathroom and checked the stalls, making sure we were alone. He told me that a few weeks earlier, his team was told to prepare the spacecraft for transportation of a group of five astronauts. He said the mission had changed, and we weren't sending just the robots first, but a full crew to Mars. But get this—the two astronauts that were carried on were replacements."

"What do you mean by replacements?" Gordon asked.

"Well, replacements. There were two astronauts that weren't too happy to be sidelined after all of the training," Alex said. "That's what my friend said."

"Where did the orders come from and why?" Gordon asked.

"He heard the orders came from high up in the White House, maybe even the President. NASA's command had put up a fight and were pressured to do what they were told. Even when the White House was told of the risks involved on such short notice, that it could cause a mishap," Alex said.

"Come on, pick up your ball—those women are too close. Let's move out of this area." They both jumped in the cart and were about to turn around when a branch cracked loudly from above the golf cart. It fell, almost hitting them.

"What was that?" Alex asked, ducking as more branches started to fall. Turning his head, he saw one of the women pointing what looked like a gun in their direction. "Gordon, get low in the cart!"

"What's happening?" Gordon shouted, holding on as Alex turned the cart and pressed the pedal, taking the cart up to full speed—not in the direction of the clubhouse, but toward the women. Gordon didn't have time to say anything, he just held on and watched as Alex swerved the cart and jumped a small hill. They were airborne for a few seconds before hitting the women's golf cart, ramming the woman with the gun. She fell to the ground and Alex smashed the cart into their cart, knocking it over. It landed on the other woman's legs and they heard her cry out in pain. Alex turned the golf cart, moving at top speed they raced to the clubhouse. Gordon looked behind them; the woman with the gun limped to help get the cart off her friend.

"What's going on, Alex?" Gordon yelled, holding on tight when they hit the asphalt parking lot.

"Grab your bag and get home—lock all your doors! Someone has been following me for the past few days and you might be in danger as well. Someone doesn't want anyone to know who is on that spacecraft," Alex yelled, stopping at Gordon's car and dumping his clubs into his back seat.

"I think I know at least two of the people on that spacecraft on the way to Mars!" Gordon said, now mad. "My assistant and her husband are missing," Gordon jumped into his driver seat, starting his engine.

"Why them?" Alex slammed Gordon's door. "Go home!"

"I'm not sure...but I'm going to find out." Gordon shouted out his window.

chapter 90

Gordon pulled out of the parking lot, leaving a dirt cloud in the air following him. Quickly he jumped on the highway and instead of making his way home, he turned the car toward work. Calming himself with pleasantries, he talked to the day guard and moved forward to his parking spot. On the drive, a plan had formed in his mind.

He worked his way through the complex toward his office. A few people were working on a Sunday. NASA was good with flex time. Finding his office, Gordon checked his device, finding nothing had changed. He unhooked the wires, putting everything into a small box. Before he left the office, he filled out a form for time off. He said he had decided to surprise his wife and take her to Rome for their upcoming anniversary.

Gordon knew that his job would be all right; his boss had suggested he take some time off. Better now before they got busy. When the spacecraft made it to Mars, they would be smashed with work for a long time. He needed to make sure his family was safe.

He dropped the form on his boss's desk, grabbed the box, and left the building. Gordon reached home with time to spare. He found his place on the front porch in plenty of time to hug his daughter and throw rice. After the young couple entered the white limo taking them to the airport, Gordon hurried inside and pulled out his and his wife's suitcases from the attic, shaking off the dust and tossing them on the bed. He was halfway packed when his wife entered the room after saying goodbye to all the guests. The house was now silent and she stood in the doorway wondering what he was up to.

"Honey, what are you doing in here?" She asked. Gordon hadn't heard her enter the room and jumped in the air at the sound of her voice.

"I don't have a lot of time to explain right now! But I need you to pack a bag—no questions asked!" Gordon said, tossing more clothes on the bed.

"Honey, what's going on? No questions!" She asked, "What has gotten into you? I know the wedding has been stressful, but now it is over," Jane stated, not moving.

"I need you to listen to me! I need you to do what I say! Do you hear me? Do you hear me?" Gordon raised his voice and she saw the seriousness in his face. She shut her mouth and started quickly packing. When they were finished, he took her purse and left her phone on the side table by the bed and put his with it. He went to their closet safe and pulled out a bundle of cash that he had put there for emergencies. She watched, tears in her eyes.

"Jane…not now. Please trust me…please." Gordon whispered in her ear. "It's going to be all right." He took her hand and pulled her along behind him, locking the house. He put the bags in the trunk of her uncle's parked convertible. "He won't care…remember he will be gone for a few days to your sister's house." Her eyebrows lifted but she remained silent as she climbed in the front seat and buckled herself in.

Gordon ran back, forgetting his box, and checked the house making sure everything was off. He tossed his car keys on the table and locked the house up tight. Her uncle would just have to use his car. Then, he reconsidered, *That might not be a good idea if someone is watching my car.* He retrieved his car keys, leaving a note that they borrowed her uncle's car. He would have to get a ride home. Gordon put the box in the backseat and got in the driver's side. He pushed the button lifting the convertible top, putting it back in place, and pulled out of the driveway, turning toward the highway heading north to Connecticut. As he maneuvered out of the subdivision, taking the turns a little faster than he wanted to, he felt the car grip the road. He took out his wallet and fumbled through the business cards until he found the scrap of paper he was looking for. He took the first exit, heading for the gas station, and pulled into the first pump.

"I'll be right back, Jane." She looked out the side window saying nothing...just waiting. He had never talked to her like that and she knew something big was wrong and knew he would tell her soon. But right now, he was in a state and she knew it was best not to say anything and remain quiet so he could focus.

Inside the store, Gordon approached the attendant.

"Hey, son, could I use your phone? Mine is dead and I have an emergency and need to make a phone call," Gordon asked.

"I just can't loan out my phone to anyone...sorry," the attendant, turning his back to look at the monitor when a truck pulled in.

"Son, please…I'll give you a $100 bill if you let me use it for five minutes," Gordon said. That got his attention.

"Five minutes and I get $100? And you won't steal my phone?" The young man said, thinking it over.

"I'm not the stealing type," Gordon said.

"Okay, Mister…five minutes. But let me see the money first."

Gordon pulled out a $100 bill and pushed it through the small hole in the protective window, then put out his hand, waiting. He saw the attendant trying to decide and finally the young man put his phone through the small space into Gordon's hand. Gordon walked a few feet away and turned his back, dialing the number. It was picked up on the second ring; the voice listened as Gordon whispered into the phone. He jotted down an address onto the scrap of paper and hung up the phone. He handed the phone to the young man and as a final thought, deleted the number off the phone.

"Thank you, son!" He laid an extra $50 on the counter with the phone, pushing it toward the kid. "For being kind."

"No, I can't take it—I wasn't really kind," he said, pushing all the money toward Gordon.

"Yes…you were a life saver." Gordon left the store, leaving the cash and got in the car, heading back to the highway.

After thirty minutes Jane could wait no longer.

"Gordon Turner! I think I deserve to know what's happening. Have you done something wrong?" Jane asked.

"No, Honey. It's a long story and I guess we have time. We have a long drive ahead of us." He talked until he had told her everything that had happened and was pleased when she wasn't mad and had soon fallen asleep.

chapter 91

Gordon wasn't tired; thirteen hours of adrenaline and coffee had kept him wide awake. There was no way he would sleep anytime soon. His mind kept going over everything that had happened and he wondered why Eve was put on the ship. When they reached the area around Yale, Gordon shook his wife and watched the sleep leave her beautiful face. She was still the woman that he had loved all those years ago.

"Honey…Are we there?" Jane sat up, grabbing her purse and searching inside for a compact.

Gordon watched Jane pat her face with pressed powder, checking it in the side mirror. Putting on her lipstick, she smiled and sat up straight, touching her husband's hand. They rounded the corner, following the car's GPS, and stopped at a pair of giant iron gates.

"Are you sure this is it? It looks like a celebrity's house, look at those huge pillars!" Jane said.

"Hold on, let me check the address again," Gordon said, eyeing the scrap of paper. "Yes, this is the address…oh boy!"

"Honey, I think you need to pull over there. Do you see the keypad with the monitor?" She asked.

"I see it. Let me straighten the car out." Gordon pushed the button and heard a distant ring.

"Hello," a voice came out of the speaker.

"Hi, it's Gordon and my wife Jane," he said, leaning out the car window to get closer. The large gates started to groan as the heavy metal screeched across the pavement. They waited until there was enough room to go through the opening and paused until the gates started to close behind them before moving forward.

Gordon pulled around the circle drive close to the front door. The house looked larger the closer they got. The porch was huge and overpowered the dark double oak door. On each side of the porch, six thick white pillars stood tall, carved with cherubs. Each were positioned at the bases, giving the illusion that they were holding the pillars in place. It was quite grand.

Before Gordon and Jane could get out of the car, the front door opened wide and Eve's parents made their way down the steps.

"What happened?" Janet asked, "Did you hear from her?"

"Dear, let them get out of the car!" Michael said, pacing the driveway…waiting.

"I'm so sorry! Where are my manners?" Janet said. "Yes, you're right! Hello…I'm Eve's mother, Janet," she said, pulling open the passenger door.

"Hi! I'm Jane. Sorry to intrude. My husband had thoughts that we might be in danger," Jane said.

"No! No…Gordon did the right thing in coming here! We have plenty of room. Here, let me take your coat. You can have a seat by the warm fire and I'll get you some wine," Janet stated.

"Yes, please," Jane said, looking around the room at the high ceilings and large stone fireplace with the bright logs lighting the room.

After they were all seated around the fireplace, Gordon told them everything that had happened. He tried to play down the women on the golf course. It had happened so fast, he wasn't really sure what happened or maybe he wasn't ready to admit that they had tried to kill the two men.

"Why would they want to kill you or Alex? Are you sure?" Jane asked, giving her husband a worried look.

"Yes! I think they were real bullets! But maybe they were just trying to scare us. We were lucky to get out of there in any case," Gordon said.

"Why would someone want you dead?" Jane asked.

"Because I think someone might know that I'm suspicious about Eve's disappearance. If she is on that spacecraft, I'm sure someone doesn't want it to get out that the United States of America kidnapped two of its citizens and put them on a one-way trip to Mars. They might not want anyone to know and will do anything to prevent the news from getting out," Gordon said.

Janet let out a shriek, "What! I'm to never see my daughter again?" She sank into the chair and sat staring at the fire. Michael patted her hand.

"Don't worry—we'll figure it out," he said gently. He looked in Gordon's direction. "Are we sure that she's on that ship?"

"Everything that has happened in the past 48 hours leads me to believe that Eve and her husband have been taken and are on their way to Mars. I think the best thing for us to do now is to start with trying to contact them. Using the device that connects us with one of the trucks on that spacecraft, we might have a side channel that we can use to talk to the astronauts and Eve. Then we can really know what is happening out there.

"I need a place to hook it back up. I went and removed it from work. The receiver is implanted on one of the module trucks that we designed. I was going to tell NASA that it would be a good safety procedure to have one in all the trucks, but we were under a rush to just get them prepared in time. I figured by the time we sent the astronauts next year, it would be easy to show them how to install the devices in all the trucks," Gordon said.

"Let's go to my office to hook it up! Come with me. I have an office upstairs that should have everything you need," Michael said. "This way please."

On the stairs, Gordon was surprised when the small woman popped out of nowhere. He noted that her hair was longer than he would have anticipated; it flowed down her back in a wild manner.

"Yes, you're here," Sarah stopped mid-step and touched her forehead. "It worked," Sarah said, pleased as she passed Gordon. He stopped trying to understand what the odd woman was saying.

"Yes, very well," he said.

"I'm sure she understood…this time," Sarah said, "They are all right and have a secret to tell! I couldn't see what she was thinking," Sarah continued down the stairs. "But I know they are all right! I'm off to tell the ladies!" She coasted by, almost floating.

"You'll get used to her," Michael said to Gordon.

"I hear you!" Sarah called.

PART THREE

MARS

chapter 92

Eve woke abruptly; stretching her arms, she tapped Scott's shoulder, waking him. He turned over, ignoring her.

"I know what we can do!" Eve said, "I now understand."

"Honey…can we sleep just a few more hours?" Scott groaned, "It's too early to get up."

"Wake up! Hurry!" Eve said, already struggling into her sweats. "I just got a telepathic message from Sarah! I felt her in my head—come on!" Eve said, excited.

Scott opened his eyes, checking to see if she was joking. He wasn't sure he believed her and thought Eve was just trying to give him hope. He had been reading about some people having six senses instead of five. He was trying to understand Eve and her capabilities. He remembered reading that telepathy was mind-to-mind communication, and that is what he thought Eve was talking about with reaching out to Sarah. He had been surprised that scientists already understood a lot of what certain people's brains could do. Then there were other people who were clairvoyants. These special people had the ability to gather information at a distance from objects or events. He wondered if that was like when you take a test and you can visualize your notes and read them in your mind. He wasn't sure about that one; maybe that was just memorization. The other idea he was learning about was precognition. He wondered if that was what happened when Eve was talking to her "space being" father and her voice changed to that of a child's. Eve had gone to different places in her mind, making her feel as if it were really happening. She went into that state when collecting information, perhaps using visions from ancient places from the past. Other times, the "space being" seemed to be trying to tell Eve about some event in the future.

Scott wondered about when Eve had used her mind to interact with the team and seemed to stop time and freeze the team in place. Was that a form of psychokinesis? The last form of mind management that was on his list was ESP; he hadn't seen Eve use that ability to get information in an extrasensory manner by using a sensory process of the brain, tapping into other realities…or had she? It was all really confusing; he wished he knew more about how the brain worked. He remembered reading a story of a man getting hit in the head by a horse hoof and being able to speak a different language when he came to.

It was all interesting, the untapped junk DNA that seemed to lay dormant in humans brains waiting for the right time to be unleashed. Scott knew that humans were the only creatures on Earth that could communicate with writing and remembered recently they had identified a specific gene. It allowed humans to speak and communicate with written language. It was a gene only found in humans. Scientists had found 223 genes that were different from anything else living on Earth. It made him wonder about the possibility that human life might have started somewhere else and had been brought to Earth. What had made humans evolve so much faster than the other species on Earth? The big question that kept going through his mind was: *Why were these space beings trying to help the human race survive?* And thus, move them forward in their evolutionary process. Whatever the case was, because he loved Eve, it had made him think of the world around him in a different light. He knew Eve would think him odd if she knew he was studying her. But he had lots of time on his hands.

Scott dressed quickly, finding his discarded clothes from the day before. He floated, pushing his way off the walls, following Eve through the spacecraft. He followed the dim lights that turned off behind Eve as she passed.

They stopped in the storage room. Chuckling to himself, Scott made a stupid joke in his head, then hoped that the time in space wasn't messing with his thought process. He knew that parts of the brain gave off electricity or light at a certain frequencies. Markus had told him that sometimes the elongated space travel affected people differently. Scott was told that Markus and the women had been tested to see how they would react when preparing for the mission. Scott hoped that he was mentally strong enough; he had to be! He had to watch over Eve and the child she was carrying.

chapter 93

By now Scott felt he had grown very familiar with the ship and the small amount of space they had to move around in. He found himself doing the same thing every time he entered the storage room where the semi-gravity made them able to walk after they had just floated down the halls. He had gotten used to the process and found himself tapping each of the robots on their heads as he passed. It was his form of saying hello to each one of them. He stretched his long limbs while he waited for Eve, watching her check each rover for the hundredth time. After the first four, she called out, excited. Scott joined her and moved to the driver's side door, looking inside to see what she had found. Not knowing he was there, Eve called out again and Scott jumped in the air, caught off guard, and hit his head. Rubbing the soon-to-be lump, he tried to see what she was looking at.

"This is the one! Look!" Eve said, excited.

Scott leaned inside to see what Eve was pointing at. They had been checking all the rover trucks for months, because she was confident something had to be there. He wasn't so sure after not finding any sign indicating that Gordon had installed anything special. Eve pointed to the dashboard and on the left side was a small white flower sticker that was the same color as the interior and could be easily missed. It wasn't in any of the other rovers, so maybe she had found something. He leaned in, watching. Eve gently worked one side, then the other, and was able to pull it off intact.

Underneath was a small folded piece of paper in the shape of a square. Eve smiled, now satisfied. Her hands were shaking as she pulled it free of the dashboard. Gently Eve unfolded it, reading the contents, making sure she understood each word and its meaning. Typed in a small font were instructions of how to turn on the communication device.

"Here, let me see it," Scott said. "I'll read it to you. It says to look under the passenger seat up in the coils." Scott was closer and reached down to pull out a small ziploc bag; he handed it to Eve. She dumped the contents on the front seat and turned each of the parts over a few times in her hands, inspecting each one, trying to figure out how it went together.

"Okay…give me a clue," Eve said.

"It says all you have to do is plug it in right there."

Scott said, pointing to the middle consule. "And connect the red wire there. It should start after connected," Scott said, making sure it matched the tiny diagram.

"Nothing is happening," Eve said. "Wait! Look at the tiny solar panel! I think it's dead. We'll have to take this truck outside when we reach Mars to recharge the battery… it looks solar like about everything else."

"Well at least we found it!" Scott said, "Undo it and we will hide it back under the seat. At least we know it's there and we'll be able to use it. For now, I think it is best to keep it to ourselves. I've been reading how space travel can change people in different ways. We don't want anything to happen to the device if someone loses their mind," Scott said, laughing, now happy.

"I agree. We have to be careful," Eve said.

She put the sticker back where it was on the dash and smacked it before closing the door, making sure it was pressed down tight. They were both happy, relieved that they might have some control over their destiny. Together they floated, holding hands in the microgravity out of the storage room, making their way back to their sleeping pod.

chapter 94

With the lithium batteries replaced on the ship's solar panel, everything was functioning to full capacity and the astronauts found the ship back on a steady course. Time had gone by as they traveled, everyone settling in to their daily routines. Days passed into weeks, until the spacecraft was finally just a few days away from Mars. The crew had been excited until NASA reminded them how hard it was going to be to slow down the spacecraft while trying to land in the exact spot that had been calculated.

Unlike Earth, Mars hardly has an atmosphere. Scientific thoughts were that at one time Mars had an atmosphere consisting of gasses like Earth. This not only protected the planet from radiation but regulated the planet's temperature. Thoughts were the atmosphere had somehow been destroyed. Even with the thin atmosphere, it now had seasons, polar ice caps, extinct volcanoes, and canyons. One idea was that a large comet might have collided with Mars, ripping apart the atmosphere and making it uninhabitable. But scientists have found on Mars evidence of a nuclear signature relating to testing of nuclear bombs, similar to what we did on Earth in the Nevada desert. When a bomb goes off, it leaves behind a gas called Xenon 129; the only way to produce this gas is with a nuclear explosion.

Lacking an atmosphere to slow the spacecraft down, the astronauts were going to do everything in their power to decelerate. They would have to circle Mars, rotating around the planet behind one of the moons, then go in sideways. Then they needed to upright the vessel to put her down on the surface. It sounded almost like an impossible task to Eve.

"Okay! We get one chance to do this! If we don't get it the first time, it hasn't been predicted what will happen. We need to get ready. We need to check and lock everything down, then strap ourselves in our chairs," Britney stated. "Once we're secured, I'll turn off the atmospheric pressure. You might feel different because it puts pressure on our organs, it's what keeps them in place. Without the pressure, our internal organs would separate and move apart with no force holding them together. But don't worry...you might feel your heart beat faster, because in space the atmospheric pressure isn't the same as Earth so your heart beats slower."

"Good to know. But what kind of gravity is on Mars?" Eve asked.

"From what I understand, the pull isn't like the gravity on Earth. As you know from your studies, gravity is the force of attraction between two objects such as planets and stars or moons. The force felt on Earth pulls everything toward its center," Britney explained. "We have been living mostly in microgravity as we traveled. You know, the condition where an object appears to be weightless or floating. The bad thing for us is the blood normally flows downward in our bodies on Earth, because of gravity. But in microgravity the blood flows upward, slowing the heart. The higher pressure can affect your vision. So we have been told that it is close to Earth's gravity, but not as much pull," Britney said.

"I understand…everything is going to be different and in time our bodies will evolve to adapt to the environment." Eve said, wondering what would happen to her child with all the changes. She put her hand over her stomach in a protective gesture and pushed those thoughts to the back of her mind. Eve didn't want to think about what *could* happen and tried to focus on what was about to happen.

The small group was prepared and ready to get to Mars; it had been a long eight months in space. Everyone was dressed in their white spacesuits, helmets ready to be put on. The anticipation and excitement filled them all.

"Okay, it's time to put on your helmets and make sure that your oxygen is working correctly. Don't forget to check your O-rings. Is everyone good? If you're having trouble, please raise a hand," Britney said, looking around. Everyone was watching her with intent looks on their faces. "We have been training for a long time and it will be an honor to land on Mars with each one of you. See you on the surface." Britney said, taking her seat behind the large control panels.

They all watched the timer counting down and heard NASA in their headsets giving orders. Eve had thought that communication would be delayed because of distance but the feed must have been coming from the space station. She felt the excitement grow in the control room. When the timer hit two minutes, there was a brief silence and a man started rapidly giving the astronauts directions.

Eve felt the ship start to shake; the vibrating was intense—it made her teeth rattle. She tried to turn her head to the side, but the pressure forced her back hard in her seat, taking her breath away briefly. It was so loud even with her ears covered she could hardly hear what NASA was saying. In the raspiness of the reception, Eve made out the blare of an emergency siren going off and yelling in her headset from NASA.

She looked over at Scott and saw his eyes were open and he was mouthing something to her. Eve looked in the direction he was trying to motion with his head. She saw that Britney's eyes were closed, and her head was leaning to the side. Eve could tell that she had been knocked out. Panic filled her, she tried to yell out for help, but no one could move or just couldn't hear her. Eve tried to pull away from her seat, but the force was so intense that it glued her to her chair. Eve closed her eyes, reaching out to her "being" father. She felt him in her head and a surge of power heated her body, hitting her hard in her chest. The medallion under Eve's suit had turned the material dark as if on fire. She could feel the metal burning her skin. Her breath was taken away for a moment as the medallion touched the area over her heart.

Very slowly, Eve unhooked the straps of her harness, freeing herself from the chair. Against the velocity of the pressure, she pulled away from her seat inch by inch. She leaned forward, fighting the pressure surrounding her, feeling the molecules of the space pushing her back. With small steps, Eve tuned out the noise around her and was able to move forward. She focused with determination toward the control panel that was in front of Britney. As she calmed, Eve was able to hear the voice in her headset and began to understand what was being said.

"Angle 45 degrees! Slow her down! You're going to burn up!" NASA yelled over and over. The ship robots rolled around the panels, doing their part to take control of the ship. But they had been programmed to assist the astronauts, not take over, and could only help a small amount.

chapter 95

Eve suddenly felt a calm come over her as a blueprint of the control panel visually entered her mind. She absorbed the information within seconds and took the handheld controls, turning the wheel gently, angling the ship to go in sideways to slow them. The ship fell behind the larger moon, letting it block some of the resistance.

"Okay, you're doing a good job. In thirty seconds, I need you to straighten her out and break away toward the surface. Ready...okay! Now!"

Eve turned quickly, up-righting the spaceship's direction. She pulled hard on the controls, holding on tight, trying to straighten the ship out. She could hear the suspended dirt and small rocks hitting the ship's sides, sounding like they were in a sandstorm.

"Straighten her out! Hurry! Here we go—gently pull the fuel in the last compartment...it will distribute the weight. Hold on! You're doing it!" NASA directed.

The ship hit the surface of Mars with a thump that brought Eve to her knees. She could feel them sliding and she held on tight to the controls, not letting go. Tears streamed down her face and she continued to hold on, then there was silence. Eve fell to the floor, breathing hard. She looked around the cabin and stood, testing her legs. She wasn't hurt but her legs were very weak and she managed to drag herself along the hard surface holding on to the walls, making her way to Scott. By his side, she removed his helmet, checking to see if he was breathing and pulled the side oxygen, putting the mask over his face.

"Take some deep breaths," Eve whispered, "Please Scott!" He breathed a deep inhale without opening his eyes. Eve let out a sigh of relief when she saw his chest rise and fall, knowing that he was okay. She then crawled to Britney and found that she was waking up and watched her start to look around the cabin.

"What happened?" Britney mouthed inside her helmet.

But Eve left the question unanswered as she moved to Markus, finding him fine. But when she took off Courtney's helmet, blood was dripping from her forehead and Eve checked her pulse.

"I need some help over here!" Eve yelled. Markus and Eve pulled Courtney out of her chair, moving her to the floor. "She's not breathing! Get the side oxygen!"

Eve began to give her CPR, blowing in her mouth to clear the passage and then together she worked with Markus like a rehearsed team.

"One-Two-Three-Four-Five...breathe!" Markus counted and put the oxygen over Courtney's nose and mouth. "One-Two-Three-Four-Five...breathe."

They kept at it until Courtney coughed and they rolled her on her side. Scott had crawled over to help and checked Courtney's pulse, nodding at Eve. Courtney looked up, dazed. Her eyes were glossed over, but she put up her thumb in an "I'm okay" sign and sucked on the oxygen for a few more minutes. Everyone sat on the floor around her, exhausted, and looked up when Britney spoke.

"I'm so sorry! I've never passed out on a mission!"

Britney said, tears streaming down her face. "Eve, how were you able to do that? The force must have been so strong." Brandy said wiping her tears with the back of her hand.

Eve looked at Scott and he nodded. "There's something that we think you all should know. I think I know the reason we were placed on this ship instead of the rest of your team. And now we need to find a way to return to Earth in the next 22 weeks," Eve said. The room was quiet as everyone looked in Eve's direction.

"What is the reason?" Markus asked, confused.

"Well, for the past year I have been solicited by a company that is working with NASA. I know it is because last year when doing my dissertation, I came up with an anti-gravitational device to move matter. I made a video showing my results and the back story on my…origin."

"What do you mean by 'origin'?" Markus asked.

"This is going to be hard to understand because it's a long story, but I turned over this information to the President of the United States. I think he wanted me on this mission and Scott was brought along to keep me happy."

"I don't understand. Why would he kidnap you guys and change the mission that was in place?" Courtney asked. "It was a real risk sending us with the robots. We might have better prepared if we had known in advance. But we were just happy to be going, with most astronauts it is our life goal to go to space."

"I think the President not only wanted to put humans first on this planet, he needed it to be me just in case. I kinda have special...let's just call it talents that might prove to be an advantage to making this mission successful," Eve said.

"Well...okay...I still don't understand," Britney said.

Eve glanced at Scott, who gave her the look that it was up to her to reveal herself. "I'm a Star Child," Eve stated. Everyone was silent, trying to digest what she was saying.

"What does that mean?" Markus asked.

"I know this is going to be hard to believe...but I'm part Human and part space being," Eve said. When no one said anything she continued. "I think having RH negative blood is because space beings have mixed their DNA with humans, thus causing a problem when having a child. I'm pregnant and need to get a shot as I get close to having a baby or it could kill me and the child. It's like two different species mixing. So now you know the reason we are here and the problem we have," Eve said.

"You're pregnant?" Markus asked, "Well no one tells me anything! Congratulations!"

"Well glad someone has been enjoying themselves on the ride here!" Brandy said, "But really happy for you both."

"That's GREAT!" Courtney said. "Being the ship doctor I'm sure we will find a work-around."

"It's all right. We are going to be fine," Scott said, "Look—all of us need to be proud. We are the first to make a landing like this. Because of all of you I'm sure they will collect all the data and the ones that follow will have an easier time. This is a great day!"

chapter 96

Everyone looked at Scott and hope filled their faces, making them realize what they had just done. "Now Britney, tell NASA that we are all okay," Scott said. "We can't have them think we crashed."

Britney picked up the headset and put it back on.

"NASA, are you there? We are all okay and have landed on Mars!" A cheer went up inside the ship from the small group. "NASA, are you there?" The connection was silent.

"What happened?" Scott asked.

"I think our position has turned away from the space station so we will have to wait about 13 hours before we are in a place to get reception; remember a Martian day is 24.7 hours. But we do have a list of things that need to be checked." Britney said, pulling a chain out of her spacesuit; dangling on the end was a key. Britney crawled to a panel and unlocked the drawer, pulling out a thick pamphlet.

"Okay…first, we need to evaluate the spacecraft and see if there was any damage. Let's start with checking inside with each lab. Markus, you come with me and Courtney, you go with Eve and Scott. You guys check the greenhouse and the storage area, and we will take a look at the engine room. Report back here when you finish," Britney ordered and disappeared down a side hallway.

"We're on it!" Eve said. She stood slowly, feeling her legs were weak even in this Mars gravity. Scott and Courtney had more trouble; it was like learning to walk again.

"This is crazy," Scott said. "My legs feel like lead."

"Yes, it is really hard to lift my feet for each step. I think we will really be sore tomorrow; this is like a major workout," Courtney said.

They made their way down the long hall, leaning against the walls and stopping from time to time to catch their breath. Anyone watching them would find it amusing. Every step left them breathless. They went first to their lab, the greenhouse. Inside, one of the 20-pound buckets of sand had left a trail across the floor as if it were dragged. But for the most part the plants were secure. Scott had the idea to use some of the extra netting to cover over the plant pots; this allowed for the plants not to move, locking them in place. A few of the tomato plants had broken branches and lost a few green tomatoes, but most were unscathed.

"Good idea on tying them down!" Eve said, "It could have been a disaster!"

"You guys ready to move to the storage room?" Courtney asked. "I'm getting hungry and it will take us at least thirty minutes to get there."

"You guys go ahead…I'll catch up. Let me grab some fresh food for our meal tonight…a celebration!" Eve said, grabbing a cloth bag hanging on the wall.

Once they were out the door Eve loaded the bag up with some of the spaghetti sauce and weird shaped pasta that she and Scott had attempted to make. The best items were what she harvested to make a salad. She plucked some of the outside leaves of the lettuce. Eve remembered reading that the plant would grow replacement leaves once some were removed. A tomato, one onion, one orange pepper, one cucumber. Eve looked around wondering if there was anything else. She remembered finding a drawer with dried fruit and hadn't told the others. She removed dried apples, adding some cinnamon and brown sugar to her bag. She would rehydrate them for dessert and surprise everyone. Leaving the greenhouse, she remembered that she was eating for two and hoped that the baby was getting what nutrition it needed. She had felt a flutter last week but knew it was too soon to feel a kick. They had 22 more weeks to get home to Earth.

With this in mind, the walk to the storage area felt like it passed quickly. She entered to find Scott and Courtney struggling to put one of the robots back on its rack. It had come loose, and she knew it wasn't light, even when they all had their strength.

Eve set her bag on the floor by the door so she wouldn't forget it and soon the three of them had the robot back in place.

"Wonder what the plan is with the robots now that we're here? I thought they were to be directed remotely," Eve said. They waited until they all caught their breath before seeing what else needed to be done.

"I'm not sure…the robotics class we took before leaving showed us how to turn them on and I guess it has been built into their software that they are to do what we tell them and they can't harm us," Courtney said.

"Well, that's good—they're stronger and outnumber us.

Just in case, tell me—is the way you turn them on the same way we turn them off?" Eve asked.

"Yes, I think so. See this button on the back? We just have to type in a number for both," Courtney said. "Do you want me to turn one on and show you?"

"No, we can wait and deal with them later. Right now, I'm tired, and we are going to cook dinner tonight." Eve said, feeling a flutter in her midsection again. She put her hand over her stomach.

"Is everything all right?" Scott asked, concerned.

"Yes, I'm good," Eve said.

"What's wrong?" Courtney asked, "Can you feel the baby moving already?"

"No, I'm good! Just a flutter," Eve said.

"Well I need to check you anyway—doctor's orders!" Courtney said, stepping in front of Eve and starting to unzip the front of her suit. "We can remove these when we get the clear from Britney that the levels are stabilized on the ship."

"No, really—I'm fine." Eve said, looking at Scott for some help. But it looked like he wanted her to be checked also. "Look—it's nothing!" She paused. "Courtney, please…I'm just pregnant."

Courtney hesitated. "But I'm still checking you. How about we move to my lab; it will be more comfortable." Courtney looked in Scott's direction.

"Yes, Honey—it won't hurt to let her check you out. If you were at home, you would have already gone to the doctor by now." Scott said, moving by Eve's side.

"All right! Fine! Scott, get the food!" Eve said, now mad at all the fuss.

"Come on...this way," Courtney said.

It took them about twenty minutes of taking baby steps to make it to Courtney's lab. Scott and Eve hadn't been there and looked around at the small tidy area full of cabinets packed with equipment.

"Is there anything different Eve should be doing being RH negative?" Scott asked, waiting to see if Courtney had any information that might help the situation.

"Everything is the same as a normal pregnancy, we just need to figure out what's in the shot that they give women in this situation. But I will work on it to see what we can do," Courtney said.

"Yes," Scott said, looking hopeful.

"I guess that they didn't think of everything when preparing for this adventure," Courtney said. She looked at Eve, seeing she was nervous. "Everything will be okay. We'll think of something. How far along are you?" Courtney said, patting Eve's arm in comfort.

"I think we have 22 weeks before I'll need the shot," Eve said.

Courtney checked Eve's pulse. "Well, let me take a look. Let's do an ultrasound...it might be too early to hear anything, but we'll see."

"Okay," Eve said, not knowing the process or what to do.

Scott paced the room, waiting. Now that they were on Mars all he could think about was what they were going to do to get home.

chapter 97

Light had started to filter in the large round window in the portal room. The group sat watching the sun rise, wondering about the new world. The filtered light was dimmer than on Earth. It was almost like an overcast day. Eve had to remember the distance that the light had to travel. Soon they would be the first to walk on the surface. Well, the first in a long time.

They had landed just a half mile from the targeted area in a region of Mars called Ares Vallis. It was close to where NASA had put down the Pathfinder in 1997. Its mission was to look for signs of water. Scientists believed that at one time, Mars was close to Earth's atmosphere, thus full of water and life in the oceans. The Pathfinder was equipped with an x-ray spectrometer and high-powered camera to look for ancient life forms. NASA was sure Mars had a wet past.

It had taken all night to make sure all the spacecraft living areas, research labs, sleeping areas, airlock for docking the spacecraft, advanced life support, oxygen generators, water recycling, treadmill, toilet, and the 3-D printer, Roboaut (robot), were all checked. It looked like everything was in working order as the team huddled around the porthole, watching the surface start to lighten as the sun rose on the horizon.

"It looks different, almost like a desert with no vegetation and a lot of rocks," Markus said.

"Yes, look at those large rocks just laying scattered about." Courtney said, "It looks like something just picked them up and dropped them where they lay now...really weird."

"NASA said that they have found ice at the poles and at one point there were active volcanoes," Britney said.

"Are those mountains over there?" Eve asked, pointing to the large mounds popping out of the flat, sandy landscape.

"From what we were told, there isn't any volcanic activity in this area," Britney said.

"Well, I think we are looking at the mountain range named the Twin Peaks area. It's not known for volcanic activity. They do look like mountains, sitting there all alone in the middle of nowhere. We will have to investigate them closer and see what they are. It's on our list of information that NASA wants us to send back," Courtney said.

"How were they formed, I wonder," Scott said.

Courtney, Britney, and Markus looked at each other. Courtney answered, "Well, thoughts are that even with the million years of erosion, for at least the past two billion years Mars has been a cold desert where only the wind and dust has carved out the landscape. Its light and dark markings showed the changing of seasons. It is said that the rocks from Mars show an ancient magnetic field. Here on Mars, water forms in ice clouds daily around the Olympus Mons as the moist air rises and cools. It is the tallest volcano in the solar system. They think the atmosphere is so thin on Mars that any water evaporates or freezes. Today much of the water remains frozen in the polar caps in ice deposits just below Mars' surface. The north polar cap has thin layers of ice that has built up deposits. It has clean and dirty layers because it depends if there is a dust storm happening while freezing and is added to the layer.

"Besides all that—sorry, I got sidetracked—the twin peak area is thought to resemble the pyramids and Sphinx of Giza," Courtney took a breath.

"Yes, if that's the case, it would be interesting to know if they are also aligned with the three stars of Orion's belt. Did you know they have dated the pyramids and Sphinx back to 10,500 BC, when the pyramids lined up with the belt stars of Orion? At the same time, the Sphinx looked out at the constellation of Leo," Eve said, looking in Scott's direction. "I wonder if they are on the same longitude and latitude lines that are around 30 degrees? Or if the navel of Earth lined up perfectly from the north, south, east, and west. I wonder if what we are looking at is the same as it is on Earth." Eve said, thoughtful, "Sorry—just thinking out loud."

"Can I borrow those binoculars?" Scott asked Markus, "I just want to get a good look." Scott took them and stepped up to the window. The area was lit enough outside that he could see the large hills in the distance. He focused on the smaller rocks that were where the Sphinx would be and noticed a shape that really could be the size of a Sphinx. He visualized the area, seeing that it could be true, visualizing where part of it could be buried in the sand. "Yes, I think it looks like that to me," Scott said. Everyone took a turn with the binoculars.

"I think you're right," Britney said. "We will have to take a closer look. Hey...the connection should be up soon, and we will be able to run a check on the outside of the ship to see if we are intact. We will have to wait at least an hour. It looks like a sandstorm is moving in. In 2001 a huge storm sent dust into the atmosphere where it circulated around the whole planet for months and stayed hazy for a long time. But this one looks small; they said this happens daily. It is best for us to wait until it's finished before clearing the panels.

"I think all of us except Courtney are going to have to suit up and go outside. I'm sure after landing like we did the panels are covered in Martian dust and some could be buried," Britney said.

"Okay. I wonder if we need to do that before we can make contact—we might not have enough power," Markus said. "And I think you're right to leave someone on the ship just in case. Good plan!"

"I understand, but I wish I could go out with everyone," Courtney said. "How about if everyone suits up and you guys take one of the trucks out and drive around the ship first?"

"Yes—that's a great idea!" Eve said, taking Scott's hand.

"Okay…point taken. You're right—that would be the safest way to explore first," Britney said. "How about we meet in the storage area in an hour suited and ready to leave the ship?"

The group left to get ready; Scott and Eve went to their sleeping area and dressed quickly, wanting to get to the storage area first to make sure the rover they wanted to use was pulled to the front by the large door.

"Are you ready?" Scott asked.

"Yes…come on." As they passed the kitchen area, Eve grabbed a package of dehydrated milk and mixed it with cereal. She added water and waited while the hot water expanded the package and she carried it with them, sucking the contents.

"I'm really missing real food about now!" Eve said.

"Well, just keep eating as much as you can. I know they developed these packs full of chemically treated nutrition… who knows what is really inside those." Scott said, kissing her and then pressing the packet back to her lips.

"Don't worry, Honey—I'm eating!" Eve said, kissing him as she went by.

He licked his lips, tasting the sweet flavor. He had been feeling a little out-of-control in this situation and he was the man! The basic instinct to take care of his wife—and now family—was constantly on his mind. What were they going to do? With his extreme intelligence he was having a hard time trying to figure it out. He didn't want to talk to Eve about it, because she knew the situation already, why rehash it and add extra stress?

chapter 98

When they arrived in the storage area, the lights were a little dim. The robots' metal gleamed in the soft light and were really a little creepy; their rows of large eyes lay in wait, giving the couple the feeling of being watched.

They found the truck with the communication device and Scott read the directions while Eve hooked it back up, putting it under the driver's seat and attaching the little solar panel to the dashboard under the large window. When the others arrived, she was adjusting the seat to fit her long legs.

"I take it you're driving," Britney said, climbing in the passenger seat beside her.

"Yes, I thought it would be best until you guys get used to the controls." Eve said, "I'm ready when you are."

Scott and Markus slowly climbed into the second row. The moving was slow with all the extra weight of the suits adding to their strained muscles. After the door closed, they all heard Courtney talking in their headsets.

"Check your seals and make sure the oxygen is flowing inside the cab. Don't remove your helmets this time around, until we are sure everything is functional," Courtney said. "If you're all good, I need a thumbs-up from each of you."

"I'm good!" Eve said, putting her thumb up.

"Okay!" Britney said.

"Markus and Scott?" Courtney waited.

"Yes, clear!" Scott said.

"Party on!" Markus said, "Now we are the aliens?"

"Eve, start the engine," Courtney said. They all held their breaths, hoping that the vehicle turned over after sitting for so long. Everyone relaxed when they heard the soft purr.

"I'm now moving outside the room so I can open the hatch so you can drive out. Shutting the door now. Pushing the button to open the hatch now," Courtney said.

They all heard a grinding sound as the door started to lift, then it stopped.

"Stand clear! I'm re-hitting it." Courtney said, "It seems stuck."

The door went back down and started to lift again and this time it rose just enough for the truck to clear. Eve moved the truck slowly forward and was soon outside.

"Courtney, it looks like we're low on power. Leave the door open to save what we can. We are moving in position to check the outside of the ship," Britney said.

"Okay…I'm moving to the control room. I need to check the in-house robots to see what they can do to help us," Courtney said.

"Roger that," Britney said.

They pulled outside, observing the topography features of the surface of Mars. They had landed in a flat area and noticed to the west was a mountain range with a huge mountain. To the south were the "Twin Peaks."

"I think that must be Olympus Mons," Markus said, pointing.

"It's huge!" Eve said.

"Well, Mars has the highest mountains in the solar system. Olympus Mons is 15.5 miles high so there had to have been volcanic activity at some point," Markus explained.

"It's incredible!" Eve said. "How far away do you think it is?"

"I'm not sure, maybe a distance of at least 20 miles? I think if we were at the base, we wouldn't be able to see the top," Markus said.

"Well I can't see the top from here!" Eve said.

"Look at the snow or ice on top," Scott said. "Did NASA know that? It means water on Mars other than at the poles."

"Honey, that's the clouds!" Eve said, laughing.

"Yes, they know. We haven't been the only ones with probes on Mars. I'm sure the Russians and the Chinese are also gathering information. Soon they will be making claims to certain areas. Most likely we will mark the areas we explore with U.S. flags. We have a whole container of them. That probably explains the rush to get us here first. That might have been NASA's reason to send us now instead of waiting. Others must be coming soon," Markus said.

chapter 99

"Why don't we make a slow circle around the spaceship first and see how we're sitting?" Britney instructed and pointed the direction she wanted Eve to drive.

"Here we go." Eve moved forward; the terrain was vacant of vegetation and reminded her that they weren't on Earth. It looked almost like a barren Arizona desert without the cacti. Small and large rocks were scattered all over and Eve drove around many, not wanting to challenge the vehicle. But she knew that Gordon's baby would be able to climb just about anything.

"Look, some of the panels are buried and the others are covered. We are running on our back-up power generator right now. We have a lot of work to do or we are going to be dead in the water soon," Markus said.

"Eve, continue around and let's see if we have any damage," Britney ordered. Eve went left, staying about six feet away from the craft.

"Everything looks intact. We're just a little tilted…but for the most part we really didn't do too badly," Markus said. "Eve, could you pull back by the hanger and park? We're going to need some tools and help."

"What is that?" Britney asked, seeing the solar panel on the dash.

"It's a safety device that my mentor planted in the truck," Eve said. "It's for emergencies if something happens when we are far from the ship."

"Okay…cool. Let's do some work, gang. Remember to keep the visors on your helmets down. Just reminding you that the radiation is said to be intense because of the thin atmosphere around this planet," Britney said.

"Yes, you're right. Parts of this planet might look like Earth but we can't forget how intense the radiation can be on the human body, let alone our eyes. We don't want to go blind!" Markus said. "How about I activate a few of the robots to help? It looks like a big job."

"Good idea—I think they were completely powered before we left," Britney said. The group checked each other to make sure that every suit was working correctly.

"Here we go. Scott, press the airlock," Britney ordered.

"Yes, Ma'm." Scott said and the truck door opened.

"Everyone…follow me," Markus said. He moved back inside the hanger and found the stored tools. "Could you take these outside?"

Scott and Eve struggled to lift the picks and rakes and small shovels.

"I can't believe how heavy these are!" Eve said.

"Yes, I know. This space travel is something else." Scott pulled Eve into his arms and patted her helmet, looking into her green eyes.

"I don't think they believed me…" Eve said. "Now they might think that I'm a nut!"

"Don't worry, Honey, with time they will see. Come on,

let's see how the robots work." Scott said, pulling her along behind him in Markus' direction.

Markus had already turned on two of the robots and was working on the next one. They watched as the large pieces of metal lined up patiently waiting for their orders.

"How many are you turning on?" Scott asked.

"I think six will do it. They really work fast," Markus said, moving to number four.

"Almost ready?" Britney asked, coming inside covered in Mars dust. The static made the dry dirt cling to the outside of her suit and when she brushed it off it reattached.

"Yes, almost…I thought six would be good," Markus said, moving to number six. When finished he stated in a loud voice, "Martian number 1, 2, 3, 4, 5, 6 please go outside and clear the solar panels. When finished come back for your next orders." They all watched as the lights in the robots' eyes glowed and the line moved outside in a formation. A compartment in their arms opened and a brush appeared at the end of their hands. The six robots lined up and started to brush the panels, gently removing the dust and dry dirt. As soon as one was clear, the six would move together to the next area. The astronauts all watched in amazement at the organized robotic team moving around the ship.

"It's incredible how they work together…I guess we supervise?" Eve asked.

"I don't totally trust them left alone. Just like any machine. For instance, think about the Roomba vacuum; it's programmed to pick up everything on the floor and underneath furniture. It always gets stuck, then you have to find it and set it back in motion and empty the waste it picked up," Markus said.

"Haha—you're right!" Scott said, "I saw those on TV."

"What about the part that needs to be dug out? Do we want to work on that? Or you will have them do it?" Eve asked.

"I'm not sure…let's see how bad it is first," Britney said. "You guys want to ride around and take a look?"

"I'll go with you," Eve said. "The boys can stay here and monitor the robots."

"Okay, come on," Britney said.

"Scott, I'll be right back," Eve said, patting his helmet, and got back into the driver's seat. She observed a green light on the dash and fumbled under her seat and pulled out the device.

"Is that the safety communication port?" Britney asked.

"Yes, and it looks like it's charged. Hold on, let me take a look here." Eve noticed that words were playing a message over and over like on a ticker tape. "It's a message from Gordon! He's been visited by my parents and all are worried that we have disappeared and on our way to Mars!" Eve chuckled.

"What is it?" Britney asked.

"He made a joke and I have to bring him back something interesting," Eve said, "Hold on—I'm sending a message back."

"What are you going to tell him?" Britney asked.

"I'll read it to you…Gordon—Yes, we are on Mars now and all is safe. We are working on a quick return…any ideas? Problem pregnant…love to my parents and Sarah, tell her… I heard her." Eve said and pressed the send message.

"What do you mean you heard her?" Britney asked.

"Well I kind of have a sixth sense. I know it's weird," Eve said.

"Do you mean you can read minds?"

"I'm not sure; it's all new to me. Are the Russians really dropping exploratory rovers and supplies in about a month?" Eve asked. She drove around the spacecraft and found the area that looked to be buried. "It doesn't look bad; nothing appears to be broken."

"That is good news! We'll bring the robots around when they finish their task. I was told we have to give one order at a time not to confuse them. Then we have to set up the satellite dish and cables. It will help with the reception and powering the extender pods we have to attach. We have a lot of work to do before we are set up to be 100 percent functional. There are dust storms here on Mars and we will need to store energy. The whole planet can stay hazy for months at a time. It won't be good if something happens before we are ready.

"But for your question…I did hear that the Russians were launching around the time we did. So, I would think that they would be close in the next few weeks. We have a lot to do before they arrive. We need to get everything functioning and go out and flag as much land as possible. We were told documentation and photos are going to be necessary to prove that we were here first. Now I'm not sure if it is only rovers and supplies that might be coming. Who knows what to expect? We are on a need-to-know basis, even with us being the ones risking our lives! I know what you're thinking—if it is possible for a workaround to get on that craft and if it is returning to Earth…. Right?" Britney asked.

"You're right…that is what I was thinking," Eve said. Britney patted Eve's arm, showing compassion for the first time. Eve tried not to tear up, discovering that there was a heart under the tough demeanor.

"We'll find a way," Britney said, back to her bossy self. "Pull back around to the hanger and let's check their progress."

chapter 100

Back at Eve's parents' house, a cheer went up when the message came in. "They are safe on Mars and pregnant!" Janet said, happy and relieved.

Everyone was dancing around the computer room. Janet stopped and looked across the room at Sarah, who was leaning against the wall with her fingers to her temples. She wasn't joining the group and Janet wondered why.

"What is it, Sarah?"

"It's good news that the device works, but there is a problem that Eve isn't telling us. Gordon, when you send back a message…tell her…to tell us what she isn't saying. Tell her I see it." Sarah said and left the room.

The group looked at each other and the excitement was crushed with the realization that something was wrong besides the obvious.

"Are we sure that Sarah is right? Maybe she's just being paranoid?" Gordon asked.

"Well…Sarah has never been wrong. All these years…she really has a talent that is hard to understand." Michael said, hugging his wife close. "Do as Sarah asked, please. And tell Eve also that we love her! Ask what we can do to help," he said.

"Okay, I'll send it now," Gordon said, "I'm not sure how long it takes to go back and forth. I'm going to hook a loud buzzer that will go off when messages come in, so we don't have to remain in the room waiting. Honey...Jane...could you go help make breakfast?"

"Yes, I can do that!" Jane said, putting her arm around Janet, pulling her toward the stairs, leaving the men alone to rig the device.

"Don't worry! Everything is going to be all right," Jane said, when they were alone.

"What are we going to do? What if I can never see my daughter again?" Janet choked back the tears that had caused her voice to shake.

"We're going to figure it out! Everyone will work together and come up with a solution," Jane said.

"Yes of course...sorry for my weakness, I'm glad you're both here! Come on, I have a great quiche recipe that the boys will like." Janet led her guest to the kitchen. They didn't see Sarah; she had disappeared.

"Good—I love new dishes! Gordon is always a good trouper when I'm making new things for dinner. But I think he keeps protein bars in his office in case he is still hungry afterwards," Jane said, laughing.

They walked arm-in-arm into the large kitchen.

chapter 101

After clearing the spacecraft of all the dust and dirt, the astronauts were able to fill up the generator's storing power for the ship. It was enough to make it for the next few weeks before the veiled overcast atmosphere allowed small amounts of light to be gathered by the solar panels. The robots had done well and returned to their stalls to recharge. Tomorrow they would clear the area and start setting up the module pods, creating the team's living space away from the ship.

They had worked all day, setting up many of the satellite dishes and preparing the area. The transmitters were also fueled by the solar panels, thus making them able to communicate with NASA daily. It took about 32 minutes for NASA to receive a message sent from Mars and about 32 minutes for the team to get the response. They took turns checking for the messages about every hour. Then everyone would gather around and talk about the response they would send back.

The team had voted to not tell NASA about Eve being with child and not to question the reason that she and Scott were there. They knew that if they revealed the secret,

NASA's agenda would take priority over Eve and her unborn child. NASA might not care about risking Eve's life.

They made a plan of their own. They had been tracking the Russian ship that would be in Mars' orbit in two weeks. They had a couple escape pods and figured if they could get one of them to go high enough, it could get towed in by the Russians' craft. If that were the case, it would allow about 20 weeks to get Eve back to Earth.

"Won't it take longer than that to get back?" Eve asked.

"Not really. They will be a lot lighter and would already be in motion to slingshot around Mars, increasing the speed. They are dropping not only their rovers but supplies and food for later use, so will be thousands of pounds lighter," Britney explained.

"I wonder how the United States got them to do that?" Eve asked.

"If astronauts are in need, no matter where we're from, we're in this together. More of a human race survival thing, instead of country thing," Britney said. "I think you'll get back twice as fast. But we will have to figure the calculations. We need to know their ship's projected speed ahead of time."

"It's a good plan!" Scott said, looking at Eve.

"That and the only good one we have!" Britney laughed.

"We have two weeks to calculate the timing so it would put you right in its path. The best point is when it slows to drop the supplies," Courtney said, jotting down a few notes.

"In the meanwhile, we will have to pick up the pace on finishing the setup of the colony. We will need the space ready to store the food and equipment. Also, we will need to make a trip out to take a look at the twin peaks area and see if the hills are a geological feature or alien made," Britney said.

"No matter what it is, we will need to survey the area and flag it before the Russian ship is even close. I wouldn't be surprised if their rovers are dropped in the same area, with the idea of claiming it for their own. They, like us, want to see if there are any secrets left from an ancient civilization," Courtney said. Everyone nodded in agreement.

"Are you guys up to driving out today?" Britney asked.

"I'd love to explore! How about we take two trucks, just in case," Eve said. "Can you drive?" She asked Britney.

"Yes…I'll drive one and Markus can come with me and Courtney will go with you and Scott," Britney said. "Let's meet in the hanger in two hours, ready to leave."

"Sounds good!" Scott said. The group broke up, each having things to do to prepare to leave the ship. He pulled Eve behind him to their sleeping pod area.

"What do you think of the plan of connecting with the Russian spacecraft? Do you think it will work?" Scott asked.

"I'm not sure…if it works and the timing is right, it is possible," Eve said.

"You know, because of weight, the chances will be better for success if you go alone," Scott said.

"What are you saying? I won't go without you!" Eve said.

"Honey…if it saves you and the child, you will go without me!" Scott said, pulling her in his arms. "I'll come home when the next colonists arrive in two years. Tell me you see the logic in what I'm saying."

Eve held him tighter, clinging to him. "I understand what you're saying, but there has to be an alternate way."

"You'll go without me?" Scott asked, wanting reassurance.

Eve nodded, not saying the words. She knew that there was no way she was going to leave him behind.

chapter 102

The group met in the hanger dressed in their spacesuits and carrying their helmets. It didn't seem as gloomy as the day before; a good day for an adventure and the group's spirits were high with anticipation.

"Remember to keep your visors down; the radiation will be really high today, even with the special windshields on the vehicles. So today even in the cab, let's keep our helmets on," Britney said.

"Also, let's get in the trucks and make sure the communication system is working between us. Remember the microphones are in our helmets as well so we have extra backup," Courtney said, testing hers.

Eve and Scott climbed into the truck with the white flower, followed by Courtney. Britney and Markus could be heard not only in the helmets' earpieces, but through the communication system in the trucks. Before pulling out, Eve checked the device under her seat, seeing the message from Gordon. She sent back a quick message and replaced it.

The two trucks moved across the flat surface in one formation with Britney's truck taking the lead. They noticed the displaced rocks of all sizes lying scattered across the dry, desert-like surface, as if just tossed there. The area was void of any resemblance of past vegetation; the ground was just very dry. The trucks moved across the flat areas with ease, slowing at the outcropping of large rocks that appeared in their path and going around the larger ones.

They approached the tall mounds, noticing their looming size from a few miles away. They appeared all alone on the landscape, the mounds getting larger and larger the closer they got to them. The team stopped and parked for a few moments, observing the structures. Up close it was obvious that they weren't formed geographically. They were covered in surface dirt and showed evidence of wind erosion.

"Wow! These are really a lot bigger than I thought!" Markus said while pointing, "Britney, let's take a look at that outcropping over there first."

Britney lead them to the left until they were right in front of the pinkish colored stone structure. It was the size of the Coliseum in Rome.

"Circle around and let's get a better look," Markus said. Britney lead the way slowly around the base, keeping her distance.

"It looks like it's half buried," Eve said. She had taken out her phone and was filming. When they turned around the side corner, they all stopped and looked at a half-buried head of a dog with a long nose.

"My God! Is that what I think it is?" Markus asked, raising his voice in excitement.

"I think you're right! It looks Egyptian! Look at the headdress!" Courtney yelled. "What does this mean? Egyptians were here and then came to Earth? Or that this isn't the first time we've been to Mars?"

"It proves that there is a connection between Mars and Earth! Everyone on Earth is going to be tripping when they see the film footage! I really didn't think we would find anything like this! Amazing!" Britney said. "Make sure we film all the way around."

The team observed the Egyptian-like headdress that was depicted on Earth worn by the pharaohs and ancient gods. Eve recalled that type of headdress represented status, power, and authority.

"This is the same representation depicted in some of the ancient Egyptian hieroglyphics," Eve said. "Look at the details! You can tell it was once striped. I believe the headdress is called a Nemes?"

"Well I really don't care what it is called! We just made the biggest discovery of our time!" Britney stared at the sculpture.

"It is a representation of what was worn by the gods. See the lappet? It was once a decorative flap or fold in the ceremonial headdress," Eve said.

"How do you know all of that?" Courtney asked.

"I did my dissertation on anti-gravitation and did a lot of research on the pyramids," Eve said, excited.

"There are still bits of a blue color on the headdress area," Scott stated.

"Look! You can see the inlaid stones embedded in the headdress. You can still make out the different colors," Courtney said, excited.

"Sumerian texts describe the use of petroleum products in advanced chemistry. It gave the Egyptians the use of different colors of paints and pigments used in the processing of glazing. Now it seems like the space beings taught them.

Also, the use of semi-precious stones were a substitute for lapis lazuli," Eve said.

"I wonder if this proves that your research might be true?" Scott said.

"If that's the case, I wonder if underneath is the whole body of the Sphinx just like in Egypt," Courtney said, pointing to the back of the head.

"Fantastic!" Markus said, into their headsets.

"Did you guys know that they think at some point the face of the Spinx was redone to what it is today? It has been said that it was once the face of a dog like this one and then made to look like a human man," Eve said.

"So, I take it that what we just found at this site must mimic the pyramids in Egypt?" Britney asked.

"Or the other way around…maybe the Sphinx in Egypt mimics this one. Maybe someone built this one first," Eve said.

"I would say so. Can we move closer?" Scott said.

"Yes, let's take a closer look. Okay, Britney? I would like to get a sample of that blue paint," Eve asked. "You know how you can't carbon date stone, but we might be able to carbon date the paint used," she waited for a response.

"Okay, but approach slowly. We will watch you and hold back just in case," Britney said.

"You guys ready?" Eve asked, pulling up the incline toward the face. "Scott, can you take my phone and take a few pictures and film for me?"

"We have filming ability here in the cab. I can do that one," Courtney said.

"Sounds good, Courtney. I just want footage for my personal file, for a friend at NASA and my parents," Eve said.

"I'm not sure NASA would like it. They would consider anything we find theirs," Courtney said.

"Well since we aren't officially on this mission, they have no control over us! We never signed anything binding us to silence." Eve said, pulling right up to the headdress. The blue paint was worn but intact. Eve used the truck's arms to scrape a small area, getting a good amount of the blue paint. She secured it in the container before retracting the arms.

Eve had a second thought and took one more sample of the exposed rock. She believed there might be micro-organisms or fossils embedded in the rock used for the face. The pink stone was different from the rocks they had yet encountered. That might also give them some information in solving the mystery of Mars' past.

"You got it?" Britney asked.

"Yes, coming back to you now," Eve said, backing out of the space and pulling up beside the other truck.

"I take it that those huge mounds over there must be like our pyramids in Egypt?" Britney stated.

"I would say so…except I think they are much older. They think the pyramids in Egypt are as old as 10,000 to 14,000 BC and that for now is scientists' best guess. But they think that the Sphinx might be a lot older than that… I'm talking around 20,000 to 30,000 BC. Using sonar they have found a hidden underground chamber, which might contain written history of our planet and the origin of these space beings. Maybe it even has information on the lost city of Atlantis.

"As Scott said before, they are lined up with the star system of Orion's belt. You know Orion's belt is called the three sisters or three kings; it is the asterism in the constellation

Orion. Scientists say that the people who built the pyramids were more advanced with technology than we are today," Eve said.

"Do you think that there were more than one kind of space beings visiting Earth from different places?" Britney asked.

"If you're asking my opinion, I would say that there were. In my research I was focused on how whoever built the pyramids moved the heavy stones. Did the ancients have a kind of laser that could melt the rock and then put them in place with no mortar? They had to have something that we haven't invented yet, which could cut in such precise angles. And I know a gravity device is possible, because I figured out how to make one," Eve said.

"So, what you're saying is…you think that at one point these beings from the Orion constellation left their planet and came to our solar system to set up colonies like we are now doing?" Courtney asked.

"I think it is a possibility…but as scientists we need proof," Eve said.

"I didn't believe…until Eve and I were researching. We keep coming across things that made us question what we had been taught as children. There have been many stories considered myths that have been brushed under the rug by the Catholic Church and governments around the world. They think that the population wouldn't be able to handle the truth of our existence," Scott explained.

chapter 103

Markus continued their conversation as the group circled the huge monument, "I think that our government must know or have an idea of what we might find here on Mars. I wonder if it will be kept hidden from the people of Earth. Interesting conversation. You guys keep talking—I'm going to set up a flag real quick." Britney pulled up close to the buried dog head.

"I want to get a better look also," Markus said. They moved up to where Eve had just left.

"I know before, like in the 1950s, they would publish in the papers any odd stories pertaining to experiences with space beings or sighting of spaceships," Eve said.

"I remember a story of a man in 1961 in Eagle River, Wisconsin. I think it was recorded on TV—you know black and white TV in those days—not sure what show I was watching. Anyhow, it had this farmer telling the story of what happened to him. He said he saw a metallic shaped disk land outside his kitchen window. He saw a hatch open, like a car trunk, and a little man gets out—about five feet tall. He is holding up a jug motioning that he needs water. The farmer says his eyes were so penetrating that he had to look away and could feel the being in his head. He fills the jug with water and a second being hands him something that looks like a handful of wafers. After they left, the farmer tasted the wafer and thought it tasted like cardboard.

"Soon after he reported the incident, an investigation agency showed up called 'Project Blue Book.' The wafers were taken and tested. In the results they found the wafers were chemically modified with a combination of buckwheat, soybeans, and bran, but the odd thing was what they didn't contain: Salt," Scott said.

"Why would that be so significant?" Courtney asked.

"Well, because everything on Earth has sodium chloride," Eve said. "Thoughts are that the beings came from a place that doesn't have salt and that it is harmful to them. On Earth we all came from the salty oceans and salt is even in our blood."

"It makes me think of the myths of people using salt as protection. Or putting a circle of salt around you that the evil sprints can't cross," Courtney said, laughing.

"I know, right!" Scott said.

"Okay guys—are you ready to roll?" Britney asked.

"We got the flags down and documented our findings and took pictures that are time stamped. Let's check the mounds."

"We'll follow you guys," Eve said and moved again behind the other truck.

"What about the idea of astronauts in space and the challenge of feeding us for extended space travel? It really gives us three choices: Bring food; terraform a planet, like we are going to try to do here on Mars; or change our own metabolism. Maybe it wasn't the salt that they were afraid of but the modification of the body to survive. Back to that theory that we are what we eat! Ha ha ha," Courtney said.

"Moses was in the desert for 40 years with the Israelites—what did they eat? They said Manna came from the sky and fed them. Was Manna supplied from the space beings using a kind of mechanical device? Maybe based on algae cultures?" Markus wondered.

"There is a kind of modern Manna machine being developed by the astronauts at the space station. They are growing hydro algae and say it grows fast in that environment," Britney said.

"That is interesting!" Scott said.

"Okay…as we get closer, let's start with the smaller mound; it is the farthest away and we can work our way back to the two others. I don't know what they were thinking when they tried to play down the idea that these mounds might be pyramids. It looks quite obvious from here," Britney said.

"Doesn't it?" Markus chimed in.

"Very grand! I really find it hard to believe, even with all our evolved ideas of our evolution as humans," Courtney said.

They circled around the smaller mound and were able to see part of the base was buried. They stopped along the circumference and Markus got out and pounded a four-foot stake into the ground. He attached an American flag to each post. He put a post on each corner of the smallest square structure.

"Okay, let's move to the next one…I'm ready," Markus said, getting back in the truck.

"Do you need some help on the next one? I feel funny sitting here watching you do all the work," Scott said.

"Na…it's all right. It's quicker with just one of us getting out," Markus said. "Anyhow, think of the workout I'm getting!" He laughed, "The big question of the day is: Did life start here or on Earth? Or did it come from somewhere else?"

"I'm going to vote that it started here—not on Earth!" Courtney said.

"I say…I might agree!" Markus said.

"I'm not so sure…maybe the same time?" Britney said.

"I'm going to branch out into the larger picture. We know that there are many places in the galaxy that are in the goldilocks zone for life. So our dilemma is not the idea that other life exists out there. It's the idea of time travel and how did they come here in the first place," Eve said.

"Yes, I get it," Scott added. "If we agree…as we see here, there were others before us. How did they travel the distance through space from faraway places and remain alive when they reached Earth? What was their life span? Were they in a hibernation? How were they able to travel faster than the speed of light?"

"If we had some of those answers then we would be able to do it ourselves and visit them," Eve said.

Chapter 104

The second mound was larger and took the group an hour just to go around the base planting their flags. Because of the distance, they decided it was best to put the flags along the sides. They noticed giant statues carved into some of the stones around the base. They were clearly relics of a lost civilization that occupied the planet Mars.

"Look at the size of the rock blocks! It is hard to understand how they would ever be able to lift those...even with an anti-gravitational device," Courtney noted. "Some are the size of a VW Bug!"

"Well, my theory is that the ones who built the structures had a device that made moving matter easy. A kind of technology that we are now just discovering. It also has to do with sound waves at a certain frequency," Eve said.

"Look around...see how flat the plane is around the base? Where would they even be able to find all the stone to build the structures? They must have had to bring them a great distance! Look at those blocks—how tightly they fit together!" Markus said, excited.

"In Giza, it's said you can't fit a piece of paper between the blocks, they so perfectly fit together. You know they didn't even use mortar to hold them together," Eve said. They finished the second mound and moved to the largest and waited, staring at its size.

"What do you guys think? Do we have time to do the last one or should we wait until tomorrow?" Britney asked.

"How's your truck on energy? Ours looks like we are good for five more hours," Courtney stated.

"Yes, we're showing we have about the same amount of time left. And it will take us an hour to get back. Okay, let's try to finish," Britney said.

Britney led the way to the base of the largest pyramid, bringing the trucks closer than the others because of its size. They started the same procedure as before with Markus getting out each time. The others waited, amazed at the size of the structure.

"Guys, look!" Eve pointed. "I wonder..." Eve had noticed a hole-like arch, cut out in the side of the pyramid, about one-third of the way up.

"It looks like an entrance. Remember we were able to go inside the structure that was on the moon," Courtney said. "What do you guys think?"

"I'm not really sure about what we saw on the moon because it was so dark. I just remember the inside," Markus said.

"Well, what do you guys think? We still have three hours. I wouldn't mind taking a look," Courtney said, excited.

"I'm not sure..." Britney said.

"Let's vote," Courtney suggested.

"Well, I would like to take a look," Eve said. "If we do it quickly it will be okay with time."

"I'm curious too," Scott said.

"Yes...I want to see what's up there! Besides, fellow astronauts—we are adventurers here to discover other planets and beyond," Markus joked.

"You're silly! But I really want to see what's up there!" Courtney said.

"Well, it sounds like we all want to go," Britney said. "Let's do it. We're wasting time talking about it. Park facing the colony in case we have to make a fast exit. Now make sure all your equipment is good and let's go. Just in case we will leave one of the trucks running. Turn yours off, Eve." Britney ordered.

"Okay, Commander." Eve laughed, excited to go inside the pyramid.

Chapter 105

Back at the house in Connecticut, a bell rang through the house and the men hurried to the upstairs security room. The women came moments later, breathless. Everyone held their breath, waiting for Gordon to read the message.

"Hello All, we have found the device and are glad to be in contact. We had no idea we would be taking this trip and are trying to come up with a solution to make it back to you soon as possible. Yes, I'm pregnant and have about 22 weeks to come home to get a shot. We will be in touch soon. Eve."

"What is she talking about?" Michael asked.

"She's being careful what she says," Gordon said. "Smart girl! She is protecting them and us at the same time."

"What is this about getting home in 22 weeks?"

"She is RH-negative!" Sarah said. "And many of the abduction cases reported are said to have RH-negative blood!"

"Well, what does that mean?" Jane asked.

"It means that my daughter is going to need a shot or she and the baby are in danger and we have 22 weeks to figure something out," Janet said.

"Okay, so we do what we do best," Michael said.

"We research until we have an answer."

Chapter 106

The team climbed and climbed, working together over the large stone blocks. It took about thirty minutes of strenuous activity to make it to the landing of the largest pyramid. At times they had to wind their way back, looking for the path that others had taken long ago. At the entrance they all stood, overwhelmed at seeing the large arches. The perfectly built structure hadn't moved since the original builders had put the stones in place. The arches showed the perfect angles and precision of the entrance. The opening was larger than anticipated and had grown taller the closer they had gotten. The group stood in place for a moment, catching their breath and looking into the dark space beyond.

"We have to remember that we are carrying about eighty pounds on our backs," Britney gasped between deep breaths.

"I know...back on Earth, none of us would have even been winded, because we are in good shape," Scott said, leaning over to catch his breath. He had fallen into the way he finished runs in college. That position didn't help him at all while in his spacesuit.

The entrance looked dark, like a black hole, but a glow of defused light came from far inside. Stepping through the entrance, they noticed notches had been cut into the stone. Each cutout held a different colored mineral that had been injected into the wall, fitting perfectly. As they stepped forward, the stones started to illuminate. The colors of a rainbow filled the space.

"It activated when we crossed the threshold," Courtney said, looking at the others.

"Yes—I think you're right. Does anyone feel an energy or a kind of frequency filling the room with power?" Eve asked. She could feel something, like a buzz pumping her blood as if it were mimicking the rhythm of the lights. The faint drumbeat of a distant people played in her head. Eve took a breath and pushed the sound to the back of her mind, trying to focus on the present. She didn't want to go to that distant place in front of the others. Scott saw that something was wrong and moved to her side, looking at her face behind the protective shield.

"I feel it too! Stay close. Remember to use your mind to push against it," he said.

"My necklace is heating up under my clothes…I can feel it pulsating," Eve whispered.

"What did you say?" Britney asked.

"I think this is technology not understood on Earth," Eve said. "Come on, let's continue and then get out of here."

"You're right! We don't want to waste time," Britney said, moving forward.

chapter 107

Inside, hieroglyphs could be seen from the entrance. The bright colors were still intact and depicted bearded figures in their travel clothes. The appearance of technology hung from their bodies. The group stood looking inside, wanting to move forward but unsure for a few moments. Now that they were there, the unknown frightened them all a little. Eve moved to the front, taking the lead beside Britney.

"We are on the discovery of an amazing historical event to share with the human race. We are the first ones from Earth to cross this arch," Markus said.

"I'm going to record with my phone. I think NASA would like to take a look, if you guys have your gear to record," Eve said.

"Yes, I have it," Courtney said, taking out the film and video cameras. Markus took out a digital camera as well.

"Okay, we are filming!" Courtney said, moving to the front with Eve.

Eve stepped forward with Scott on her other side. She brushed her fingers on the wall, removing some of the dust from the surface. Looking on the ground she saw a stone that seemed to change colors in the light, making rainbows dance on the wall around it. Eve picked it up, stuffed it in one of her outside pockets, and snapped it shut. She took many pictures and then filmed from the beginning to the end, making sure to get all of the hieroglyphics. The mural stopped abruptly and then there were just smooth walls ahead leading to the inside of the structure.

"Does this remind you of something that we saw when researching?" Eve asked Scott.

"That is weird—I was thinking the same thing. Remember the pictures we saw of the Anunnaki that were etched in stone? Look at the beards…I remember at the time thinking they were unusual. The style was different than the way the artist depicted the men represented in the mural. Remember they were thousands of years old, but they were wearing clothes and gadgets on their wrists that looked like watches," Scott said.

"Yes…I remember now. They were written about in the Samaritan's text. Remember my…ah…father said something about these beings coming from space to colonize Earth and Mars—the Anunnaki! So it must be true! And here they are on Mars," Eve said.

"I wonder if these beings of yours are from there?" Scott whispered.

"What are you guys talking about?" Courtney said, "I'm confused."

"Nothing…just research," Scott said. "Hey Eve, take a look at this…"

"What is it?" Eve asked, stepping by Scott's side, winking at him through their protective shields.

"You're in a good mood! Hold on, Honey, look at that," Scott said, pointing to the back corner.

The area had a high rounded ceiling and at the back was a stone doorway. Cut into the rock was an entrance that didn't go anywhere. The rainbow lights converged, making a white light and creating a beam of brightness that hit the doorway in the center. A black discoloration shadowed around the outside of the doorway, causing a contrast with the surrounding stone.

"That's weird. It looks like a doorway but it's solid smooth rock," Eve said, running her fingertips over the surface. Touching the cool stone, Eve felt a spark go through her body, catching her off guard, making her jump in the air a little. It was like a shock from an electrical current. She felt a slight burning sensation on her chest where the medallion hung inside her spacesuit.

"Eve, come from there!" Scott said. He had felt the power surge standing five feet from her.

"There's an energy coming from that area. It is really strong," Eve stated.

"I know—I felt it too!" Scott said. "I just didn't want something to happen. We don't have much time with our air supply. Come on—we'll come back when we can stay longer."

"You're right," Eve said, understanding what he was trying to say in front of the others.

"We're ready...what about you guys?" Eve asked.

"We've filmed enough and time has gone by—we need to get back," Britney said, moving toward the entrance.

"We will have to come back to explore more. We have a sandstorm coming in fast," Courtney said, looking down at her device.

"I hate to leave! But we have to remember safety first!" Markus said, "Come on, guys."

When they passed over the entrance, Eve felt a snap or a disconnect with the energy inside the pyramid. It was weird, as if it were alive and sending her a message. She remembered reading a study that they were doing on quantum waves and how they were like transmitters to every neuron in the human brain. Maybe that was what had just happened to her. She thought of how radio waves worked and how sound traveled where people could tap into shows played in the '60s…*Crazy,* she thought.

Courtney led the way down the weathered stones, weaving through them until they reached the bottom. It didn't take as long as the climb and they were inside the trucks heading back to the colony within twenty minutes.

Chapter 108

Behind them, the storm was coming fast from the west. They could feel the ground vibrating beneath them. It sent shock waves from the direction of the pyramid. They heard a loud hum as the energy spread across the flat surface of the desert. The sky had changed to a blood red color, darkening the iron oxidized sand. The pace of the trucks increased to full force, moving across the packed surface of the hard soil.

"We might have to outrun her! Fall in line! We will push the pedal to the metal!" Britney yelled above the noise of the wind.

"Here we go! Don't want to get caught out here at night. It gets down to at least -72F. Freezing my balls off isn't the way I want to go!" Markus yelled back. "Sorry ladies!"

"We understand!" Eve said, pushing her truck to top speed. "We'll keep up…hurry! I see the storm catching up! We need to lock down the colony." Eve yelled as the noise intensified.

"Eve! Help! We're running out of power! Come up beside us and open your door," Britney yelled into the wind.

"Hold on, guys!" Eve screamed and pulled up beside them. "Ready?" She opened the door and Britney moved against the wind into one of the back seats. Markus jumped out, pulling the solar panels behind him and staking them to the ground. By now the wind had picked up and they felt the truck start to rock. The intensity of the air current made Markus fall to his knees. He was having trouble fighting the strong wind, making the sand and dirt stick to his helmet. It was making him lose his bearings.

"Open the door! Open the door back up, Eve!" Scott shouted.

Reluctantly Eve pushed the button and felt the wind fill the cab, almost toppling the truck on its side.

"Girls! Move to the right! Use all your weight to keep us upright!" Eve yelled. She watched as Britney and Courtney understood, moving their bodies against the right side of the truck.

Scott jumped out, leaning forward into the wind and taking small steps toward Markus. Reaching him, he pulled Markus to his feet and turned, dragging him back in the truck's direction. Courtney and Britney were ready, pulling them both into the truck and activating the oxygen and air seal lock. When the door closed, it drowned out some of the outside noise. Eve pushed the gas pedal to the floor.

"I need a rope or a belt," Eve screamed to be heard.

Courtney found some rope in the back. "Tie it here to the door handle and here to the wheel. The wind is pushing us to the right and we are going to miss our base if it isn't held stable," Eve directed. "I can't see too much in front of us."

"We only have thirty more minutes. I have locked in the GPS locator so we know where we left the truck and you're right, Eve, we were going slightly east. It looks like we are lined up now on a direct path with the colony," Britney said.

"Okay! You guys okay—Markus?" Eve asked above the noise.

"I'm good…just a little embarrassed that I went down!" Markus said. "Thanks, Man—for coming for me!"

"Dude, we're a team! I've played a lot of sports. If something happens to one of us, it happens to us all!" Scott said.

"We aren't out of it yet!" Courtney said, looking to the west out of her binoculars. "A really dark cloud is moving fast this way. It reminds me of a storm cloud full of rain or snow but this one is traveling on the ground."

"We're going as fast as she'll go!" Eve yelled.

"Britney, can you tell the onboard robots to open the hatch when we are a few minutes out so we can just pull inside?" Courtney asked.

"Yes…good idea!" Britney said.

"Remember to close it as soon as we pull inside," Courtney directed.

"Also be sure the robots activate the oxygen as soon as it closes," Eve added.

"Yes! I'm on it, ladies!" Britney said.

When they reached the outskirts of the camp, Eve couldn't see anything out of the windshield and had to slow to a creep. The wind was blowing so hard it now rocked the truck from side to side.

"Look over there!" Courtney yelled over the noise. A yellow light could barely be seen. The wind had slowed for the moment, almost like they were in the center of a tornado.

"Hurry—move inside!" Britney directed.

"I'm trying…I'm going straight into the wind! She's doing her best!" Eve shouted. "Come on, baby!" she whispered to the truck.

Eve pulled into the hanger; equipment had fallen or gotten blown around the room. Scott and Markus jumped out and started moving the things out of the way, making room for the truck.

"Shut the door!" Britney yelled, but nothing happened. Something was wrong and it was stuck.

Scott ran to the robots, working a few off their racks and turning them on. "Jump up and pull the door closed!" He ordered.

Understanding, the three robots moved toward the door and jumped to grab the top, manually using their weight to pull the large door to the ground. A foot of sand had blown in its path.

"Remove the sand." Scott yelled. The robots got on their knees and started moving the sand with their hands, clearing the area below the door. The door moved into place and Scott pressed the latch and it sealed the door. He pushed the button that allowed oxygen to fill the room.

chapter 109

The team had gathered around the door. The light on Scott's suit had changed. It was flashing orange, meaning he was about to run out of oxygen. He went to remove his helmet.

"Wait on it," Eve yelled, panicked. "The light hasn't turned green for safety of the room. Hurry—follow me!" Eve took Scott's hand and moved to the door that connected the room with the ship. "Come on, everyone! Robots, power down." The robots stopped in place, slumped next to their stands.

The group moved into the inside room and closed the door behind them as it filled with oxygen. Scott slumped to the floor and Eve fumbled with the latch on his helmet, pulling it from his head. She turned on the oxygen tank that was for emergencies and covered his nose and mouth, watching his eyes as he took deep breaths. He put up his hand.

"I'm okay, Eve. Please let me go!" Scott mouthed.

"Sorry...I was just making sure," Eve said. Seeing the light was now green, she took off her helmet. Tears flowed down her cheeks. Still holding him tight, she kissed his sweaty forehead. She moved the long wavy hair out of the way, stroking his head.

"Sorry, my emotions are out of control right now!" Eve said, wiping tears with her gloved hand. She looked around the small space, seeing the small group that had become her family. They paused, listening to the sound of the storm outside. The lights were blinking on and off as the backup generator turned on.

"Is everyone okay?" Britney asked, "I know it has been an eventful day. But we are going to have to do a complete check tonight and see what kind of damage we have. I know it's a pain, but we are going to need to stay suited up just in case," she said, checking everyone's eyes to see if they understood. "Everyone change out your oxygen tanks so we are all full. I'm sure Scott isn't the only one that's low."

"Is the hanger green?" Eve asked.

"Yes, it was a smart move, Scott. That would have been a real problem if we couldn't have closed it."

"How long does these storms usually last?" Scott asked.

"We don't know. Some last a few days and others a few months," Courtney said.

"That isn't good with the Russians coming," Eve said, looking down at Scott, stroking his hair still in her lap. He smiled, a little embarrassed at her public display of affection, and struggled to sit up in his heavy suit.

"Okay…I'm good," he said, seeing the smiles on the others' faces as he pulled on his helmet.

"All right, I'm checking the control room. Markus, check the generators. Courtney, check the living spaces and Scott and Eve, please check the garden and put the robots back in place in the hanger. Everyone report to the control room when you're finished with a damage report," Britney directed.

The group helped each other to their feet, changing out their oxygen tanks, ready to do what the captain had requested.

When Scott and Eve were alone, she turned to him. "Scott—never do that again! You don't need to be the hero!" Eve said, making a kissing noise. "I love you!"

"Honey, I just was reacting to the situation…I really didn't have time to think about the danger. I wasn't about to leave Markus out there to die!"

"I know…I just don't want anything to happen to you!" Eve said.

"And if something does happen to me…you have to promise to go on without me."

"I wouldn't be able to!" Eve said, feeling sad. *Why am I feeling so emotional…ah my hormones must be crazy,* she thought.

"Promise me," Scott said, intense. "Listen to me, Eve. I need you to promise me!"

"Scott, I can't promise. I'm not sure of the uncertain future," Eve said, looking in his eyes and feeling the tears forming.

"Honey, you have to promise me this one thing…please," he pleaded.

"Okay, my love…I will promise." She pulled him close, feeling she couldn't get close enough in their suits and just wanting to feel his skin against hers.

"Come on. Let's do our check," Scott said, moving to the door that took them back into the hanger room.

Inside the room the trucks were fine and still in place, but tools and stainless steel workbenches were blown against the back wall. Scott took charge of the robots and had them clean and sweep the space, putting it back in working order.

Eve parked the truck they had used back in its parking space. She pulled out the communication device, seeing that there was no message, and linked it to her phone. She decided to send part of the video she had taken inside the pyramid of the walls and the colorful hieroglyphics. She typed a short message telling Gordon and her parents what they had found, wanting them to take a look and see what they thought. Also love to Sarah telling her that she was right.

"What are you doing?" Scott asked, approaching the driver's side of the truck.

"I just sent part of the video that I took in the chamber and the footage I took on the moon. Gordon and my parents will love seeing it. Scott, lean in here…let's take a selfie," Eve said.

"Okay, but I'm not looking my best!" Scott said.

"Smile…like we are on vacation and didn't just outrun a dust storm," Eve laughed.

"Ready," Scott said. Eve clicked a few photos and sent the one where she thought they looked cute.

"Come on, time to check the garden room. If all is well, we can take a washcloth bath—exciting, I know! I can't wait to return home and sit in a hot tub with bath salts and sweet lavender. Sounds divine right now!" Eve said, closing her eyes and remembering the feeling of comfort and the smell from recall.

"Yes, that would be really nice! Come on, Honey! Let's do it." Scott said; hand in hand, they left the room.

chapter 110

The bell dinged upstairs. The group had been having wine and appetizers in front of the fireplace while they passed the time playing a board game called Ticket to Ride. At the unexpected sound, Jane jumped nervously in the air, knocking the game and dislodging the pieces, many falling to the floor.

"I'm so sorry, everyone," Jane said, picking up the small trains that were now all mixed up. The men had rushed from the room as the bell rang as if in a race. Janet put their glasses and plates on the side table and the ladies quickly moved upstairs to see what had come in from Eve and Scott.

"Okay—what have we got?" Gordon said. "Looks like we have three files coming in."

"Yes...I think if I connect this here, we can get a digital download on the larger monitor," Michael said.

"I think one might be a video," Gordon said.

"Yes, they're slowly coming in." Michael adjusted the computer to face the room so everyone could see. They all gathered around the large monitor awaiting the results. The percentage of the download increased as it grew closer to completion.

"That one is 60%!" Janet said, excited.

"And that one is 90%," Sarah said. Just as she spoke a picture opened on the screen. Eve and Scott stood smiling in the camera through their space helmets.

"Eve face looks slender," Janet said, "And look at how long Scott's hair is! The waves are fantastic! I've never seen it that long before!"

"They also took that picture inside one of the trucks," Gordon stated. "I recognize it."

"Look—a different one is opening," Jane said, and they all turned to study the video slowly buffering. It would play a small amount and then stop and start back up again.

"What is that?" Sarah asked, studying the frozen photo on the screen. The third file opened with a message, which Gordon read out loud.

"Hello all! We made a discovery today on Mars and I would like to know your insight and thoughts on what we found. We have experienced a sandstorm and how long it lasts will determine our plan to connect with the Russians' spaceship. In a week when they are in the right position, we will try to get on that ship and make it home. We think that is our only chance to make it back. Any information or ideas that you might have would be helpful. Love, Eve and Scott.

"What are they going to try to do?" Janet said.

"It will be okay, dear!" Michael put his arms across her shoulders, pulling her close, wanting to comfort her.

"Hey look! The video is finished!" Sarah stated. The film had started on its own and they all gathered around to watch the grainy footage as pixels were slowly added while it buffered. Then it returned to the beginning and stopped, ready to view.

"Okay, let's see what we have here." Michael said, clicking the arrow to make the video start.

They saw the outside of a large step pyramid.

"Is that what they call a Ziggurat?" Jane asked Gordon.

"Yes...they say those were built to serve as a stairway to heaven for the gods," Janet answered for him.

"Look!" Sarah interrupted. A frame showed a few of the astronauts climbing over the huge stones, making their way up the pyramid. The camera lens moved to the peak of the pyramid and slowed down and settled on an entrance in the side of the structure.

"I can't believe it!" Gordon said. "I always thought of the possibilities. At some point in the past few years, I have seen footage sent back from Mars from the rovers. The United States has a few on the ground and so do the Russians and Chinese. But NASA always played the still shots down as just shadows on Mars' surface."

"Look at the size of the stones compared to the height of the kids. Scott is 6'6" and he isn't much taller than the stone blocks," Janet said.

The filming stopped and then continued, showing the entrance into the pyramid. Large arches were intertwined, making a basketweave pattern. The selectively placed pieces of cut stone made a formula for architectural beauty.

"Whoever built that really knew what they were doing... think how old this site must be, just to be still standing. This looks like it hasn't been touched in hundreds if not thousands of years!" Janet stated, not taking her eyes away from the screen, afraid to miss any little detail.

"Oh my! Look at that!" Michael stood and paced, excited.

The lens had stopped and focused on looking inside the opening. The video camera adjusted to the dimmer light inside and then focused on the images on the walls. The picture focused as the phone adjusted to the light. The brightly painted hieroglyphics on the walls became clear.

"I wish I was there to see this in person!" Janet said. "Could you imagine being able to touch them and be the first to figure out what they are saying?"

"Yes…I told Eve that I wished I could have gone to Mars! But I knew it would never be possible because of my age," Gordon said.

"I didn't know that you would have wanted to go…" Jane said.

"Well…just the thought of the adventure and what would be found there. But seeing it this way is almost as good. At least we are seeing the truth of what is really on Mars before all the politics get involved and information is only disbursed for a select few to see," Gordon said. He touched his wife's arm, reassuring her that he would never leave her, even if he could.

"Look at the men in the mural; they all have beards. I think that I have seen that style of petroglyphs before! We might have some photos in one of the books we have around here!" Janet said, excited.

"Yes…I don't remember off the top of my head where that archaeological site is…Turkey? We have gone to so many," Michael explained. "But I know the book you're talking about!"

"Look! That looks like one of those doorways that they call Gate of the Gods," Janet said, looking at her husband to confirm she was right.

"I remember reading scientists thought they might have been ancient portals or star gates. You remember like the one we saw in Mexico?" Janet asked. "Honey…play it all again," she instructed.

chapter III

"What is that?" Gordon asked, staring at the grainy video.

"Some say that these doorways were a way that the ancient gods moved between worlds. I'm not an expert, but the idea from what I have read talked about somehow being able to bend time...something to do with quantum physics? I know it sounds crazy...but scientists have found places on Earth that have high levels of magnetic energy. In some of those places, people have gone missing and time has been lost. This looks like some of the doorways that we have seen in places we've visited," Michael said.

"It's an interesting theory," Gordon said. "I think I have heard stories from time to time. Disappearances around the world, in certain areas or hot spots, where victims don't remember where they've been, and a large amount of time has gone by. Sounds like the same thing you're talking about?"

"Right—that's it. I remember this one story about a Michigan student who went hiking after a storm. The searchers tracked with dogs and found his shoes near a body of water. It looked like the guy was walking in the snow and then the tracks just stopped. He was just gone," Michael said.

"How could that be?" Gordon asked.

"There are many things that can't be explained; it doesn't make them impossible," Sarah said. Gordon looked away, dismissing her comment, believing that everything had an explanation.

"Just because we can't see something with our human eyes, it doesn't mean that it isn't there!" Sarah said, reading his mind. "Even other mammals—cats, dolphins—all can see things that we can't."

"That's true, Sarah. Look—there's more," Michael stated. "The student showed up a year later wandering around the same area. He was discovered on one of the back roads. He was wearing the same clothes that he disappeared in and thought only an hour had gone by. He didn't recall anything that had happened in the past year or where he had been. It was like his brain had been wiped clean."

"Remember when we were researching some of the ancient tribes in Alaska?" Janet asked.

"Oh yes..." Michael nodded.

"There was a trapper who had hiked into this small Eskimo village where he would trade food for animal skins. When the trapper arrived, he found the village deserted; even the dogs for the sleds were missing. The fires were still smoking with pots of food cooking over them. Their belongings were still there inside each hutch. The thing that the trapper found really odd was that the Indians' gravesite was completely empty. The graves had all been dug up and the bones were gone along with all the people. The trapper said it was if they had all just disappeared into thin air," Janet said.

"What are you trying to say?" Gordon asked.

"That anything is possible if you open your mind," Sarah said, not liking Gordon's skepticism.

"There have been reported sites around the world that have had unusual energy. The Bermuda Triangle for one… many weird disappearances for ships and planes. One ship was found floating empty with nothing wrong, but the crew had just disappeared. Many have seen weird lights and energies in that area," Janet said.

"One of the big mysterious places is in northern Mexico—Ceballos, Mexico—called the Zona Del Silencio, meaning the Zone of Silence. In this area cell phones just stop and compass needles just turn in circles. There are also weird mutations of animals. When you are there you can feel a tingling in your body," Janet continued.

"Scientists say the Zone of Silence draws things into the area and is loaded with meteorites. It has been tested and the energy has a magnetic signature. But get this…it is on the same 26th and 28th parallels as the Egyptian pyramids," Michael said.

"Are you serious? I'm seeing that there is a lot we don't understand." Gordon said, trying to be agreeable but not totally convinced.

"What do you think it is?" Jane asked. "A vortex? Dimension? Or something like a black hole sucking everything into it?"

"I'm not sure. You're right, Gordon, there is a lot that we don't understand," Janet said.

"Well I suggest we copy all of this on to a memory stick and delete any traces off our devices," Michael recommended. "Just in case…we've found it is best to be careful with our research and the information that we uncover. We had a problem a year ago and had to really step up our security. I had a program written for me by a retired programmer friend that takes any of the ghost copies off the hard drive."

"Upstairs we can look at the video frame by frame and see if there is anything we can come up with," Janet said.

"What is upstairs?" Jane asked.

"Let's just call it our house's panic room. It's a safe place where we can hide within the walls of the house. We keep all our research and findings there. The room is full of information we have found in our research; most is top secret or controversial. We have to keep the information safe—even with our security system at the house," Janet said.

"When we're researching, we spend a lot of time upstairs in that hidden room," Michael said.

"If you guys are up to it, we'll head up there. Just grab your coffee and a sandwich and meet back here in fifteen minutes," Sarah said, leaving the room. Everyone looked at each other.

"Yes...well...let's do it!" Gordon said.

"Yes...I haven't been involved in any research in years...I look forward to the challenge," Jane said. "Just let me change and grab a pillow."

chapter 112

The group met at the top landing and followed Michael to the picture of an ancient relic at the end of the hall. He bent over and released the spring and the picture frame swung from the wall on hinges, opening wide to allow the group entrance.

"Everyone, move inside. Honey, can you lead them to the door? I'll close us up," he said.

"Yes, Dear. Everyone, come with me," Janet said, stepping forward into the dark space. "It isn't far…hold hands if you must or grab the back of my shirt. That's it—just take small baby steps." She moved them forward.

The door closed behind them, making the area completely dark. They blindly took small steps forward. After the passage rounded the curve, Janet stopped short at a solid wood door, bumping into it. Fumbling with her key, she finally found the hole for the lock. In the silence the lock turned and the heavy door swung opened into the room inside. They all stood for a moment, peering in the entrance before moving inside. Sunlight shone from the skylight in the middle of the room, illuminating the small crushed velvet couch.

"Here we are; come inside," Janet motioned. She closed the door, locking it, and flipped on the lights.

"Wow! What a nice little hideout! It is beautiful!" Jane said, stepping into the comfortable room and finding her way to the couch where she sat directly under the sunshine. She looked up, noticing light snow had covered it and was now melting, sending small rainbows reflecting off the water droplets. Sarah took the other end, putting her small socked feet on the square glass table that was in front of the couch. It left the long table with the padded chairs for the ones who would be really doing the research.

"Thank you!" Janet said. "We tried to make it comfortable. We have spent many long nights up here. That couch pulls out into a bed and over there is a storage stash and kitchen fully stocked, just in case we really have to stay here for great lengths of time. Last year we had men saying they were from the FBI trying to find us. Well, that's what they said. Turns out they were from some special government organization that was monitoring us because of our research. They scared my Eve to death." Gordon looked at Michael and watched him nod his head in agreement that his wife had spoken the truth.

Gordon didn't say anything; he just observed the room, wondering how hard it would be to build one at their house. The walls were covered with bookcases full to overflowing. On the vacant walls were painted diagrams of the earth and solar systems. He noticed the bright note tabs running down the walls holding pieces of information and wondered what they were working on. The walls looked almost like police departments he had seen on TV. There they had an idea board connecting all the pictures and information of a crime scene.

"Gordon, You can sit here," Michael said, moving the stacks of files to the plastic containers that lined the side of the table on the floor.

"Yes, we aren't going to need these," Janet added, trying to help straighten and clear a working space for them.

"Let me try to find the book that I was thinking of. It has the same kind of style painted on the walls we just observed," Michael said. He moved to one of the bookcases and turned on a small light so he could focus on the titles. After searching, he found what he was looking for and returned to the table with a few books.

"I think I saw it in one of these." He thumbed through the one on top, looking at the pictures. "Here it is—I got it!" Michael said, handing the open book to his wife.

"Yes, you're right! Now I remember! This is one of the books written by Zecharia Sitchin. The man had some weird ideas at the time…I think his first book came out in the 1970s and was called 'The 12th Planet.' He was an expert on ancient Sumerian text. In his interpretations he found the story of the Anunnaki, a race of space beings that brought civilization and technology to Earth," Janet stated.

"The Sumerian text that Sitchin interrupted told the story of the visitors from Nibiru, the Ancient Gods, and the Anunnaki. The word Anunnaki means 'Those from Heaven who to Earth came.' The Anunnaki text gave the Sumerians' tales of creation and how Earth was created. Also, how Adam was created and what happened in the Garden of Eden, the deluge (great flood), and the tower of Babel."

"Sounds like some of the same stories that were in the Bible," Gordon said.

"Well, it says here in his book where he quotes from the

Bible, Genesis chapter 6 verse 2. It reads that the 'Sons of gods seeing the daughters of man, that they were fair...' the word fair translated from Hebrew also means 'compatible,' meaning genetically compatible."

"Meaning capable of having intercourse and creating offspring," Jane said.

"Okay...this is really mind blowing! No wonder the governments are holding information from the masses. People that aren't intellects or scientists wouldn't be able to digest the information or evaluate it. It might bring mass confusion and chaos," Gordon said, questioning his Protestant upbringing.

"No worries, Gordon. We have been questioning the unexplained for twenty years since we had Eve, and this is all new to you and Jane. It is a lot to take in at once. It helps us to talk about everything out loud, even if we believe it or not at the time...it makes us think," Michael explained. "Here, look at this. I found what I was looking for. Look at these pictographic (hieroglyphics) carved into stone. I was wrong—it wasn't Turkey—they were found in today's Iraq." Michael flipped the page over his wife's shoulder and showed it to Gordon.

"Honey, can you guys set up the video feed on the TV? We can start by going frame by frame and compare the two," Janet said.

"Okay...good idea." Gordon moved to help do what was asked.

Chapter 113

"Sarah, here...take one of these books. You too, Jane. We need to speed-read them all and see if we come up with anything that might help us." Janet said, passing two of the books over to the women who both found their reading glasses and started flipping the pages.

"Okay, listen to this," Sarah said, reading out loud. "The Sumerians' society was known as the Cradle of Civilization. It says here that in the Sumerians' documents, everything that the Sumerians knew came from the Anunnaki."

"Who are these Anunnaki?" Jane asked, looking up from what she was reading. "And where did they come from?"

"According to this, it looks like the Anunnaki have been around for a while. This is weird—there is a picture taken from a Sumerian cylinder seal dated to 4,500 years ago. It shows our solar system and included in it 10 planets, sun, and the moon," Sarah said.

"Why is that so weird?" Jane asked.

"Because we hadn't even discovered the outer planets at that time! I believe Pluto was discovered in the 1930s and then classified as a dwarf planet," Janet said.

"In his book, Sitchin states that the Anunnaki had been traveling to Earth for a very long time. In fact, his theory is that the Anunnaki were traveling through space from a suggested twelfth plant they are calling Nibiru. The author states the planet Nibiru has a great elliptical orbit around our sun and passes between Mars and Jupiter!" Sarah stated.

"Gordon, how could there be a planet in our solar system that we didn't know about?" Jane said.

"Well...I'm trying to come to terms with everything myself. I'm thinking that the things that we do know for sure might be outnumbered by everything we don't know," Gordon said.

"Listen to this!" Sarah said. "Thoughts are that the elliptical orbit around the sun not only passes between Mars and Jupiter, it takes 3,600 years to do it!"

"What! Are you serious?" Janet stated.

"If that's the case, I can understand why we might not know about the planet; our lives are so short in comparison," Michael said, thinking.

"The author's idea is that the Anunnaki have been traveling from their planet to ours and Mars every 3,600 years." Sarah said, slowly putting her fingertips to her temples and sitting in silence for a few moments. Eve's parents stopped and watched her. Gordon and Jane looked to see what was happening. Sarah opened her glossed-over eyes and the room waited until they were clear. "Yes, it is true," she said. Eve's parents nodded, believing her, and turned back to what they were doing.

"If that's the case, maybe the Mayan calendar was read wrong by the people who interpreted it. Think about it... you have stories in almost every civilization about the returning of the gods, even in the Book of Revelation. What if these so-called gods were astronauts and thought of as gods because of their advanced technology? Maybe the Mayan calendar wasn't counting years, but using a different method of counting time. Maybe it was all about timing, when the twelfth planet would arrive with the Anunnaki. Maybe the last days in the Bible refer to the time when they return and there is a great war as predicted," Jane said.

"Dear, I don't think that's what they're talking about," Gordon said gently.

"No, I think she has a point. Let's think about this. What if the time predicted isn't Mayan time (Earth time), but Anunnaki (Nibiru time). If they are coming back every 3,600 years (Earth time) and visiting our planet, maybe they were to return in 2012 when the Mayan calendar ended. Then the Mayans thought Earth would end. What is the reason? Why was their calendar for that time period so advanced? The timing had to be just right," Janet said.

"It says here that the twelfth planet, Nibiru, moves around our sun in a large ellipse that is in a clockwise direction. That's different—all the other planets in our solar system rotate in counterclockwise around the sun, right?" Sarah asked.

"Yes, you're right," Gordon said.

"Is it possible that because it rotates clockwise that time could be different than ours? Where maybe it goes backwards? Maybe the Mayan calendar that made all the stir in 2012 might have to go backwards as well? I know that probably sounds far-fetched," Sarah said. The room was quiet, considering what she had just said. It was mind-blowing to think about it.

"I have something here. I think I found the reason that the Anunnaki came to Earth. See this cross symbol? It was the sign for Nibiru. It says here the word means Planet of the Crossing. The symbol looks just like the cross that we are used to seeing. It says here that the Anunnaki came to Earth in search of gold," Jane said. "Why would they need gold?"

"From the interrupted text, I think I found the story in here as well. Listen to this," Sarah read.

"The Anunnaki came to Earth in search of gold. They were using suspended gold particles as a shield to protect the dwindling

atmosphere of their planet. Tired of mining for gold themselves, they had the idea of genetically engineering the humans found on Earth. The genes of an Anunnaki were mixed with the egg of an ape woman, creating the Adam 250,000 years ago."

"That is hard to believe, but it kinda does make sense," Gordon said.

"Here's something else," Jane said, excited. "The Anunnaki started coming to Earth thousands of years ago and changed the course of human evolution—so about the same thing."

"I found something...I think it pertains to the problem at hand. According to the Sumerian text, the Anunnaki used Mars as a port station on the way from the twelfth planet (Nibiru) to Earth," Sarah said. "Maybe the pyramids on Earth and now on Mars might both be Anunnaki spaceports?"

"The pictures I saw of the surface of Mars did have features that showed what looked to be actual structures half covered. It could have been a spaceport at one time," Gordon said.

"Looking at this, it seems that the author is saying he thinks the Anunnaki built the pyramids to be used in communication to help with space travel. It says the pyramids were landmarks that indicated the incoming flight path for spacecrafts coming to Earth. He thinks at one time they contained equipment for communication and technology to defend the pyramids from rival Anunnaki who wanted to control them. The pyramids of today were empty when entered, but that wasn't always the case." Sarah said, taking her fingertips from her forehead again.

"Interesting...last year they found chemicals inside the cubic, foot-size vents. They thought at the time they were just air vents. But after testing the inside walls of the shafts, chemicals were found. Apparently different chemicals were being put down the shafts leading to the King's Chamber. It was discovered that when you put the two chemicals together, it would create fusion, thus making hydrogen. This could have been coming out the top of the pyramid, creating a powerful light beam. I wonder if the beam was so strong that it was like a laser light and could be seen from space?" Michael stated.

"All I know is the pyramids weren't tombs for a dead pharaoh! That is what archeologists first thought. But not one body or tomb has been found in any pyramid!" Gordon said.

"You're right!" Janet said. "So here we have space travelers from a distant planet in our own solar system, visiting our planet every 3,600 years. They seem very advanced and if we believe what the author says…this race of beings intermingled with humans, changing our DNA and teaching us technology. But why? To help the human race advance?"

"Maybe they were on a dying planet and came to Earth to mine for gold to save their planet. Maybe it was to survive and find a new place to live? The humans think they're gods because of their technology, which allows them to do things that are incomprehensible to human brains at the time. You know the references to fire and noise…sounds like a launching spaceship to me! The humans are sad when their gods leave, but the gods promised they would return," Michael said.

"Remember the Book of Enoch that was found in the Dead Sea Scrolls? There was a chapter where he had been to the heavens and was again leaving Earth and asked if he would return. He said he would return, but not in their lifetime," Janet explained. "Maybe he knew he would be gone for 3,600 Earth years—time in space is different than time on Earth."

"What I would like to know is when were they here last? That way we can try to predict when the Anunnaki will return," Jane said.

"I think we would all like to know the answer to that question. But some of the facts are that humans' intelligence took a major leap 5,000 years ago," Gordon said. "Maybe we could go from there?"

"Also, the RH negative blood that Eve has just showed up 3,500 years ago." Sarah said, "Maybe we could also go from there with the timing of the twelfth planet coming back around?" She took her fingers from her forehead.

"Where did that come from?" Gordon asked.

"It just came to me," Sarah said. "But it does make sense."

"I'm thinking if any of those dates are close, it will be passing between Mars and Jupiter sooner than we think. I wish we would be here to witness that! It would really blow people's minds," Jane said. "If their planet was advanced then, what will it be like now? Think about it...if they started coming to Earth 450,000 years ago, I can't imagine their technology now!"

"I see your point, Dear." Gordon said, not used to having this kind of dialogue with his wife.

Smiling when Gordon looked her way, Jane continued. "What if their atmosphere didn't hold up? What will be coming to Earth when they arrive? Robots? I remember this story—the Epic of Gilgamesh. It describes an artificial man, like a humanoid robot," Jane said. Everyone was quiet, thinking if it could be possible and what might be coming.

"Okay, true or not true...how does this information help us?" Gordon said.

"Well, if we believe any of this, it helps us understand the ones who were here before us, the Watchers/Angels/Anunnaki or the gods as history calls them. By understanding, we might be able to figure out how to use their technology and get my daughter home!" Janet stated.

chapter 114

The days slowly passed; the team had been hunkered down in the spacecraft for a week now as the storm outside continued. The winds had slowly decreased, but the dust, sand, and minerals still floated in the atmosphere, blocking out most of the sun. Britney had ordered that the isolated spaces that weren't essential be powered down to conserve energy. Eve and Scott had to suit up every morning in their spacesuits and make their journey to the grow lab/garden to check and take care of the plants. Instead of turning down the grow lights, they had to turn them up to full force, re-configuring the timers, turning them on for two hours and off for an hour. This process continuously kept the lab warm; they were afraid the plants would freeze and die if the lights were left off for too long.

"Do we want to check the truck communication system again today?" Scott asked.

"Yes, I guess we better. I don't look forward to the long haul in these suits, but we should just in case," Eve said. "This weather has really messed things up! It has been a week now since we talked to NASA; we haven't even been able to tell them about what we discovered!"

"Maybe that is for the best! But the Russian ship should be here in about six days according to the calculations. I think I would rather get you on your way before they try to mess things up!" Scott said.

"Now about that..." Eve said.

"I don't want to hear it. We've made a decision. It's best not to talk about it and get yourself worked up!" Scott touched her face with his glove and looked into her eyes. "Come on, don't be sad. Put your helmet on—we need to go."

Eve did as she was told, saying in her head, *I'm not sad because I'm not going without you!* They found their way to the storage area. Inside, the metal of the trucks, robots, and walls were covered with what looked like frost. A few days before Scott had to use a robot to help him open the frozen door of the truck so they could check the device, finding nothing. They had left the door ajar, unscrewing the cab light, making sure not to drain what was left of the battery.

"It looks like everything else," Scott said, pulling it out from under the seat. He brushed the components off, seeing that it wasn't going to work even if it was a clear day until it was warmed up. "I have an idea—let's take this inside where it is warmer and see if we can figure out a way to use it. It doesn't have to be in the truck to work, right? Don't we just need to charge the power?"

"You're right—I don't know why we didn't do that before," Eve said. "Saves the trouble of coming here until we can power the whole ship."

"Wait a minute—maybe we need to move a couple robots as well. Or soon they won't have enough power to move at all. We might need them for something and if they are all dead weight, we could have a bigger problem," Scott said.

"You're right! Most likely the door to this hanger is even frozen." Eve said, watching Scott change out the dead batteries with the last live ones. Two of the robots came to life. They did as Scott instructed, moving stiffly behind them to the inside of the ship. Once inside the living space, Scott powered them down by the entrance.

"What are you doing with those?" Markus asked.

"We thought it would be best inside the warmth just in case. I brought a few of the battery packs that are out of power. Is there a way to recharge them?" Scott asked.

"Yes; here, let me take those. I can rig something up," Markus said. "How's the garden?"

"We also brought this box of what we have been canning and dehydrating just in case the power goes out," Eve said.

"I know; we are at 50% and we have everything turned down as much as possible. If this weather doesn't clear so we can get our solar cells to capacity, we are going to need to move all the plants and grow lights to the main living space. And turn us down to one room for us to survive," Markus said, concerned.

"We will be okay!" Britney said.

"We could start now by moving one grow light and plants at a time. It will be a big task, but if we start now, we should be able to save more of our power sooner," Scott said.

"Let's power up those batteries and start moving the plants. Start with the algae and potatoes first. If we have to, we could live on them for a while," Britney said.

"We could start with hanging the lights around the edges of the room about a foot off the walls. Feel this," Courtney said, touching the wall. Eve touched it as well and felt the cool surface.

It took two days to move all the plants and lights, crowding them into the small living space. The strong grow lights had heated the room and saved them lots of power. With the ship powered down only leaving the control room and living space heated, they hadn't gone below 46%. Britney had calculated the usage and estimated they were roughly okay for two months.

The days ticked by and they were 48 hours until the Russian ship would be in position. The weather still hadn't cleared, and the team was restless knowing that if it didn't change soon, there was no way they would be able to get Eve on that ship.

chapter 115

Almost two weeks had passed since the group at the house had heard a word from Eve and Scott. They had been researching everything they could and hadn't found an answer to their dilemma. Everyone had started to worry.

"Why haven't we heard from them? How do we find out what is happening?" Janet said, pacing the room. "How can we find out if NASA has heard from them? Gordon, do you know anyone you can trust inside?" she asked.

"I do, but I don't want to endanger anyone. I think I should take a road trip tomorrow. I am due to be back to work in two days. I could just show up as if coming back from vacation. That way I would be able to see what people are talking about from the inside. You know—shop talk. We aren't moving forward and maybe I could get some answers," Gordon said, looking at his wife.

"No! That's not a good idea!" Jane said from her position back on the couch. "It's too dangerous!"

"She's right…what if someone is still trying to hide the fact that they sent astronauts to Mars?" Janet said, looking hopeful.

"Well, I think right now it's our only way of finding out. I will not leave Eve to die on a faraway planet! At least I can find out when the Russians are making their drop," Gordon looked at Jane, challenging her to disagree with him. She looked down and a tear fell in her lap. He moved over and rubbed her shoulder. "Everything will be all right! I won't stay overnight…just there and back…promise." Gordon said.

Sarah grabbed Gordon's hand and the room fell silent as she closed her eyes. Gordon looked down at the small women with the wild long hair and was still, waiting for what she had to say. His respect for her had grown as the weeks had passed. He didn't understand her talents and didn't even know if he believed in psychic mumbo-jumbo. But he had found her extremely smart and most of what she predicted had turned out to be true. He needed all the help he could get. He waited until she opened her blue eyes, staring into his.

"You will be safe! Don't trust the messenger…dig deeper," Sarah said, removing her fingertips from his arm and her forehead. "I saw it!"

"Okay…what does that mean?" Gordon asked.

"Trust…no…one! Friends can't be trusted! Tell her just what you have to," Sarah said.

"Well then, we'll need a good plan, because you aren't driving down there alone." Jane said, standing and straightening her wrinkled clothes, moving to the table.

"Okay! Let's do it!" Gordon said, taking a seat next to his wife.

chapter 116

Two days had passed, and they still hadn't been in contact with NASA. They had been following the Russian spacecraft for the past 18 hours when it started its orbit around Mars.

"It should be in our area in about two hours," Britney said. "It's time to prepare yourself. We will meet you at the escape pod in 30 minutes."

"Okay…we'll see you there," Eve said. They left the control room, moving the short distance to the living space, working their way through the small aisle of plants.

"What do you want to eat first when you get home? I think I would like a t-bone steak with mashed potatoes and gravy and a really big salad," Scott said.

He had tried to keep the conversation light, not saying what he really wanted to say. He wanted to keep her mentally strong and not let her see the panic he was feeling. Inside he was mourning, knowing the odds were that he would never see her again. All he wanted to do was hold her tight, but time had run out. He knew this would give her and his child a chance to make it back to Earth alive.

They dressed in silence; he noticed that she had started to show. A small pooch had begun to protrude from her lower belly. He couldn't stop himself and he reached out to touch her stomach, feeling her soft skin. He looked in her eyes and pulled her to him, holding her tight. They stood half-dressed for a while, just swaying back and forth. Still neither spoke. There were no words left to say. Scott broke the embrace and they finished dressing in their spacesuits. It was time to make their way to the escape pod. They moved through the halls of the spacecraft, trying not to touch the walls, staying in the center of the passages. Now the walls were covered with the crystallized frost and were quite pretty in the reflection of the lights. When they rounded the corner, the others were already there waiting. They smiled at them both and looked away, knowing the situation.

"All right—you know what to do. We have been able to tap into the Russians' computer on board. We will be able to control the pod somewhat, but you will have to make sure when we guide you to get in her path. We will get you up there and then you will have to wait until you see her coming. We have a ten-minute window," Britney explained.

"Come on, Eve, let's get you strapped in." Courtney took her arm, leading her inside to the small space that allowed six astronauts to sit side-by-side around the circumference.

Scott came inside and sat next to her. "Eve, I need to say something. We don't have much time."

"What's going on?" Eve looked around and noticed that the others had left, and she couldn't see them from her position.

"I want you to listen to me! I love you, Eve…I don't regret anything that has happened in our lives. But now you're going to go! This isn't about us anymore, but the child that you're carrying!" Scott said, choking back a sob.

“No! I can’t do it! Let me loose! I won’t go!” Eve screamed.

“Honey…yes, you will!” He put both his large gloved hands on each side of her helmet, and they locked eyes through the glass. Tears streamed down both their faces. “No more crying. You know this is the right thing.”

Eve gripped his gloved hand with hers, not wanting to let go. “I love you, Scott. Please don’t make me do this.”

“It is time.” Courtney said from the hatch, motioning for Scott to hurry.

“Tell the child I loved his mother!” Scott said as he turned and left.

The hatch closed and Eve was left with a sadness that filled her soul, causing her heart to hurt. She watched the timer in front of her through swollen eyes. Two minutes… one minute…30 seconds…10, 9, 8, 7, 6, 5, 4, 3, 2, 1. A loud rumble filled the space, shaking the pod. Eve could feel the capsule rocking and she could see the smoke outside the small window. She waited, ready for the pressure and the rush of being shot out of a canon.

From the control room the small robots raced around. A red light had started blinking and the pod wasn’t releasing.

“If we don’t get her out of here in the next two minutes we’re going to have to abort!” Britney said.

“What is happening?” Scott yelled, panicking.

“It’s not releasing!” Markus said. “I think it’s frozen! We didn’t think of that!”

“Abort!” Courtney said. “Something else might be wrong. Watch the Russian ship for the food dump. We can’t lose sight of that!” She yelled into the communication device in her helmet. She rushed behind Scott, who put his helmet on and tried to run to the pod with Courtney behind him.

They heard Britney ordering the robots behind them aborting the mission. They moved quickly, opening and closing areas behind them on the parts of the ship that had been closed down to save energy. Entering the pod area, they opened the door and felt the strong current of smoky air pressing them backward.

"Close the door behind us!" Scott yelled to be heard. Courtney did as he directed, and they felt the wind calm just a little. Observing inside the pod, they noticed that the round chamber had moved off its base a few inches, allowing the outside atmosphere to blow in through the small gap.

Inside they noticed that Eve's eyes were closed and she wasn't moving.

"Is she okay?" Scott asked Courtney. "Does she have air?"

"I'm not sure. The glass of the window looks cracked—it might be letting out the oxygen," Courtney said.

"Let's get her out of there!" Scott yelled, panicking.

"Scott—you're going to have to calm down. Please pull yourself together! I need your help."

"Okay…tell me what we need to do." Scott said, knowing if he didn't get himself together Eve could die.

"The pod is off its stand. We are losing oxygen and so is Eve. The remote door isn't going to work so we need to manually open the door. I need you to use your muscles to help me open it…okay?"

"Yes, I'm ready—show me what I need to do."

"Okay…I'm opening the latch…now push!" Courtney yelled, pressing her small body against the door. It moved about six inches and stopped. They both breathed hard, trying to catch their breath.

"Markus! Can you hear me?" Courtney said into the microphone in her helmet.

"Yes, I'm here. We have the drop tracked and it's looking like it is going to be close to the twin peak area. What's wrong?" He asked.

"We need some help! We can't get the door open to get her out!" Courtney said.

"I'm on my way! Britney, you got this?"

"Yes! I got it…hurry!"

Markus found Scott and Courtney pushing on the door and saw that they had only gotten it open about a foot. He moved the exhausted couple out of the way. He laid on the ground and was able to use his legs to push the door open another foot. He undid his oxygen tank and crawled under the opening, pulling his tank behind him.

Markus moved in front of Eve and tapped the glass on her helmet, not getting any response. He undid her harnesses and pulled her to the ground, dragging her toward the opening and removing her tank. He pushed her through the opening to Scott and Courtney, who pulled her under the hatch.

"Open the outside door and pull her into the hall," Courtney ordered. Scott picked up Eve, moving her to the hall where Markus joined them. They were able to close the door behind them, making sure that the airlock was secured tightly.

"Wait! Make sure the light is green before you take off her helmet!" Courtney ordered.

They waited, circled around Eve, for 30 seconds until the signal was clear and they could remove her helmet. Courtney put the oxygen mask over her face and checked her vitals.

"She's breathing! Look at her chest! Feel this," Courtney said. "It's warm…that's weird."

The material on her suit had darkened over the area on her chest. Markus and Courtney didn't understand and started to back away.

"That isn't normal...what's happening?" Markus said.

"You guys have watched too many alien movies," Scott said. "Eve is special. Her necklace must have heated up."

At that moment Eve's eyes opened. She saw Scott and a weird, dolphinlike, child's voice penetrated each of their helmets.

"What's that noise?" Markus said, putting his gloved hands to the side of his helmet. "What is wrong with her?"

"It's okay," Scott said. "She's okay." Scott removed his helmet. He looked in her eyes and could see when Eve returned to him and the child had disappeared. He didn't say anything, but his thoughts were that her "being father" had just saved Eve by shocking her heart.

"What just happened?" Markus asked, still keeping his distance with Courtney. Neither had taken their eyes off Eve, as if waiting for her chest to burst open and a creature to pop out.

"I'm okay," Eve whispered with a now hoarse voice. "I think there's something that we might need to tell them," she looked at Scott and watched him nod his head. "You better never make me do anything like that again! We are leaving here together or not at all! You hear me, Scott?" Eve scolded and sat up, pulling him down and kissing his lips. "Now get me up. We need to get to the control room to see what happened with the drop."

Courtney and Markus were quiet, following the pair. They both weren't sure what just happened and wanted to keep their distance.

chapter 117

Gordon pulled up at the front of NASA headquarters and got in line with the other cars waiting for entrance. It was 7 A.M. and he wasn't used to having to wait. He spent his time observing everything around him, not taking safety for granted. When it was his turn, he pulled up and recognized the familiar guard that he always saw on the day shift.

"Good morning, Mr. Turner," the guard said, writing Gordon's name on his clipboard alongside the code on Gordon's laminated entrance pass. "Been on vacation? I see you're back a day early. Hope you had a good time. Where did you go?"

"My daughter got married and we went to Barcelona. It was really nice," Gordon said.

"Good to hear—been wanting to take the wife there."

"Yes, a very nice place; you have a good day," Gordon said, moving forward. *No wonder the line is long if this guy knows and talks to everyone.*

Gordon's heart was beating fast, not knowing what to expect as he made his way to his section of the building. He passed his boss' office, seeing his door was open and he was on the phone. Noticing Gordon, he signaled with his hand for Gordon to come in and wait.

"How was your trip?" He asked, once off the phone.

"It's been an eventful time this past month. What's been happening around here?" Gordon asked, sitting down in the chair in front of the desk.

"It looks like the transport with all the equipment for the colony landed close to the target spot. But that's about all the information that has trickled down from upstairs."

"When do you think they will need us to help check the trucks?" Gordon asked.

"I think it might be a while. There was a duststorm on Mars a few weeks ago and they haven't been able to make contact with the ship since then. We will fall in last after the ship is checked and the colony remotely set up by the robots. After it's all functioning, they'll call down for us to do our part."

"What is your expected time frame on that?" Gordon asked.

"I'm not sure; it could be a few months is what I'm thinking. Why do you ask?" He said.

"I was thinking…I have a lot of accumulated vacation and sick time that you know I never use. I was wondering if it would be a problem to take some time off? I know once we are in the mix upstairs, we'll be working non-stop for months with plenty of overtime."

"What's going on, Gordon? You never take time off."

"My wife has been upset since my daughter left. It's the reason we ended up going to Barcelona as well. She and my daughter are really close and she keeps saying how she feels she has lost her best friend. I thought, anticipating the work ahead, that it might be best to spend some time with her," Gordon said, feeling that it was a little lie and not a big one.

His wife would most likely be feeling that way if she weren't distracted at the moment.

"Yes…I understand; I should probably do the same. My wife tells me when we are in the crunch that she feels like she's single. I told her she can feel it all she wants, but she better not act like she is! Ha ha ha. Yes, that's fine with me if you want to take some time."

"Thank you, sir," Gordon said. "I might take one more trip; she was talking the romantic ways of Paris. How about I check in every week with you to see the progress?"

"Yes, that's fine…I'll send the papers over to the office clearing your time."

Gordon stood, shook his boss' hand over the desk, and left the office.

Relieved, he picked up his pace, not wanting to run into co-workers and having to explain his absence. He found the elevator that went to the top floor. The door opened and he looked around at the four halls that lead away from the main lobby, trying to remember. *Dang—which one was it?* Gordon took the one to the right, moving down the brightly lit hall. He passed the blowup black and white prints of space missions, each with their gold plaques underneath telling the dates of every mission. He remembered this area and moved forward, now knowing the way.

The last door on the hall was closed and he tried the knob. Finding that it was unlocked, he moved inside the robotics lab. Inside scientists were already at work and nodded as he passed, making his way to the back office. He knocked and the door opened, revealing a brown-haired women in a lab coat looking over some data spread out over her desk.

"Gordon!" She said, looking up over her dark, thick glasses. "What brings you to my neck of the woods?"

"Connie…I need some information," he said, closing the door behind him.

"What kind of information?" She asked, smiling at him.

"Secret information," Gordon said, smiling but not trying to overdo it. He didn't want to give her the wrong idea. Connie had told him once that she was attracted to him and he had laughed, playing it down, as if what she had said was a joke.

"That sounds interesting," Connie flirted. Seeing his face, she got serious. "Okay—what's going on?"

"I need some help. This is too big to just trust anyone, so I've come to you. Can I trust you, Connie, to say nothing and to help me?" Gordon asked.

"Is it anything illegal?" Connie asked.

"No…well not on our part…far as I know…" Gordon said.

"Okay, what do you need?" She asked.

"I need to know about the spacecraft that we just sent to Mars. Is there anything that you've heard that might have changed from the initial plan?" Gordon asked.

"I heard that the weight was changed at the last minute and they were afraid that it might complicate the mission. But it landed close to where they had calculated…why?"

"Okay, what I'm going to tell you can't go any further." Gordon said, waiting for her response, until she nodded. "The reason the weight was dramatically changed at the last minute is that Washington gave the order to put astronauts on that craft. Right now, I think they are in danger and I need all the information that you can get to help them." He watched her face moving from silly disbelief, to thinking he was pulling one on her, to sitting up straight, then standing and pacing the small office.

"Are you sure? How do you know? No, I don't want to know. Best that I don't know details," Connie said, nervous. "What do I need to find out?"

"I need to know if they've been in contact since the dust-storm on Mars. Also, where did the Russian ship drop the supplies? That would be helpful. But whatever you do, you have to be safe. There are people out there who don't want the information to get out that we sent astronauts. If you feel any danger, you have to back off." Gordon said, standing, "I'm serious."

"Okay—how will I contact you?" Connie asked.

"Take this and I'll be in touch with you. Is this your cell number here?" Gordon dug in his wallet, searching for the scrap of paper he was looking for. He found Michael's number and wrote it on the back of one of her cards and handed it to her, taking an extra card for himself.

"Yes, that's it…I'll be in touch," she said.

"Thanks, Connie, I really appreciate the help." He awkwardly patted her shoulder, then backtracked his way to the elevator and back to his car. Finding the highway, Gordon felt he had done what he could and headed north. The sooner he reached his wife, the better.

chapter 118

The control room was silent; there was a real elephant in the room. Courtney and Markus were off to the side whispering, while Scott and Eve were at the other end of the room doing the same thing. Britney looked up from the computer wondering what had happened that she hadn't been able to see from the monitors.

"What's going on? You're all acting weird!" Britney said. "I know we didn't get the desired results, but we are all okay...right?"

Eve took a deep breath and explained, "As you know, I was trapped inside the escape pod..." The room was still silent, Eve could feel the fear coming from Courtney and Markus. "All right. There's something that we need to tell you guys. It's a long story so you might want to get comfortable," Eve said, looking in Scott's direction.

"Are you sure?" He asked her.

"Yes, they deserve to know the truth. We should have told them long before now," Eve said.

"What is going on?" Britney asked.

"Well...we think we were put on this ship by the President of the United States. It really is my fault for letting him know of my strange abilities." Eve said, motioning for everyone to sit down. "You see, it all started when my parents, who were retired science professors, disappeared..."

Eve talked and talked, telling them everything that had happened in the past two years. How it was hard to believe it all at first. As Eve spoke, she pulled out one of their few bottles of wine, pouring them all a small cup. Eve also explained how the necklace came to be around her neck and was a kind of metal that couldn't be broken or removed.

"So…you think that you are really a hybrid of human and these beings that visited Earth long ago? I thought you were joking when you said that before! And somehow you have contact with the aliens through this necklace? You might be reincarnated from a child that at one time had been on Easter Island?" Markus asked.

"Yep, that's about it. From what we've discovered in our research and all that has happened since, I say Yes. Not that I understand it all, but I'm 90% convinced," Eve said. "Everyone, drink up…remember the studies they did on wine!"

"What are you talking about?" Britney asked.

"Are you serious? You don't know? Red wine in space helps prevent muscle and bone loss because of the effectiveness to preserve health in a weightless environment," Eve said.

"Hate to tell you, star girl, we are not in space weightless!" Britney said. "Now don't get it twisted, I like the wine."

"Ladies! Stay focused…I like the wine too! It was a stressful day." Courtney said, "And having just the taste of wine is a luxury."

"Listen, I know it's hard to wrap your minds around something so far-fetched as what we just told you. I had the same doubts, but after I saw these beings myself, I started to change the way I thought. I also have seen the way Eve changes when she goes back in time. Not physically—it's like a different person is in her body. Her voice changes, she acts differently, and she even recognizes this being as her father. I might not understand what's happening at the time, but by what I've seen in the past few years, I know that it's true."

"I know this is the reason that I was put here on this ship. I'm here to help make this mission a success. I think Scott was put here to make me happy, because I would have gone crazy if we were separated and they probably didn't want to take that chance," Eve explained.

"I thought that as well…I'm not sure if I told you that at home, I'm a lawyer. Probably the last person they would really want to put on a trip to Mars," Scott said. "Especially if my wife's life would be in danger if she got pregnant."

"Well…after everything we've seen here on Mars…I believe you," Markus said. "I was just a little tripped out when I heard that voice thing. I thought that some kind of Mars micro had got you. Maybe I've watched too many alien movies. This makes more sense."

"Yes, I'm sorry we didn't get you to the Russian ship. But that really was iffy getting you back in time anyway," Courtney said. "And then you would have been all alone."

"I didn't want to go alone!" Eve said, looking in Scott's direction. "I won't go without him. So, we're going to have to prepare for what might happen with me and the baby. We have about 20 more weeks," Eve said.

"Don't worry! We'll keep trying to think of something! I'm working on a shot that might help," Courtney hugged Eve.

"Now that you all know everything, what happened with the drop?" Eve asked.

"The embedded tracker landed close to the pyramids in the twin peak area. One of them looked like it might have bounced and rolled for a while so that one I'm not sure about, but the other two looked to be stationary," Britney said.

"How long do you think until we go retrieve them?" Scott asked, "How long does the locator beacon last?"

"As long as the tracker isn't damaged it could last for years. With any luck, the dust in the atmosphere will be settled soon and we will be able to go out in the next two days. Today we are going to need to get all the robots that we can power up to clear the solar panels. Also, the escape pod needs to be put back onto its base and the damage assessed," Britney said.

"I think that when that's done, and we are at full power, we'll need to finish setting up all the satellite dishes that will give energy to the extended living pods. Because they will run separate from the ship, we will be able to use them when the next storm passes through," Markus said.

"Yes, you're right! The last way I want to go is freezing to death," Courtney said.

"I hate being cold!" Eve added.

"It will be a lot of work for the next few days, but it has to be done before the next storm sets in. Then after that's finished, we will go out and bring back the drop and pick up the other truck," Britney said.

"It's a great plan! I'm just happy to be alive with you all and my perfect husband!" Eve said, kissing Scott's cheek.

"All right!" Scott said, wiping the side of his face, feeling the leftover moisture. "Stop all this sweety stuff!" Everyone laughed at his discomfort with Eve's open affection.

"Okay, let's take a break, eat, and do whatever you need to do and we will meet down in the hanger in one hour!" Britney said. The room cleared out, leaving the small robots to monitor the computer systems.

Chapter 119

Gordon returned to Connecticut, and relief filled the house. He had kept checking to see if he was being followed and didn't notice anything as he had made the drive north.

"Honey!" Jane said, opening the front door and running into his arms.

"Jane! Come on…I'm fine!" He hugged her quickly before pulling away and retrieving his bag out of the back of the car. He had stopped by their house to grab some extra clothes, finding the house empty, and locked up tight. His car was gone from the garage and he assumed Jane's uncle had taken their sedan. He had enjoyed the convertible and had thoughts of buying one, thinking it was just the two of them now.

"How did it go?" Michael asked, shaking Gordon's hand and taking his bag.

"It was good. Jane, you might want to check on your uncle. He must have found my spare keys. You know him—not wanting to spend any money when I'm sure he has a million in the bank.

"Okay, Honey, I'll call him, but what happened?"

"Sorry…I was able to talk to a friend who is in the loop on the top floor. That's where everything happens, and she is going to do some checking for me. I trust her; I've worked with her for many years. I know Sarah said trust no one, but she is the only person I think will be able to have access and do it for me. Also, I was able to see my boss and take some time off. I told him to just call me when they were ready for me to work with the remotes connecting the vehicles. One thing I am sure about—no one has any idea that we landed astronauts with the spacecraft on Mars.

"I did learn that the Russian ship was able to complete their mission and is on the way back to Earth. The food and their probes were dropped close to the target area. They were lucky that they got as close as they did. A large duststorm had hit the week before leaving the visibility terrible. The Russians had to go into the atmosphere heavily saturated with particles blown around from the storm. They almost did it blindly, using mostly just their GPS to show where the surface was. It was a real blind dump, but it sounds like it was a success. I just wonder if the drop is intact. I was told they had to recalculate the distance," Gordon said.

"That is really impressive! All remotely!" Michael stated, "Do we think the kids are on the Russian ship?"

"I'm not sure at this point but I should be able to get more detailed information on the ship; it's in my classification. I have access to that level of information. But the idea of people being on Mars is the big secret. Makes me wonder about what we have been doing in space lately that is kept secret even from people working at NASA. Everyone was surprised when Vice President Pence announced a new arm of the military, Space Force. There was a lot of talk at work, wondering what the United States is hiding. Why all of a sudden do we needed a military force in space? And why was the secret being kept from the very people that were working on the logistics to make it happen? What are we covering up?" Gordon said.

"The government is always hiding something for one reason or another. I would like for once just the truth... instead of waiting fifty years for it to be deemed safe for us to know," Michael said.

"So Eve and Scott aren't on that Russian spacecraft?" Janet asked.

"It's hard to say if they made it. But as far as I know, my best bet is that the craft didn't get close enough for them to be able to get towed in. It was quite a storm and there wasn't a lot of visibility." Gordon said.

"Okay, we'll find a different way," Janet said, keeping a firm upper lip. "We have a few ideas. We have been looking at different concepts while you were gone...just in case that one didn't work." She motioned them to follow her to the upstairs room. Once everyone was seated, she started the conversation again. "Let's all assume that they aren't on the Russian ship and work from there."

"What are you thinking? Anything interesting?" Gordon asked.

"Well, maybe..." Sarah said, smiling.

Gordon had moved to the other side of the table, keeping his distance from the small woman, knowing he was a little afraid of her. He hoped she couldn't read his mind. He looked in her direction and quickly turned his head when he saw her smiling at him. He didn't understand people like her and sometimes not understanding made him nervous. He had always believed that there was a logical explanation for everything. All Gordon knew was he didn't want to get on the strange woman's bad side.

chapter 120

Janet continued, "We have found something interesting. What do you know about portals, or the idea of different dimensions? You know—traveling through time?" Inside the comfortable room, she pulled out a file.

"Let me think…I've heard about wormholes that were Einstein's solutions of his field equations for gravity. The idea is that they act as 'tunnels,' connecting points in space-time," Gordon said, looking around the room at their blank faces. "If two points are connected through a wormhole, it takes less time than traveling through normal space."

"I get it!" Sarah said from the couch, "It's like taking a shortcut in space-time," she sounded pleased with herself.

"Yes…it's a concept that allows for time to go backwards. If we could travel faster than the speed of light, we could communicate with the past," Gordon explained.

"I see," Michael said. "It takes a moment to wrap your mind around that concept…but I think I understand."

"There are possible quantum fluctuations in various fields that might make it possible," Gordon said. Seeing he had to make it simple, he walked over to the whiteboard and started to draw. "Look at it this way…a wormhole has two mouths and is connected by a throat," Gordon drew the wormhole as he spoke.

"I recognize that!" Janet screeched, running to one of the bookcases and finding a large book. She started flipping through pages covered in hieroglyphics until she found what she was looking for. She set the book in the middle of the table and everyone gathered around to see what she was pointing at. On the right page was a photo of what looked like a wormhole with Egyptians riding on it as if going on a journey.

"Maybe this was the way they depicted traveling through time," Janet said.

"Yes, you could be right!" Gordon said, surprised that it looked like what he had drawn.

"It is interesting how everything seems to tie back to the ancients who were here before us. I don't understand where all the information was lost. Why we are just now rediscovering things from the past?" Jane said.

"We think that at some point, maybe around the last ice age or the great flood, civilizations were destroyed, and information was lost. Around the world many sites are being discovered because of aerial programs that take pictures from satellites. They are able to see under the thousands of years of vegetation," Michael explained. "So...scientifically, how do these portals even work and how do we find them?"

"I'm sure someone, somewhere, is doing experiments trying to make time travel possible. There are many different ideas out there. From what I understand, the portals are a kind of magnetic reconnection. They are lines of magnetic force that crisscross and where they join together, they create an opening," Gordon said. "It is an energetic gateway. It has to be open at both ends for it to work; then it is a doorway that you are able to pass through."

"What happens if one side isn't open?" Janet asked.

"Time will be lost until the other side opens." Sarah said, removing her fingertips from her forehead. "I saw it!" Sarah's eyes rolled back, showing just the whites of her eyes. Gordon quickly turned his head, moving a step away from her.

"That might be true; it's hard to say. There are people who disappeared and showed up years later, wandering around disorientated. Most couldn't remember what had happened or where they had been," Gordon said.

"There are certain people who have an energy signature that is recognized by the gateway. If they are close to the area, it draws them to the doorway. The openings connect the two locations in the star system. This is where the creators reside. There are many places on Earth hidden within the magnetic fields." Sarah said, opening her eyes.

"Okay, that makes sense." Janet said, putting her arm around Sarah.

"I'm not sure where that all that came from," Sarah whispered. "They also said that certain places and objects are portals. Do you think Eve can feel it when she is near a portal?"

"That's a good question, dear. We will have to think on it," Janet said. "Gordon, is that all you know about portals? You seem to know more information than we found."

"Well…let me think. There is an idea that portals relate to black holes in space. By falling into a black hole vortex, you could travel inter-dimensionally through the vortex to a certain location." Gordon grew silent when he looked at Sarah, "Sarah, you're freaking me out!"

"I'm okay, Gordon! Sorry! I do weird things when I'm thinking…things just come to me and I have to filter what I'm going to say. Sometimes they are talking to me and the idea just pops in my head. Right now, they are telling me that it has to do with frequencies at a certain location. It is a kind of energy signature for that location. The frequencies equate the 'signature' soundwaves that come from that location. Once the established mass (person, animal, or object) is caught up in the signature flow, they can physically be transported between the two spaces," Sarah said. Gordon was quiet, thinking about what she had said.

"That is like the pyramids. They aren't only in Giza—they line the whole Nile River coast. Did you know they each have a frequency signature and their own distinct sound? I wonder if in the past they were all different portals?" Michael said.

"That's really interesting! Who would have known that was possible?" Jane said.

"I think I read that some gateways are ancient fake doorways cut into solid stone. It was said that these false doors were gateways to the Egyptian underworld. The imitation doors were all facing the East. The Egyptians said they were passages from the world of living to the world of the dead," Janet offered. "Maybe they were portals, too!"

"What about monolithic doorways that are found around the world? They could also be portals!" Jane said excitedly.

"So now we need to start looking into magnetic fields that have had disappearances over the years, like the Bermuda Triangle," Janet said. "We need to study where these gateways might be."

"Also, we need to send a message to Eve to take a closer look at that doorway in the back of that opening in the pyramid," Michael said.

"Yes! That's a great idea! Eve might feel the energy and it might recognize her," Sarah said.

chapter 121

Janet looked up from her computer, "I have been taking a look at the hieroglyphics Eve sent in the video. They look a lot like the drawings that were left by the Sumerians. I know I'm not a linguist, but if we interpret what is written there we might have a clue to the lost technology. I contacted a professor friend of ours from Brown University. I sent him a few still frames to see what he might come up with. What he translated might have some bearings here."

"He translated that it was talking about vibrations that appear at different frequencies and create their own sound. Just like what we're talking about. He relayed that he thinks the hieroglyphics describe each planet having its own signal or tone and the sound goes out into space. What we all found amazing was the idea that they were talking about the 'string theory' thousands of years ago," Michael said.

"String theory?" Jane asked.

"It is a theory that there are strings (particles) that propagate through space interacting with each other. They cause the universe to be made up of vibrations," Gordon said.

"Yes, and from what he quickly interpreted, the vibrations

are even given off by singing and prayer. Through these signature vibrations you can have a direct connection to the gods," Michael said. The room was quiet for a while as everyone digested the information.

"I wonder if these wormholes go to these beings on their planet? What if Eve finds the portal and ends up who knows where?" Jane said.

"That's a really good question, Jane…I guess we are going to have to step out by faith that this portal/wormhole is connected to one on Earth," Janet sighed.

"Okay…it sounds like Eve needs to find a high-density magnetic field," Sarah said. "Let's see what we can do to find the ones on Earth."

"I know it is a long shot…but what else can we do?" Janet said.

Chapter 122

It had taken longer than the astronauts had thought to restore the colony to one hundred percent. The module living quarters had all been set up, allowing each of them to pick one as their own. They were as big as a one-bedroom apartment and it was nice to spread out and have some privacy after months in close quarters.

The worker robots were now all powered up and hung back on their racks. The whole spacecraft had been thoroughly cleaned and disinfected. They decided to leave the garden where it was in the main living space just in case.

After the sand and dust had settled, they had been able to make contact with NASA. A cheer had gone up that everyone was all right. NASA had been concerned because the Mars mission team had been out of contact for over three weeks. Britney passed on the status of the ship and what had happened while communication was out. They decided to leave out what had happened with the escape pod, not wanting to tell NASA about Eve.

The day had finally come where the sun had broken through and they prepared to take their journey back to the twin peaks area. Today they would again take two of the trucks. First they would locate the truck that they had left and see if it had power. Knowing how fast the weather changed on Mars, they didn't waste any time, leaving right after breakfast.

Scott rode with Eve and they once again picked the truck with the flower. They hadn't been able to power the communication device. Eve now put the small solar panel in the filtered light and watched the light start to blink as it gathered energy.

They followed Britney's truck as she took the lead. The tracker beeped in their helmets from the radar leading them to the location of the truck. Courtney sat up front and Markus was alone in the back. The day was bright and clear and they all looked at the landscape as they passed, traveling in silence.

"It says that this is the location, but where is the vehicle?" Britney said into their headsets.

"Look—there's the solar panel! Over there," Courtney said.

"Come on, we need to get closer," Eve stated and pulled up beside the half-covered panel. Part of the USA flag blew in the wind, the red and white stripes showing brightly in the dull terrain. There was no sign of the truck.

"Let's park here and investigate," Britney said, stopping beside Eve. "Leave your engine running."

"Dig right there!" Markus said. "I'm sure I put that flag only about five feet from the truck." The small party got out and checked the area, not seeing the truck anywhere.

"That's weird," Courtney said. "Britney, let me see that device." She took it out of Britney's outstretched hand and started adjusting it. "It's showing that it is far away from here. It must have gotten blown away in the storm."

"We can go check the food dumps first; they are closer." Britney said, heading for the truck.

"Hold on, let me get the flag and panels!" Markus said, digging it out and seeing that it was still intact. "Why would the truck be missing and the flag and solar panels still here? It seems odd."

"I know. I'm starting to wonder if there is someone else on Mars. We need to move west," Courtney said.

"You guys lead, we'll follow," Eve said.

They traveled for about ten minutes and found the drop. This one was still intact; the honeycomb air pockets that surrounded it had held. A few had deflated under the impact and made the package slightly lay on its side, but nothing had broken through the seals.

"Let's try to save the air pouches—we can reuse them for something," Britney said.

"How about we use them like bags and load everything inside?" Courtney stated.

"That's a good idea. Be careful and just cut one end when you take them off," Britney ordered.

"Sounds good!" Scott said, grabbing his knife.

It took them good hour to load everything into the trucks. To conserve energy, they took turns turning off their trucks until they were ready to go.

"We have the other two about 30 minutes away. The other truck looks to be 15 minutes away," Courtney said.

"We should go for the truck first if it's okay. We will need it to haul the supplies," Markus said. "What do you guys think?"

"I think that makes sense," Britney said. "Courtney, direct us to the truck."

"We need to go back east, but more southeast will cut a few minutes," Courtney said. They traveled at a fast pace, finding that the surface sand was loose after the storm and when they slowed the truck, they would sink a little in the loose soil.

"It looks like we're going toward the pyramids. Do you guys see them on the horizon up ahead?" Courtney said.

"They look to be fine. They are so solid that nothing seems to affect them here on this desolate place." Scott watched the structures loom larger and larger as they approached.

"Hey, look over there!" Eve directed and everyone turned in their seats. They noticed that the missing truck was parked right on the side of the pyramid that they had climbed.

"Do you think after it had energy that it retraced its steps on its own?" Scott asked.

"I don't think we implanted that kind of program, unless NASA moved it remotely," Eve said.

"That's the only way it could be here. Look—it's perfectly parked a foot from the bottom of the pyramid!" Britney said.

"That might not be the only way," Eve whispered to Scott.

"What did you say Eve? I couldn't hear you," Markus asked.

"Well…I don't think that it was blown here," Eve stated, feeling a little skeptical.

Chapter 123

They parked beside the lost truck and everyone climbed out and checked the tires and inside, not finding anything unusual.

"Okay—this is just a little weird," Courtney said. They were all thinking the same thing, afraid to say it out loud, but wondering if they were the only ones on this planet.

"Do you think it could have been the Russians? Maybe they have people here as well. I remember seeing a picture of one of our rovers with a shadow. The shadow looked like a man in a spacesuit fixing the solar panels."

"If that's the case, they're really wrong not to tell us!" Markus said.

Just at that moment they heard a rumble in the distance and felt the ground beneath their feet shake a little.

"What was that?" Markus yelled, above the noise.

"I'm not sure," Courtney said, looking at her device. "Great! I think we have a storm moving rapidly this way. It's weird…my GPS is just showing ripples."

"Quickly turn off your vehicles and put out your solar panels. Put them deep! We can't lose any! Scott, there's an extra pair in your truck…grab them just in case. Markus, get one of the bags of food and the extra oxygen tanks! This isn't good!" Britney yelled. Everyone moved into action, racing around. "Come on—we are going to have to take shelter, we can't move fast enough to beat this one! Get up the pyramid to the opening." Britney directed and they all started climbing, carrying the extra weight of the supplies on their backs.

"It's a good thing that we're in better shape than we were a few weeks ago after being on the ship so long!" Markus said, carrying two of the tanks like they were 10-pound dumbbells.

"Yes, I'm not as winded!" Courtney yelled. "Beat you to the top!"

By the time they reached the entrance, the wind had picked up and the ground had started to vibrate. They had turned from explorers to survivors. They burst inside the entrance, dropping everything by the sidewall, and sat, catching their breath.

Scott could feel his chest burning for lack of oxygen and tried to slow his breathing. He felt a fire running up his arm from his chest. He remembered seeing Eve's soft face through the glass of their helmets before he passed out.

Eve noticed his distress and not thinking, took off his helmet. She grabbed the oxygen tank, turning the airflow on, and covered his nose and mouth with the plastic cup. Scott's chest rose and fell quickly at first, then went back to normal. He opened his eyes.

"What happened? Did I have a heart attack?" Scott whispered.

"No, just a panic attack," Courtney said at his other side.

"Okay, that's good." He slowly sat up, coming around.

"Well, we just learned there is a high oxygen level inside this pyramid. We can breathe in here! Eve forgot when she removed your helmet," Britney said. "But quick thinking, she got you the oxygen."

"That's good, right?" He looked around and everyone had now removed their helmets.

"It's new to us all. Let's just keep our oxygen tanks close by. They should issue smaller ones in the trucks, because these emergency ones are heavy."

"I'll take note of that," Eve stated.

"These have to be eighty pounds. But I'm sure they aren't supposed to leave the vehicles," Markus said.

"Okay! What was all of that? The weather prediction from NASA said that today would be good all day, no storms on the horizon at all," Scott stated. "It sounded like an earthquake or what would we call it? A Mars quake?" Scott asked.

"I thought there's no volcanic activity on Mars because of a lack of dynamic tectonic plates and a magnetic field," Markus said, looking in Britney's direction.

"Well there was something...one of our rovers picked up a tremor in April of 2019. It detected a quake just below the planet's surface. I think it was the first evidence that Mars is still geologically active," Britney said.

"You're right...I remember reading something about a seismic zone that was found on Mars in the Cerberus Fossae area," Courtney said. Looking around the enclosure, she noticed a brightness coming from the back of the room. She moved forward toward the light. It was part of the enclosure that held the crystals and minerals embedded in the walls. "I think something is going on! I can feel a static in the air."

"Scott, get up! I need you to stay by my side. Something is...happening. I can feel it." Eve looked in the direction that Courtney was talking about and felt a warmth inside her suit over her chest start to heat. "Hurry! Scott!"

"What is it?" He asked, but as soon as he touched her arm, he could feel the heat pulsing through his body as well.

"He's here," Eve stated.

"Who's here?" Britney asked, moving forward as well.

"My Father Is Here!" A child's voice echoed off the walls sending chills down the team's spines, scaring them.

"It's all right," Scott whispered, looking at Britney, Courtney, and Markus over his shoulder. He held Eve's arm tighter as she started to move forward. "You might want to hang back. On Earth if you see them, they don't let you go."

"We'll be right behind you," Markus said. The two women moved beside him.

"Okay, here we go…" Scott said. "Put on your helmets! Eve, you too!" Scott helped her into hers, seeing the wild look in her eyes. It was as if she didn't totally recognize him. He snapped on his helmet and took her gloved hand in his. Together they slowly moved into the now bright room.

The minerals inlayed in the walls were all lit up, sparkling different colors of every spectrum. The rainbow of colors covered every space in the room, bouncing off the walls. It was as if they had a surge of energy and light was shining from behind them. In front of the stone doorway, small crystals in the pink granite sparkled, making the walls look like they were wet. The energy was creating transparent colors that distorted the space around them. It covered the walls with beams of sparkling light, making the area look as if it was floating in space. The astronauts saw the whole galaxy surrounding them, the images transferring to the walls.

Chapter 124

In front of the stone doorway was a fifteen-foot-tall white transparent creature; the energy illuminated through his alabaster skin, making him glow. He had the same features as a human, but his head and body were elongated; his skin and hair were all white, like an albino. Around the sides of the room sat others like him that were not as large in stature. They watched the newcomers with interest but said nothing and just waited to see what was about to happen.

"Daughter! My special girl!" He said, moving in Eve's direction with his arms open.

"Father!" Her voice screeched the high pitch like a dolphin. The sound bounced around the room, causing the space around them to vibrate as the beings along the wall sounded the same greeting.

"I told you we would be together again soon!" He drew her into his arms and Scott moved along with her, keeping his hand on Eve's wrist. He held tight, not wanting to break contact. He would not lose her now.

"Father—is it true that we come from far, far away? Are we the Annunaki that the Sumerians talk about?" Eve asked in her child's voice. "Are we who the Bible describes in

Revelation returning one day to take those that are worthy up to the heavens? To take them back with us?" The child's voice asked.

"Somewhat, Daughter. There is more to it," he said.

"What will happen when our people return?" Eve asked.

"Some of us have never left and are able to travel in this dimension. We have been watching this planet you call Earth for thousands and thousands of years. Our planet started to lose its atmosphere. Our planet is in your solar system but goes undetected because it doesn't move in the same orbit-rotation around the sun. It takes an Earth year 364 days to go around the sun. It takes our planet 3,600 Earth years to orbit around the sun. At that time, we are close enough for others from our planet to make the journey to Mars and then on to Earth.

"We searched for a place where we could live without too many complications. When we first came to Earth, we stayed deep in your oceans undetected. But every 3,600 years, we would have to take humans home with us to help repopulate our planet. Because they didn't live very long, we would put them in a deep sleep, a hibernation process that still isn't understood on Earth. Then we wake them years later when we reached home. That way we were able to mix our species on our planet and at the same time speed up man's evolution on Earth. It made both our races stronger. After upgrading man's DNA, we taught mankind what they needed to know to advance in science and technology." He spoke quickly, as if trying to convince her that they were doing the right thing.

"When are they coming back? When are they going to be close again?" Eve asked again.

"Daughter, don't you understand? You are the upgraded version of us. There are many living in plain sight among your kind on Earth. When they arrive many like you will get to choose to stay on Earth or come to our planet," he explained.

"I just want to go back to Earth…to live out the rest of my life," Eve said, and she saw sadness fill his eyes.

"Maybe we won't be able to be together for as long as I thought. Child, you have always had the ability to go home," he said sadly.

"What do you mean, Father?" Eve's child's voice asked.

"The necklace you wear, remember the one I gave you? It will allow you to travel between the hot spot areas in this solar system. But why do you want to go back? You have your human man." He closed his eyes, reading her mind.

"Ah, I see…a baby! Yes, I understand. A shot is needed… I know our beings were working on a solution for that problem when the planet was last near 3,500 years ago."

"Is that when the planet was close enough to visit Earth? I now understand—that's where the RH negative blood came from! A mixing of two different species. Science hasn't been able to detect where the RH negative blood came from 3,500 years ago; it just showed up." Eve said over her shoulder to Britney who hadn't moved and stood like a statue listening to the interchange.

"So, you're saying there are less than 100 years before the planet is close enough and they will come?" The child asked.

"Yes, my daughter, they are coming," he said.

"I wish I was going to be there to see it!" Eve said.

"You could be, daughter. We have some ambrosia that could prolong your life. It works on those that are hybrids.

You could live as long as some of the Sumerian kings that lasted three hundred years. It works like some of the treatments they are now doing in your California, called reverse aging blood transfusions. It would reverse the aging process. This is a procedure where the blood in the body is totally replaced with younger blood. Most likely their experiments won't really work to prolong life. They need our blood, or maybe yours."

"Thank you, Father, but I would like to just live out my human life. You said I could go back to Earth?" Eve asked.

"Yes…you have always had the ability to go home to Earth. Don't you feel the pull toward the doorway?" He asked.

Eve allowed the energy to pull her forward into the giant transparent being's arms, holding him tight, she wept. "Will I see you again?"

"Yes, until they come, then I will go home. Maybe your grandchild will come back with me." He looked over her shoulder at the man tightly holding her wrist. "Your son's son will be able to choose of free will to leave Earth. Prepare him with the truth," he directed.

"I will," Scott promised. "Keep them safe!" He said, looking over his shoulder at Britney, Courtney, and Markus. "We are ready."

"Good-bye, my daughter…until we meet again! A portal is hidden your necklace. You don't need to be at a certain place to move between dimensions!"

chapter 125

The group heard an electromagnetic storm outside and a rumbling sound vibrated under the astronauts' feet, making them grab the sides of the walls to stay upright. A vortex had formed in the room and started spinning faster and faster.

"Stay back!" Scott yelled above the sound of the wind. The extra dirt and sand inside the pyramid started moving, turning into a dust tornado inside the room. "Try to move to the area by the entrance! You don't want to get sucked in!" He screamed to the astronauts.

As soon as the others were in place, Scott pulled Eve behind him into the center of the vortex. They were right in front of the stone door. It started spinning faster and faster; darker flashes of lightning swirled inside the circular cylinder creating a strong electrical magnetic vortex and making a swirling cloud of gray smoke.

Eve and Scott were pulled inside to the middle, disappearing into the center of the cloud. They were inside the storm, rotating counterclockwise. The strong wind tried to rip them apart and Scott pulled Eve into his arms, holding her tight. Their eyes held each other as well through the dirt-covered glass of their helmets. The wind was so strong that it wanted to rip their spacesuits from their bodies, but the material held under the strong pressure. They looked down and saw the white cloud start to collapse. Like a door shutting and connecting them to a different place, they together fell through into darkness.

Chapter 126

Eve and Scott lay still, tangled and discombobulated. Darkness surrounded them and neither could speak nor move. At first, they just listened to each others' breathing inside their helmets.

"Eve, are you okay?" Scott whispered.

"Yes…I'm good." Eve said. Her voice had returned to normal. Both sat up and Scott noticed that Eve's helmet was cracked and had a small hole in the faceplate.

"Are you able to breathe?" He asked.

"Yes…why?" She asked.

"Check your oxygen level," he ordered.

"It seems fine," Eve said.

"Okay, I'm taking mine off. Just wait until I see if we can breathe." Scott took off his helmet and smelled moist dirt. "I believe we're good." Scott helped Eve take her helmet off.

"I think we're underground. Do you think we're in the bottom of the pyramid?" Eve asked.

"I'm not sure where we are…but we are alive and can breathe." He softly kissed her, "Maybe we are going to be all right. Come on, let's see if we can get out of here." Eve took

Scott's hand and let him pull her toward a dim light that became brighter the closer they got to it.

Soon they were standing in the entrance of a large cave mouth. It was a sunny day and they could feel the warm breeze caressing their faces and the smell of the ocean.

"I think I know where we are," Eve said, looking at the large scattered stones toppled around the entrance. Eve went to the left side and searched the wall, finding the symbol of the cross identifying the Nibiru people. "It is the same symbol on the back of my medallion. We are on Easter Island! We are home on Earth! And the aliens are among us!" Eve said, patting her stomach. Laughing, she moved his hand to her stomach, where they both felt the kick. Eve wrapped her arms around Scott's waist and held him tight. They stood for a while, feeling thankful and happy to be together and alive.

"Now…how are we going to get off this island?" Scott said.

References within this work include:

Ancient Aliens Unclassified, The History Channel (Information combined and current information originated from "Ancient Aliens" History Channel Seasons 1-14

Easter Island a Novel by Jennifer Vanderbes, ASIN BOOOQCQ9AW

Discover Magazine June 2018 "Beyond time" pg. 57-60

The Day After Roswell, By COL. Philip J Corso with William J Birnes, ISBN 978-1-5011-7200-7

Air Space Smithsonian Magazine, March 2019 Article "Signs" By Mark Kaufman

The Anunnaki Chronicles A Zecharia Sitchin reader, Edited by Janet Sitchin ISBN 978-1-59143-229-6

The 12th Planet (Book one of Earth Chronicles) by Zecharia Sitchin, ISBN 978-0-06-137913-0

Astronaut Aquanaut (How space science and sea science interact) by Jennifer Swanson, ISBN 978-1-4263-2867-1

Atlantis The Antediluvian World, by I Donnell, ISBN 10-1906621276

Remnants of the Gods by Erich Von Daniken ISBN-13-978-1601632838

Chariots of the Gods by Erich Von Daniken, ISBN 0-425-16680-5

Almanac 2019 National Geographic, ISBN 975-1426219818

The Book of Giants the Watchers, Nephilim, and the book of Enoch by Joseph B Lumpkin, ISBN 9781936533497

The Books of Enoch The Angels, The Watchers and The Nephilim by Joseph B. Lumpkin, ISBN 978-1-936533-07-7